THE
ENDLESS
GAME

ALSO BY BRYAN FORBES

FICTION

Truth Lies Sleeping
The Distant Laughter
Familiar Strangers
The Rewrite Man

NONFICTION

Notes for a Life (autobiography)
Ned's Girl: The Life of Dame Edith Evans
That Despicable Race: A History of
  the British Acting Tradition

CHILDREN'S BOOKS

The Slipper and the Rose
International Velvet

THE ENDLESS GAME

BRYAN FORBES

RANDOM HOUSE NEW YORK

Library of Congress Cataloging in Publication Data

Forbes, Bryan, 1926–
The endless game.

1. Title.
PR6056.063E5   1986   823'.914   85-10761
ISBN 0-394-54849-3

Manufactured in the United States of America
2   3   4   5   6   7   8   9
FIRST EDITION

THIS BOOK IS FOR BRIAN GARFIELD,
A TRUE WRITER AND A TRUE FRIEND

Who shall stand guard to the guards themselves?

—JUVENAL

Tyranny is always better organized than freedom.

—PÉGUY

1

IN THE ORDINARY course of events Calder denied himself any form of pity for others, yet that morning he was uncharacteristically moved when he found a colony of spiders in his bath. He counted seven, seemingly all identical, clinging to the tub's vertical sides like stranded mountaineers. Sinking to his knees, he examined them at close range: did they really climb up through the plug hole, or was that just an old wives' tale? The oddest thing of all was that one never saw them appear; they simply manifested themselves during the night.

He turned on the cold tap, hoping the noise would disturb them, but it had no effect. Were they aware of him, what messages of alarm were being transmitted by their minuscule brain cells, had they congregated in this one spot for mass suicide? Drowning them was no answer, for he remembered how, when sodden, they disintegrated: he would be left with a bath full of dismembered legs, like scattered false eyelashes in a whore's bed. Revulsion rather than compassion dictated his final solution. Tearing off a length of toilet paper, he carefully scooped and removed each spider, allowing the entire colony to escape towards the dusty skirting.

After he had sluiced the tub and while waiting for it to fill, he shaved himself with a disposable razor, studying his image in the steamed mirror like a painter sizing up a new model. The moustache he now sported seemed alien to the rest of his face, and this pleased him. That and the darker rinse he had given his hair the night before subtly changed his otherwise bland features. He had always had a soft skin with no appreciable beard line, and now the moustache gave him a certain sporty air. I look like the bloody subaltern I once was, he thought, and memories of another era, a simpler life, came crowding back: a time when he had first learned his trade. In many ways it was a face on which nothing had been written, the face of a man ten years younger.

After taking his bath he doused himself with cheap cologne bought especially for the occasion, pungent but ordinary. Then he gave his wet hair a middle parting, thinking, It's small touches like these that set me apart from the rest. Yet there were tiny cracks in the plaster of his self-satisfaction. He felt uneasy, not about the job he had come to do, but because he was back in a country he had never expected to see again.

Donning a pair of surgical gloves, he cleaned the bath and washbasin thoroughly, paying particular attention to the taps. He placed a used lipstick on the windowsill and dropped the cardboard protective shell of a Tampax in the toilet bowl before lowering the seat. Then he put his own razor, soap, toothpaste, toothbrush and the bottle of cologne in a plastic bag and carried this and his soiled towel into the adjoining bed-sitting-room.

Before dressing he examined his naked body. He found something erotic in the contemplation of the pinkness of his skin and the tautness of his muscles. Always at moments like this, just before setting out on an assignment, he fell prey to an intense sexual need. There had been times when the feeling was so strong he had been forced to masturbate. It was yet another aspect of the whole secrecy of his life. Looking at the crumpled bed, he almost yielded, then reminded himself of the strict timetable he was committed to.

He put on a nondescript suit at least a size larger than he normally wore. It had been purchased several weeks earlier from an Oxfam shop in Liverpool, his port of entry. His regular, tailor-made clothes were already packed in an airline holdall. When finally satisfied with his appearance and still wearing the thin surgical gloves, he wiped every surface in the room. Then he placed other false clues: a cigarette butt picked from a gutter, some book matches advertising a hotel in Palma, Majorca, an airline brochure giving details of flights to the Middle East and finally—the crowning touch—an address book he had found by chance in a public urinal and saved for just such an occasion. Though it was unlikely he would be traced to this rented room, it was his custom to leave nothing to chance: should the authorities come looking for him, they would have several excited hours of false hope. He checked once again, then left the apartment, locking the door after him. Before descending the carpetless stairs, he stripped off the surgical gloves and placed them in the holdall.

Outside in the street a group of immigrant children were playing a noisy game of cricket, using a bat crudely fashioned from a piece of planking. Before the last war the area had been a respectable dormitory for London East Enders with pretensions for climbing into the middle class. Most of the terraced houses, identical with the one Calder had just vacated, had been solidly built at the turn of the century and sported angular bay windows and small front gardens. In their heyday they had been religiously painted every year, the entrance steps burnished with pumice, but now the doors were like rotten teeth in the mouth of a derelict. The few remaining privet hedges clung to life in a thin layer of powdery earth, their only nourishment the excreta of tribes of pet dogs. The majority of the front gardens had been concreted and were used as off-street parking spaces for a collection of rusting hulks. What had once personified genteel suburbia was now a ghetto; apart from the odd old-age pensioner too impoverished to flee, the entire district had been colonized by the postwar flood of immigrants. Not that Calder had any overt racial prejudices: he was in the business of retailing the hates of others, and had no interest in buying for himself.

Assuming a slight limp as he left the house, he picked his way through a minefield of petrified dog turds and discarded junk-food containers. Just as he was turning the corner he was struck from behind by the cricket ball. Old instincts rather than the force of the blow made him drop to his knees. The key to the apartment flew out of his grip as he put out his spare hand to save himself. The children stood transfixed, expecting some violent retaliation, but Calder merely retrieved and pitched the ball back to them. They said nothing, and he had a sense of their silent victory. As they resumed their game he searched for the key and dropped it through the grille of a storm drain in the gutter. The feeling of unease returned; he had not wanted any contact with strangers, however trivial.

Still maintaining the limp, but quickening his pace, he hurried to the nearest Underground station. There he purchased a ticket at one of the automatic machines and descended the escalator. He was first amazed and then appalled by the decay and filth, recalling other times when these labyrinthine caverns had promised safety from the German bombers during the worst of the London Blitz; the sleeping bodies, layered in the bunks like clothed corpses in a catacomb; accordion music, the fretful cries of children; sandwiches at midnight made with bread the color of Army blankets; and pervading all the stale sweat of human fear.

Now the curved walls seeped rusty water and there were missing tiles above his head, giving him the feeling that the teeming city above was pushing down. Only the wind was the same, rushing at him from distant tunnels. He walked with fastidious care to avoid the sea of plastic flotsam; filth had always appalled him. The torn posters on the walls were defaced with obscenities, as though the purveyors of hate and envy were determined that nothing, however innocent, should escape their anger.

After switching trains twice, he finally alighted at Hammersmith.

Above ground once again he purchased a half-pound box of Cadbury's Milk Tray chocolates from the station kiosk, then boarded a bus, which crossed Hammersmith Bridge and took him as far as Richmond. From Richmond he doubled back to Kew Gardens, getting off at a deserted stop and walking the rest of the way through a series of back streets until he arrived at the prearranged location. There, as planned, he found a nondescript 1979 Ford Consul waiting for him in a lock-up garage. The car had been stolen the previous night from outside a block of high-rise apartments in Brixton chosen because of its ethnic inhabitants.

Calder checked that the car had a valid license, then, donning leather gloves, recovered the ignition key from under the driving seat. As he drove away he passed a milkman serving two women festooned with hair rollers, but despite a full description of the stolen vehicle being given on television at a later date, neither the women nor the milkman ever recalled the incident.

Picking up the M4 motorway at Chiswick and remaining on it until he reached the Datchet exit, Calder cut across country, skirting the walls enclosing the grounds of Windsor Castle, and taking the Thames-side road until he reached Runnymede. There he switched to the main A30 artery and headed west, observing the varied speed limits with scrupulous care, doubly cautious because an early application of the brakes had revealed their shortcomings. The last thing he wanted was any sort of accident.

Thorough in everything, he checked out the glove compartment and the side pockets in the doors. These all proved empty, but he noticed with distaste that the previous occupant had chewed gum: the ashtray was filled with dry, gray pellets that reminded him of rabbit droppings. He had a sudden, vivid recollection of a pet Angora buck he had kept as a child: the crude hutch fashioned from apple boxes by his father, the floor drilled with holes in one corner for drainage. Remembering those times, he wondered what hidden needs had determined such a placid, uninteresting pet. A rabbit was no substitute for a dog; just a fur-matted face staring through the bent chicken wire of the cage, chewing, end-lessly chewing and defecating. No, no real pleasures, only the Sunday-morning chore of cleaning out the urine-blackened straw, and feeding the eating machine with cabbage stalks and dandelion leaves. The longed-for dog had never been his. Perhaps that was the beginning of it all; perhaps in the end it all came down to that first sense of deprivation.

The sight of the discarded wads of gum disgusted him after a while, and he wound down his window and tipped out the contents of the ashtray. Calder had a horror of dirt and squalor. The apartment he maintained in Zurich under the name of Miller was as pristine as an advertisement in *House and Garden*; nothing was ever out of place there. Thinking of the moment when he would return to it as he steadied the speedometer on 40 mph, he was reminded of one of his dead mother's often repeated homilies: "Whatever else you do, never go out of the house in dirty underwear. You never know when you might be knocked down in the street, and then think of the shame when they take you to hospital." The strangeness of her reasoning had fascinated him as a child, and it still retained some of its original mystery. The fears of others were always fascinating. Useful too, of course, extremely useful. Calder collected fears as other men collected postage stamps.

Now, on the outward journey, he registered and memorized every landmark, filing them away in reverse order. He had never trusted to luck. It was not a word in his vocabulary.

Although it was July, allegedly one of the English summer months, sheet rain began to fall from skies of unrelieved gloom. Reducing his speed, he said a silent prayer for his own Mercedes 500 SLC. That's all I need, he thought, to skid now in this clapped-out old banger.

The rain ceased as suddenly as it had begun, like manufactured film-studio weather. He switched on the radio, and found it tuned to a local commercial station. A phone-in program was in progress, and the irritation he immediately felt at the banalities being exchanged kept his adrenaline flowing. His gloved hands tightened on the steering wheel and several times he gave his own obscene answers aloud. How could people live day in and day out with that mindless pap? Dreary little suburban housewives droning on about their colorless lives, fouling the airwaves with their marital dirty linen, their phobias and prejudices. Mental acne. The show was being hosted by a DJ with a patronizing, fake American accent. "This is your own Tuesday talkathon," the DJ intoned, pronouncing it Chewsday, "when all you gorgeous little sweethearts out there can tell it like it is." Calder wondered how anybody worth anything could continue to live in England. Every small town he drove through had the same faceless High Street: betting shops, uninviting pubs, takeaway Chinese restaurants, the pavements scarred with refuse spilling from plastic bags, as if the only growth industries left were those propagating ugliness and sloth. It seemed that the England he had once known had deliberately effaced itself. He switched off the radio, conscious that his anger and disgust could make him careless.

A few miles outside Farnham he pulled into a lay-by and bought a bunch of flowers from a roadside stall, paying for them in coins. Before

7

driving off he took a disposable hypodermic syringe from his holdall and put it in his jacket pocket.

His destination, the Fernwalk Nursing Home for the Elderly, was situated about five miles outside Farnham. It had once been a private family residence and stood in spacious grounds, obscured from the road by a tangled screen of rhododendrons. As Calder approached it he noticed that the squall of rain had flattened the remaining purple blossoms so that they seemed as devoid of life as the inmates they shielded from public gaze. A weeping ash stood close to one of the brick pillars of the main gates, and the branches trailed across the roof of the Ford as he drove in. The sudden, sinister noise made him duck his head, and he felt foolish. There was a notice asking visitors to observe a 5-mph speed limit; another, closer to the house, stated that children were allowed in only by prior permission of the Matron.

Like the majority of such establishments, the house itself immediately suggested a last resting place. It was red-brick, late Victorian, smothered in places by creeping fingers of ivy. There were bars on the windows—more appropriate to a prison than a quasi-hospital. Huge Scots pines dripped their acids onto the potholed drive; it was the season for the cones to fall, and the wheels of Calder's Ford flattened them in their dozens as he carefully reversed into the parking space nearest to the front entrance. He noted that there were only two other vehicles, almost certainly belonging to members of the staff, since relatives affluent enough to afford the fees of such a place would hardly aspire to Datsuns and Mini Minors. He left the key in the ignition and picked up the flowers and box of chocolates. At no time in the journey had he ever removed his gloves. Now, once more assuming the limp for the benefit of anybody who might be observing him, he made his way to the front door and pulled the wrought-iron bell handle.

Nothing happened for fully half a minute; then a shape appeared on the other side of the frosted-glass panel set in the center of the door. He took in the fact that the door was fitted with a well-known security lock, and heard two sets of bolts being shunted free.

When the door was finally opened he found himself confronted by an elderly man in a tweed suit. The old boy was wearing an obvious toupee at a slant (it could have been back to front), which gave his face a lopsided appearance. He was clutching a paperback edition of one of Enid Blyton's fairy tales, and waved it like a flag.

"Have you read this?" There was violence in the voice. "Everybody should read this! It should be compulsory reading in schools. Because it tells the truth. It's my Bible. I get all my knowledge from this book.

While I've got this they can't pull the wool over my eyes"—all this delivered with a maniac grin, a grin that was suddenly wiped out as he removed his upper set of dentures. "You got here just in time, you know. Their latest idea is to try and take these away from me. They've stolen everything else, and now they're after these. That gives you some inkling of what I'm up against, doesn't it? But this book gives me the edge, that's what they don't realize. While I still have this I can always keep one step ahead."

The words were spattered straight into Calder's face at close range. Suddenly the old boy gripped Calder by the upper arm and pulled him across the porch and into the hallway. Despite an appearance of feebleness he had the disturbing strength of the insane.

"But we'll talk about that later on the journey up to town. So glad you got here, dear fellow. So good of you to respond to my letter. Had to send it in code because they read everything. Still, I knew I could rely on you, and I shall make it worth your while. I'm not short of a few sovs, you know."

Excitement and the absence of teeth had made him dribble. He tightened his hold on Calder's arm. "The vital thing is to get me out of here so I can retrieve my papers. I can prove everything once I get my papers. We'll leave at once, shall we? Did you come in the Roller?"

A voice said, "All right now, Lord Orchover, that's enough!"

A young uniformed nurse came into view, and with practiced ease loosened the old boy's grip on Calder's arm. "Put your teeth back in, there's a good boy. Otherwise I shan't read you a story tonight."

She gave Calder a quick smile. "Come on, do as you're told. In they go. Snap, snap." She lifted Orchover's hand to his mouth and pushed the dentures back into place. "That's better. Don't look your handsome self with those out. Now, back into the television room or else you'll miss *Blue Peter,* and then you'll be all upset. I'm going to bring you your tea in a little while."

"Will I have dippy soldiers?"

"Yes, if you're good. Two brown eggs and lots of dippy soldiers."

"My lawyer here will also require refreshment," Orchover said. "He's made a special journey from chambers to discuss certain confidential matters with me."

The nurse faltered. Odd, Calder thought, how any mention of the law makes even the most innocent uneasy.

"Are you his lawyer, sir?"

"No, I've come to visit a relative," Calder said, speaking with a slight brogue.

"There! You're telling fibs again, trying to catch me out just because I'm new. That's naughty, very naughty." She guided Orchover towards an open door leading off the hallway. Calder glimpsed four or five other elderly men sitting in a row of armchairs like figures in a fairground shooting gallery. "Naughty boys don't get any treats, don't get any dippy soldiers, naughty boys don't."

"I want to do potty. Number twos," Orchover whined, regressing into childhood.

"Not having me on again, are you? Because I shall be really cross if you are."

"No, I'll do it this time. Do proper number twos."

"All right, I believe you. Let me just attend to this gentleman, then I'll come and see to you."

Calder waited until she had settled Orchover in his chair. "Sorry about that," she said, returning to secure the bolts on the front door. "I heard the bell but I couldn't get here quick enough. I was upstairs cleaning up after another one. You need eyes in the back of your head for this job." Then, suddenly conscious that she might have been indiscreet, she added, "We're short-staffed at the moment, I'm afraid. I'm only a temp myself. Now then, sorry, who is it you've come to see?"

"My cousin, Mrs. Nicolson," Calder said, still using the brogue.

"Oh, yes. Now, she's no trouble, unlike some. Well, she will be pleased. Matron told me she doesn't get many visitors."

"No, well, I think I'm the only family she's got left, sadly, and you know how it is, it's difficult to get time off. My work takes me abroad a lot."

"Somewhere warmer than this, I hope? What a summer we're having."

"Yes. Well, the Middle East is certainly warmer."

Calder noted that she had pale blond hairs on her upper lip, a characteristic that always attracted him. Her uniform was clean, the bib fastened over her bosom heavily starched so it was difficult to speculate on her true shape. Nurses held a certain fascination for him. Perhaps it was their apparent purity. He guessed her age to be no more than twenty-two or twenty-three, a shade too old for his tastes, though she looked as though she might be a good sport off duty, not averse to a quick tumble. At another time and in another place he might have tested her.

"I hope I'm not breaking the rules, arriving out of normal visiting hours?"

"Oh, they're not that strict here. Matron's very flexible. As far as visitors go, that is." She smiled at him, but it was the smile of somebody conditioned to turn compassion on and off like a light.

"Nanny!" Lord Orchover shouted from the television room. "Potty! Can't wait much longer."

"Oh, God!" the nurse exclaimed. "It's one of those afternoons. Look, excuse me, I'll have to deal with him, otherwise there'll be an uproar in there. The others don't care for him overmuch. Can you possibly find your own way? First landing, second room on the left. You'll find Mrs. Nicolson's name on the door."

Left to himself at last, Calder mounted the oak staircase to the first floor. The hideously patterned carpet was stained and worn bare on the treads; a pungent smell that he could not place at first permeated the upstairs region. And then it came to him: it was that same fetid smell of the first schoolroom he had sat in as a small child—part human, part disinfectant. A reproduction of a popular religious painting faced him on the landing: Christ idealized, unmarked by agony, resembling some modern pop star, blessing a cluster of children gathered around His feet like stage-door groupies. Below it was a notice giving the fire drill in the event of an emergency.

As he took stock of his surroundings Calder became conscious of a continuous background noise. It suggested a number of small, fractious birds settling down for the night.

He found Mrs. Nicolson's name on the door he had been directed to, but was disconcerted to see that two other names were also listed. That hadn't been allowed for in his brief. A piece of cake, they had said; nothing to this one, just a quick in and out. But none of them was ever a piece of cake.

When he touched the door gently, it swung open to reveal a metal-framed institutional bed placed at right angles to the entrance. On it, curled up on a patchwork quilt, was an elderly crone in the fetal position. Her nightdress was drawn up to expose heron-thin legs. The crone's eyes opened and fixed on him.

"Doctor? Are you the doctor?"

Calder faltered, momentarily at a loss.

"I can't have any more children, you know, if that's what you've come about. You must make my husband understand that. I don't want them. I never did want them, only little Bertie, and he died."

Becoming more conspiratorial, she pushed herself upright on scrawny elbows. "The fact is, and I can tell you because you're a professional man, he took me against my will. I suffered him. I was his wife and I suffered him." She sank back again as though the effort of confession had drained her.

11

Calder looked across the room to where a second old woman was sitting in the bay window. This one had the soft, bloated look of an imbecile, and like her companion by the door she was semi-naked, draped rather than clothed in an odd assortment of garments. As he stared at her, taking in the catheter tube connected to the plastic bag taped to the leg of her chair, Calder felt strangely disturbed. For the first time in many years he experienced something approaching panic. As though reading his mind, the woman in the window waved to him. The sudden movement of her lolling head brought her into a shaft of weak sunlight, catching her fine white hair and giving her a wispy halo. It was like an omen.

He turned his attention to the third occupant, the one marked for a quicker release, but nothing he had been told had prepared him for the change in her appearance. The woman they now called Mrs. Nicolson was sitting in an armchair by the side of her bed, and as Calder edged closer he saw that she was held in place by leather restraining straps around her middle. He knew her real age, and he remembered only too well what she had looked like the last time he had seen her in another country. Now, as he knelt in front of her and began his pantomime of concern, he found the change in her more shocking than he could ever have imagined.

"Hello, precious," he said, employing a term of endearment he had not heard since his own childhood, "did you think I'd never get here, then?" He raised his voice for the benefit of the other two women. "Sorry it's taken me so long, but I brought you these"—holding up the box of chocolates and the flowers that were already wilting—"brought you your favorites. Didn't forget those."

The woman known as Mrs. Nicolson raised her head until her watery eyes were level with his; their two faces were hardly more than eighteen inches apart, and Calder could smell sour milk on her breath. A slow flicker of perception, like the action of a lazy shutter on a camera, passed across her features.

"You," she whispered, framing the word through toothless gums.

"That's right, precious," Calder answered. "It's me, Martin."

Her eyes focused, searching his face.

"Not . . . Martin," she said finally.

"Yes, it is. Martin, turned up to surprise you."

She twisted against the straps, rocking her head from side to side. Calder looked around to see if the other two had noticed anything, but both appeared to be asleep.

"Come to make sure you're okay. Comfortable here, are you? Nice

12

room they've given you. And some company. Nice to have friends you can talk to, have a little chat with."

He leaned across her and placed the chocolates she would never eat and the flowers she would never smell on her bedside table beside a Mickey Mouse clock that showed the wrong time. He checked his own watch to make sure, conscious that he was running behind schedule. "You'll enjoy those later."

His trained eye missed nothing. There on the bedside table, together with the enamel spittoon dish, the false teeth in the glass of water, propped against the jar of boiled sweets, was a photograph of a young girl. It had been taken on a lawn in front of an imposing country house, and the girl was dressed in white tennis clothes. A man whose face was familiar to Calder had his arm around her waist, and his hand rested just beneath her full breast. The girl stared straight at the camera with the arrogance of somebody who knows her beauty will open most doors. There was a hideous comparison to be made between her youthful sexuality and the three occupants of the room.

"Treating you well, are they? Looking after you? They tell me you're making good progress."

Now he worked with the skill of a cardsharp, quickly extracting the hypodermic syringe from his pocket, then reversing and securing the needle. With his hand held low and shielded from sight, he tested the already charged chamber of the syringe to ensure there was no air lock.

"Nice friendly staff. I met one of the nurses downstairs, not been here long, she told me, but a very jolly girl, I thought, a cut above the usual." He kept the chatter going like a warm-up man on a canned television sitcom. "Some of them can be real dragons, but she's got a very pleasant personality. I'll get her to put your flowers in water when I go down."

"Flowers," Mrs. Nicolson said, sagging forward against the leather straps. Her voice had gained in strength, and there was an echo of times past in it that Calder remembered. "Just like you to think . . . to think of flowers." He thought, They did a very thorough job on her, but love was always the last thing to be eradicated.

"I remembered, didn't I? Remembered your favorites."

Ready now, he took one of her hands in his and eased back the cuff of her flannel nightdress. Her fingers were crooked and cold to the touch. Then, as if seeking to massage some feeling back into her wasted arm, he searched for the vein. The contact of flesh to flesh produced a reaction: she moved her fingers to explore the texture of his jacket in the way a blind person traces the contours of a stranger's face. Just as he was poised for the final act the woman by the door suddenly cried out.

"Doctor! I need you, Doctor! Look at my baby!"

Calder swung around, almost losing his balance. The woman was holding up a disintegrating teddy bear. It had one button eye missing and straw padding bulged from a torn shoulder joint.

"He's dying, he's dying," the woman wailed.

"Shut up, you silly old cow!" Calder hissed. He listened for any sound of the young nurse returning before reaching up and pushing the needle home in one movement, stroking the liquid into Mrs. Nicolson's vein, urging it towards the tired heart.

Caution dictated a gentler approach when next he trusted his voice. "Just attending to this lady, then I'll be with you to take care of your baby," he said, keeping the lies flowing as the syringe emptied. He watched Mrs. Nicolson's face. She raised her head again, looking into his eyes for the last time as the final realization crowded out all previous doubts.

"Why . . . now?" she whispered, the two words expiring on a whistled breath. She appeared to Calder to be shrinking, and like the professional he was he leaned forward to press his lips against her parchment cheeks, acting his role to the end. She made no other sound as the toxin took immediate effect, but gave a barely perceptible shudder before her body sagged in its bonds. Calder took his face from hers and pulled the needle free, carefully reversing it again before secreting it in his pocket. Then he gently eased Mrs. Nicolson's dead body back into an upright position, tucked her blanket around her knees and brought her hands together on her lap.

"That's my lovely girl," he said. "Feeling sleepy, are you? Well, you have a little catnap until your tea comes."

Tension had cramped him. He got to his feet and bent to knead the muscles in his calves. As he straightened up he became aware that the woman in the bay window was observing him.

"Is it the holidays?" she asked. "Are we going home for the holidays?"

"Soon."

"Oh dear, oh dear, I didn't want to go away this year. Do I have to go?"

"Not if you don't want to," Calder answered.

He still had two tasks to perform. There was a clue to be left behind and a clue to remove. He took a used envelope bearing an Irish postmark from an inside pocket, crumpled it and placed it under Mrs. Nicolson's bed. Then he reached across her for the photograph of the young girl, and in so doing knocked over the Mickey Mouse clock. The jolt caused the alarm to go off, and he clamped a hand over the exposed bell until the sound petered out. He froze, listening intently, but there was no indication that any of the staff had heard. He put the photograph into his wallet.

The tension was broken by the woman with the teddy bear moaning, "What about my baby boy?"

Calder bent and kissed Mrs. Nicolson on the forehead.

"Now that I'm back in the country I'll try and come more often, precious. Let me know if there's anything you want, anything I can bring you."

He moved to the door, but bony arms holding the teddy bear barred his way. "He's dying. Bertie's dying."

"No, he's fine. Just fine." He took one last look at the woman he had just murdered. A splinter of justification entered his mind: perhaps he had done her a favor after all.

He pushed the other woman down onto the bed and she cradled the bear, loosening the neck of her nightdress and exposing a surprisingly full breast.

"Perhaps if I feed him. They said I didn't feed him enough before." She pushed the dark nipple into the bear's face as Calder made his escape. He descended the stairs two at a time, relieved to find the hallway deserted, and had almost gained the front door when Lord Orchover suddenly materialized, moving with disturbing speed to waylay him.

"Weren't leaving without me, were you? You wouldn't leave an old chum in the lurch, surely? Not an old Carthonian?" He had been eating a piece of buttered toast dipped in egg yolk, and his slack mouth glistened. "We wouldn't care for that at all."

Calder managed to get a grip on the top bolt of the door, but Orchover restrained him.

"Talking to you, chummy. I insist you take me with you!"

"Get out of my way, you stupid old cunt!" Calder hissed. He used all his strength to push Orchover aside, but like some dog who has never learned when not to jump up, Orchover came back for more. The top bolt was free now, and as Calder stooped to slip the second one Orchover grappled with him. Calder hit upwards with the flat of his hand, the blow striking just above Orchover's Adam's apple. Bits of half-masticated toast flew out of his mouth, splattering the lapels of Calder's jacket, but the door was open now and he was outside before Orchover's body hit the deck. Behind him there was a shout from the young nurse. The Ford started at the turn of the key and he gunned the engine, sending a shower of loose gravel winging towards the house. One of the flints cracked the glass panel in the front door, but kneeling beside the retching Lord Orchover the young nurse scarcely registered the fact. Later she was to have no clear recollection of the car driving away.

"You bad, wicked boy!" she was saying. "Trying to get out again, weren't you? Well, just serves you right. I've had enough from you for one day. You'll get me in bad with Matron, you will."

As though picking up an offstage cue, the Matron emerged from her office. "What on earth's going on, Nurse?"

"He was making a run for it again, Matron."

"Not me," Orchover gasped before a fresh choking fit denied him speech.

"He's lying, as usual. It's the second time he's tried it today."

"I can never snatch half an hour's rest in this place without something happening. When he's having one of his turns you should never leave him alone."

"Well, I can't be everywhere at once. I was getting their teas ready."

"That is not part of your duties. Mrs. Mason is responsible for afternoon teas."

"Bit difficult, though, if she doesn't show up, isn't it? Be a riot if they didn't get their teas on time."

The Matron stared her out. Insolence was something she had to live with in these enlightened days. "Well, just get him into bed. Can't leave him lying there."

"He's a dead weight. I can't lift him on my own."

"Take his head, then." The Matron bent to help, putting both arms under his knees, her starched cuffs crackling with the effort. Together they dragged Lord Orchover upright. His dentures fell to the floor.

"Leave them," the Matron ordered. "He's safer without them. Don't want him choking to death in the state he's in. Put him in Number Seven down there, that's empty. Then give him two Valium and make sure he's locked in."

"He'll only pee the bed if he can't get to the bathroom."

"Then he'll have to pee the bed, won't he? That's the least of our worries."

"Not the least of mine," the young nurse muttered.

"What was that?"

"Nothing, Matron."

They manhandled the old man along the corridor and into the spare room, dumping him fully clothed on the bed. At a later date the Matron was to regret not having examined him more thoroughly. Had she done so, she might have noticed the bruise forming on his throat, though she was to justify her professional lapse by stating that in itself the bruise would not have aroused any undue suspicion: old people often knocked themselves and bruised at the slightest touch.

"How far did you get with the teas?" she asked when they had locked him in.

"I've done all the ground floor and prepared the trays for upstairs."

"Well, give him his Valium, stay with him until he's calmed down, then relock the door and return the key to me. I'll attend to the rest of the trays."

The young nurse pulled a face at the Matron's retreating figure, then went to the drug cupboard. Opening it with a second master key, she extracted the Valium and signed the drug register.

"Got me in proper Dutch, you did," she said when she returned to Lord Orchover. "I treat you special, as you're my favorite, and this is how you repay me. Well, no story tonight, my boy. Come on, swallow these two sweeties. Open up. Quick, down the little red lane."

He swallowed the tablets with some difficulty.

"Got tummy ache."

"No wonder. Well, you just wait for a change. Behave yourself for once." She plumped the pillows and pushed him back into them. "You're a silly boy, giving Maureen all this trouble."

"Kiss, kiss."

"You don't deserve a kiss."

Tears rolled down his cheeks, and she relented. "All right, just one. Now you just lie quietly. I'll look in presently."

As she left the room the Matron was mounting the stairs with one of the prepared tea trays.

"Can I help, Matron?" she asked in her contrite voice (no point in staying on the wrong side of the old bitch).

"No, this is the last. But check that lot in the television room. Specially Mr. Goldman. See if his bag needs emptying."

It wasn't until she had given the other two women their teas that the Matron noticed anything odd about Mrs. Nicolson. More from habit than any other consideration, she pulled a screen around Mrs. Nicolson's bed before slipping a hand inside her nightdress to feel for a heartbeat. If she was honest, she felt a sense of relief; her charges usually died during the night, an added and unwelcome disturbance of the routine she set such store by. In her student days death had often horrified her, especially the death of a small child, but ten years of running a geriatric home had changed that. Now it was just a matter

17

of filling in forms and a telephone call to the next family on the waiting list to tell them a bed had become vacant. She had developed a landlady mentality, thinking of the inmates as temporary lodgers rather than patients—for that was all they were, lodgers deposited with her by sons and daughters with more money than conscience.

Even so, she had not expected Mrs. Nicolson to go so suddenly. Not that the poor soul had much to live for. Given the choice, there were others she would rather have seen the back of, but there was never any textbook to explain death. She came out from behind the screen. The other two women, bent over their food bowls like battery hens, seemed unaware that anything untoward had taken place.

Returning downstairs to her office, she made the obligatory call to the duty doctor of the day. He took her professional word that Mrs. Nicolson had departed this earth and promised to look in and sign the death certificate when he had finished his evening surgery. The Matron then noted the details in her logbook before summoning Maureen. Together they went upstairs and laid out Mrs. Nicolson, sponging the corpse and dressing it in a clean nightdress before placing it on a rubber undersheet and covering it with a fresh counterpane.

The death had smothered the Matron's previous irritation. "Take a tip from me," she said, "it's always worth doing this properly. The relatives are always more concerned with the welfare of the dead than with the living."

"That so?"

"Very much so, believe me. Make me puke, some of them. Though in poor Mrs. Nicolson's case, I don't suppose there will be many mourners."

"Well, he'll turn up, I imagine," Maureen said. "Be a right shock to him."

"Who?"

"That bloke, her cousin, who was here."

"Cousin? What are you talking about?"

"He was just here this afternoon."

"Her *cousin* came here this afternoon?"

"Yes, Matron."

"This afternoon?"

"Yes."

"Why wasn't I told?"

"You was resting. You said not to disturb you. He arrived just as his Lordship was trying to do a bunk."

"And . . . this man told you he was Mrs. Nicolson's cousin?"

"That's what he said."

"Did he give his name?"

"No. Well, he might have done, but what with Mrs. Mason being away and dealing with his Lordship I had my hands full."

The Matron stared at her, then lifted the counterpane from the corpse.

"I mean, he had flowers with him. . . . What's wrong, Matron?"

The Matron did not answer. Instead she stripped back the nightdress and carried out a more thorough examination of the corpse.

"What did I do wrong, Matron?" Maureen repeated.

"Nothing, nothing, child. You're new here, you're not to blame. Just tell me one thing. When you came on duty, did you give Mrs. Nicolson an injection for any reason?"

"Injection? No, why would I? She wasn't down for any on her chart."

"You're absolutely certain?"

"Course I'm certain. You can look in the book."

"People have been known to forget logging these things in the heat of the moment."

"Well, I didn't and I don't want to be accused."

"I'm not accusing you, Nurse. I'm merely asking you. What else did this man say to you?"

"Nothing much. Apologized for coming out of normal visiting hours. Said he worked abroad and that was why he hadn't been before."

"How old, would you say?"

"In his forties, maybe. That's just a guess."

"Did you see him leave?"

The girl shook her head. "But he must have gone by the time we dealt with his Lordship. He couldn't have gone after, could he?—because we were there in the hall."

"That's right," the Matron said slowly. "So we were." She pulled the nightdress down again and replaced the counterpane.

"Now, I want you to listen very carefully. I have to tell you certain things. It'll all have to come out sooner or later, but I wish to God . . ." She left the sentence unfinished.

The girl watched her as the Matron moved around and opened the top drawer in the bedside chest. She took a small box from it. "Have you ever seen this before?"

"I don't ever touch their things unless they ask me to."

"I believe you, Nurse, there's no need to be defensive." She lifted the lid of the box and displayed the contents. "Do you know what this is?"

"A medal."

"Not *just* a medal. The George Medal. It's only given for acts of conspicuous bravery."

"Was it hers?"

"Yes."

"Fancy. Old Mrs. Nicolson. I never would have guessed. She didn't seem the type for anything like that."

"No. Except, she wasn't Mrs. Nicolson. She wasn't married. Nor was she as old as she looked. They gave her this medal for what changed her, or so I'm told."

The Matron replaced the box in the drawer. "The reason I questioned you, the reason I'm telling you these things, is to protect you later."

"What have I got to be protected from?"

"I don't know yet. All I do know is that the man you let in was not her cousin. She does have a cousin, her only remaining relative, but he's seventy and bedridden. Now, I'll tell you what you've got to do. Move those other two into Room Sixteen and don't touch anything here. Don't touch the body, or the chocolates or the flowers. Nothing."

"What d'you think happened, then?"

"I've no idea, but if I were you I would start trying to remember exactly what her visitor looked like and everything he said to you, because whoever comes is going to ask you more questions than me."

The Matron went downstairs to her office, sat behind her desk and collected her thoughts for a few minutes. She rang the doctor again and told him to cut short his surgery. Then she dialed a number she had never used before.

2

WHILE THESE DEVELOPMENTS were taking place Calder was driving to Heathrow Airport. There he checked the stolen Ford into the multiple car park adjacent to Terminal 3. On his way across the covered bridge to the actual terminal he dropped the ignition key into a waste bin, together with the torn-up parking ticket.

Inside the terminal he made his way to the nearest toilet and locked himself in a cubicle. Using a pocket mirror, he carefully shaved off his moustache, then changed into his normal clothes and packed the Oxfam suit in his holdall. This done, he visited the bookstall, and there purchased the raunchiest girlie magazine on display, together with a copy of that day's *Times.* Concealing the magazine inside the newspaper, he threaded his way through what appeared to be a crowd scene from *Gandhi,* descended the escalator to street level and stood in line for one of the coaches that ferry passengers to Central London. He was fortunate enough to obtain a seat at the very rear, and during the journey made a close study of certain advertisements in the magazine while giving the impression that he was engrossed in the newspaper.

It was only now, as the coach approached the outskirts of Kensington, that some of the fear he had carried so far began to fade. Not that he ever felt completely safe, or allowed himself to become complacent, but he harbored the promise of momentary pleasures to come, pleasures that he owed himself when a job had been completed.

At the coach terminal he walked a few blocks, taking the opportunity to dispose of the spent syringe and the magazine in a bin bearing the legend KEEP LONDON CLEAN. He smiled to himself as he walked on, enjoying the private joke, then caught a double-decker bus, which took him in the direction of Soho. Alighting at the junction of Oxford Street and Tottenham Court Road, he went into a sports outfitters and made a few purchases, paying cash as always. Then he crossed into Charing Cross Road and took a route that eventually brought him to the sleazier end of Berwick Street and an address he had memorized from the discarded magazine. A flickering neon sign over the doorway displayed the words IMPERIAL SAUNA CLUB.

Inside, sitting behind a table in what passed for the reception area, a bored-looking Cypriot watched television on a miniature receiver.

"Can I help you, friend?"

"I would like a sauna," Calder said.

"This is a private club. You a member?"

"No."

"You like to join?"

"Do I have to? I'm just a visitor to London."

"We have temporary memberships for visitors."

The Cypriot produced a card and rubber-stamped it. "What's your name, friend?"

"Whittaker," Calder said, choosing it at random.

"Spell it."

Calder dictated each letter, but even so the Cypriot made two mistakes.

"Okay, Mr. Whittaker, that'll be a tenner for the membership, and another tenner for the first visit. You get ten back on your second visit. As a member you can use the Vestal Bar, which has topless hostesses, and if you want food we can have it sent in. Drinks and food are extra. Okay, friend, all clear?"

Calder nodded.

"Now then, let me show you the other facilities available and you can make your choice. You look like a man of the world to me."

He offered a battered brochure to Calder. Listed on it were the various specialties of the house: *Luxurious Roman Foam Bath plus Perfumed Oil Massage, Caesar Massage (to make you feel like an Emperor), Nero's Beauty Treatment (the hottest experience around), The Hides of March Skin Rejuvenator, Claudius' Champagne Bubble Bath.* It looked and read like the tired menu of a restaurant that always had a table available.

"Plenty of choice there, friend, so take your time. Course, if there's something extra you fancy that's not on the list, just ask. You're a valued member now, friend, and we do our best to please." During this his eyes constantly flicked from Calder to the television screen. He made the same speech to every punter.

"What extras aren't on the list?"

"Well, we can arrange specialties. Depends what you fancy. Might cost you, but nothing we enjoy is free, is it? Now, I'm going to take a risk with you, friend. I think I know a sport when I see one. I'm going to take a risk and let you take a look at something very confidential."

He reached under the table and brought out an album. It contained a dozen or so Polaroids of nude girls.

"You realize, I don't do this for everybody, friend, so don't let me down, will you? All our staff are fully trained. Fully. But we never have any trouble here, get my meaning? Right now Number Two there, Marlene, and Number Seven, Trixie, aren't available. They're with regulars, but you can always have a drink in the bar and wait for them if they take your eye."

Calder turned the well-thumbed pages.

"Lovely clean girls, all of them, no problems."

"I'll take Number Nine."

"You've made a good choice, friend. Betty is one of our most accomplished technicians. Now, I've done you a couple of favors and I don't want to push you, but since this is your first visit, let me guide you. You want the best, right? I saw that the moment you came in, and I'm never wrong. Be guided by me, take this week's special offer. You get the lot —sauna, foam bath, perfumed oils and the full massage." He lingered

22

over the word "full" and exposed gold-filled teeth as he smiled. "That's the one to go for, take my word for it. And because I want you to keep coming back, I'm going to go mad. Normally the specials cost another twenty-five. Give me another tenner and we'll both be happy. We take credit cards, by the way."

"Yes, fine," Calder said, anxious to terminate these boring preliminaries. "And I prefer to pay cash."

"Your privilege, friend," the Cypriot replied, but he had a hurt expression, as though Calder had cheated him out of a haggle. He counted the money, then pressed an intercom button. A girl's voice crackled a response.

"Betty, you got a special coming down. Mr. Whittaker, a new member, so treat him good." Then to Calder: "All arranged. Through that door and down the stairs. Betty's waiting for you."

The basement area into which Calder descended had at some time been given a vaguely Roman décor, but by now Rome was on the decline: crude murals depicting scenes of Pompeian lust lined the passage leading to the rabbit warren of cubicles. Some of the murals were peeling from damp, and others had been defaced with graffiti. One wit had scrawled THIS IS WHERE I SPENT MOST OF MY CHILDHOOD, and another, obviously a true Roman scholar, had written IN MEMORIA AETERNA ERIT JUSTUS.

Calder's chosen girl was waiting for him at the end of the passage. It came as no surprise to him to find her older than her photograph; still, he felt he had made the best selection from those available.

"Hello, I'm Betty." She gave him the smile of an airline hostess who has just flown eleven hours with a capacity load in a Jumbo. She held out a small towel. "Take a shower before your sauna."

"I don't want the sauna. Just the massage."

"It's a house rule to take a shower."

"I imagine the house rules can be bent a little, can't they?" Calder waved a twenty-pound note. The girl hesitated, then took it, slipping it into the pocket of her flimsy cotton gown.

"What's your first name?"

"Martin," Calder answered and immediately regretted it, remembering the last time he had used it, seeing again that other room where senility was the only membership fee.

"Oh, nice. Ever had a massage before, Martin?"

"Once or twice."

"When you needed to relax, I expect. You married, Martin?"

"No."

23

The cubicle she led him to contained a plain divan covered by a sheet, a small chest of drawers with a bottle of baby oil on it and a chair piled with towels. A coat hanger bearing the words SAVOY HOTEL DO NOT REMOVE was on the back of the door.

"You paid for the special, right?"

"Yes."

"Did they tell you what the special is? Want to start taking your clothes off? Did him upstairs tell you?"

"Not exactly, no."

"Well," the girl began, reciting it like a grocery list, "you can have half and half, or just a French, a hand job and I give a really nice rub, or you can go the distance but only straight, nothing kinky, that's my house rule . . ." She broke off: "You shy, Martin? Shall I help you take your clothes off?"

"How old are you?"

"How old am I? Guess."

"Seventeen," Calder said.

"Oh, yes? You trying to get a reduction or something?"

"You're seventeen," Calder repeated.

"I am? Okay, the customer's always right. You got it, seventeen. Now, let's get those clothes off you."

"No, I'm fine. But you can put these on."

He opened the parcel of the purchases he had made, taking out a white tracksuit and a pair of white socks. The girl edged towards the door.

"Listen, Martin, what's your game?"

"No game."

"You're not into anything rough, are you? What have I got to do when I put those on?"

"Nothing. They're just to make you look pretty. Prettier."

"You're sure, now? Because I'd hate you to get the wrong ideas. Like I should tell you, we got protection here. See this?" She put her hand to a switch on the wall within reach of the bed. "This is the panic button. I press it once and they come running for you. And they don't mess about."

"There's nothing to be afraid of," Calder said. "I just like seeing girls in pretty things." He held out the white tennis socks.

"Well, okay." She took them from him. "But you've been warned. No funny stuff."

She untied the cord around her waist and let the gown slip to the floor. Her skin was unhealthily pale, as though she had lived all her life hidden from sunlight. Calder could see her rib cage as she sat on the divan and started to pull on the socks.

"There. That what you wanted?"

"Don't talk. Now this." He offered the tracksuit.

"Still got the price on it," the girl observed.

"I asked you not to talk."

"What am I supposed to be, a seventeen-year-old dumbo?"

"Just do as I ask."

She stood up and stepped into the tracksuit, then worked the zipper halfway up.

"Right to the top," Calder said.

She did as requested, then came and stood close to him. "This what gets you off, is it, Martin? Making believe you're back at school? Afraid of big girls, are you?" She rubbed her body against his.

He pushed her from him. "Don't behave like a whore. I'm not paying you to be a whore." He tossed the towels to one side and sat down on the chair. "We're going to act a little play, you and me."

The girl's eyes flicked to the panic button. "You haven't bought me for the whole bloody night, you know. How long is this going to take?"

"Don't swear. I don't like to hear those sort of words coming from a young girl."

"Okay. Sorry. Tell me. What play are we doing?"

"You've just come home from school and you find me here. Your mummy and daddy are out, there's just me here. I'm an old friend of the family, somebody you like. You've been playing tennis. You're hot, so you want to take your clothes off and have a bath, but you don't want to be rude to me, because you like me. You know your mummy likes me too, and you're jealous of her. You'd like to get even, put one over on her."

His voice took on a more urgent note. "So when you come in and find me here, you undress in front of me, because you're a little tease, you want me to see you naked, and make me do nice things to you."

She hesitated, still unsure of his real intentions. "That it?"

"Yes. It's only a game. If you act it well, there's another twenty pounds in it for you."

Despite many years of catering to a bizarre variety of sexual tastes, she was strangely embarrassed by his request. She preferred the known to the unknown.

"Just one thing before you start," Calder said. "Your name. You're not Betty now. You're Lucy. Pretend to come in the door. Wait a minute until I'm ready."

He turned away from her. She went to the door, opened it a fraction, then closed it again, standing with her back to it. Calder turned at the sound. "Hello, Lucy. You're back early. I'm afraid Mummy and Daddy aren't here. They've gone to do some shopping. What have you been up to at school today?"

"Just playing."

"Playing games?"

She nodded.

"Made you hot, I expect?"

She nodded again. She was like somebody at the first rehearsal in an amateur dramatic show being fed lines she had no idea how to react to.

"Well, don't mind me if you want to get out of those hot clothes."

She began to unzip the tracksuit, her movements awkward, as though what he asked of her was alien to her normal way of life, revealing first her pale breasts, then the stomach with the appendectomy scar running towards the sparse pubic hair. Exposed in this fashion, her nudity seemed the more obscene.

"That's lovely," Calder whispered as the garment fell to her feet and she stepped clear of it. "Keep those nice white socks on for a moment. You've grown into a very pretty girl, do you know that?"

Again she merely nodded.

"Not frightened of me, are you?"

"No."

"No, of course you're not. Why don't you come and sit on my lap?" He patted his knees in the way one beckons a cat to jump up. She walked to him and straddled his thighs, facing him.

"There! That's comfy, isn't it?" He put a hand on her breasts and stroked the nipples. "Such sweet little titties you've got. With little buds on them. Is that what you call them?"

She had no idea how to answer him.

"Have you ever been kissed on your titties?"

Is the Pope Catholic? she thought, but dutifully shook her head, humoring the poor sod.

"Well, I might have to kiss them in a minute. I bet lots of boys at school try and kiss them, don't they?"

"Some," she said.

"But you don't let them. I'm going to be the first. What else do boys try and do?"

"The usual."

"What sort of things? Dirty things?"

26

"Course."

"They want to touch you down there, don't they? In your secret place."

"Yes."

"You like my hand there, don't you? I'm different from those boys. I only do nice things to you. Soft, gentle little touches, like that. Do they ever ask you to touch them?"

"Yes."

"And what happens then?"

"I run away," she said, thinking, Only a couple more hours and that'll be it for the day, deciding that he was harmless after all, just another retarded bloody case. She squirmed forward on his lap, hoping she could speed the ultimate conclusion. There was no real difference between any of them, except perhaps a few unfamiliar words to disguise all-too-familiar urgencies. This one was a shade kinkier than most, but at least he had promised to be generous.

"What would you do if I did kiss these?" He circled one of her nipples with a finger, and for some reason that she could not explain to herself the caress disturbed her; ordinary lusts had less menace to them. "Would you tell Mummy and Daddy?"

"No."

"All right, I will kiss them, but only if you ask me to."

"Yes, okay."

Calder's expression changed.

"No, you have to say it. Say, 'Kiss my titties.' "

"Kiss my titties," she repeated flatly.

"That didn't sound as though you mean it. You have to mean it." His voice grew more insistent. "I'm different from those dirty boys at school. I would never do anything unless you asked me."

"I am asking you." She knew what was required now. "I want you to suck them, suck my tits, make me come."

"Oh, you know all about that, do you? And who taught you about that?"

"You did. The last time, remember?"

He smiled then and pressed his lips to one nipple. We know your problem, the girl thought, enduring it. We've met you before, Martin. I've got your number, wait until I tell the other girls. She sat patiently while he warmed to his ministrations, her mind going to mundane matters.

After a while he moved to her other breast until finally satisfied; he

27

looked up into her face and said, "Was that nice? Like that, did you?"

"It was lovely."

"Glad you came home and found me here?"

"Very glad."

"Do you love me?"

"Yes."

"Say it."

"I love you."

He suddenly gripped her tightly, pushing her down into his lap and holding her there pressed against him until the spasms finished. When his grip loosened she eased herself away and bent to pick up one of the towels. Calder sat with his eyes closed and she realized he was crying. She put on her gown again, then folded the tracksuit neatly. "Feel better now?" she asked.

She removed the white tennis socks and placed them with the tracksuit. "You can still have your massage, you know. After all, you've paid for it. Want to get your money's worth. And you did say you were going to give me a little extra. I acted real nice for you."

Calder opened his eyes and stared at her as though he had never seen her before. They were all the same once it was over, she thought. They can't wait to get out. She touched the twenty-pound note in her pocket. Easy come, easy go, pity they're not all like this one, allowing herself a small private joke.

Then Calder seemed to recover. He got up from the chair and picked up his holdall.

"Don't forget these, you might need them another time." She held out the tracksuit and socks, but as she made the movement towards him Calder turned quickly, pushing a short knife in under her heart, then withdrawing it and plunging it in again several more times with terrible force, his actions so swift, the knife so sharp that she was scarcely aware until seconds later when the pain struck her. Shock took all the strength from her and she pitched face downwards onto the divan, muffling the last cry she made before losing consciousness.

Calder stood looking down at her, then wiped the knife blade on the sheet before replacing it in his holdall. He stepped outside into the empty corridor, closing the door after him.

The girl was not the most requested choice on the list, and it was more than an hour before another client picked her. By then she was beyond help, sharing death with a stranger just as she had shared the rest of her life. The last thought she'd had was to remember what it had been like when she was really seventeen.

28

3

AS A RESULT of the Matron's second phone call a certain chain of events had been set into motion, and barely four hours later, roughly at the moment when Calder was entering the massage parlor, the corpse of Caroline Oates, G.M. (née Nicolson), duly certified as dead by the local G.P., had been removed from The Fernwalk Nursing Home to an unlisted address in north London. There, Dr. Colin Hogg, Fellow of the Royal College of Surgeons and a Commander of the Most Excellent Order of British Empire (Civil List), immediately began his postmortem. As the senior pathologist at the disposal of the Security Services, he was no stranger to the many vicissitudes that human flesh is heir to. Caroline Oates, spinster, was his third cadaver of the day; the other two had been officers of the Special Branch, brought to him in plastic bags, the victims of a bomb outrage. He was exhausted and somewhat irritable.

As was his custom, Hogg kept up a running dictation of his findings while working, and his assistant, a recent and still queasy recruit to the trade, found it difficult to keep pace with him. The atmosphere in the dissecting room was hardly conducive to small talk, and Hogg prided himself on his speed with the scalpel. He was also a stickler for accuracy in all things.

When he had completed his main examination and had removed the viscera, he stitched up the corpse with a panache that had long been his hallmark and the wonder of visiting students. In his closed circle he was highly respected but not liked, for he had little natural sense of humor and bristled if ever an acquaintance was brash enough to venture even the mildest of jokes about his calling. A lifelong bachelor (which led many to speculate, wrongly, about his sexual proclivities), his main form of relaxation was the cultivation of particularly garish dahlias, a choice that his more snobbish friends derided behind his back; gardening, like other hobbies, is not without its pedants. He kept three books by his bedside—Stevenson's *Quotations,* Debrett's *Correct Forms of Address* and Lord Wavell's *Other Men's Flowers*—but seldom, if ever, read a newspaper. "All the news I need to know is brought to my slab" was another of his bons mots to his students.

Having made the last stitch and cut it neatly, Hogg stepped back from the table and removed his bloodstained apron. Ignoring protocol in his own domain, he lit his sixth cigarette of the day, exceeding his usual quota by two. Extensive studies of the bared human lung had long since convinced him that the official health warnings were not without foundation, but he was too set in his ways to change. He usually began his lectures to students with the words: "There is no truth to the rumor that man is immortal." The facts were that he relished a cigarette with his two cups of early-morning coffee (Blue Mountain beans, freshly ground, filtered and served black and sugarless), just as he revered his claret and port. He kept the cigarette between his lips while completing his customary thorough postoperative ablutions, blowing the long cylinder of ash into the washbasin before donning his MCC tie and jacket. Then he went outside to join the two men who had been patiently awaiting his findings.

One of them, Alec Hillsden, was a past, though casual, acquaintance. He was of average height, wearing a blue two-piece suit that had obviously been bought off the rack when he was several pounds lighter. Hogg put his age in the mid-fifties, though from a lifetime's study he was aware that the human face is notoriously unreliable as a barometer of the years, the naked body being the only true test. Although Hogg never inquired too deeply about anybody who did not come under his knife ("I deal in ends rather than means" was another of his more quoted and quotable sayings), he was well aware that Hillsden's description of himself as "a very minor cog in the War Office machine" was less than accurate. It was Hogg's deduction that Hillsden worked for B Division of M16, and that his presence that night, together with his companion —now introduced as Sir Charles Belfrage—indicated that the late Miss Oates was no ordinary corpse. Hillsden had the look of a man who took nothing at face value; it was a quality that Hogg admired. Sir Charles, on the other hand, had Foreign Office written all over him—the built-in arrogance of somebody who still believed that his class administered the world.

Hogg extended a hand still warm from his ritual scrubbing. It was one of his private pleasures to note how strangers reacted to a handshake that came fresh from the dissecting room. "I can tell a man's character from that simple social gesture" was one of his boasts. Sir Charles, who had officiated at two Commonwealth Independence ceremonies and had shaken innumerable and often suspect hands during a lifetime's devotion to the Crown, passed the test with flying colors.

"Good of you to accommodate us at such short notice," Sir Charles said. "I know my Minister will be most grateful." The Whitehall gamesmanship was not lost on Hogg, but he had an almost unlimited scorn for politicians of any hue and had not voted for twenty years.

"Have you anything vital to tell us?"

"What sort of question is that?" Hogg replied.

Sir Charles gave his thin smile. "I'm sorry if I put that crudely. I meant, have you formed any definite opinion as to the cause of the lady's death?"

"I'm not in the habit of forming anything else. I practice an exact science, Sir Charles, one that is seldom diplomatic and frequently alarming to laymen. The full report will be in your possession as soon as my assistant has typed up my notes. We happen to have been at it all day. This was our third in a row."

"I appreciate that," Sir Charles answered, deflecting the barb and employing a tone of voice that had placated everybody from rabid members of the Primrose League to Third World dictators. "It's just that there happens to be a particular urgency in this case, and it would help if you could bend the rules."

"What rules?"

"Should I have said 'habits'?"

"I've no idea what you should have said."

Sir Charles tried again, the smile now permanently in place. "Well, I wonder whether you could find it possible to give us a verbal summary of your conclusions? Always assuming that such a request doesn't run counter to your normal, high professional standards, naturally." He took out a small Georgian snuffbox and helped himself to a pinch, afterwards clearing his nostrils on a patterned handkerchief.

Oh, God, Hogg thought, why do they always have to be *characters*? "I think we could stretch to that," he answered.

"Did you find anything untoward, for instance?"

"Most deaths are untoward."

"Yes, of course." Sir Charles blew his nose a second time. "I'm not doing very well, am I? A little out of my depth. Please forgive me."

"Miss Oates was prematurely senile," Hogg said. "Age? I'd put her real age at somewhere between forty-eight and fifty-two."

"Forty-nine, actually," Hillsden murmured.

"Well, there you are. But she looked considerably older. Some hardening of the arteries. Visible, and in the case of the kidneys, pronounced deterioration of the viscera. Total hysterectomy carried out anywhere from six to eight years ago. Little body fat, some calcification, advanced spondylitis of the fourth and fifth vertebrae. Evidence of past fractures of the tibia and four fingers of the left hand. On the index finger the entire nail was also missing. Pronounced dental decay throughout the mouth. Brain volume greater than average. Of course I wouldn't dream of anticipating what the pathological tests will produce. They won't be finished until late tomorrow afternoon."

"You didn't find any evidence of recent damage?"

"The term 'recent damage' doesn't convey much to me, I regret."

"Again, forgive me. As you say, we've all had a long day. What I was trying to elicit was . . . Well, let me put it this way: it would put my Minister's mind at rest to be assured that death was from natural causes."

"You actually believe in putting Ministers' minds at rest, do you?" Hogg said at his most arch. "I can't help thinking that's a big mistake. You and I haven't crossed paths before, Sir Charles, so perhaps it isn't entirely clear to you that I don't spend my waking hours removing warts or conducting postmortems on ingrown toenails. I'm seldom asked to investigate 'natural causes,' as you so charmingly put it. But if it is imperative for your Minister to retire to bed with his Horlicks and a clear conscience, show him the local G.P.'s certificate. He will find it states that death was due to cardiac arrest, a bold and concise verdict which reflects the utmost credit on the workings of the National Health Service."

"But . . . ?" Sir Charles let the word dangle in the air. "Bold and concise it may well be, but I would guess you have your doubts, and that's why we are here, soliciting your vastly superior judgments."

"What you're really asking is, will this turn out to be a murder inquiry?"

"It would be most helpful if we could positively eliminate that possibility. In other words, the truth as you see it."

"There's a great deal of truth in a corpse," Hogg replied, enjoying the debate. "However, let me state categorically that the lady was not shot, stabbed, strangled or suffocated, if you'll pardon the alliteration. On the other hand, I did find evidence of recent injections."

"Injections?"

"Yes. Though one should not draw any early or sinister conclusions from that. She was in a private nursing home, was she not? I'm told that in many of those places they inject everything and everybody at the drop of a hat, just to make life easier for the staff. Nothing against that; hope they do the same for me when the time comes."

"Dr. Hogg," Alec interrupted, sensing that at any moment Sir Charles would blow a fuse and scotch any possibility of getting closer to a definitive answer. "It's already been established with the Matron of the home that Miss Oates was given an unknown and unauthorized injection sometime today. That's the one we'd like to specifically identify."

"My dear sir, I am not a prophet, nor am I given to inspired guesses. If the said Matron is correct, and if the said recent injection was not administered by a member of her nursing staff, then it is always possible that my lab technicians will isolate a toxic substance that hastened the good lady's departure from this planet. There was little wrong with her heart; it appeared remarkably normal, in point of fact, considering her general condition. But I repeat, I am not gifted with ministerial infallibility."

"Thank you," Sir Charles said in a voice full of pebbles. "Then I must tell my Minister to await your full report with all the patience he can muster. I apologize for pressing you so hard at the end of an exhausting day." He gave a look to Hillsden and reached for his bowler and topcoat.

"Pompous little fart," Sir Charles observed as they both got into Hillsden's BMW. "Is he always so boringly pedantic?"

"His bile is worse than his bite; an irritating sod when he gets on his high horse, but he's the best we've got."

"Has he been positively vetted recently?"

"No idea."

"Well, treat him to an update. I haven't been lectured like that since Idi Amin demanded to know why he hadn't been knighted. And speaking of honors, you'd better have this for safekeeping." He handed over Caroline's George Medal.

Before starting the BMW, Hillsden glanced inside the box. A dead moth was partially powdered on the medal ribbon. That's all there is to show for what she went through, he thought, that and the mutilated corpse in Hogg's freezer.

"Do you imagine he sits down to a three-course meal after a day like this?" Sir Charles remarked, trying to fasten his seat belt.

"Probably a vegetarian. I know I would be." He put the BMW into gear and swung out onto the North Circular Road. "Most of them go round the twist in the end, you know. His predecessor topped himself. Did it the messy way, too, which surprised us all. You'd imagine that chaps like that would have some foolproof, painless method. Very ironic, like something Evelyn Waugh might have written. Do you read Waugh?"

"No," Sir Charles said, still fiddling with his seat belt. "Saw him throw up at the club once. Put me off. That and his tiresome Catholicism. What is this car?"

"BMW."

"That's a Kraut make, isn't it?"

"Yes. Bavaria Motor Works."

"You lot are a law unto yourselves. No chance of us being allowed a foreign car, though come to think of it, most of the bloody things are made abroad these days."

"Where are we driving to, by the way?"

"Oh, didn't I say? Chalfont St. Giles."

"In that case we're heading in the wrong direction. Hold tight and I'll put your theory to the test. Watch this for a law unto itself." He executed a neat, illegal U-turn at the next available gap in the dual carriageway, then accelerated in the direction of Hanger Lane.

Sir Charles reached for his snuffbox. "Don't object, do you?"

"Not at all."

"Filthy habit, but marginally safer, according to the statistics. Ever tried it?"

Hillsden shook his head.

"Noticed old Hogg puffed away. Made him vaguely human. You don't smoke at all?"

"Never my own. Gave it up three years ago. Now I just scrounge and feel holy." After Belfrage had finished blowing his nose, he continued, "What's he like, our new Home Secretary?"

"Haven't you ever met him?"

"Oh, I seldom move in your exalted circles."

Belfrage took his time before answering. "Difficult to say, really. Early days, feeling his way. How do you read this business?"

"It would seem to point to murder. My hunch is that the lab tests will throw up one of the new toxins. Remember that job outside Bush House a few years back?"

"Remind me."

"BBC journalist in the Overseas Service got shafted by an umbrella with a poisoned tip."

"Oh, yes, I do recall. Very James Bond stuff. Ian didn't exactly do you boys a favor, did he? Too vivid an imagination. Reduced the whole thing to a kid's game. Bad thing, imagination." A fresh intake of snuff produced a resounding sneeze. "Excuse me. I've always thought the really lucky ones on this earth are those born without any. Tell me again, what witnesses were there?"

"Witness, singular. The young nurse who let him in. Well, that's not strictly true. There was some old titled coot who got in the bogus cousin's way and was thumped for his pains, but apparently he doesn't know his arse from his elbow anymore."

"Who is he?"

"Lord Orchover."

"Good God! Is that where poor old Archie ended up?"

"You know him, do you?"

"Years ago. Mad as a snake, always was, though quite a dab hand with the ladies in his distant youth. Mind you, most of the time he could never identify himself, let alone anybody else. We were in the Grenadiers together, but he got involved in some frightfully sordid divorce case and had to resign. Fucked the GOC's sister at some garden party. He was never a good picker. How about the nurse and the Matron?" Belfrage asked with disconcerting abruptness.

"We ran them both through the Central Computer. Nothing."

"Too much technology," Belfrage said. "Starts with seat belts and will end with Big Brother. Can't think how Orwell ever got to Eton." He stared out of his side window. "Mind you, he guessed right about some things. She was one of yours, wasn't she?" The sentences had been deliberately run together; obviously part of his usual technique, Hillsden thought.

"Yes, at one time."

"Where?"

"Berlin to start with, and Berlin to end with. Austria in between."

"Had to attend the Berlin film festival once, God knows why. Frightful place, packed with hideous people."

"Nothing but Germans, I suppose?"

"Germans and film types, nauseating combination. What happened to her?"

"She went back once too often. They were waiting for her the last time. The file's still open as to how."

"You're referring to the East sector, presumably?"

"Yes."

"When was that?"

" '79. We managed to do a trade four years later, but by then they'd done more than their usual thorough job on her."

"Hogg's medical summary, that was part of it, was it?"

"Yes." Hillsden did not want to dwell on that part of it, but Belfrage was relentless.

"Did she crack? Not that I'd blame her."

"The whole East Berlin network fell apart, so we have to assume that, yes, she did."

"Then what? Sorry to push you, but I don't want the Minister to catch me out."

"Then nothing. We got her home without any publicity. There was no immediate family to look after her, so it was decided to swap a Russian prison for a British nursing home. More comforts, but the same bars on the windows. Not that she was too aware by then. I guess, by then, everywhere seemed the same. And there, until today, was where she remained."

"How important was she?"

"Well, since the war we haven't run too many Grannies."

"Sorry?"

" 'Grannies' is the Firm's slang for the fairer sex."

"Extraordinary names you lot think up."

"Probably because it's an extraordinary business we're in."

"But all that *Wind in the Willows* stuff. 'Moles' for example—such an infantile media word. I prefer the old-fashioned 'traitor.' "

"I don't disagree," Hillsden said. "Maybe that's because it all seems so *Boys Own Paper* on the surface. We cling to juvenile code names to keep us sane."

Belfrage was silent for a while, then inserted the probe once more. "So can we take it that during the years she spent in our care she was not party to any new information?"

"She was a vegetable," Hillsden answered, forcing himself to use the word, remembering too much. He thought of a particular safe house in West Berlin, and of a castle set in the middle of a lake close to the Austrian-Czech border, and of how different Caroline had been then. He tried not to think of the corpse on Hogg's table.

"So no threat?"

"Hardly."

"Therefore if she wasn't murdered for conventional reasons, what are we left with? Revenge? But revenge for what? Presumably they'd extracted all they wanted. What else was there? The letter? Irish postmark, you said?"

"Yes, but that's too obvious a plant. I can't buy the Irish connection in this case."

"I don't go armed with very much then. That won't please the Minister. He was very edgy on the phone. Doubtless because of the Glanville affair breaking the very day he took office. Tricky one, that. Why didn't your chaps pull in Glanville years ago? You must have had his card marked."

"Don't blame us. It was your department who insisted he be given immunity."

Belfrage stared straight ahead.

"Did you know Glanville?" Now it was Hillsden's turn to press home a question casually.

"Met him a couple of times. Fearful old woman, I thought. Queer as a row of tents. Why d'you think so many of them were?"

"Perhaps they were afraid of getting girls pregnant." The mild joke brought no response.

They arrived at the Uxbridge intersection, and Hillsden threaded his way through a maze of bollards and road signs. "Are we still heading in the right direction?" he asked.

"Yes, take the Oxford road." Belfrage hummed a few bars of a vaguely familiar tune before reverting to the subject of the Home Secretary's personality, as though this, far more than the mystery of Caroline's death, was the only vital issue. "You asked me what our friend Bayldon is like? Ambitious, naturally."

"Ambition is the curse of the political classes."

"Anxious to score quickly, as they all are in this day and age. Well-heeled, which is par for the course, otherwise he couldn't afford to be in the Labour Party. Never blossomed while Wilson was at Number Ten. They loathed each other, I'm told. But he rode that out, kept his face in front of the public, made the ritual appearances on the picket lines and attended all those frightful anti-nuclear rallies."

Belfrage hummed the same tune again, then gave directions for the last stage of the journey.

When they arrived at the Minister's house, two uniformed policemen stepped out from the shadows to check their identity before allowing them in.

"Thank you, sir," the senior policeman said, saluting. "I don't know if you're aware, but there's a Red Alert up tonight, sir."

"What brought that about?" Belfrage asked.

"Bomb at Paddington Station, sir. About ten killed and twice as many injured. Seems we got off lightly, considering."

"Anybody claimed the credit?"

"Not so far, sir."

The double gates were closed after them, and word was relayed ahead to the house that they were on their way.

"So much for a Red Alert," Hillsden remarked. "You noticed how thoroughly they searched us. Christ! For all they knew we could have a Nike missile on board."

They passed a police dog-handler halfway up the driveway, which was three or four hundred yards long, lined with pollarded lime trees, and widened into a turning circle in front of an elegant Queen Anne house. The instant the car came to a stop the front door was opened by a butler, and they were ushered into a paneled study. A few moments later their host joined them.

The Right Honorable Toby Bayldon, Privy Counsellor and Member of Parliament, Her Majesty's Home Secretary, had, it was maliciously said, surrendered everything to the Labour Party except his wife's inherited wealth, having never felt the necessity of approaching a political career with an attitude of sincerity. From what he had closely observed, the only rewards for sincerity were thirty years on the backbenches and a knighthood if you didn't make waves, or a life peerage when the Leader felt the time had come to shunt you off down one last cul-de-sac. Bayldon's elevation to Cabinet rank after the last general election had been the major talking point of the new government, but only those close to the fountainhead realized that the appointment was the most cogent example of the Prime Minister's ability to move horizontally and vertically at the same time. Labour had been returned to office after nine years in the wilderness with a slender majority, and the country more or less in a state of siege. Although Bayldon had ensured that his standing with the grass roots of the Party meant he would be less of a menace inside the Cabinet than out of it, he had underestimated the Prime Minister's cunning. He had expected to be made Chancellor, but the P.M. was too old a hand to give his most obvious successor to the throne exactly what he wanted. Instead, obeying the first golden rule of politics, namely, "Always convince those you are about to deceive that you are acting in their best interests," he had offered the hot seat at the Home Office. It was an object lesson in outmaneuvering: at this particular juncture in the country's fortunes, the Home Office was the last place where Bayldon would have the spare time to plot a palace revolution.

"I expected you both earlier, Sir Charles. Now I've got my boxes to get through, so I can't spare a great deal of time."

Bayldon crossed straight to his Carlton House desk and sat down, establishing his territory like a bloody tomcat, Hillsden thought; those newly introduced to power could never resist parading it.

"I don't think you've met Alec Hillsden, Home Secretary."

"No, I don't think I have. Though I will say that in the short time I've been in office, I've already become aware of the shortcomings of your outfit, Hillsden. There are some shake-ups on the way."

He did not look directly at either of them, but busied himself shuffling through a sheaf of official papers. "Did my chap offer you a drink?"

"No, as a matter of fact."

"He doesn't speak any English, that's the trouble. Impossible to get proper staff these days."

"Good for security, though," Hillsden observed blandly.

Bayldon raised his eyes for the first time, then addressed Belfrage. "What will you have?"

"Gin for me, thank you."

"How about you, Hillsden?"

"Nothing for me, sir. I'm driving."

Bayldon opened the doors of a cabinet built into the paneling, revealing a well-stocked bar. He poured Belfrage a generous gin and a glass of decanted port for himself. When he was on public view and the Nikons were pointing in his direction, he always drank beer.

"Now then, what's the score on this business?"

"Nothing much at the moment," Belfrage said. "In fact, the reason we're late is the postmortem took a fair old time and in the end told us very little. Hopefully, the lab tests, which will be with us tomorrow afternoon, should come up with something."

"God! Why does everything take such an age? If I worked at their speed the whole country would grind to a halt." He savored his port and paced a little. "Well, we have to live with inefficiency, I suppose. Now, granted it is always a mistake to be wise before the event, from what I've gathered so far there doesn't appear to be any major threat to the security of the nation from the death of some decrepit old woman, even if she was at one time working for your organization, Hillsden. Am I right in saying she was a burnt-out case? That's the jargon, isn't it?"

Hillsden made a conscious effort to keep the anger out of his voice when he replied, "After the Russians released her she was of little use to anybody, Minister."

"Why d'you say *Russians*? I understood she was held by the East Germans."

"Initially, yes."

"Well, let's be accurate, shall we? What sort of stuff was she handling when she was active? How would you classify it?"

"As classified," Hillsden said. "She wasn't a filing clerk or a charlady; she was out in the field, taking her chances. Contrary to popular fictions, Minister, we don't operate a finishing school for Mata Haris. Miss Oates was a key figure in the Austrian station during the time some people describe as the good old days when the cold war was officially below zero."

"We don't use that term anymore," Bayldon snapped. "I would

remind you that the avowed policy of this government is to mend some of the fences, repair the damage done by the last two Tory regimes. Let me ask you this, is there any CIA connection that I don't know of? We don't need to inherit any more skeletons in your outfit's cupboards. The P.M. and I are not prepared to stomach a repeat of the Glanville fiasco, and the public at large is sick and tired of these frequent security scandals. It's a measure of my resolve to get on top of the situation that you are both here tonight."

Hillsden had partially switched off during this tirade. It's amazing, he thought, how quickly they all slip into old molds—*"a measure of my resolve"* and other such beauties, covering their nakedness with such tired fig leaves.

"I can assure you, Minister, that my department is not aware of any CIA interest in Miss Oates since her return to this country. Naturally, while she was in the field she would have been in contact with our American counterparts in the course of her duties."

"Yes. 'Duties' is an odd word to employ where spying is concerned, I always think."

"What would you call them, Minister?"

Sir Charles took down a good half of his gin.

"It implies something worthwhile," Bayldon replied. "I've always felt that the whole espionage industry is a squalid waste of public money." He stared at Hillsden's face as though it was an Autocue and he was reading off a party political broadcast. "From the first day we took over the reins of government we have moved for closer ties with the Soviets. Détente wasn't just a cynical electioneering ploy. We meant what we said in our manifesto. Coexistence has to become a peaceful reality. Now, I'm not suggesting you chaps don't have your uses in wartime, and obviously we have to remain vigilant, but the paranoia has to go. In the past most of it has been counterproductive."

"Nobody would be happier than my department, Minister, if the scenario was suddenly transformed into *Where the Rainbow Ends.* The only slight snag, as I see it, is that the KGB is not noted for its willingness to embrace such revolutionary concepts as peaceful coexistence. I'm given to understand that espionage is the only growth industry in Russia."

"Well, everything's relative, isn't it?" Belfrage interjected, his antenna warning him that it would be as well to head the dialogue in another direction. "I think the point Hillsden is trying to make, Minister, is that the late Miss Oates did, at a certain moment in time—and it's refreshing to hear from your lips that those times are behind us—prove herself to be a very courageous woman who finally paid the price of her patriotism. When she was returned to us from Lubianka—"

"Where is Lubianka?" Bayldon asked.

"Moscow. It's a prison."

Bayldon recovered quickly. "Yes, of course. I hadn't heard that pronunciation before. Go on."

"They did a very thorough job on her there. The least of which was breaking four fingers."

"Did she talk?"

"The technology of persuasion is highly sophisticated these days. Bravery is no longer finite, if indeed it ever was. Yes, we have to assume she did talk at some point."

"Why assume?"

"Our entire Berlin network was uncovered," Hillsden said, reentering the conversation. "Though it was never established that Caroline . . . Miss Oates . . . was the prime source."

"Very distressing, I'm sure, all that. But what I don't follow is that presumably in this prison you mentioned they interrogated her until there was nothing more to extract. Otherwise they would not have traded her, as you put it. That being so, why this present panic? Of course one is horrified if it's proved she was murdered, but that's a matter for the civil police to solve . . . unless—and I stress the word 'unless'—certain facts are being withheld from me?" He looked from one man to the other. "One would not be well pleased to subsequently discover that this 'incident' is the tip of another iceberg that could sink us all."

Hillsden deferred to Sir Charles. You're the bloody diplomat, he thought, you handle that one.

"There's no question of concealment, Minister. I have to admit that the circumstances as we presently know them give rise for concern, and as such we would be failing in our responsibility if we did not pursue the investigation to the hilt. As you rightly say, on the face of it there appears to be no plausible explanation, and maybe it will prove to be an isolated, possibly never fully explained incident that fades away."

Bayldon pondered this for a moment, then got up, rising from behind his desk as if to an imaginary dispatch box. "I would like to take you both into my confidence," he began pompously, then caught himself out and switched to a more conversational tone. "As I am sure you realize, any new administration needs to be granted a certain breathing space.

41

Without playing party politics, I can admit to you that when we finally got a chance to examine the books, we were horrified at the magnitude of the problems we had inherited. That's by the way, but coming back to my own position, the office I hold is delicately poised at the moment. That wretched Glanville business was dumped in my lap before I was scarcely through the door. It's my view that the country needs a period of stability. We've had our fill of spy scandals. These regular exposures have become a positive cottage industry. I've also had to deal with the Monarch's lack of security at Windsor and widespread corruption in the Met, none of which can justly be laid at my feet, but which nevertheless I have to cope with. Now, it would be utterly improper—utterly improper, I repeat—for the truth ever to be cynically concealed. At the same time, we all have a duty at this critical stage in the nation's situation to proceed with circumspection. No good purpose would be served if the unfortunate death of Miss Oates was blown up into front-page news for the Tory gutter press. So, if a proper and honorable way can be found for the poor woman to be buried without further ado, so much the better. We do, after all, have ample justification in the wording of the doctor's death certificate. Should questions be asked, we can say with a clear conscience that she died of a heart attack."

He had made frequent little stabbing gestures with one hand throughout this speech. Just as if we're two traffic wardens, and he's trying to talk his way out of a parking ticket, Hillsden thought.

At this point they were dismissed, though Bayldon did unbend enough to see them to the front door. "You chaps okay for transport?" he said as he shook hands.

"Yes, we came down in Hillsden's car. Though, come to think of it, it would be more convenient if I could go straight to Whitehall under my own steam."

"Well, use my chap," Bayldon said. "I won't be needing him again tonight."

"That's exceedingly kind, Minister. Much appreciated. And thank you for seeing us. It's been a most useful meeting."

As they walked to where the vehicles were parked Hillsden said, "If you don't mind, can you ride with me until we reach the motorway? There are still a couple of things I'd like to discuss. His car can follow us."

"Fine. Let me find his driver and tell him."

They set off when the arrangements had been explained, and as soon as they were past the police checkpoint Hillsden said, "She was murdered. I can always smell murder. I only half listened to him spouting all those fucking platitudes, because all the time I was trying to remember something Caroline said to me the last time I saw her."

"Did you 'run her'—that's the expression, isn't it?"

"No. But we were both in the Austrian station. She thought she was onto something big; that's why she went in again. I think she knew her luck was running out, but she went in anyway. It wasn't my decision. I might have stopped her if I'd been there, but they'd lifted me by then."

"Did you remember back there?"

"What?"

"Well, whatever it was she said?"

"No, it started to come back and then I lost it again. But I'll dredge it up in time. Bayldon isn't my cup of tea. Is he yours?"

Sir Charles shrugged and reached for his snuffbox. "They come and go. I've served quite a few in my time. We remain neutral, you know. Doesn't do to form opinions."

"Oh, you Civil Service types, you're so cagey."

"Question of survival."

"What he was really saying was, Don't rock my boat."

"Nothing unusual in that. That's standard dialogue. What else did you want to discuss?"

Hillsden activated the windscreen wipers before answering. "I don't have your broader view of events, nor do I have your patience. All we ever get is bits and pieces of the jigsaw puzzle. Sometimes they slot in, sometimes they don't, and sometimes pieces are deliberately mislaid."

"Meaning?"

"Well, he touched on something. What piece of the puzzle did they miss in Lubianka? Why would they take a risk now? Why would they go to the trouble of killing her so long after the event?"

"Good question—always assuming they did."

"They killed her, all right."

Sir Charles wiped his nose with the patterned handkerchief. "Correct me if I'm wrong, but I get the impression that your interest is not entirely professional. There seems to be an element of a more personal involvement." He closed the snuffbox and tapped the lid twice.

"Why wouldn't I be personally involved? We shared the same risks. And unlike some, I don't give a damn about rocking Bayldon's boat or anybody else's. For my money, politicians are like drunks. We're the ones who have to clean up after them." He glanced up into his rearview mirror. "We seem to have lost his chap."

He eased his foot off the accelerator. Belfrage twisted around, constricted by his seat belt, to look back at the road behind them. It was then that they both noticed a red glow in the sky. Neither of them spoke, but Hillsden executed a textbook three-point turn, slammed the BMW into third gear and gunned it. Less than a mile down the curving road they came upon what remained of Bayldon's Ministry Jaguar. It was end towards them, and the explosion had turned it over so that the encased belly was exposed and petrol was burning for twenty yards all around. Hillsden ran with the fire extinguisher he carried under the front passenger seat, but it proved totally ineffective against the blaze and they could only retreat and watch as one last guttering explosion rocked the blackened shell. Then an eerie silence. When the heat allowed they again approached the wreckage, but what was left of Bayldon's chauffeur looked like a heap of charred offal.

Belfrage walked away and stood staring across the dark fields while Hillsden used his car radio to alert the local police. He was still talking to them when he saw the headlamps of an approaching vehicle. It proved to be a large truck loaded with vegetables.

"Christ!" the driver exclaimed. "What happened to that poor sod?"

"No idea. We just came across it," Hillsden replied. "You'd better back up. The police will be here shortly."

"Bleedin' roll on! Not much left, is there?"

Two police cars arrived simultaneously and behind them a police recovery truck. Hillsden identified himself and instructed them to crane the smoldering wreck off to one side of the road. "Wave that character on. As far as he's concerned it was just an accident, got it?"

One of the patrolmen beckoned the truck driver to proceed as soon as the road had been cleared.

"Now, I want this whole stretch of road sealed off," Hillsden ordered the police sergeant in charge. "Have your blokes get diversion signs into position. Nobody, but nobody, is to touch anything until the Bomb Squad get here."

"Bomb Squad, sir?"

"That's what I said."

"But wasn't it an accident, sir?"

"No."

The sergeant looked dubious. He was a married man with only eighteen months to go before retirement. Hillsden's manner and credentials impressed him, but he also had a healthy respect for his own Chief Constable, who deeply resented any intrusions into his manor.

"I'll have to get my own authority for that, sir."

"No! Don't waste time farting about with permissions. Do it, man, and don't argue. And stop your mob tramping all over the bloody place. Just get your roadblocks into position."

"How do we treat this, then, sir?"

"Treat it?"

"Yes. I'm thinking of the press. As you know, they often monitor our 999 calls. What's the form if they get wind of it?"

"It's your job to see they don't."

"I'd still like some guidance, sir, against the eventuality."

"It was just an accident. He skidded, went off the road and the petrol tank exploded."

"I wasn't only thinking of the driver, sir. There's yourself and the other gentleman."

"There was nobody else in the vehicle. Sir Charles was my passenger and we just happened to be passing the scene and raised the alarm."

"Right. Got it. Thank you, sir. Fortuitous, wasn't it, sir, you being on the spot like that?"

"Yes," Hillsden said. "Quite a coincidence."

"Just one last thing, sir. When I make out my report, I take it I don't use the term 'accident'?"

"You'll get further instructions on that, Sergeant. Let's just deal with the immediate, shall we?"

The sergeant finally seemed satisfied he had put himself in the clear and went to carry out his orders.

"I think we should get the hell out," Belfrage said, rejoining Hillsden.

"Yes, it probably would be a good idea if you made yourself scarce. I'll hang about until the boffins get here, just to make sure these characters don't foul it up. Take my car; I'll have it collected tomorrow. Where will you be first thing?"

"In my usual watering hole, writing a letter to the chap's widow, I expect." He looked towards the wreckage again as an ambulance pulled in. "I wrote quite a few of those in the war."

He got in behind the wheel of Hillsden's BMW, and this time fastened the seat belt without difficulty. "What do you believe in, Hillsden?"

"Religion, you mean?"

"No. Belief. What holds you together?"

"Oh, that. I just believe in evil. Good old-fashioned evil. That way you never get disappointed. Expect the worst, and all the rest is a bonus."

4

IT WAS WELL into the next day when Hillsden finally reached home, having cadged a lift in a Thames Valley squad car. During the journey he stopped to buy an early edition of one of the tabloids, not expecting to find any mention of the car bomb, but more concerned that there had been no leak of Caroline's death.

Understandably, the front page was given over to the Paddington Station nightmare. The death toll had now risen to eighteen and there was a horrifying photograph of a mutilated child being cradled out of the wreckage by a young policeman, himself one of the injured. The caption beneath the photograph, for once employing a sub-editor's inspired irony, read, "Fascist Pig at Work." Scanning the inside pages, Hillsden was relieved to find no mention of Caroline or the death of Bayldon's chauffeur. The only other item that merited a banner headline concerned the murder of a prostitute in a Soho massage parlor, predictably raising the question, IS THERE ANOTHER RIPPER LOOSE?

Before entering his house, an anonymous semidetached on the outskirts of Wembley, he got down on his knees and checked the underside of his wife's Ford standing in the forecourt. He was conscious that, like the majority of people, his vigilance relaxed in the lulls between terrorist attacks. It was only when a new outrage occurred that he religiously observed the security procedures. All he found was an oil leak and a fresh dent in the back fender. He made a mental note to have the car serviced. His wife was one of those women who regarded anything mechanical as having eternal life.

He went into the kitchen, where their cat, an enigmatic neutered tom with hair that was always clotted, sat Sphinx-like on top of the breakfast bar. It had obviously sampled the cold supper left out for Hillsden the previous evening and which now looked singularly unappetizing. Going to the fridge, he took out a packet of processed Cheddar cheese, but the plastic wrapping resisted his efforts to tear it open and he resorted to a knife. *Eat Before JUL 14* was stamped on the label. He checked his watch, found that the cheese was a week over the limit, but decided to try it anyway. It tasted of nothing and reminded him of the bland, yellow bars of Sunlight soap his mother used on laundry days. Scenting a titbit, the cat came to life, but having been offered a morsel, rejected it.

"All right for some, isn't it?" Hillsden said aloud.

The cat regarded him with resentful eyes.

Hillsden was of two minds whether to go to bed or not. From long experience he knew he could exist on no sleep at all, or else needed a full eight hours. Anything in between disoriented him. While munching on the cheese he read the newspaper again. A new group calling themselves the People's Revolutionary Party had claimed credit for the Paddington bomb, though a spokesman for Scotland Yard's antiterrorist squad discounted this, stating that the outrage bore all the hallmarks of the IRA. That must be a comfort for the victims, Hillsden thought. Turning the page, he studied the sad, bovine face of the murdered prostitute. The owner of the massage parlor had denied his premises were ever used for immoral purposes. "We cater to an exclusive clientele," he was reported as saying. "Our members include several members of Parliament, film stars and the clergy. My staff are all highly trained in the Swedish technique and are strictly forbidden to cohabit with the customers."

As Hillsden leafed through the paper his thoughts switched from the pointless death of the child in the policeman's arms and hints of low vice in high places to the more personal events of the last twenty-four hours. Could there be any possible connection, other than coincidence, between Caroline's murder and the bomb in Bayldon's car? The only common link was himself, yet logically the bomb could not have been meant for him. Belfrage, maybe, though even this was a long shot and presupposed that Belfrage would request use of the car. Most acts of terrorism were random, but to select a career civil servant out of the public eye seemed more random than most. The most obvious deduction pointed to Bayldon as the prime target, with the unfortunate chauffeur thrown in for good measure, yet even this seemed arbitrary. Murders of political figures and members of the judiciary had been the IRA's specialty in the past, but on this occasion Hillsden was inclined to deny them credit. Given that the aim of any subversive organization was to provoke maximum horror and outrage, then the blowing up of crowded pubs, railway stations and discos would seem to give better value than the elimination of a politician with no particular claim on the public's affections. Even the killing of Earl Mountbatten had not been capable of sustaining public outrage for long. The sexual peccadilloes of some actress in a television series commanded more sustained attention.

Inevitably, his thoughts swung back to Caroline; how ironic, he thought, that unknowingly her death had saved a life tonight. If we hadn't had cause to discuss Caroline, poor old Belfrage would have been scraped off the road along with the chauffeur.

He carried a past image of Caroline with him as he extinguished the ground-floor lights and mounted the stairs to the bedroom. He took in the Laura Ashley wallpaper and matching curtains, the framed set of Wyeth prints his wife had ordered from one of the Sunday color supplements. There were times when he felt his entire marriage had been assembled by mail order. Margot could never resist any gift offer. As a result, they had a set of the world's hundred great books, not one of which she had ever read from cover to cover; they were preserved in a custom bookcase in the living room next to a miniature dresser holding a collection of the world's greatest thimbles. If only there was a special offer on love, he thought, going into the bathroom to undress so as not to disturb her.

The scar that ran from his left shoulder under the armpit showed up lividly in the cold fluorescent light. When he was naked it gave him a slightly lopsided look, and his nakedness was a further reminder of times past when both body and mind had been unscarred. Caroline saved *my* life that particular night, he thought, memories coming full circle. That had been in the Austrian days, in Vienna, both of them staking out a dead letter box in the Prater, so nearly an apt description: the sudden flash of a knife coming out of the darkness as, Harry Lime–like, a teenage mugger attacked from the shadows. He had been taken completely off guard, and only Caroline's swift and effective intervention had saved him. Now the image in the bathroom mirror taunted him; he was still living, but her nakedness was alone in death, rigid beneath Hogg's shroud on the marble.

He sat on the toilet, but irregular hours and gut-rotting snatched sandwiches and junk food had cemented his bowels. Even so, he did his best thinking on the old thunder box in the throne room where all men were finally equal. Was it the Sun King who gave audiences perched on an enema bowl? That I wouldn't care for, I'd draw the line at that, Hillsden thought with the first glimmer of humor he had permitted himself since the news of Caroline's death. There was a musical toilet roll by his elbow, another of his wife's jackdaw acquisitions, and the toilet paper itself had wise sayings printed on every sheet. He suddenly felt a desperate loneliness, a sense of loss, a feeling that nothing in his life had meaning any longer.

All those years that Caroline had been shut away, first in Russia and then here at home in that last staging post for the dotty and infirm, he had clung to the remembrance of things past, and at least while she had been in Russia he had not been denied all hope. From time to time word had filtered through that she was keeping the faith. That was a mockery, of course, a convenient sop. Faith for what? Not something basic. Not Christ on the Cross, or the Virgin with the bleeding heart, the promise of a better life hereafter. Just another ideology as twisted as the one that sanctified the placing of the bombs, just a blind faith in the morality of Us as opposed to Them. All of the participants on both sides of the dividing line playing the same endless nihilistic game.

Pain gripped him, not the needed pain in his bowels but the spasm that memory always had the power to induce. Sitting there, he was wracked with silent sobs, unable to control the sudden fit. I'm nearly fifty, he thought, seven years still to go on the mortgage, no children, anonymous, wiping my arse on Christmas-cracker jokes.

He recovered quickly, seeing the irony of it all, forcing himself to scorn his mounting self-pity. God, he thought, I wonder how long I would have lasted in the Gulag? Crying in the bog like some snotty little schoolboy. No wonder they pulled me out of Vienna. Poor old Alec, not up to it anymore, didn't go by the rule book: Thou shalt not commit weakness, nor cohabit or have carnal knowledge of a fellow operative, male or female, in sickness or in health. *But I loved her.* Love, the last treason we embrace. I offer that in mitigation. The castle by the lake in Krumpendorf, that's where we said good-bye; then I came back to this, the patterned wallpaper, the trendy furniture from a Harrods sale, the Teasmade by the bed, cheese that always tastes of soap, marriage on the installment plan, a wife who deserves better.

He brushed his teeth with a brand of paste that guaranteed morning freshness. There was promise in everything but his own future. Then, still naked, he switched off the remaining lights and entered the bedroom. As he slipped between the sheets his wife moaned in her sleep and turned towards him. He felt the warmth of her body as it touched his colder flesh. How easy it would be, he thought, if death blotted out the desires we once felt instead of bringing them closer.

5

IN ANOTHER PART of London, in a self-appointed three-star hotel that catered mostly to a Middle Eastern clientele, Calder slept peacefully.

The previous evening he had dined well in a small Greek restaurant in Moscow Road, getting quiet satisfaction from the joke. On the way back to the hotel he had disposed of the murder weapon and the Oxfam clothing in one of the rubble-filled builders' tips that seemed to have proliferated all over the city since his last visit. Before going to bed, he had rinsed the remaining dye out of his hair; he was confident there would be a different desk clerk on duty when he checked out. He had registered under the name of Holgate, and affected a North Country accent. Now he slept without dreaming.

It wasn't until the following morning that he encountered the first hitch in his careful, prearranged plans. The hotel had no room service. He hesitated, but after giving it some thought discounted the risk of using the dining room. As he was shown to a window table he felt justified in his decision: the room was filled with Arab families, the women fat and veiled, the children consuming vast quantities of food, replenishing their plates at regular intervals from the self-service buffet. Calder observed them without rancor, though he was amazed that anybody could start the day by heaping cheese and pineapple slices on top of kippers; it seemed a desperate attempt at Westernization. For himself he merely took yogurt, fruit and toast, suffering the unspeakable coffee.

While he ate he studied a later edition of the same newspaper Hillsden had bought. The Paddington bomb still occupied the front page, though the photographs had been changed, and on the inside pages a suitably somber Bayldon was featured visiting the scene together with the Commissioner of Police. The lead story held little interest. He scanned it briefly, then searched for any mention of the Soho killing. This had now been updated to include a different picture of the dead girl, showing her wearing a sash in some beauty-queen contest she had never won. Her obituary now described her as a home-loving girl for whom great things had been predicted, and the theory that a new Ripper was operating was given added prominence. Calder read every word, then satisfied by the absence of any reference to the identity of the killer, he turned to the sports pages. Even in Zurich he kept up with the County cricket scores, and during the winter months enjoyed an airmail subscription to an Australian paper in order to keep tabs on their season. Cricket was the only thing he missed about England.

The photograph he had taken from Caroline's bedside table was in his wallet, together with a Swissair club-class ticket booked in his passport name of Miller. He was looking forward to the flight home, to returning to his pristine apartment and unsuspecting neighbors who matched and respected his own reserve. Once home he could resume his ordered existence and disappear into the pleasing dullness of life in Zurich until the next call came. He nibbled on the funereal toast, thinking longingly of the fresh croissant that would shortly be his to enjoy again. Croissant and decent coffee, served piping hot, not the cup of lukewarm, bitter dregs he now pushed aside.

Having checked the standing of his favorite cricket team in the league tables, he turned his attention to the financial pages, noting with satisfaction that the price of gold had moved up a few points as a result of the latest Middle East oil crisis. For the rest the commentators sang their usual lament about the state of the home economy. The British disease of industrial stagnation and labor unrest still appeared to be endemic despite the recent change of government. How gullible they remain, he thought; they still cling to the belief that parliamentary democracy controls their destiny. The Trades Union Congress was promising closer cooperation with the newly elected Labour Cabinet, trotting out the hallowed platitudes, the same stale old panaceas to cure a condition that had long been terminal. Calder folded the paper and placed it to one side, reminding himself to buy a few of the latest hardback novels at Heathrow. No sense in paying those inflated Swiss prices. His taste ran to historical romances. Jean Plaidy was one of his favorites—she always provided a good solid read; her heroines had an innocence that never failed to excite.

Then, with that instinct for survival that so far had never betrayed him, he became aware that across the room he was being observed by one of the Arabs. He had nothing but a gut feeling to go by, and even as the warning note sounded, the man, who was alone, got up from his table and walked past without a glance. Calder tried to isolate his suspicion; was it because the man was wearing a Savile Row suit rather than the traditional dress of the majority in the room? Or was it something more familiar, like the scent of a woman one has once slept with yet cannot place accurately? As much as the coffee diluted with long-life milk, the thought left him feeling queasy. He lingered over the remains of his breakfast a short while longer, keeping the man in sight in one of the wall mirrors. The Arab had gone to the reception desk, presumably to check out, though there was always a more sinister explanation. Calder waited until the man had disappeared from view, then left a tip by his plate and moved swiftly to the elevator. Once in his room he rang down to the desk and asked for his bill to be made up and held ready for him. He checked the room with his usual thoroughness, and again wiped all surfaces he might have touched.

51

The Arab was nowhere to be seen when he left the hotel, but as he stood waiting for a taxi a police car drove up and stopped in front of the entrance. There was a moment when Calder believed the police were going to approach him, but they walked past to examine a battered Austin Mini parked on a double yellow line. He saw them crouch down to inspect the underside of the car before one of them produced a bunch of keys and started to try them on the locked driver's door. When he finally obtained a taxi, he made a point of saying "Harrods, please" quite distinctly for their benefit.

He entered Harrods by the main door fronting onto Brompton Road, then walked through the shop to the Men's Department. From there he exited at the rear of the building, crossing into Hans Place, where once in his student days he had taken a girlfriend for an illegal abortion. He was fortunate enough to find a second empty taxi, and this time gave Heathrow as his destination.

"Hope you've left yourself plenty of time," the taxi driver said.

"Why's that?"

"I've just come back down the M4 and the traffic's something brutal. Two-mile jam-up, mate. Roadblocks all around the bleeding airport."

"Roadblocks? What for?"

"Well, all these fucking bombs, aint' it? Like fucking wartime all over again. They've just announced another one on the news. They've done the sewage works right by the airport. Three killed and about fourteen injured, so the radio said. Still counting them. To say nothing of the fucking health hazard. All that Tom Tit blown up in the air to land you know not where. I know what I'd do. Bring back fucking hanging. Except hanging's too fucking good for that shower. Which terminal you making for?" he rattled on without pausing for breath.

"Number One."

"Well, we might be lucky. I'll try and dodge round the worst of it, keep off the main roads. Might cost a bit more on the meter."

"That doesn't matter. Just get me there."

"Do me best. If I had the money I'd join you, get the fuck out of it."

The man was as good as his word, driving like one possessed through a series of back streets, but proved to be an irritation as he kept up a monologue in a pronounced Cockney accent Calder found difficult to follow.

"Not worth a toss these days, this country. We've 'ad it, if you arsk me. Nuffink but bleedin' grafters and wogs. I do a full ten hours a day, pushing this bleedin' motor around, and I still can't make a fucking living. But bet your life there's fucking layabouts just off the banana boat taking home more than me from the bloody Welfare, and moonlighting on the side. Know what I mean? It's 'appening all around, take my word for it. No, doncha talk to me about this country, because I'll give you an earful."

He hunched over his steering wheel, clutching it to his chest like a football, punishing the diesel engine and threading his way through the heavy traffic with fearful abandon. When they finally reached the outskirts of Heathrow, they hit the first of the roadblocks and joined a long line of cars waiting to be checked. Calder could see the flashing blue lights of several police vehicles; inside the perimeter fence of the airport was an Army tank, its serrated gun pointing skywards. Soldiers armed with automatic weapons were posted at intervals. As the taxi edged closer to the head of the queue it became obvious that the police were carrying out thorough searches, not just going through the motions. Calder made a mental check of everything he was carrying. There was only one dangerous item: the photograph of the girl. With his eyes on the driver he extracted it from his wallet and slipped it into the crack between the leather cushions of the seat just before it became their turn to be inspected.

One policeman addressed Calder while a companion asked the taxi driver to step outside the cab and produce his license.

"You traveling to the airport, sir?"

"Yes," Calder said. "What's all this in aid of?"

"Just routine precautions, sir. In view of the recent terrorist attacks. Is this all the luggage you have?"

"Yes, just the one case."

"Would you mind opening it, please, sir?"

Calder complied and the policeman riffled through the few articles of clothing, then opened the waterproof bag containing toiletries.

"Are you a British citizen, sir?"

"No, I'm Swiss."

"Speak the language very well, if I may say so. Well, thank you, sorry to have troubled you."

His companion had gone around the vehicle to open the trunk. The taxi shuddered as it was slammed closed.

"Okay, cabbie, on your way."

"Bleedin' waste of time," the taxi driver said, immediately resuming his criticism of life in general. "Not gonna find anything in a fucking cab, are they? What they should be doing is running all the foreigners out of the country. That's the fucking answer. Except *we're* the foreigners now. Proper fucking outcasts of the island. Going somewhere exotic, are you?"

"No. Just a business trip to Brussels, I'm afraid."

Calder took out some notes from his wallet in preparation for the fare, then retrieved the photograph he had secreted. He was careful not to overtip; taxi drivers remembered such things. Entering Terminal 1, he immediately noticed that more police were stationed at the Departures escalator. He went to one of the bank counters and requested the exchange rate for Belgian francs. The teller punched a computer button and gave him the figure.

"Is that all? Okay, I think I can do better when I get to Brussels."

He left the building again, threading his way through the diverging traffic to Terminal 2. For as long as he could recall, the authorities had been adding to Heathrow, and most of the buildings looked as though they had been put together from a child's Lego kit. The lack of any unified design irritated him.

Having no luggage to check in, he went straight through Passport Control and Security without incident. After purchasing a duty-free bottle of Scotch, he visited the bookstall. To his disappointment there was no new Jean Plaidy, but his spirits rose again when he spotted a number of reprints of Victorian pornographic novels. He selected one entitled *Lascivious Scenes in the Convent*. The promise of excitements to come relaxed his customary guard, and it wasn't until his flight had been airborne for ten minutes and he was enjoying the first hospitality drink that he recognized the same Arab from the hotel sitting a few rows ahead in the opposite aisle.

6

AT ROUGHLY THE same time as Calder's flight to Zurich took off, Hillsden was given two pieces of information. The first came from the Bomb Squad, informing him that the explosive device used on Bayldon's car was of a type not previously encountered. It was judged to be superior to anything employed by the IRA in the past. A painstaking examination of the wreckage had established that the detonating mechanism had been connected to the car radio.

"That's probably the reason why the explosion didn't happen immediately you both drove off," Hillsden was told. "It's a technique that's been used before. Said to have been perfected by the PLO, but who knows? The reasonable assumption is that, since he was driving alone, Bayldon's chauffeur switched it on for a late-night news bulletin."

"All the news that's fit to hear," Hillsden remarked, and then regretted the flippancy. "I take it you've discounted any possibility of the bomb being planted while the car was on Bayldon's property?"

"Yes, absolutely. The car was under constant surveillance from the moment he arrived home until you two left."

"How about his staff? Anything there?"

"They have a French cook who's been with them for five years. We're waiting for Paris to come through on her. There's the butler, who is almost certainly gay, but otherwise nothing known, and a gardener that Bayldon swears is as clean as the Pope."

"What about the dead chauffeur himself?"

"Ex-Army, clean discharge, nothing except a couple of speeding tickets on his license. Married, but living apart."

"Blanks all round, then?" Hillsden said. "Where was the bomb? Under the hood?"

"No, packed into the core of the spare wheel. Which makes it a certainty that it was planted earlier."

"What type of explosive?"

"Sodium chlorate."

"The car came from the Ministry pool, I take it?"

"Yes and no. It was a pool car, but Bayldon had insisted that it be reserved for his use exclusively."

"So who are you putting your money on?"

"Well, we've been wrong as often as not, but we don't reckon the Irish mob this time. They've been favoring remote-control hits in recent months, and, as you know, they're creatures of habit. Unless, of course, this is the start of a new cycle."

"Has Bayldon been questioned?"

"You don't 'question' Ministers, Alec. You interview them. Yes, we saw him this morning."

"He seemed pretty shaken last night when I broke the news to him on the phone."

"Well, the upper lip was stiff this morning. Nothing like a few television cameras to bring out the best in politicians. Gave us the standard speech about figures in the public eye being vulnerable, et cetera. Stirring stuff."

"And he didn't volunteer anything out of the ordinary?"

"Gave us a bit of tongue-lashing about the need for extra vigilance. In turn, we advised him to vary his routine every day from now on. Special Branch are doubling protection for him and his wife."

While Hillsden was mulling over these various bits of information, he got a call from Hogg.

"Sorry I'm taking so long," Hogg began with uncharacteristic politeness, "but I wasn't convinced by the first batch of tests, so I went back and ran some of my own. There's something that puzzles me."

"Can you tell me what?"

"I'm not certain yet." Some of the old brusqueness returned to Hogg's voice. "When I am, I'll let you know. I want to talk to a chum at Porton first."

As soon as he had hung up Hillsden relayed both conversations to Belfrage.

"Interesting," was Belfrage's only comment.

Why are all these official types so bloody noncommittal? Hillsden thought. He wanted to hear the echo of his own pain in the other man's voice. "How are you feeling?" he asked.

"Wired up to the radio, you say?" Belfrage replied, refusing to be drawn. "That's a new one, isn't it?"

"Not really." Hillsden could not resist elaborating. "We used it years ago. Remember Krakov? He was the great classical-music lover, if you recall. We fixed it so that he got the last night of the Proms for his swan song. He went out on 'Land of Hope and Glory,' one of the Firm's more inspired private jokes."

"Don't tell me things I have to forget, Alec."

"Oh, aren't we on scrambler?"

"Yes, but I still don't want to hear it. Officially, we don't stoop to such things."

"*Officially* the world is still flat. People still fall off the edge; didn't you know that either?"

But it wasn't Belfrage's unemotional responses that Hillsden pondered when he replaced the receiver. He sat at his desk and drew patterns on the dusty window. From where he sat he could look down the river in the direction of the Tower of London. Treason had once been a simple matter, solved quickly on the block, where now fatted ravens strutted as a tourist attraction. Now treason was a Rubik's Cube that nobody solved. There had been a time when operatives were paid in cash and received no income-tax demands; hoards of gold sovereigns had been kept for the sole purpose of rewarding especially successful ventures, but those halcyon days were gone. We're just civil servants now, he thought, subject to the Whitehall rule book and pay scales; it won't be long before we're on the same level as sewage workers, and maybe that's where we should be. Keep it neat.

The room he occupied was on the second floor of a converted warehouse in a derelict dock area. Above him a onetime lucky film producer occupied a luxury penthouse complete with roof garden and Jacuzzi. Below, on the ground and first floors, a firm of chic interior designers had their offices. Hillsden's outfit, sandwiched in between, had a sign on the door which stated that Porter, Forsyth and Newhouse, Ltd carried on business as wine importers. The sample crates of cheap wine to give credence to the enterprise, should any stranger try to place an order, were the only perks he and other members of the Firm ever enjoyed. "At least," the office joke ran, "we don't run a dry ship."

He switched on his television monitor. It came up with a picture of the fake reception area. All the technical gimmicks introduced after the last security shake-up amused rather than annoyed him. Like his ex-chief, the illustrious and sorely missed George (Gunga) Dinnsbury, he had no great faith in electronic gadgetry. "Show me a machine," Gunga had been fond of pontificating, "and I'll show you how to crook it. Put not your trust in that which works on batteries. They haven't yet invented a camera that can photograph a man's beliefs. When they do, I'll capitulate gracefully. Total vetting, lie detectors, all bullshit—window dressing for politicians and the media boys. You're never going to lick human deviation, human fallibility, the natural-born treasonous mind. Even J.C. was betrayed, and nobody saved him from the Cross."

The picture on his monitor showed an averagely attractive young woman sitting behind a modern desk in the act of touching up her nail polish. An attempt had been made to convey an impression of legitimacy: several framed posters on the wall showed views of the great wine-growing regions, and a display rack contained catalogs listing the contents of a fictitious stock. They'd had fun with that until the top brass put a stop to it. Hillsden had collected the office prize for his winning entry: *Château de la Vulva, Premier Cru '69—a fruity Rosé from the Black Forest which will age well.*

Ms. Glazer, the averagely attractive young woman in question, was a flaps-and-seals operator, adept at opening and resealing intercepted correspondence and well able to take care of herself. Her critical knowledge of the noble grape was sketchy, to say the least, but she could hold her own in any drinking session. Nobody in the Firm had ever got to first base with Ms. Glazer, who, if she had it, did not flaunt it. Speculation about her extracurricular tastes among the junior members of the Firm was rife, and despite their lack of success she was generally reckoned to be worth continued exploration.

Hillsden buzzed her on his intercom, watching her on the monitor as she answered.

"Glazer, dear, I'm going to take a ride down to that nursing home, so if Dr. Hogg—or maybe he likes to be called Professor, use your well-known discretion—when or if he rings, be sure and get word to me on the bleeper. It's *très important.* What color is that you're using?"

"Adorable Peach."

"Silly me for asking. Oh, and one other thing, do me a small favor and—"

"Ring your wife."

"Right first time. Tell her—"

"Not to expect you for dinner."

"Right second time. You have just won yourself a weekend for two on the cross-Channel ferry."

He took the private elevator down to the basement garage, using a code to operate it. There he was greeted by Hanson, the Firm's mechanical whiz kid, waiting for him by an Opel Monza.

"Oh, hell, nobody collected my BMW yet?"

"Give me a chance. I had to service three this morning. What's wrong with this?"

"I'm a reactionary, I don't like change. Have you checked the spare wheel?"

"What am I, an amateur?"

"Last night's firework was packed into the spare, wired to the radio."

"Neat but not original," Hanson said cheerfully. "Salamander used that in Rome."

"You're right. Why didn't I remember that?"

"Because you're not as bright as me."

"They got the chauffeur, you know."

"Yeah. High-risk business, chauffeuring."

"That's why I drive myself," Hillsden said. As soon as Hanson triggered the automatic doors, he gunned the Opel, and, after satisfying himself that it was tuned to his usual specification, drove out. He stayed on the South Bank heading west, not crossing the river until he reached Battersea Bridge. There he was forced to slow down while a procession of demonstrators, escorted by mounted police, filed across the road carrying banners proclaiming JUSTICE FOR LEE WAKEFIELD. Wakefield had been a professional agitator alleged to have met his death at the hands of the Special Patrol Group during the previous year's riots in Trafalgar Square, and had quickly been elevated to the status of martyr by the Trots, the Workers Revolutionary Party and other sundry groups on the Far Left. In their election manifesto the new government had given an undertaking to disband the SPG, but had yet to implement the pledge, having swiftly found that being in power was a different ball game than being in opposition: power needs protection.

He sat and listened to the ritual chanting, staring dispassionately at the hate-distorted faces. One of the demonstrators thumped the roof of the Monza as he passed, and stuck a pamphlet under the windscreen wiper arm. Wakefield's doomed face stared at Hillsden as he was waved on by police motorcyclists bringing up the rear of the procession.

He welcomed the long drive ahead, feeling a need to isolate himself and think things out without interruption. The memory of Caroline was still too raw—not the Caroline still in Hogg's keeping, but the woman he had once loved.

As he came off the flyover and accelerated into the fast lane of the motorway, a sudden gust of wind removed the pamphlet and the sun hit the windscreen at an angle, momentarily blinding him until he pulled down the visor. He was suddenly reminded of reflections on a lake. Why a lake? he wondered, and then he remembered.

7

AUSTRIA

"COME OFF IT, Alec, I don't believe you," Caroline said. "It's just one of your typical scare stories."

"Not a bit of it. Not even I would invent something as improbable. I'm just repeating what I was told."

Caroline searched his face before replying, "You're saying—let me get this straight—that all the flies return to this one particular room every year, and die?"

"I'm not saying it; I'm saying that's the tale Jock sold me."

"Oh, well, Jock! *All* the flies, he said?"

"Not all of them. Not even Jock would go that far. Just all the local flies, presumably."

"And you believe him?"

"You know me," Hillsden said. "Never rule out anything until proved false."

"He's seen this amazing phenomenon, has he?"

"No. He was told about it by a Herr Dr. Lehmann."

"Who's he?"

"Local historian with dubious medical qualifications, carrier of gossip and, according to Jock, victim of lethal halitosis. You know how Jock treasures such characters."

"Boy, you two are really gullible."

"Jock credits the same bad breath with telling him the phenomenon only began after a Gestapo officer was murdered there towards the end of '44. That was when the flies started their pilgrimage towards this particular Valhalla."

"I bet that's just Jock's usual embroidery."

"Listen, I haven't bought it yet, but anything is possible. Elephants die in one spot, why not flies? They must die somewhere, why not here in the castle tower?"

"Okay, you're on. Want to bet?"

"Sure."

"How much?"

"A hundred?"

"Pounds or schillings?"

"Native currency. Don't want to be too hard on you."

"Listen to the patronizing sod."

They climbed the curved stone staircase cantilevered into the massive walls of the tower. By the time they had got halfway Hillsden was complaining of cramp in his calf muscles. "They must have been bloody keen to get to bed in olden days," he panted.

"Depends who was waiting between the sheets, I suppose."

"She'd have to be something special." He rested his head against the cold, serrated stone and put his arms around her. "Now, if it had been you, you wouldn't have put me through this, would you? You'd have let your golden hair down from the turret window in the best tradition of fairy tales."

"Have to grow it first."

They kissed and he said, "How about if I just paid you the hundred and we forgot about the flies?"

"Oh, you're going to chicken out, are you? Gone cold on the idea."

"Cold on *that* idea. Distinctly warmer on a better one."

"You're going to push me to my death in a minute. These stairs were not designed for necking. No, come on! We've got this far, and I'm such a good loser."

They resumed the climb and eventually found themselves on the small topmost landing. Whether through damp or old age or a combination of both, the door facing them was twisted out of true, and Hillsden had to exert considerable force to lift it clear of the flagstone floor.

"Add a hernia to my heart attack," he gasped as the door finally gave way.

They both stood transfixed and revolted by what was revealed. The small room was literally obliterated by an undulating blanket of torpid flies. A cold breeze blew in off the lake through the broken window, and even as they watched, more flies arrived on the sill and began their slow crawl into the room, like cripples dragging themselves to a casualty station. The room might well have served as a staff bedroom in bygone days; the iron frame of a single bed still remained in one corner. It had a typically Austrian headboard with marquetry flowers set in the center, but parts of the design had been eaten away by termites. The flies were piled inches high on the bed, coagulated, dark and thick as pig's blood. The only other piece of furniture was a small washstand with a water jug standing in front of a crazed mirror. A long line of flies moved upwards towards the lip of the jug, giving the impression that it was pouring them like some foul, viscous liquid. The walls had patches of diseased plaster; in places this had crumbled away completely to reveal ancient laths, and another stream of flies moved steadily towards a last resting place in these wounds.

Suddenly a living wodge of flies broke off and fell from the bed to the floor, there to be absorbed into the shifting carpet.

In shock, Caroline jumped back, almost knocking Hillsden down the stairs. "Close the bloody door!" she screamed.

Hillsden maneuvered himself in front of her and attempted to pull the distorted door shut, but it resisted all his efforts.

"Leave it! You'll agitate them. They might start to come after us."

They backed down the stairs until they had room to turn, then began a reckless descent.

"That was really gross!" Hillsden said when they were finally out in the fresh air, both gulping it in like children after a long run. Caroline crouched down, her head between her knees as though about to vomit. "Darling, you all right?" She gave no answer and he knelt beside her. "I'd no idea it was going to be like that." As he comforted her, taking the weight of her head, it occurred to him that this was the first time she had ever shown fear of anything. "Listen, I'm sorry, I wouldn't have let you in for it if I'd known. Bloody Jock! You going to be sick?" She shook her head, though he could feel her body shaking as though she were in the grip of some fever. "Gave me a turn, too." He cradled her in his arms until she was calmer.

"It was like the nightmare I used to have as a child," she said. "Only then they weren't flies, they were a tide of faceless people and we were all running away—Mummy, Daddy and me—and I always just escaped, but they caught Mummy and Daddy. I could see him fall and the faceless people closing over him. Mummy turned back to help him and they got her, too. They were both gone, swallowed up as though they were being eaten alive. I did nothing, I just kept running."

"But that was a long time ago, sweetheart, and only a dream," Hillsden said gently. He stroked the damp hair from her forehead.

"Yes. Yes, I know. Didn't you ever have nightmares when you were a child?"

"I still do. Mostly about you and me."

"It all came back to me up there. Thank God it's my last night here. If I'd ever known that was going on above our heads I'd have died of fright."

"No, not you."

"Yes. There's no way I'd have slept here. The final horror would be if you were sleeping in that room when it all began. Just sleeping normally, unaware, and in the middle of the night they started to arrive and crawl over you! Promise you'll stay with me tonight."

"Try and stop me. Tonight and every night, if you'd only let me. But that's a lost cause, isn't it?"

"Not lost, just put on hold," she said, and he wished he could believe her.

When she had recovered they walked across the drawbridge and took the narrow path that ran alongside the lake. The bracken fronds were turning brown, and already the first leaves were drifting down from the huge trees.

"Lakes are depressing," Caroline said after a pause. "I've never liked lakes."

Hillsden nodded. "They always remind me of a poem I learned in school. Something, something 'The sedge is withered by the lake, and no birds sing.' "

" 'La Belle Dame sans Merci.' I learned that too. No, they depress me. The sea, yes, I'd love to live by the ocean."

"So, what's to stop you?"

"Money. Because I don't want some leaky cottage in Sussex or Norfolk, not one of those little 'snips' you find advertised that are 'badly in need of sympathetic renovation.' We all know what that means: an attic full of pigeon shit, rising damp up to the rafters, cold as buggery and a view of that monotonous gray expanse we call the English Channel."

"What's your fancy, then?"

"I want to wake up somewhere remote, with the sun blazing down, white sand and nothing but blue all the way to the horizon."

"Sounds reasonable."

She stopped and stared across the still waters of the lake. "Ludwig died in one of these."

"Ludwig?"

"The Dream King. Wasn't that what they called him? Not too far from here, in a spot just like this. I visited all his mad castles when I was a schoolgirl. We came on an exchange trip, a whole coachload of giggling sixth formers wearing boaters and thick regulation knickers with elastic in the legs."

"Don't tell that to Jock."

"Why d'you say that?"

"Just something he once let slip when we'd hung a few on. The usual chauvinistic stuff about sexual tastes. He confided that he'd always had a hang-up about gym slips. Not that I think he's ever done anything about it. I suspect it's all in the mind."

"That's the most dangerous place," she said. She wasn't looking at him. "They've never found out the truth. About Ludwig. His death— that last walk he took by the lake with his doctor keeper. *He* drowned too. Funny, they hated Ludwig at the time, and now he's their major tourist attraction. I've always had a sneaking regard for him. I mean, if you're going to blow the taxpayers' money, blow it on magnificent follies rather than shitty little council houses."

"Not exactly a vote catcher, darling, in this day and age."

"Well, what are *we* going to leave behind? The National Theatre, Centre Point, Kensington Barracks, all those featureless postwar concrete blocks. I'll take Ludwig's fantasies any day."

They resumed walking, and after a pause Caroline said, "I wouldn't choose that method."

"What're we talking about now?"

"Suicide. If it *was* suicide. Not drowning, that wouldn't be my choice. Oh, maybe if one was suddenly swept under in a great surge of warm foam . . . Not somewhere like this. All that eternal darkness closing over you. It would be like those flies."

She shivered and he went to put his arm around her, but she quickened her pace and the comforting gesture was lost.

"Don't go back to that. I know what you're really thinking about," he said.

"Do you?"

"You don't have to go to Berlin, you know. I could work it with Control."

She shook her head.

"They're lifting me home," Hillsden persisted, "you could come out too. Control could be persuaded. He's never been happy about the East German scene, not since Henry was blown."

Again she shook her head. "I have to."

"Why?"

"Because when I do finally come in, come home, I want to come home with something that makes it all worthwhile."

This time Hillsden stopped her and pulled her around in an embrace.

"Don't," she said. "Not here."

"What bloody difference does it make? If anybody's looking, it's just a lovers' quarrel."

"Is that what we're doing, quarreling?"

"You know what I mean. Haven't you done enough? Haven't we both done enough for all the lost causes?"

"They're not lost for me."

"Hate doesn't bring back the dead. I could make the decision for you, if that makes it easier. I could get it stopped. I love you." He had a sudden premonition that this was the last time he would say those words to her. "We could come out together, go home, retire, hibernate, finish with the whole bloody thing, live in that dream cottage by the sea."

"You've got a home, and you're already sharing it with somebody."

"That could change too."

"Swap one life of deceit for another, is that the exchange?"

"I meant I'd get a divorce."

"You'd have got one a long time ago if that was the answer. I'm not your first infidelity."

"Oh, darling, what an old-fashioned word."

"It's an old-fashioned sin," she said. "The only difference in our case is that you broke a new set of rules. We can't be what we are and have the easy life. We're not two rookies in the police force, swanning around in a Panda car looking for a few drunks to breathalyse. We are what we are: the watchers and the watched."

He tried to stop the torrent of words with a kiss, but she held her head rigid. "I'm going in once more because I still have a reason to hate. That's the game we're in, Alec dear. Not the love game, the hate game."

Now it was Hillsden's turn to stare across the lake, silenced by her terrible logic. On the far side a small boat chugged a diagonal course; moments later the waters began to gently lap against the shore.

"Anyway, you're wrong about Control," Caroline said. "It was his decision to send me back. He knows about us. We haven't been that clever."

"Control decided?" Hillsden could not keep the surprise out of his voice. It was like being told that one had caught a venereal disease from a faithful wife.

"Of course."

"How long has he known?"

She shrugged. "Does it matter?"

"Yes, it matters." He thought how hideous it had all become, how deeply the many deceits had bitten into their lives.

"Remember the last time I went to Salzburg? Control was there. He had the seat next to me at the opera—his sense of the theatrical, I suppose. He told me then, during the interval, choosing his words very carefully. Together we were a risk. Divide or be conquered. All said into his program as though he was explaining Mozart's plot to a niece on her first outing, but really being the prison governor bringing the news that a reprieve had been refused and the law must take its course—his law, naturally."

"Okay, so he knows. Maybe that makes it easier."

"Oh, darling, why pretend that anything's easy?"

"Then put it this way: nothing's impossible. Control isn't God, he's not even Jesus Christ! Just because he offers you the sacrament, you don't have to take it. Doesn't what we have count for anything?"

"That's unfair."

"I'm not in this to be fair, I'm in it to keep you."

She looked at him for a long time before answering. "Perhaps I want to go. Didn't that ever occur to you?"

For a moment he could not trust himself to speak. The day suddenly seemed heavy with the sense of something fateful coming closer. He picked up a flat stone and attempted to skim it across the surface of the lake, but it hit a patch of water lilies and plopped out of sight. The disturbed water threw back a blurred image of them both. Her calmness, the fact that she could deliberately choose a path that excluded him, seemed incomprehensible. He turned to her, envying her certainty. It wasn't a beautiful face, just a face whose image he wanted to retain forever.

"Don't look so sad, darling, I can't help what I am."

"Give me some hope, then. I'm good at waiting, if nothing else."

Caroline thought how quickly their roles had been reversed. They were both trying to keep one foothold in the normal world. "We're a pair, aren't we, you and I? I can't stop you waiting any more than you can stop me going."

"I wanted everything to be perfect today, and I ruined it all, taking you to that room. I love you, and I'm afraid of losing you—that's my nightmare. The only belief I have left is you."

"Don't make it sound so final. They go together, hope and love." She went to him and they kissed with a shared desperation.

"We'd better be getting back, then," he said finally. "Jock will be waiting for us. Wouldn't do to be late for the last supper, would it?"

They walked back to the castle without speaking, touching each other like the blind. Across the lake they could still hear the sound of the small boat's two-stroke engine. It had the beat of a funeral drum.

JUMBLED MEMORIES OF everything they had once shared still troubled Hillsden as he drove up to the nursing home he had never had the courage to visit while Caroline was alive. All unknowing, he parked in the identical space that her murderer had used. A uniformed policeman was posted outside the front door, and as Hillsden identified himself he noticed the telltale bulge inside the man's jacket.

"They've issued you with a peashooter, I see."

The policeman colored, as though caught out in some shameful habit. "Oh, yes, sir. It's that obvious, is it, sir?"

"Maybe only to me. Make sure you've got the safety catch on, otherwise you'll be ending your days here too."

He was shown straight into the Matron's office.

"I've already told two other lots of detectives all I know," she began, and Hillsden thought, somebody's put her nose out of joint. "I don't know what else I can tell you."

"It's often necessary, if boring, to go over the same ground more than once. Sometimes, in the retelling, something new emerges, something that previously everybody has overlooked."

The Matron sniffed.

"Can I start by asking you whether you were Matron here during the entire period Mrs. Nicolson was in care?"

"Yes. She arrived—I looked it up—two months to the day after I took up the post."

"You signed the Official Secrets Act, did you not?"

"Yes." He could sense her underlying hostility.

"And therefore you knew she was not in fact Mrs. Nicolson, but a Miss Caroline Oates?"

She hesitated before answering, "Yes."

"You never imparted that knowledge to anybody else?"

"Not until she was dead. It didn't matter then, did it?"

"No, I daresay it didn't. Tell me, where were you before you came here?"

"I've given all those details."

"Yes, I'm sure, it's just that I'm with a different department."

"I trained at St. Thomas', then went to Barts. I became a ward Sister there, and eventually I was offered a post as matron in the North of England."

"That was where?"

"Liverpool."

"What made you change?"

"When my husband died I found it difficult to manage on my National Health salary, so when this post was advertised I applied and was lucky enough to get it."

"How much were you told about Miss Oates?"

"You mean her medical history?"

"Yes."

"I was informed she'd suffered a severe nervous breakdown during her service in the ATS."

"Nothing else?"

"Only what drugs had been prescribed before, things like that."

"She was on drugs constantly, was she? Because of pain, or what?"

"I don't think she suffered much physical pain, but she needed tranquilizers. I have the list if you wish to see it. I know establishments like this come in for a lot of criticism, most of it uninformed and unfair, but I can assure you that in any hospital I run, drugs are never administered except under the strictest supervision and only on doctor's orders."

"I'm sure. What state was she in generally?"

"Better during the days than at night. She couldn't bear the darkness, so at night we used to put a screen around her and keep a small light burning by her bed. The drugs we used were mostly to help her sleep."

"Did she ever discuss her past with you?"

"Everything they talk about here is in the past. She had her lucid moments, yes, but they were few and far between. Though, curiously enough, I formed the opinion that she was more rational in the past few weeks than she had been for years."

"And what did she talk about on those occasions?"

"Nothing very coherent. Sometimes she'd mention names, not that they meant anything to me."

"Do you remember what names?"

"Bailey was one of them, I seem to remember. Or it could have been, it sounded like Bailey. And Jock. She mentioned Jock several times, that I do recall."

"Were you never curious to learn more about her background?"

"There's a difference, Mr. Hillsden, between compassion and curiosity. I knew she was a special case. People don't get the George Medal for nothing, do they?" she said, looking him straight in the eye. "But in my position you learn to be discreet."

Hillsden smiled. He felt she was beginning to thaw a little; her answers were less abrasive. "Can we just go back to something you said a moment ago? You said you felt she improved slightly in the past few weeks?"

"Yes, I got that impression. I said as much to her invalid cousin when he phoned."

"Her invalid cousin?" Hillsden tried to keep the surprise out of his voice.

"Yes. He phoned at regular intervals asking about her condition. He always seemed very concerned about her."

"Can you remember the last time he rang?"

"No, I don't log such things. Relatives ring up constantly—not always for the best motives, I might add."

"Roughly, then," Hillsden persisted.

"I really couldn't be sure. Perhaps ten days ago."

"And you told him her condition had improved, that she was more lucid?"

"I told him the truth. No more, no less. Nothing wrong in that, was there?"

"No, not on the face of it. Perhaps you should have been more thoroughly briefed. That was our mistake."

For the first time since the interview began the Matron looked troubled. "I don't understand."

"There is no cousin," Hillsden said slowly, "bedridden or otherwise."

"That can't be," she said. "I spoke to him myself on half a dozen occasions."

"I didn't say he doesn't exist, only that whoever phoned is as bogus as the man who murdered Miss Oates."

Wishing to give himself time to think before framing the next questions, Hillsden sipped the weak instant coffee she had provided. The rim of the coffee cup tasted of disinfectant.

"Now, please don't think I'm trying to trap you. Your little knowledge in this case was definitely a dangerous thing, as it happens, but that's not a criticism. What we must know now is the sort of questions this man asked you. Try to remember."

"Never anything that aroused my suspicions. What I've already told you: he asked whether she was comfortable, whether her condition was the same, just ordinary questions like that. The sort of things all relatives ask."

"And on the last occasion, what did you tell him? Take your time, there's no hurry. Just think. Did you, for instance, say there was some slight improvement?"

"I think I said that she was more lucid than she had been. I can't be sure. I treated him like any other relative inquiring. I never raise false hopes, I just report the facts."

"And the reason he gave for never visiting her was that he himself was bedridden?"

"Yes."

"And he was the only outside contact?"

"Yes."

"You never discussed Miss Oates with anybody else outside this building?"

She hesitated, color flooding into her cheeks.

"Not as Miss Oates. I did mention her George Medal to my best friend, but of course I always referred to her as Mrs. Nicolson."

"And who is your best friend?"

"Somebody I've known all my life. She's a schoolteacher—or was. She's retired now and a widow like me. We usually take our holidays together."

"Can I have her name?"

"Molly. Molly Flute."

"Unusual name. What is it, Irish?"

"I believe her family originally came from Ireland. I wouldn't call her Irish, though. She's never lived there, and she certainly doesn't speak with an accent."

"Do you think I might have her address?"

The Matron looked unhappy. "Is that necessary?"

"In a case like this we have to follow up every contact, I'm afraid."

She took a sheet of headed notepaper and wrote the address on it.

Hillsden thanked her. "So that makes two people who knew of her condition, your friend and the bogus cousin. Did she ever have any visitors?"

"Not visitors as such. The social worker saw her regularly, of course."

"Ah, yes. I'd better have her name as well."

"Well, it isn't always a her. They change, you see. Come and go. Sometimes it's a woman, sometimes a man. I must confess that I'm not a great admirer of the system. They're mostly young—too young, in my opinion—and often inadequate. In my day we had to learn our profession before we practiced it. This generation seems to think that reading a few books on old age qualifies them as experts. I'm sorry to be so vehement, but it's something I feel strongly about. Added to which, the local Health Authority is predictably critical of this home. They're always hoping to catch us out."

"Why is that?"

The Matron seemed genuinely amazed at his naïveté. "This is a *private* nursing home, Mr. Hillsden, run outside the National Health Service. It runs counter to all the current militant theories. All men are meant to be created equally ill, didn't you know?"

"And do they catch you out?"

"Not if I can help it."

"So when was the last time one of these social workers saw Miss Oates?"

The Matron consulted her desk diary. "Eight days ago. That was Mr. Timpson. He's been coming for the past six months. To be fair, I consider him a cut above the average. At least he has short hair and wears a suit."

Hillsden noted the name alongside that of Molly Flute. "Did you ever think it odd that she was to all intents alone in the world? Allowing for the fact that you believed in the existence of the bedridden cousin."

"Not really. I hope I don't sound cynical, but you'd be surprised how few of my patients get regular visits. Once they've been dumped here —and I do mean dumped—it's out of sight, out of mind for most of the poor souls."

"What about mail? Did she ever receive any letters?"

"Not to my knowledge."

"I understand you found an envelope with an Irish postmark under her bed after she died."

"Yes, and I can't explain that. All the post comes straight to this office. That doesn't mean I censor it, but some of my patients are blind, and, naturally, we open their letters so that my nurses can read them aloud. With the more disturbed patients, I take the sensible precaution of ensuring that their post does not contain anything that might upset them. You would scarcely believe what some relatives write, especially if they smell some money eventually coming their way. I daresay I've developed a less generous opinion of human nature since I've been here. It's an entirely different world from that of a general hospital, you understand?"

Hillsden nodded. "And when you're not here, when you take your holidays, what happens?"

"Nothing changes. The normal routine is strictly adhered to. My senior Sister has been with me for years and knows my ways."

"I think I'm right in saying that on the afternoon Miss Oates died you were on the premises, but not on duty. Is that correct?"

"I'm always on call, but, yes, it so happened I was taking a short break."

"Who was in charge, then?"

"Nurse Malcolm."

"On her own?"

"For a brief period. We are understaffed at the moment, but the afternoons are usually our quietest times."

"And until the incident everything had been normal?"

"I don't know what you consider 'normal,' " the Matron replied, and Hillsden caught an echo of Hogg's fastidiousness. "Your ideas might differ from mine."

"Let me put it another way: had there been anything untoward?"

"No. An establishment like this has to be run on very rigid lines, otherwise we'd have chaos. Many of the patients are incontinent, some

71

bordering on the insane, some with terminal conditions. So it would be dishonest of me to contend that everything goes smoothly all the time. We often get a collective fretfulness, call it no more than that. One sets off the rest. In particular we do have one patient, a member of the aristocracy, as it happens, quite harmless really, but now and then he flies off the handle and that does cause problems."

"That would be Lord Orchover, I take it?"

"Yes."

"And he was the one who first admitted the bogus visitor?"

"Yes. Most unfortunate."

"In your opinion, would I be likely to get any additional, useful information if I questioned him?"

"I doubt it. But providing it's under supervision, you're at liberty to try. The reason this . . . this horrible thing happened was that he told Nurse Malcom the man was his lawyer. He's got an obsession that his family is plotting to disinherit him, and I suppose Nurse Malcolm, who's fairly new here and not aware of how cunning he can be, got flustered. I'm not excusing her, but I can understand why she acted as she did. I insist that all visitors are escorted to the rooms. She didn't do that. Not that I exclude myself from blame. I should have spotted the injury to Lord Orchover immediately and alerted the authorities quicker."

Much to Hillsden's surprise he saw that the Matron was crying. "I still can't believe that such a dreadful thing could happen here," she said. Hillsden handed her his handkerchief.

"Oh, dear, what will you think of me? I don't usually behave so stupidly. And look what I've done to your clean handkerchief, I've gone and got lipstick on it. I'll have it laundered for you, otherwise your wife will be after you."

"How d'you know I'm married?"

"I can always tell," she said, drying her eyes. "Nurses have second sight."

"I must remember that."

"Perhaps I could be told when the funeral's going to be? I'd like to pay my last respects. Especially since she had no family." She stopped suddenly. "Now, that's odd."

"What is?"

"I *have* remembered something I haven't mentioned before. She had a photograph on her bedside table. A picture of a man and a young girl."

"Herself as a young girl?"

"No, no, it was quite modern. That is to say, the girl looked contemporary."

"Do you have it?"

"No, that's the point, you see. It disappeared."

"When?"

"It wasn't there . . . after she died."

"Could one of the other inmates in her room have taken it? Old people are often jackdaws."

The Matron shook her head. "They're both more or less bedridden. When I found Miss Oates dead in suspicious circumstances, I had them both moved to another room. Even if one of them had taken it, I'd have discovered it then."

Hillsden was silent for a few seconds. "Well, thank you, Matron, you've been very frank and I'm most grateful. You see, I was right, you did remember something new after all. Now, if I could just spend some time with this Nurse Malcolm."

They found the nurse spoon-feeding Lord Orchover a cup of Bovril in the "sun lounge," as the Matron proudly described the three-sided glass extension to the dining room.

"I'll take over, Nurse. This gentleman would like to have a few words with you about recent events."

"Don't want you!" Lord Orchover shouted, immediately becoming excited. A mouthful of Bovril dribbled down his chin. "Don't like you, don't like your manner, madam. Who's this fellow? Have they sent him? Because if they have, he can damn well clear out now. They're not getting another penny. Not a penny!"

"Off you go, Nurse. You can use my office again, Mr. Hillsden."

As they walked away Orchover yelled, "I shall raise this matter in the House!"

"He's quite harmless, really," Nurse Malcolm said. "Just a baby most of the time. Are you from the police?"

"I work closely with them. I'm from the pensions department of the War Office."

She seemed satisfied with this explanation. Having got over the first shock of Miss Oates' death, she was now savoring her moment in the limelight and seemed only too delighted to reel off her story.

"He seemed so genuine, see? What with the chocolates and flowers. Nice-spoken. Trim. Not badly dressed. Looked as though he could do with a bit of fattening up. His clothes sort of hung on him, know what I mean? Not that you want to know all that, but the real police were very pleased with me. Said I gave a very good description."

"I'm sure they were. Did you notice whether he had any sort of accent?"

"Yes. Yes, he did. A brogue. Could have been North Country, I suppose. Sounded a bit like James Mason—that's what I told the police. They thought that was very helpful. Course James Mason's dead now, but that's what he sounded like when he was playing those parts. He was a lovely actor, wasn't he?"

"One of the best."

"Will I have to say all this in court when they catch him?"

"It's possible."

"I don't know how I'd do there. I mean, I've never been in trouble before."

"Well, you're not in trouble now."

"No, but at the same time—it makes you feel queasy, doesn't it? Just thinking about it."

"Because she was entitled to a disability pension," Hillsden cut in, anxious to get back to the point, "my department has to establish whether or not there are any relatives still living that we don't know of."

"He wasn't what he said, what he told me, was he? The cheek of it, taking me in like that! But I think anybody would have been taken in, don't you? I acted with the best intentions."

"Yes, I'm sure. We understand that Miss Oates did have one genuine relative who used to inquire after her health from time to time."

"That's right."

"He couldn't visit her, apparently, but he used to ring here. Did you ever speak to him?"

"Yes, come to think of it. I did take a call recently when Matron was out."

"How recently?"

"Oh, I'm terrible on dates. Let's see, it must have been within the last three weeks, because I've only been here three weeks."

"And what did you tell him?"

"You always try and be cheerful, don't you? No point in depressing them. I expect I said she was coming along nicely. What else can you say?"

"And he was the only person who ever rang about her? You never took a call from anybody else?"

The nurse shook her head.

"I only ask because Matron said something about a photograph she kept by her bed. A photograph of a young girl."

"Oh, the photograph, yes. Nice photo, pretty girl."

"Miss Oates never told you who she was?"

"No. And I didn't ask. Doesn't do really to pry into their personal affairs, not unless they ask me, because some of them are funny about those sort of things. Get touchy, and one doesn't want to start them off. I used to chat with her, naturally, when I was bathing her or making her bed, but she didn't talk much, poor dear. Didn't read, just sat there. In fact, and this is a funny thing, or it struck me as funny at the time, the only time she ever really talked was about flies."

"Flies?"

"Yes. Couldn't bear them near her. If there was just one fly in the room, she'd spot it and get very agitated. I used to spray around her bed. Spiders I could have understood, because they give me the creeps, but I mean, flies, you've got to live with those, haven't you?"

"You have indeed. Well, thank you for all your help."

"When d'you think they'll want me in court?"

"That's hard to say. They have to catch him first."

"I can't get over the fact that I was the one to let him in. I go all cold when I think about it. You don't think he'd come back, do you?"

"I'd say that was highly unlikely."

Before leaving, he asked to see Caroline's room. It had been left empty since her death and he did not linger long; there was nothing in the room to connect with the girl he had once known, and the only thought he had was to wonder why anybody had felt the necessity to murder a vegetable.

9

CALDER'S PLANE LANDED in Zurich three minutes ahead of schedule, a fact that the Swissair stewardess announced with studied pride in three languages. Calder was in no hurry to disembark, allowing the Arab to go ahead of him. Having only hand luggage and a Swiss passport, he passed through Immigration and Customs without any hassle. There he lost sight of the Arab, but he took no chances and went into the toilet, locking himself into a cubicle for ten minutes before emerging and making for the Avis counter. It was another of his precautionary rules never to bring his own car to the airport; a vehicle parked for any length of time could arouse unwanted curiosity. He rented a 280SE Mercedes saloon, using an American Express gold card issued under the name of Miller. By the time the car was delivered to the pickup area he had convinced himself that the presence of the Arab on the same plane was mere coincidence.

Some forty minutes after the plane touched down he was on the road, driving with his customary skill and immediately adjusting to being on the right-hand side. From long habit he did not take the direct route to his home, but as usual made a detour around the outskirts of the city. He had covered some ten kilometers before he became conscious of another Mercedes in his rearview mirror. Recent suspicions surfaced, and to test whether he was being tailed he maintained his speed, then turned off into the forecourt of the first roadside restaurant he came to. The other Mercedes sped straight past. Was he being too jumpy? No, better be safe than sorry. He ordered an espresso and a slice of chocolate cake, glad to be back in the land of efficiency and cleanliness. The rich smell of freshly ground coffee and the starched neatness of the young waitress who served him had a calming effect. Admiring the tight pertness of her figure—the curve of her legs where they disappeared beneath the skirt was especially erotic—he began to plot future pleasures, to speculate how and on whom he would spend his fee. He dropped three lumps of sugar into the froth of his espresso, awarding himself extra calories for a job accomplished without mishap.

It was in this frame of mind that he lingered over the chocolate cake, letting each forkful slowly dissolve in his mouth. His thoughts switched from sex to the coming enhancement of his bank account. I must put some of it in Krugerrands, he thought. Always keep 10 percent of one's assets in gold, wasn't that what all the big operators preached? And they knew; the manipulators always came out on top, whatever the state of the market or fluctuations in the international scene.

He left the amount of his check plus an exactly calculated tip, and strolled outside to his parked car. The far carriageway of the road ran alongside a small river fed by a waterfall. Calder stood by the Mercedes and listened to the pleasurable rush of water, becoming hypnotized by it. He was still absorbed when a sibilant voice close to his ear said, "I think you've kept us waiting long enough, Mr. Miller," and he caught the scent of some strong cologne.

Swinging around, he came face-to-face with a blond young man with the unblemished complexion that, during the war, would have been automatic poster material for the Hitler *Jugend*. The youth wore a smart Burberry trench coat, though the weather hardly justified it.

"Enjoy your cuppa tea, did you?" The voice was affectedly British.

"In England everything stops for tea, doesn't it? But we're not in England, and you're expected elsewhere, so get in, sweetheart, and drive."

Calder scanned the car park, but apart from a family of tourists unpacking the trunk of a Fiat, there was nobody to save him.

"You're looking in the wrong direction," the youth said. "Didn't think I was alone, did you? I never go out alone, even in broad daylight, because there are so many nasty men about these days and Mummy always warned me. I'm terrified of being raped, so I always bring a strong friend. He's sitting over there in that Mini Cooper with the pop-star black windows. Very butch, and he's got a gun trained on your winkie. One of those guns you see in spy movies. The kind that goes 'pop' and doesn't frighten the neighbors."

As he spoke the Mini eased out and came alongside the Mercedes.

"So you just drive. We'll follow."

"Where are we going?" Calder asked.

"Curiosity killed the cat, dear. You'll find out soon enough."

The arch voice and camp language gave additional menace to the scene. Calder got into his car, but deliberately left his seat belt unfastened. As he pulled out into the road his first instinct was to put his foot down and lose them, but he rejected the idea: the Mini would almost certainly have a souped-up engine and be fully capable of keeping pace. For the moment he was defenseless.

After both cars had traveled a few kilometers he saw the following Mini flash its headlamps twice. The Mercedes that had been behind him earlier pulled onto the road ahead of him, so that he was now effectively sandwiched between the two vehicles. Shortly after this the lead Mercedes turned off the main highway and he was led up a series of hairpin bends, climbing all the time. He made a determined effort to memorize the route they were taking. Eventually the secondary road leveled out at the top of a mountain range; below was a valley dotted here and there with small estates grouped around a lake. With Calder still boxed-in, the small convoy descended into the valley, and while he struggled to formulate a feasible plan of escape the lead car pulled up in front of some imposing iron gates. These swung open, activated by a remote-control device, and the three cars proceeded up an immaculately kept driveway.

The sun had gone off one side of the valley, and the first thing Calder saw was a clay tennis court, half in shadow, with a couple playing on it. Then he glimpsed the lake through a sheltering screen of conifers until finally the house itself came into view. It was built in the conventional chalet style, but larger than average, the overhanging eaves painted in bright colors, making it look like an advertisement in a travel brochure. He also noted a tall mast with a television satellite disk mounted on it. At this point the Mini suddenly darted ahead, squeezing past him at speed with only inches to spare. The moment it stopped, the blond youth jumped out and indicated where Calder was to park. As he cut the engine the blond opened his door.

"Enjoy that, did you, dear?"

"I love mystery tours, especially when they include pretty blonds."

"Don't be too cocky, dear. Otherwise I might forget myself and slap your wrists. My friend likes it when I get rough. Turns him on, and when he's turned on it's difficult to turn him off. It might all end in tragedy."

The driver of the Mini joined them. He was roughly the same age as his blond friend, but heavier built and dressed in identical fashion, even to the striped shirt and pink tie. Together they looked like a gay cabaret act.

The other Mercedes had parked a short distance away, and only now Calder saw that the driver was the Arab. The man gave a small, mocking bow as he approached. "Well, Mr. Holgate, or, rather, Mr. Miller, here we are again. If you hadn't been so cautious at the airport, I could have saved you the cost of a hire car."

"Let's cut the bullshit, shall we?" Calder said. "I've met the Dolly Sisters here, and I can do without your jokes."

Without warning the blond youth threw him against the side of the car and carried out a thorough body search. Calder offered no resistance, and when it was over he said, "Oh, you're good. You must have been practicing on choirboys."

"Just a house rule," the Arab said. "Nothing personal. Let's go inside."

He led the way into the chalet. Calder stepped straight onto deep-pile carpet that lapped against his ankles. The interior of the chalet consisted of one enormous main room with an open staircase leading to a gallery that ran around three walls. On the ground level the walls were hung with huge modern paintings which demonstrated that size is not commensurate with talent. There was also an abundance of hi-fi equipment and a giant television screen. Two double-glazed windows slid open as the Arab approached them, activated, like the main gates, by some hidden electric beam.

The blond and his companion disappeared into another part of the chalet while Calder followed the Arab onto a stone patio that extended in gentle tiers to the edge of the lake. Two men were lying on brightly cushioned sun-loungers, wearing florid sports shirts and checked trousers. Standard rig, Calder thought, for a Miami golf course, but on these two more like stage costumes. One of them, the seeming elder of the pair, was biting on an unlit pipe, but it was alien to his face, as with a theatrical prop some actors use to give themselves poise. The whole scene suggested a posed photograph in one of the snob magazines for the good life.

The man with the pipe lifted himself out of the lounger. "Ah, Ronnie," he said, addressing the Arab, "you finally brought our friend. We were getting anxious."

"Mr. Miller stopped on the road for a cup of tea."

"Well, he wasn't expecting our hospitality, Ronnie, so we must make allowances. Do sit down, Mr. Miller. A pleasant flight, I trust? So efficient, the Swiss, and I'm all for efficiency, very little of it about these days. Can I offer you something stronger than tea?"

"Yes, I'll take a drink."

"What would you like?"

"White wine."

"Ronnie, will you take care of it, please?" The Arab withdrew. The man returned to Calder with a smile, exposing teeth that looked as though they belonged in another mouth. "I think congratulations are in order."

"Are they? You want me to congratulate you on the efficiency of your two storm troopers? This seems to me a rather futile exercise. Didn't you trust me to make the drop as on other occasions?"

"I merely thought it was time we met. And I meant congratulations to you on your usual excellent job. From all accounts everything went very smoothly."

"I did what I was asked to do—no more, no less."

"Well, slightly more, perhaps. But we'll get to that later. Meanwhile, you have something for us, I believe?"

"The arrangement was payment with delivery."

"Oh, come now, Mr. Miller, we're both too old to play games, aren't we? And you're not in a position to demand favors. You have a photograph. Give it to me."

Calder reached into his wallet and extracted the picture. Now the other man bestirred himself for the first time. "Can I see?"

His accent was not as perfect as his companion's; it was Calder's guess that he was Russian. Perhaps they both were; it was difficult to judge. He tried to think why they had chosen this particular moment to come out into the open: ever since he had taken up residence in Switzerland all previous transactions had been conducted through dead letter boxes.

There had to be other hidden dangers in the encounter, dangers he had yet to identify. He watched as the other man examined the photograph closely. "Very good, a collector's item," the man pronounced. "Well worth your trip, Mr. Miller."

"Worth the price you agreed to pay, I hope?"

The elder man opened a Chinese lacquered box on a small table between the two sun-loungers and took out a bulky envelope. "Small-denomination Swiss francs, as you stipulated."

Calder slit the envelope with a finger and glanced at the contents. He had more style than to count the notes in their presence, and in any case felt the need to somehow regain the initiative.

At this point the Arab incongruously called Ronnie returned with a bottle of chilled wine. He poured the wine and then withdrew again.

"How was England?" the second man asked. "Such a backward country in so many ways, still clinging to the belief that it has influence in world affairs. Was it strange for you, going back after such a long absence?"

"Yes and no. I prefer the plumbing here."

The first man took over again. "Old habits die hard though, don't they? Especially the ones we try to keep hidden."

"What's that supposed to mean?"

"Did you read your English papers this morning?" He picked up a copy of the *Daily Telegraph*. "Unfortunately, we didn't receive our copy of the *Times* today. The printers there are on strike again, showing the world how well democracy works. Still, the *Telegraph* is really superior when it comes to reporting lurid crimes. Perhaps you noticed this account of the murder of a young prostitute in what the British euphemistically call a massage parlor?" He let this sink in, but Calder remained expressionless. "We chose you for this assignment because we felt you had special qualifications, and you executed it faultlessly. It was what took place afterwards that gave us cause for concern." Again he paused. "That is why we decided to vary past procedures and bring you here." His delivery was so devoid of menace that its very blandness chilled. He might have been a schoolmaster giving an end-of-term report.

"You are not the only one who doesn't leave anything to chance, Mr. Miller. We monitored you every inch of the way. And, please, don't for one moment imagine I'm about to criticize your sexual tastes. I like them young and pliable myself. It adds spice to an otherwise monotonous aspect of life as one grows older. No, what disturbed us was your timing, though I appreciate that having completed your assignment you felt the need for some relaxation. There were, after all, unique pressures attached to this particular job, and we all have our lapses from grace. However, historically, one mistake has a habit of leading to another, something I am sure we would all wish to avoid. Your past contributions to the cause have been invaluable, and we would hate to lose you. I trust you get the point I'm making?"

Calder merely nodded; he sensed that the real message was still to come.

"Good. Just to make sure, we thought it might be instructive if we not only convinced you of our own diligence in these matters, but also gave you a practical demonstration of the way we deal with carelessness. We want to bind you even closer to us because we still have uses for you."

"Am I going to be asked to sign a morality clause?"

"Such a sense of humor. That's very British, is it not? Unfortunately, in addition to seeing the humorous side of everything, you British also have this mistaken gift for combining pleasure with business. There's a definite pattern about the way in which you contrive to destroy yourselves. I'm sure I don't have to remind you of what happened to some of your distinguished predecessors. It would be such a tragic waste if a man of your talents took himself out of circulation for the same reason."

"Moscow had me killed off once," Calder said with feigned calmness.

"That was for mutual convenience—hardly the same thing. But we're not here to discuss such final solutions, just to give you advice. We've always known your tastes, and it would be a simple matter to provide for them without placing anybody at risk. You have only to ask."

The sun had dipped perceptibly lower by now and most of the lake was in shadow. From where Calder was sitting the tennis court was out of sight, but from time to time he could hear the two players calling out the score.

"It boils down to a question of priorities," the elder man continued, refilling Calder's glass. "As with wine. Which grapes to nourish, and which to sever from the vine. In other words, what is most expedient to protect the vintage. Patience, that's the key word. We let others make all the first moves, because time is on our side. You're a perfect example. We didn't hurry you, did we? We arranged for your public withdrawal, kept you in luxury and then, when the time was right, reactivated you. Perhaps in the end it's all a question of national characteristics."

"Is that why you had me brought here? For a philosophical discussion?"

The elder man turned back to his companion. "Our friend still hasn't appreciated the true meaning of my words. Part of him still thinks in the old ways."

"Perhaps he will be convinced shortly."

"Yes. You see, Mr. Miller, your problem is that you still ask why? and for what reason? We never do. There are too many questions in your head. Why was I brought here? What was the real reason for my last mission? I can see those questions in your eyes. Don't ask them; they are no concern of yours. Relax, you have been paid, you have a glass of wine in your hand, and very soon we're going to enjoy a meal here in the open. On these fine evenings we usually have a barbecue, a few steaks cooked on charcoal, American style. What could be more pleasant?"

Calder shrugged. "I'm your guest, willing or unwilling."

"Don't be so guarded. Had we thought it necessary to kill you, we would have done it in London. In London you were never safe, but here in the land of the cuckoo clock you have nothing to fear."

He broke off as the Arab returned, wheeling a portable barbecue complete with an electric-fan attachment.

"Well done, Ronnie. Very good timing." He went to the barbecue and donned an apron. As Ronnie retreated into the chalet again he sprayed the bed of charcoal with a can of firelighter fluid, then ignited it.

"The Swiss can do a lot of things, but they can't produce steaks like the Americans. I have mine flown in from Texas. Certified U.S. prime."

When Ronnie returned he brought with him a small table on which the steaks were arranged like dark red books in a library. The collected works of American cuisine, Calder thought.

"How do you prefer yours, rare or ruined?"

"Half ruined," Calder said.

"Let us have some more wine, Ronnie. Bring the Margaux. You should find three bottles already opened." He switched the fan on and the charcoal began to glow.

"There's something so satisfying, so basic, don't you think, about eating in the open air? Most of us have grown to neglect the simple pleasures of life." He seemed like some huge parody of a housewife. Some of the heat of the barbecue traveled to where Calder was sitting. A lone seabird swooped in low overhead, scenting future pickings as the first slabs of meat were forked onto the grill above the hot charcoal. A slight breeze coming off the lake carried the smell of seared flesh to Calder, and for the first time since his arrival he relaxed slightly, the domesticity of the scene combined with the wine blunting his usual reflexes. Fat from the meat dripped onto the red embers and a smoke haze drifted across the patio.

Ronnie returned to place the bottles of wine on a second table, and as he did so the blond youth and his companion appeared out of the chalet, treading silently like ballet dancers emerging from the wings, and pinioned him from behind. With the blond's hand clamped over his mouth he was casually frog-marched down the shallow steps to the edge of the lake. Any distant, casual observer would have taken them to be three men out for an evening stroll. Ronnie stumbled once and managed a cry for help before being silenced again, but the sound he made was little different from the call of a sea gull. The two young men held him firmly, compelling him towards the untroubled waters. In the fading light and through the haze their outlines blurred. Calder sat upright in his chair as the full implication of what was about to happen hit him. When the group reached the water's edge, Ronnie's captors forced him to his knees, pressing his head down and submerging it. To Calder the scene was like the moment before a car crash when everything appears to go into slow motion. The struggle at the lake's edge took hardly any time at all, yet seemed to last an eternity. When it was over, the two youths lifted the Arab's limp body and carried him back towards the house, taking a wider circle for the return journey and disappearing into the gloom.

Calder was the first to break the silence. "That was for my benefit, presumably?"

The chef at the barbecue looked up from his labors; he was sweating. "Put it this way, Mr. Miller: in view of your lapse of concentration in London, it was necessary to demonstrate our singleness of mind. You see, Ronnie, unlike you, had outlived his usefulness. He had developed that terminal form of greed, a fondness for two paychecks."

"Who turned him?"

"Happily, not the British—otherwise you, too, would be expendable. He had been corrupted by the gospel of the Blessed Khomeni, so Moscow Centre decided he would meet with a boating accident. It's well known these lakes are very treacherous."

At that moment the two tennis players, a man and a girl, joined them. The girl was dressed in close-fitting slacks and a heavy V-neck sweater that molded against her body as she walked. Calder could not see her clearly at first, but as she drew closer he recognized her as the girl in the photograph he had carried all the way from the country he had once called home.

10

WHEN HILLSDEN RETURNED to the warehouse later that same day, Rotherby was waiting for him with Hogg's written report. Rotherby—variously known as the Colonel or Lawrence of Wapping, having once unwisely confessed to a turgid adulation of T.E.—had come to the Firm from, of all places, the Treasury, and regarded anything committed to paper with unconcealed horror. "If you don't write it, they can't read it. If they can't read it, they can't copy it. If they can't copy it, they can't steal it, and if they can't steal it, they can never hang you with it. Q.E.D."

Knowing this, Hillsden was prepared for his greeting.

"Look at this bloody tome, Alec! Ten pages of the stuff, and most of it reads like *On the Origin of Species.* All he needed to tell us was How and By What, but naturally he had to air his superior fucking knowledge."

"Would you like to rephrase that, Colonel? He's brilliant at his job, but I doubt whether his knowledge of fucking is superior to yours."

"Do drop that 'Colonel' nonsense. So infantile."

"Okay, give it to me in shorthand."

"The substance injected into her has been identified as DS7. First known use 1944, when issued to SS officers. Causes complete respiratory failure within ninety seconds. Hogg's own findings checked out and confirmed by Porton. Then there's some other grisly stuff that he couldn't resist adding, such as the upper bowel containing a quantity of partially digested Farex."

"What the hell's that?"

"Really, Alec! Where were you brought up? Farex is a preparatory food normally only given to infant children. My nanny swore by it."

"I never had a nanny."

"That explains a great deal. D'you want to hear the rest?"

"No, that's enough."

"All seems a bit pat to me," Rotherby observed. "The SS reference, for instance. I never like clues that are handed to me on a plate."

Hillsden nodded. "All the same, check it out with Bonn. Ask them for every incident over the past five years involving the stuff. Ask them whether it's still manufactured in their perfect democracy, and if so where and under what supervision. And while you're at it, ask whether it's available over the counter on prescription."

"On prescription? You can't be serious!"

"Where have you been all your life? The drug houses don't miss a trick these days. Every bloody thing under the sun is available in some form or another if they can get away with it. For all we know, somebody's marketing a mild dose for hay-fever sufferers, or vets are using it to decrease the surplus canine population."

"You do amaze me."

"That's one of my main functions in life. I'm a professional amazer. Where's Fenton, by the way?"

"Out."

"Doing what?"

"The Turkish embassy sent for somebody to examine a suspicious parcel."

"That's not our bag. Since when have we been a bomb disposal unit? We're wine importers and gentlemen of leisure."

"It isn't a bomb. Just some collection of documents they seem to think might interest us."

"What language are they in?"

"English, but they don't understand them, apparently."

"Well, if they don't understand them, Fenton certainly won't. He's only just mastered the *Morning Star.*"

"That's why Control agreed for him to go. It's all part of his master plan—Control's Turkish Delight. He's never forgiven them for blowing up his sister's holiday home on Cyprus."

"I sometimes think we're all totally mad."

"Subversive talk, old son! I shall have to insist on another positive vetting for you."

"The only thing I'm concealing is an attack of athlete's foot."

"Been drinking out of dirty cups again, have you?"

"You're warm. The last cup I drank out of tasted of Jeyes Fluid. I've been down to that nursing home."

"And?"

"I dredged up a couple of things. One I don't understand at all, and one we can follow through. Apparently the staff got regular phone calls from somebody purporting to be Caroline's cousin, asking after her health."

"Traceable?"

"Doubtful, but we've got to have a shot. Is Waddington around?"

"Was."

"Tell him I want to see him." As Rotherby started to leave, Hillsden added, "And run a check on the Matron and the entire staff. Here, take this." He handed over the slip of paper containing the names he had noted down. "Especially Molly Flute. Try Special Branch first." He rummaged in his desk drawer and took out an unopened packet of digestive biscuits. "And while you're at it, run one on Bayldon's chauffeur too. Ex-Army"—but he was talking to air.

When Waddington came in, he was still struggling to rip the plastic wrapper on the biscuits. "If we could only blanket the entire country with this stuff, Wadders, we'd have one hundred and two percent maximum security. The only way you can get through it is with a chain saw."

"Another Communist plot," Waddington said somberly. "As Solzhenitsyn has written, 'They won't take us with tanks, they'll take us with their bare hands,' which, translated from the Russian, means they will undermine the very fabric of our society by attacking the sacred ritual of the British digestive biscuit."

"Don't make jokes. It's not my day for jokes. Is there anything to drink?"

"You have a choice. The corked house red or the corked house white."

"Raid the Colonel's private store."

"You can't be serious. You know how spastic he gets."

"Listen," Hillsden cut in, bored with this dialogue and changing the subject abruptly. "Apart from the Bush House killing—which in any case was done with the poisoned tip of an umbrella—the use of a hypo is fairly uncommon, at least over here. That should give us a starting point. Does the computer have anything?"

"Anticipated you. Just been there. The magic box only came up with one name. Mozhayev. He was credited with a couple, but we took him out in Belgrade last year."

"Shit! Have you read Hogg's report?"

"Yes."

"And?"

"Very thorough."

"Oh, fuck you, Waddington! Can't you ever commit yourself to an outright opinion? Nobody minds you being wrong. All we ever ask is that you take a plunge."

"We're very touchy today."

"Yes, well, I've got plenty to be touchy about." Hillsden jumped up and raided a case of wine standing in the corner of the office. "Where's the corkscrew?"

"Where would it be? Filed under C, second drawer down."

In his anger Hillsden savaged the cork, then poured the dregs of a coffee cup into a waste bin and filled the cup with wine. "Nothing makes any sense. No sense at all. Why poor bloody Caroline? And why now? Why bother to exchange her and send her home if eventually, years later, when she's gaga, you're going to eliminate her?"

"Perhaps that's the sense of it: the fact that it makes no apparent sense. The good old KGB mentality, the inscrutable Russian mind, et cetera."

"Too easy. I don't buy it. But what else could they get out of it? Why risk it going wrong? It was a clean, professional job, planned and executed by somebody who knew his way around. Yet they never do anything without a reason. Therefore"—he started to pace the room, taking frequent swigs of wine as he went from wall to wall—"therefore we have to look for something beyond the immediate. Is it something in the past or something in the future? Let's deal with the past. There's nobody left from the old Austrian station. Jock's dead, Henry went a long time ago, the stables were cleaned out years ago. There's nobody."

"Except you."

Hillsden stopped by a window and gazed down at the sluggish waters of the Thames below. "No, I was out of it by the time she went back. It was Jock's show."

"So you say."

"Well, it happens to be true."

"I repeat, so you say, but perhaps *they* don't believe that. You know as well as I do that Moscow never closes a file. The reason Caroline went back that last time was because she and Jock were onto something really big. With Jock and Henry dead and Caroline sucked dry, who else is there but you?"

"Wadders, you do talk the most unutterable balls sometimes. If they want to get to me, why kill a burnt-out case?"

"To force you into doing something."

"What, for instance? Resurrection of the dead?"

"All right, don't be so bloody high-hat. You're forgetting something. What about the bomb last night? Maybe that was meant for you."

"Oh, bollocks! Use your brain for a change. (A) the bomb was planted in Bayldon's car; (B) although I have a certain charisma, it doesn't extend to having the automatic use of the Foreign Secretary's chauffeur-driven car; (C) it was just a macabre coincidence."

"Okay, okay, but you asked me to plunge."

Hillsden resumed his pacing. "At the moment all we have is two loose ends. I got something from the Matron at the nursing home. She let drop that a photograph was missing from Caroline's bedside after the murder. A photograph of an unknown young girl. Question: Who was the girl? Second question: Why was it worth stealing? Find me the answer to those, Wadders, and I'll see to it that you retire with a knighthood. Remind me, did you ever meet Caroline?"

"No. Before my time."

"Everything's before your time. You make me feel bloody old."

But even as the words left his mouth, it wasn't age he felt, but guilt.

11

THE GIRL IN the photograph flew into Heathrow the following day. On this occasion she traveled on a legitimate British passport under her given name of Pamela Brent-Russell. Clearing Immigration, she made straight for the green Customs exit. There she was stopped for a spot check by a young Preventive Officer who made a specialty of suspecting attractive women. He searched her single piece of luggage and, when denied success, questioned her closely about her Cartier wristwatch. She further frustrated him by revealing it was a cheap fake made in Hong Kong.

"If you don't want to take my word for it, confiscate it. It will self-destruct in about a week's time. I buy one a month," she added, just to put him in his place.

After he allowed her to proceed, she made a phone call from one of the few unvandalized kiosks, dialing a number in the Belgravia area. A male voice answered.

"I'm back, darling," she said. "Have you missed me?"

"Of course. Did you have a good holiday?"

"So-so. But I missed you too. Do you want to see me?"

"Need you ask?"

"When?"

"Slightly tricky until late this evening. How about ten-thirty?"

"Can't wait. See you then."

The warning bleeps started, and she just had time to add, "I don't have any more English change," when the connection was broken. She stared at her tanned, unblemished skin in the broken mirror above the receiver. A police notice was pasted on the wall beside the mirror: BOMB WARNING. BE ON YOUR GUARD. REPORT ANY SUSPICIOUS PACKAGES OR UNATTENDED BAGGAGE. She smiled at her own image, then left the terminal building and took the Underground train to central London.

Her final destination was Notting Hill Gate. Leaving the main road, she made her way towards a row of terraced houses that had once been Edwardian artisans' cottages, but in recent years had been bought by speculators and given a face-lift. The front doors and shutters had been painted in this year's *House and Garden* colors and stood out in rainbow contrast to the surrounding drabness. She entered one in the middle of the row. Somewhere a burglar alarm was ringing relentlessly, and the sound stayed with her once she was inside the house.

"Gunther!" she called, "I'm back," but no one answered. From habit she kicked off her shoes and padded through the main room to the kitchen beyond. The rear of the house was L-shaped, the two sides facing into a small walled garden. There was a hatch for her cat cut into the kitchen door and she anticipated her usual welcome home, but the animal did not appear. She noticed that its bowl of food was untouched. "Daisy?" she said, "where are you? Come on, come on out and say hello." When nothing happened, she felt strangely cheated.

In the kitchen she filled an electric kettle to make herself a cup of instant coffee, and was conscious that the whole house stank of stale smoke. The sink was filled with unwashed crockery, and the frying pan on the cooker had a layer of congealed fat in it blackened with specks of burnt bacon rind. Wrinkling her nose in disgust, she searched for the special security key to enable her to open the kitchen window. It was only then that she noticed that most of her potted plants had died from neglect. Lazy bastard, she thought, he never lifts a finger when I'm not here, but then she saw something else and stood very still. Her ears suddenly unblocked; she was acutely aware of the noise of the city beyond and of the persistent ringing of the burglar alarm. Sudden nausea made her sway. She started to back away from the window, but her bare feet refused to grip the tiled floor.

A wooden trellis topped the dividing wall between her garden and the next. Her neighbor's tangled honeysuckle covered most of it and provided a degree of privacy for both properties. The inverted yellow blossoms gave off a heady fragrance in the evenings, but now as she stood staring out it was the scent of fear that reached her. At first she thought she was halucinating, but then the full horror struck her: her cat was pinioned to the wooden struts, its forelegs spread-eagled in a crucifixion pose, its neck squeezed tight by a garroting wire securing it to the frame.

The shock was so great that for a few seconds she blacked out. When she came to, she found herself bent over the sink, her face almost touching the unwashed dishes. She retched, then slid down to the floor, pushing her cheek against the cold tiles until the spasms subsided. Lying there, she did not hear the front door opening or her name being called, and it was not until a hand lifted her head that she was aware of anybody else in the house.

"What happened? Did you faint? Pamela, did you faint?"

She stared up into a familiar face. "Oh, it's you," she said. "Thank God."

"What is it? What happened?"

"They killed Daisy."

"They what? Who did?"

"Look out in the garden."

Gunther stared at her, then straightened up and went to the window.

"Why did you leave her there for me to see?" Pamela sobbed, shock now turning to anger. "Why didn't you cut her down, you bastard?"

"What are you talking about? I didn't know. I've been away for a couple of days."

"You promised me you'd take care of her."

"I did, I did!" he shouted, returning her anger from guilt. "She was all right when I left. I put out plenty of food."

"Her food's uneaten. Didn't you notice?"

"I told you, I've been away, I just got back."

"You just didn't care. You've never cared about my cat."

"Oh, Christ!" He went to help her up, but she spurned his helping hand.

"Get out of here, go into the other room, don't look anymore. I'll deal with it," he said.

When she was out of sight, he took a plastic garbage bag and a pair of pliers, then unlocked the door to the garden and went outside. As casually as somebody pruning roses he cut through the garrote and the wires securing the forelegs and dropped the stiffened corpse into the bag. Then he went through the house to the front and deposited the bag in the dustbin.

"All over," he said, kneeling beside where she lay on the sofa. "Look at me. I'm sorry, really I am." He kissed her, but her mouth did not open to him.

"What sort of person would do something like that?"

"A cat hater, presumably."

"Ring the police."

"You're still in shock. You're shaking. You know as well as I do we can't tell the police."

"They crucified her. It's the most horrible thing I've ever seen. I want you to find out who did it."

"Look, be sensible. I've said I'm sorry, I wish it hadn't happened, but it's done, it's over, and there's no way I'm going to draw attention to ourselves by making inquiries." Again he tried to embrace her, but she remained as stiff and unyielding as the dead animal. "You know this neighborhood. There's a break-in everyday. Listen to that alarm going off now. It was probably some shitty little sneak thief who tried to rip us off, got nowhere, and took it out on the bloody animal."

"That's what you would call it."

"Don't give me a hard time about everything I say. I'm telling you, that's the most likely explanation. Why don't you go upstairs and lie down for a bit? I'll make you a hot drink."

"I don't want a drink, I want us to get out of this place, live somewhere else. She was my cat. I loved her." She searched his face, looking for some reflection of her own anguish, but he remained impassive.

"I'll buy you another" was all he said.

"I don't want another. I never want another pet as long as I live. And I want to move."

"Okay, no big deal. I was going to move us anyway."

"Why? What else has happened since I've been away?"

"Nothing. Just time we moved on. You know that. Now, can we talk about other things? Did Miller make the delivery?"

"Yes."

"You're sure?"

"I destroyed the photograph myself."

"So cheer up, it's not all bad news."

"You make me sick sometimes," she said.

"That's right. Not being British, I lack your sensitivity, as you've often told me. But just remember one thing: because of me you're still around to feel grief."

She got up and walked past him, climbing the stairs to the bathroom. She turned on the hot tap and started to remove her clothes where she stood, kicking them to one side. After a pause Gunther appeared in the doorway. She was naked now, and he moved to put his arms around her.

"Don't. I'm not in the mood."

"I deserve some thanks, don't I?"

She slipped from his embrace and got into the partially filled bath. He sat on the closed toilet seat and stared down at her body.

"Don't I?" he repeated.

"Yes, but I'm tired right now. All I want to do is fall into bed and get a few hours' sleep. I'll be nice to you later."

"Only you British could call sex 'nice.'" He mimicked her upper-class accent. "Oh, darling, that's so naice. Put your naice thing inside my naice thing, but don't move it about too much because Mummy told me only foreigners do that."

Nothing he said had any meaning for her: she could almost make herself believe she was still at thirty thousand feet somewhere in the stratosphere, drifting in and out of that uneasy sleep that bore no resemblance to the airline advertisements. Only the familiar note of sexual pleading in Gunther's voice, and his searching hand reaching below the water to the silkiness of her groin, forced her back to reality.

"It's no use. Just hand me a towel."

He took one from the hot rail, but held it just out of her reach, so she stepped out of the bath and walked out of the room, leaving a trail of water on the fitted carpet. "Just because you can't have your own way every time." In the bedroom she took a flowered dressing gown from the back of the door. "And for your further information, I have to go out later, so you'll have to wait even longer before you get your oats. *He* wants to see me, and as you've often told me, the cause comes first."

She put her hands behind her head and flicked up her damp hair, twisting it to stay in place. He stood in the doorway watching her, and something in his face made her relent. She went over and kissed him. "I'm not standing you off, really I'm not. It's just everything—that nightmare of poor Daisy, jet lag, everything. You wouldn't want to make love to a corpse." Her use of the word brought back a searing image of her dead pet, and the return of horror gave an extra urgency to her embrace. He mistook her anguish and tried to prolong the kiss, feeling her loose, warm breasts through the gown, but again she slipped free. "Even though you make fun of me, I will be 'naice' to you"—it was her turn to parody herself—"especially 'naice.' When I get back I'll do all the things you like, all the things you've taught me. I just have to get some rest before I see him. They're anxious to know if he's kept his nerve."

"I'll keep you to that. What did you make of Miller?"

"Different." She got into the bed.

"In what way?"

"I don't know. Maybe because of his reputation I'd expected a sort of Frankenstein. But he looked like a bank clerk." She pulled the blankets up to her chin.

"Did he make a pass at you?"

"Are you kidding? Of course not."

"You're his type. He likes them young."

"Why, darling, I do believe you're jealous"—making the statement as though, for the first time, she could believe that he was human after all. "You ought to know that he's not my type. I only go for Germans like you. Especially Germans like you."

He took the compliment without smiling. "What time are you meeting him?"

"He made it late, ten-thirty, so wake me up about nine, will you?"

"Find out as much as you can. But be subtle. You've got a good excuse—you've been out of the country and you've missed all the news. Pump him."

"I'm sorry I was so grotty just now. It's just that sometimes I wonder if our luck will run out. That's why Daisy's death frightened me so much."

"I don't have luck. Luck is for amateurs," he said, but her eyes had already closed and she never heard the last comfort. She slept fitfully, and a little after nine Gunther returned to wake her. After doing her hair and applying a discreet lipstick, she dressed in fashionable but conservative clothes in strict contrast to those she had traveled in.

"He likes you like that, does he?" Gunther said, and she caught the renewed sarcasm in his voice.

"The short answer is yes. And while I'm out you might clean up the kitchen. It looks like a slum."

"I don't make homes, I wreck them."

She left the house and was lucky enough to obtain a taxi without much difficulty. It was still light but with the orange glow over the city peculiar to that time of year.

"Royal Court Theatre, Sloane Square, please."

On arrival she went inside the theater and studied the posters until she was certain that the taxi had driven away. Then she walked around the corner towards Eaton Square. She had the feeling that she was in alien country, conscious of the wealth behind the well-kept façades, the smug, padded existence of the inhabitants. When she reached Eccleston Street at the far end of the square, she crossed over and made her way

93

to one of the mews leading off Belgrave Place. Apart from a small boy trundling himself along on one roller skate, the street was deserted. Keeping her head down, she went to one of the fashionable, single-fronted houses.

The door was opened as soon as she pressed the doorbell.

"Well, how about that for timing?" she said.

"I don't deserve anybody so perfect," Sir Charles Belfrage answered. He drew her into the house as the small boy skated past.

12

CREMATION HAD BEEN Control's decision. "Much the best," he said, "in the absence of any written preference. So much neater and in keeping with current thinking. Safeguards the environment. My mother was one of the founder members of the Cremation Society; at the time it was considered very infra."

"Will you go?" Hillsden asked.

"I'm rather inclined not. I always seem to catch the most appalling colds whenever I attend funerals. No, all in all, I think your presence will suffice to do the honors for the Firm."

"The Matron at the nursing home expressed a wish to attend."

Control considered this. "Again, I think not. Just your *discreet* presence, though it might be a good idea if the wife went along with you. Make it look normal."

The suggestion took Hillsden by surprise. "That hadn't occurred to me."

"Occurred to me," Control said, cracking his knuckles; then, dispensing with any further discussion on the subject, he added, "Oil of Evening Primrose."

"Sorry?"

"Works wonders for the creaking joints our mortal flesh is heir to. I take it every day. Also retards the aging process, or so I read in one of those beauty columns."

The idea of Control studying the latest cosmetic tips in women's magazines seemed another of his many eccentricities.

94

"So be prepared, Alec, one day you might walk in here and find Dorian Gray sitting behind this desk. Imagine what that would do to Accounts! They'd get their knickers in a right old twist if they had to pay a pension to a teenager. That's settled, then, is it?" he said, switching back to their original topic with disconcerting abruptness. "The funeral's on Monday, Tunbridge Wells Crematorium. Sufficiently off the beaten track and quite a pleasant place, I'm told, as these places go. Fitting, I thought—Kent, the garden of England—as a last resting home for a heroine. A nonreligious ceremony. We wouldn't want to attract any attention from the locals."

"I'll think about my wife."

"Strikes me as a good piece of window dressing. Won't present any problems, will it? Well, none that you can't overcome, I'm sure. The end of a chapter. Well, the end of a whole book as far as you're concerned, I suppose." He cracked his knuckles again and gave his innocent, inquiring look, but Hillsden refused to be drawn. "Any further leads?"

"No. Except we do know that somebody was keeping tabs on her. Perhaps we should have done the same."

"Yes. Being wise after the event. But you're no closer to identifying the missing photograph?"

"No."

"It all adds up to something, Alec, and that's what they pay us to find out, we humble servants of the Crown."

Some of us humbler than others, Hillsden thought as he was dismissed.

He returned home later that same afternoon to find his wife still in bed asleep, expelling her even breaths like sighs. An open box of Quality Street chocolates sat on the bedside table with half the contents eaten, the discarded wrappers strewn about the floor. He bent and retrieved a paperback in their midst. It proved to be a clinical study of female sexuality, the latest in a long line of best sellers on the subject, following a familiar pattern of anonymous case histories. Margot had turned down the corner of one page: "I have been married to the same man for eighteen years, but my sex life is nil and has been since God knows when. I stay with my husband because I've nowhere else to go and I can't bring myself to look for sex outside. I'm not a swinger. I regard myself as just an object. I wish I had the courage to be a lesbian."

He replaced the book where he had found it, then tiptoed out of the room and went downstairs. From habit, for company, he switched on the portable television his wife usually carried from room to room, muting the sound to a minimum, just loud enough to catch the announcer's words. Good news or bad, it was all delivered in the same flat tone, giving the impression that every newscaster had been cloned from a prototype. As he waited for the kettle to boil he watched strange images of death replacing one another on the screen like cards falling from uneasy hands: children with pear-shaped skulls, distended bellies and matchstick legs, lifeless in the arms of their haunted mothers; what remained of a British soldier lying in a Northern Ireland ditch; a racing car exploding into flames and expelling a human torch—this last item repeated in slow motion. He thought: It's as though the only information worth transmitting is that which sickens and shocks. Maybe since the Church's version of *Paradise Lost* had become déjà vu, it was necessary to give the public a daily reminder of God's infinite mercy.

The kettle screamed, and he leaped to silence it just as Bayldon's unctuous face replaced the incinerated racing driver. Schooled in the political academy of insincerity, Bayldon stared straight at the camera wearing his most ministerial face, though as he fielded one or two awkward questions the reflection of the firing squad could be seen in his eyes. He assumed a faraway look while searching for new ways to conceal old lies. It was all verbal Muzak, piped to the masses like the soothing stuff airlines delivered on takeoffs and landings, those moments of maximum danger.

Hillsden dunked a single teabag into two cups. He had never been able to fathom why the bags did not disintegrate in boiling water; it was one of the great riddles of domestic existence. As he returned to the bedroom with both cups of tea, Margot came awake.

"I heard voices," she said.

"I had the television on downstairs."

"What time is it?"

"Not late. Just gone six. Were you having a nap?"

"Yes, I had one of my headaches."

"I brought you a cup of tea."

"Don't usually fall asleep in the middle of the afternoon."

"Does you good occasionally. Damn, I forgot to sugar yours."

"I've cut it out, I'm on a new diet." Her eyes flicked to the box of chocolates, but he affected not to notice.

"I should join you. I'm getting decidedly porky. It's all those business lunches."

"How was it today? Been busy?"

"So-so. Took a few orders. Matter of fact, I brought you a bottle of the new sparkling wine we're pushing this month. Nonvintage, but very pleasant. It's going well." He sipped his tea, glib as Bayldon. "Did you take something for your headache?"

"Yes, I took a couple of aspirins."

"Weather doesn't help, been heavy all day. Tell you what, why don't we go out tonight, have a meal somewhere? Be a change, especially if you're feeling a bit iffy. Save you bending over a hot stove."

"Well, I look such a mess."

"Not to me, you don't." It was like talking to a child who was afraid of failing an exam. "Come on, I'll run a nice bath for you."

"Don't let's go anywhere posh, then."

"What about Chinese? That little place in the King's Road? Chinese food isn't fattening, so that won't ruin your diet."

He went into the bathroom and turned on the taps, glad that she could not see his face when he shouted the next bit of news. "We don't get out enough, if you ask me. My fault. I work such lousy long hours. Still, mustn't complain, lucky to have a regular job these days, and the more depressing it gets, the more people seem to drink. But it's hard on you, dear. Everybody needs a break now and then; after all, we're only here once. That was brought home to me today. We had something of a shock at the office."

"You brought what home?"

"No, I said, we had a shock today."

"What was that?"

He sat on the rim of the bath, the reason behind the lie he was about to tell draining the strength from him.

"Have I ever mentioned a Mrs. Nicolson to you?"

"Mrs. who?"

"Nicolson. She worked in Stores."

"Don't think so. What about her?"

"She suddenly dropped dead today. One minute she was having her morning break in the canteen, and then, no warning, she just keeled over. Just like that. We got an ambulance and rushed her to hospital but she was dead on arrival. Only fifty."

"Fancy."

He tore off a sheet of toilet paper and wiped his eyes. "No age at all. You can guess what a shock it was to all of us."

"I can imagine," his wife answered from the bedroom. "Must have been a greater shock to her husband."

"She was a widow. All on her own."

He made sure of the temperature of the water, then composed himself and returned to the bedroom. The chocolates and the paperback had been tidied away out of sight. "Your bath's ready, dear." He stripped off his own shirt and went to his wardrobe. "I don't suppose you'd come with me, would you? Bit depressing to go to one of those things alone."

"Go where?"

"Her funeral. It's on Monday."

"Why do you have to go?"

"Well, somebody from the office has to go. We drew lots and I was landed with it."

"Couldn't you have made some excuse?"

"Not really."

"But I didn't know her."

"I realize that, but I just thought you would come and keep me company. We could make a day of it, drive on to the coast afterwards. They've given me the whole day off."

"Where's it being held, then?"

"Down in Kent, Tunbridge Wells."

"Funerals depress me."

"You haven't been to that many."

She had been taking off her clothes and makeup during this exchange, and now, partially naked, she left the room. "I've been to enough to know I don't like them."

"But if I made it into a treat?"

"I'm getting a lot of treats all of a sudden. Tea in bed, wine, eating out tonight, a trip to the seaside. Anybody would think you had a guilty conscience."

"I was only trying to be nice." He picked up her cup of tea and followed her, but when he got to the bathroom she had locked the door. "Don't you want this?"

"What?"

"Your tea. You haven't drunk it."

"I've drunk all I want."

"Why have you locked the door?"

"Because."

"I thought we might have a bath together. Like the old days." There was no answer. "Darling, did you hear me?"

"Yes."

"Well?" He waited. "Okay, just a thought. I'll go and make a booking for dinner. We can talk about Monday later. Perhaps you'll feel better after a nice meal."

He started to take the teacups downstairs when she shouted, "Alec!

Don't book anywhere posh, I haven't got anything to wear. Nothing fits me anymore."

In the kitchen he made a phone call to the restaurant, then sat waiting in the darkening room, dreading the treat to come.

13

"BEGIN AT THE BEGINNING," Waddington said. "Treat me like an imbecile just out of police college. I might be able to prise loose a few chips of your marbled memory."

"What a command of language you have, Wadders. You missed your vocation. You should have been an art critic."

Waddington took this as a compliment. "I won the essay competition at school three years running. It's a gift, I suppose." He and Hillsden were sitting in a cheap hamburger joint just off Covent Garden, mostly patronized by students and the odd derelict, and chosen by Waddington because it was self-service: "We won't be interrupted by waiters."

Not that Hillsden cared. He was indifferent to food or his surroundings today. Dinner out with Margot the evening before had hardly been a culinary or conversational success. Far from enjoying herself, she had treated the event as a bribe she was reluctant to accept. "You're not doing this out of the kindness of your heart, so don't pretend you are. You want something in return" had been her recurrent theme, and he had left the question of her accompanying him to the funeral in abeyance. As they both picked at Chinese food that proved the old maxim that the Far East was inscrutable, it had occurred to him how often her intuition scored a bull's-eye. There was no moratorium for infidelity; one carried it forward from year to year, an unpaid item on the human balance sheet. She could make no direct connection between the fictitious Mrs. Nicolson and Caroline, but years ago the line of suspicion had been drawn.

"I always believe in getting back to basics," Waddington continued. "Don't you think that's a good idea? For instance, remind me how Caroline was recruited in the first place. Start with the day she joined the Firm."

"No, we have to begin further back than that." He stared at the pulverized meat crammed between the two layers of soggy bun, then took a tentative bite. The act of deciding whether or not to swallow it made his speech even more deliberate. "The background, her background, is important."

"Okay. So fill me in."

"She was an only daughter, born 1938, in Finland."

"Finland? She wasn't British?"

"Oh, yes. Her father was the naval attaché at the embassy in Helsinki. She was born in the embassy, as a matter of fact."

"Born with a silver CD plate in her mouth."

"Are you going to listen or just make facetious remarks?"

"Sorry."

"When the war came, her parents shipped her home with a nanny. So she was probably reared on the renowned Farex," he added, testing whether Waddington, like Rotherby, had picked up the reference in Hogg's report. Waddington stared blankly, and Hillsden continued: "Then when the Russians invaded in November 1939 her father was posted as British liaison officer with the Finnish forces at the front. I don't know how well you know your history, Wadders, but after the war it was revealed that there was actually some half-arsed plan for an Anglo-French army to go to the aid of the gallant Finns. I believe the scheme was to send four divisions to invade Norway before the Germans did, and to take on the Russian army in Scandinavia."

"Sounds pretty harebrained."

"Well, don't forget that during the first, phony-war year we were still playing at it—dropping leaflets instead of bombs and singing comic songs about the Siegfried Line. Anyway, while London and Paris were still arguing the toss the whole situation changed. The Finns had great success at the start. They were better trained and better equipped. It was a bitch of a winter that year, and both armies were slugging it out in sub-zero temperatures. But the upshot was that the Russians regrouped, and in February of the following year they launched a massive new offensive in the Karelian Isthmus. By the time Whitehall and the Frogs had agreed on a definite plan the shooting match was over. The Finns capitulated in March 1940. Caroline's father was taken prisoner, tried as a spy and executed, although that never came out until long after the war. Until then he was merely posted as missing, and even when the truth surfaced it was officially suppressed—nobody wanted to rock the boat where our glorious Russian allies were concerned."

"What about her mother?"

"She stayed on throughout, trying to discover what had happened to her husband; she took a job as secretary or something. When she was finally convinced he was dead, she killed herself."

Hillsden broke off as a group of punks swaggered past the table. With their vivid-colored hairdos, Thirties clothes and outsize boots they resembled something out of a pantomime, but there was no mistaking their latent hostility. One of them deliberately knocked against Waddington's chair, but he and Hillsden ignored the provocation. "I suppose if I ate this food every day, I'd be aggressive too," Waddington observed as they passed. He poured a dollop of ketchup from a plastic container shaped like a tomato and encrusted with dried sauce. "There's a theory that junk food ingested over a prolonged period inflames the brain. Did you know that?"

"No, but I can believe it."

"Sorry, go on about the Finns. That's fascinating, they didn't teach that in my school."

"No—well, as I say, after Stalingrad it wasn't done to criticize the Red Army. The only rap they ever got for raping the Finns was to be expelled from the League of Nations."

"The League of Nations! That was still going?"

"Too true. I always thought that was the ultimate sick joke. For Christ' sake, stop interrupting."

"You were the one who digressed. Okay, so where was Caroline during all this?"

"She was safe in England. The nanny was one of those able characters who crop up in that sort of situation. Tough as teak. Caroline always described her as the deck of the *Victory*. There was no way she was ever going to entrust Caroline to anybody else. She brought her up without help from anybody, and she never let Caroline forget what had happened in Finland. I guess she must have done a pretty thorough job of indoctrinating the kid. She hated everything Russian with a passion. Some people refused to play German music during the war; well, Caroline once told me that Nanny Anderson—she was Scots, naturally, that's where all the best ones come from—wouldn't let her listen to Tchaikovsky, and this at a time when the First Piano Concerto was practically our second national anthem. She was a ballsy old dame, from all accounts. She supported Caroline, educated her, and instilled in her a lifelong hatred of everything the Russians stood for. So you might say it all began there, that Caroline got a good grounding for her life to come."

"She decided to get even from the cradle, did she?"

"No, come on, that would be too facile. That idea came much later, and not for the reasons I've just described. Oh, sure, she was conditioned all right, she couldn't help herself, but she never set out on that course. She was bright, learned languages quickly, sailed through her exams and was fairly uncomplicated, all things considered. When she finally left school, I think that like most kids of her generation she just wanted to have a good time."

"What year are we talking about now?"

"Around '56, '57. She had no particular ambition, took a secretarial course, got bored with that and signed on as a courier for a travel agency in order to see the world on the cheap. Hated that; said all she ever saw was the inside of a coach and complaining faces. Took another course as a manicurist, and eventually landed a job at Austin Reed's, in Regent Street."

"What happened to the nanny?"

"She died. Caroline had no other relatives, or none that she ever traced."

"How about boyfriends?"

"Plenty, I gather. You can't go by the pictures on file, but when I first met her she was quite something. Not beautiful, because it was an odd face. Lovely mouth, the sort you wanted to kiss the moment you saw it."

He pushed the uneaten remains of his meal to one side; it looked like a road accident. "How did you manage to finish yours?"

"I've tasted worse," Waddington said. "So she was a manicurist. What then?"

"That's when she got recruited. One of her regular clients was old Dinnsbury."

"The legendary Gunga?"

"The very same. He was running B Division when they first met. Not that she knew that; all she knew was that he didn't like nail polish but adored having his mount of Venus massaged."

"His *what*?"

"It's here, on the ball of the thumb, a noted erogenous zone, I'm told, though it's never worked for me. Anyway, she thought he was just some rich old buffer in the City and a good tipper. Maybe he did have the hots for her, who knows? If he did, he never made a pass that Caroline admitted to. I guess it was just hand holding. What he did do was offer her a job. Gunga was no slouch when it came to sizing up possible recruits. He looked harmless enough, but he was a real operator underneath all that cigarette ash. I daresay he nosed around, got her talking about her background, made some outside inquiries and decided she could be potential cannon fodder. You know, I've always thought that if it had been left to Gunga, our stables would have smelled a lot cleaner; I can't see him not sniffing out Burgess and Blunt and that motley gang. He was a cute old sod, whatever anybody says about him now. But he wore the wrong tie, belonged to the wrong clubs, ate his peas with a knife, so to speak. It was such a fucking closed shop in those days, before the shake-up. And, of course, they did for him in the end."

"How? He wasn't ever suspected, was he?"

"Oh, when the shit hit the fan nobody was safe. The 'super-mole' theory touched everybody of note. Parliament and the media were baying for sacrificial victims. It was bloody panic stations. Mind you, no getting away from it, we had been deeply penetrated."

"As the girl said."

"You can never resist the ghastly pun, can you?"

"Apologies. That hamburger has inflamed my brain."

"Caroline came under the shadow simply because she was Gunga's girl and tainted by association. As for Gunga, they vetted him three times, and although he was finally given a clean bill of health, he'd upset too many people along the way. They gave him a C.B.E. for appearance' sake and early retirement. After that he faded quickly—died about eighteen months later. If he knew anything, he took it with him to the grave."

"What sort of job did he offer her?"

"General shorthand typist at first. He was testing the water. He never committed himself in a hurry. Then, when he was satisfied, he made her his own secretary. That was the real beginning. The moment she got to know the ropes there was no stopping her. She told me that when she found out the real nature of his work she felt she'd finally come home. Those were the exact words she used. With Gunga's encouragement she learned Russian; languages had always come easily to her, and of course she was with the right man. Old Gunga spoke God knows how many languages: he was a sort of human Linguaphone, from all accounts. Actually knew a dozen Indian dialects, apart from everything else."

"He served out there, didn't he? Hence the nickname, I take it?"

"He served a damn good curry, that's for sure. Caroline said it was volcano heat."

"So it was all his doing? He encouraged her to break loose?"

"He approved her going to earth and becoming a card-carrying member of the CPGB. Just standard infiltration. She fed them a lot of smoke and some fire, all of which Gunga masterminded. But that really wasn't her bag, it was just a stepping-stone. It didn't fulfill her, she said. I suppose she was a late developer where hate was concerned. She'd listened to all the horror stories at Nanny's knee, but it was Gunga who showed her how to make use of them, how to get even. Are you with me so far?"

"Yes, but I could do with a coffee refill," Waddington said. "If only to remove the taste of the food."

Hillsden went to the counter and purchased two more plastic cups of the liquid they sold as coffee. "Listen," he said as he returned, "people who knew Caroline in those days said she couldn't wait to get close to the real enemy in the field. Swapping class hatreds with the Brothers was not her idea of striking a blow for democracy. You and I know that any prolonged stint in those boondocks is pretty demoralizing. To be always on your guard, to change your name, your whole life-style, avoid old friends, cultivate new habits, like drinking beer instead of gin, smoking a cheaper brand of cigarettes, taking a different newspaper, swotting up the accepted jargon and remembering to trot it out at the right moment when everything inside you is crying out to refute it. Those are the pressures you live with twenty-four hours a day. It's not the splendid romantic existence that novelists are fond of picturing. And it's especially difficult for the girls, in my view."

"Why especially?"

"Don't you think that life in general is more difficult for them?"

"Do I? I don't know."

"Bring it down to your basics, Wadders. Whatever else, they've got the old monthly burden for openers. We may enjoy the pleasure that is momentary in the position that is ludicrous, but they're the ones stuck with the consequences. Or am I going too fast for you?"

"No, I'm gaining deep insights."

"Anyway, the point I was making is that she had set her sights on a field job. Jock was the one who finally worked the oracle. He was one of Gunga's original blue-eyed boys, and he'd been looking for new blood to beef up his operation in Vienna. That was the line he shot, though knowing him as I did I'm bloody sure he had a more personal, ulterior motive. And I daresay Caroline wasn't unaware that the quickest way to Jock's heart was through his fly buttons, to put it crudely. Not that she ever succumbed to his many charms, because they were pretty evenly matched when it came to getting their own way."

"Can you be sure of that?"

"Of what?"

"That they didn't make it."

"Take my word for it, I'm sure."

"If we're treating this seriously, the object of the exercise is not to take anybody's word, but to get hard evidence."

"She didn't sleep with him. If she had, they'd have shipped him home instead of me."

Waddington nodded, but Hillsden was left in doubt as to whether he was convinced.

"Jock convinced Gunga that she would be invaluable to him; he put up a strong case. Naturally, once she got wind of the idea Caroline put in her two cents, and between them they got Gunga to agree. I don't think he was ever entirely happy about it, because he was old-fashioned in many ways, but she was his star pupil and he couldn't begrudge her wanting to fly the nest. Rumor had it that Jock clinched it by saying that if he didn't get her he wanted out. It was probably an idle threat, but Gunga couldn't take the risk. He was a tough egg, old Jock."

"I only knew him by repute."

"Oh, Jock was good. He ran the Austrian station with spectacular results during the height of the cold war. At the time he prised Caroline loose the CIA had requested our help to penetrate a ring operating out of Munich. The Yanks were getting more and more spastic about the amount of high technology they were losing to Moscow, commercial hardware that could be readily adapted to military uses, plus just plain military hardware. They knew who was running it in Munich, but they couldn't figure out how he was getting the goods to Moscow. It was pretty complicated. When it finally got unraveled, we found the stuff was leaving Los Angeles on fake invoices labeled 'refrigerators' or 'washing machines,' and being airfreighted to West Germany. From there it was transported overland to somewhere neutral—sometimes Switzerland, sometimes Austria. After that they lifted it from Zurich or Salzburg to Amsterdam, and from there to Russia with love and a great deal of profit. They worked it with multiple transactions and reams of false import licenses—enough to baffle your average Customs man. The Russians were forking out three times the retail price in hard currency, paying top dollar.

"It was beautifully thought out. At that time the Russians were light years behind. All they had was dinosaurs—number crushers, as they used to be called. We're talking, don't forget, about the genesis of the microchip revolution, when Silicon Valley was in its infancy. But it wasn't just plain industrial thievery. They were desperate to improve the performance of their nuclear stockpile, and they set about it in their usual thorough way, using the oldest weapon in the human arsenal—money. Lots of it. They splashed it about. All they had to find was a few greedy textbook capitalists, so they settled on a good German democrat, a Harry Lime, model two, and got him to set up the whole operation for them. They supplied the wherewithal and he placed the orders through one of his shell companies, of which he had dozens, all with legit-sounding names. On the other side of the pond the suppliers were just as greedy to get the business, anybody's business, with not too many questions about the eventual destination. And nobody suspected a thing until the Russians started to market their own versions at international trade fairs. The Yanks suddenly woke up to the fact that they were in competition with themselves."

"And you say Jock was the one who cracked it?"

"Jock, mainly, with a little help from his friends."

"Including Caroline?"

"Yes. Jock used her to get close to the Harry Lime character. Which she did very successfully."

"You didn't like admitting that, did you?" Waddington pushed the knife in quickly.

Hillsden stirred his coffee with a plastic spoon, then snapped it in half. "Didn't I?"

"No. I was watching your face."

"How astute of you, Wadders. Comforting to know you haven't lost your touch."

"Would you prefer me to put it another way? How about if I said she was just doing her job, would that upset you as much?"

"Oh, come on, you can do better than that! Aren't you the eyes and ears of the world, the Firm's gossip columnist? You've heard all about Caroline and me. Alec liked a little on the side. Blotted his copybook, poor old Alec, blighted a promising career, got sent home for behavior not becoming an officer and a gentleman, to say nothing of a spy."

"Take it easy."

"Fuck taking it easy. She's dead, Wadders. Hogg cut her open and then stitched her up again. She's in the deep freeze, just another fish finger, another statistic, another casualty of peace."

"Aren't we all eventually? But meanwhile let's try and find out why she ended up on Hogg's plate."

"I suppose you've never committed adultery, Wadders? Been the perfect little husband, spurned getting head in the typists' pool?"

"There's such a thing as discretion."

"And I bet you're good at it. God! You're such a pompous cunt sometimes."

106

"Probably. But I've got under your skin, haven't I, touched the raw nerve? I'll take a guess: you didn't like sharing her, did you, even though it was in the line of duty?"

"Where do you get your dialogue, out of *True Romances*? I was in love with her! Does that answer you, or is that too simple?"

His voice had grown louder during this exchange, and now he became conscious that the punks were listening to every word. One of them made a remark and his companions fell against one another in appreciation of his wit. Hillsden pushed the plastic cup across the table, knocking over the grotesque ketchup bottle, and got to his feet. Waddington tensed, sensing an explosion, but Hillsden brushed past the group and had covered a hundred yards out in the street before Waddington caught up with him.

"That was really stupid of me," Hillsden said finally.

"I goaded you."

"It was monumentally stupid. You're right, you did hit a nerve. I thought it was a dead nerve, that I'd had a root canal where Caroline is concerned, but I was wrong."

"Want to call it a day?"

"No, let's walk. You know my trouble? Even though she's dead, I'm still jealous. Jealous of time wasted, time lost."

"That's good. Gives you an edge."

"Does it? Also makes me careless."

They walked on in silence until Waddington judged the moment ripe to reopen the subject. "Where was the last time you saw her?"

"Austria. We were all three there then. Me, Caroline, Jock."

"Then she went back to Berlin, right?"

"Yes."

"Why? I thought you said the Munich network had been cracked by then."

"She was onto something else, something she and Jock had stumbled upon."

"Something she didn't share?"

"No."

"Wasn't that odd, considering your relationship?"

"Not really. Sometimes it's wiser not to know too much. I wasn't running her, Jock was, and he made it a local house rule that we didn't share more than was necessary."

"What was their relationship?"

"Close."

"Look, I don't want to press you on this, but by 'close' do you mean intimate?"

"She wasn't sleeping with both of us, if that's what you mean. What you have to understand about Caroline is that she worked by the book. I only had her body from time to time, never her mind."

"After she was taken, why didn't Jock follow through?"

"Good question. Perhaps he did, or perhaps he tried to; we'll never know. I was back here by the time Caroline disappeared, and I never saw Jock again. A month after we got confirmation that Caroline was in Moscow, Jock was dead. The whole Austrian network was kaput."

"Did it ever occur to you that Caroline might have betrayed Jock and the others?"

"Yes, it occurred to me."

"And?"

"Anybody can be broken. Ours is not an exact science, Wadders. You should know that."

They were strolling under the colonnaded entrance to St. Paul's, Covent Garden, traditionally known as the actors' church. Hillsden paused. "Pygmalion," he murmured.

"What?"

"We did that to Caroline. The Firm does it to everybody who comes within its orbit—makes them over, changes them for good." He looked up to where the army of pigeons were settling down for the night. "I've always loved this part of London, this piazza in particular, even though it's been screwed up like everything else. D'you have a sense of history, Wadders? Is that part of your secret life? Do you get pleasure from ruins —myself always excepted?"

"Not particularly, no."

"What a lot you miss. It's the only thing I cling to, history. Knowing it's all happened before keeps me sane."

As they approached one of the smart neighborhood restaurants a posse of look-alikes from the social pages of *Vogue* suddenly disgorged onto the pavement, all talking in strident voices. They blocked the way, arguing about what disco to favor next with their custom, and Hillsden and Waddington were forced to step into the street.

"Just think: our efforts aren't entirely useless—we're helping to make democracy safe for that lot."

"Alcoholism is also a major problem in Russia," Waddington answered. "We don't have a monopoly on parasites."

"It simplifies everything, doesn't it, if you believe? Like manic religion or political faith. Take whoever churns out those leading articles for *Pravda*. You'd have to have absolute belief, wouldn't you, to write stuff like that day in and day out?"

"Not necessarily. Chum of mine used to write second leaders for the *Times*. Said it became a trick after a while. The trick was to pose an endless series of questions. He told me that after doing it for a year he could turn in a thousand words on any subject they threw at him in half an hour flat."

"You've made my point for me. He *didn't* believe."

"How can you be sure the *Pravda* hacks don't have their tongues in their cheeks?"

But Hillsden had lost interest. His thoughts were darting about like fireflies. "The only clue we've got, as I said to Control, is the missing photograph of the unknown girl. I keep asking myself, why did Caroline have it by her bedside, and why did it disappear? I blame myself for not knowing the answer. I betrayed her."

This time Waddington was caught napping. He could not keep the surprise out of his voice. "You betrayed her? How?"

"I never went to see her in that home. And d'you know why? I was too bloody scared. Oh, I pretended to myself I was being noble, playing the reformed adulterer, but the real truth was I couldn't face seeing what they'd done to her. Wouldn't you call that a betrayal?"

"But you said 'blame' at first. Why 'blame'?"

"I'd have seen the photograph."

He stopped at the next corner. Across the street an old derelict was preparing to doss down for the night, covering himself with cardboard torn from cartons that, ironically, carried advertisements for merino wool blankets. Without a word to Waddington, he walked over to the old man and felt in his pockets for a coin. He held it out and the derelict took it, his grimed hand like a claw. Scabs of dirt encrusted his stubble, and he seemed to be wearing at least five layers of clothing tied together with string around his middle. The rest of his belongings were contained in a plastic shopping bag. He examined the pound coin, but said nothing.

"Your good deed for the day," Waddington said as Hillsden rejoined him.

"Nothing good about that. Just conscience money. Real charity is loving somebody without question. . . . So this hasn't been a complete waste of time for you, Wadders. You've learned I have an Achilles' heel. Let's have a drink. I've looked under enough stones for one night."

14

THE WAITING ROOM next to the small chapel at the crematorium did little to provide any solace for the passing from this world to the next. The fire in the small grate reminded Hillsden of the comforts once provided in railway stations. He picked up an out-of-date magazine from a table and thumbed through the pages.

"Not exactly the most cheerful places, are they?" he said to his wife.

"I hate everything connected with funerals."

"I know that, dear, but I'm glad of your company."

"If your firm thought so much of her, I'm surprised they didn't lay on something decent. Are we going to be the only ones?"

"Well, I don't think she had any family."

"Morbid, I call it." She took a small handkerchief from her sleeve and dabbed at her nose. She stared out of the leaded window. "It would be raining."

"I don't mind that so much. More fitting somehow. I always think there's something macabre about bright sunlight when one's saying good-bye." He glanced to see if his voice had betrayed him, but Margot was repairing her mouth with a scarlet lipstick.

"I'm sorry I let you talk me into it. I shall be depressed for a week."

"It won't take long," he said, keeping his voice even. "Then you can go straight home."

"I shall have to go to the hairdresser's after this. This damp's ruined my perm." She examined her face in the mirror of her powder compact as though she had never seen it before. Hillsden had a sudden memory of what she had been like years ago, when Joan Crawford mouths were all the rage: Margot had never relinquished her past. Time stood still for both of them in that depressing little room, and it was Caroline he saw again rather than the girl he had once courted and married. As the skies darkened outside he thought how brightness had once fallen from the air. "Now dust has closed her eyes" . . . Caroline had loved poetry, often quoting it to him in the aftermath of lovemaking, something that had curiously embarrassed him, though now, when it was all too late, he remembered it with choking sorrow.

They waited in silence until the undertaker entered the room. "Would you be the Nicolson party, sir?"

"Yes."

"Are we expecting any more, sir?"

"Doesn't look like it, does it?"

"In that case, sir, perhaps you'd care to step into the chapel." At close range he gave off an alarming scent of mothballs.

The chapel seemed to Hillsden to have been built on the scale of a doll house. There were three rows of pews on either side, but nothing to suggest any form of religious belief. The only relief from the starkness was a single vase of flowers on a corner plinth. They sat down in the front row.

"What are we supposed to do?" Margot whispered. "Who conducts the service?"

"I don't think there is a service as such."

"Nobody says anything, you mean?"

"I don't think so."

"It's hideous," she hissed, "quite hideous."

"Well, it won't take long."

He was suddenly aware that somebody else had entered the chapel. Glancing around, he saw Belfrage seating himself in the rear pew and immediately dipping his head in prayer. When their eyes eventually met, neither man betrayed any recognition.

After a short pause the undertakers carried in the simple coffin and placed it on the metal rollers that would convey it on its final journey. The team bowed to the coffin and retired.

Nothing happened for two minutes; then a hidden switch was pressed by unseen hands and the coffin started to inch forward through a square opening in the facing wall. The only sound came from the metal rollers. Once the coffin was through the opening a piece of red curtain slowly unfurled and concealed it. For all the world like a Punch and Judy show, Hillsden thought. After that, silence. *Why did I come? I said good-bye years ago, when we were both alive.* The ceremony they had just witnessed had no meaning for him. He tried hard to think of Caroline, but the image remained blurred; he could think only of the wooden box behind the curtain. Convention demanded that he should kneel and pray, but there was nothing to pray for anymore.

They sat for a while longer, not knowing what to do. "Is that it?" Margot whispered.

"I imagine it must be." He was conscious that his voice was muffled, and realized he was close to tears.

"Well, let's go, then." As she got up she caught sight of Belfrage leaving. "There *was* somebody else here."

"Was there?"

"Yes. Didn't you see him? A well-dressed man."

"Must have been a family friend."

"Wouldn't have thought she had such posh friends. You take a look at him."

They went outside into the fine, biting rain, but Belfrage was already leaving in his chauffeur-driven car.

"That was him. Posh car, too," Margot said. "Fancy rushing off like that. You'd have thought he'd at least have paid his respects, considering we made the effort to come."

"Probably, like you, he finds funerals depressing."

"Well, that was certainly depressing."

The head undertaker was loitering close to the hearse. A drop of water hung on the end of his nose.

"I trust everything went off smoothly, sir? All satisfactory, was it?"

"Yes. Thank you."

Hillsden realized what else was expected of him, and reached in his pocket for a note. He passed it over surreptitiously: it was like bribing a head waiter for the last remaining table.

"Very kind of you, sir. I hope we can be of service again."

"Those people give me the creeps," Margot said before they were scarcely out of earshot.

"Never mind, dear, it's over now. I'm sorry it was such a morbid outing for you, but I'm very grateful for your company."

"Well, I certainly wouldn't have come if I'd known it was going to be like that. Not even a hymn. Pagan. Really pagan."

Hillsden drove out onto a country road. They were both silent until he reached a main intersection. "Now then, would it cheer you up if we drove on to the coast as I suggested the other night?"

"Not much point, is there, on a day like this?"

He put the car into neutral. "Look, it's not worth having a row about. I'll do whatever pleases you most. It was depressing for me, too, but we're still alive and we still have to make a go of it. Can't you ever make the effort?"

She stared straight ahead. He found it hard to believe that once he had longed for her company, longed to make love to her. He thought, We used to do it at any time of the day, sometimes in places like this, parking the car in some deserted clearing, taking the risks that passion makes all of us disregard. Now, hunched in her seat, she was just a sullen stranger. All the familiar excuses came crowding back: Perhaps things would have been different if our child had lived, if there had been a second chance; perhaps if I had never become wedded to a life of deceits, if we had shared something other than a burnt-out lust—music, literature, even a mundane hobby like gardening; if we had been an average middle-aged couple devoid of imagination, content with our suburban lot, substituting a pet dog for the dead child and lavishing the lost affection there. It was always *if,* the perennial echo.

"Well? You choose."

"I don't want to go anywhere special. I'd rather get my hair done," she answered finally.

He put the car in gear and turned in the direction of London. As they drove in silence he sought to distance himself from the past, but his head swam with old memories and new questions. He envied Caroline her peace. Where had he once read, "No one needs the dead"? She was out of it for good. By the time we reach the hairdresser's, he thought, the fire will have consumed her. Then a surge of hatred stirred in him, a hatred for everybody who had brought him to this point in his life, and for the life itself.

15

IT WAS OUT of character for Hillsden to act on impulse, but his failure to make any sense out of the circumstances of Caroline's murder grew in him like a cancer. The conversation with Waddington had served only to intensify the loss he would always feel; nothing else of value had surfaced. There was only one sliver of light to be discerned in the overall darkness, and that came from a newspaper report of an unrelated incident. A German manufacturer who supplied aircraft components to NATO had been gunned down outside his home by a unit of the Red Army faction calling itself the Patrick Flute Commando, in honor of one of the dead IRA hunger strikers.

"Get onto Belfast," he instructed Rotherby. "I want to know if there's any family connection between the dead man and the Matron's best friend. Flute isn't that common a name, and it might give us a tie-in with the envelope found under the bed. Was that ever analyzed, by the way?"

"The envelope? Yes."

"Did they find anything?"

"Nothing to get excited about. The address was typed on an Olivetti electronic and the Dublin postmark was genuine. The only slightly unusual factor was that the paper itself was of Swiss origin."

"Swiss?"

"Yes. Only sold in the better-class stationer's."

"Well, follow up anything like that."

He took a call from Belfrage as Rotherby left the room.

"Sorry I had to dash away like that," Belfrage said. "We had a reception here for the new President of Gambia, and I had to show my face. Hope you didn't think it rude."

"Well, not the sort of place one wants to linger in. Good of you to make the effort. I wasn't expecting to see you there."

"I felt it only proper in the circumstances." Belfrage's voice was as bland as ever. "George Medals aren't tossed around. Sad end to a brave woman. Was that the wife with you?"

"Yes."

"I'd like to meet her. We should all have a meal one of these days."

"She doesn't go out much," Hillsden said, his mind working on other things.

"Any fresh developments?"

"Nothing to speak of. No breakthrough, that is."

"Well, let's keep each other posted."

As he hung up, Hillsden was aware that the real question had remained unanswered. He considered tackling Control as to how Belfrage had known about the funeral, then thought better of it: the old boys' network was better left undisturbed. All the same, it puzzled him, and he filed it away for future reference.

Next, he contacted a friend in Special Branch who owed him a favor to see who had been pulled in recently, but there was nobody remotely fitting the description given by the young nurse. In any event, the more he thought about it, the more he was inclined to discount the idea that the assassin had anything to do with local politics. For one thing, nobody had claimed the credit, and that was always a sure pointer.

"We're equally baffled by the bomb in Bayldon's car," his Special Branch friend said. "So far we've drawn nothing but blanks. It's odd that nobody wants to step up and collect the prize. We thought we were onto something with the dead chauffeur. He did a stint in Northern Ireland, but only as a batman. Bayldon hasn't been in the job long enough to warrant that sort of attention. The IRA have restricted fields of vision. Long memories, yes, but they don't usually pick off unrelated targets. Seems out of character and a bit early in the day to pick off ministers who've only just taken office."

"Talking of cars, the job at the nursing home obviously required a getaway vehicle. The home's not on any bus route. All the taxi drivers at Farnham station have been checked out, but what about stolen cars? Apart from the nurse, the only person who saw our killer was a dotty old buffer called Lord Orchover. Most of what he says makes no sense, but I did pick out something from the local C.I.D.'s report. Orchover believed the killer to be his lawyer, and was apparently incensed that he didn't come in a Rolls. Wait a minute, I've got a transcript here." Hillsden rummaged among his papers. "Yes, this bit. Question: Did you see the car he came in, my Lord? Answer: I'd given instructions for him to bring the Roller, since I don't travel in anything else, but he brought a bloody Ford."

"You want to know how many Fords are stolen every day? How about to the nearest hundred?"

"Thanks, forget it. I'm just casting about in every direction. We're totally stymied at the moment."

Maybe it was the funeral, more than the mud disturbed by his session with Waddington, that slowly convinced him the answers lay buried in the past. There had to be loose ends from the Austrian and Berlin days that had persuaded somebody that the risk was worth taking. And risk it had certainly been. For the perpetrators suddenly to have reopened a file considered dead led to only one conclusion: that they believed even a vegetating Caroline still represented a threat, and had to be eliminated. Her murder had not been an amateur operation. He paid her unknown assassin a grudging compliment; he was good, he had left no obvious clues; he had come and gone without trace, albeit with his quota of luck that everybody needed. Such operations needed backup. They needed careful planning, and from experience he knew they could not be carried out without superior resources—money, accomplices, an intelligence network.

His next move was to remind himself of recent events, and he spent long hours going through the files. The one file he studied with extra care was the Glanville case. Glanville, finally exposed as a double agent, had, like Blunt before him, been carefully hidden in a position of trust. There was a certain depressing similarity between the two, in that Glanville was also a known homosexual, highly respected for his academic calling as an authority on medieval architecture, and the holder of a Distinguished Service Cross, given for his war record in Intelligence. He had been parachuted into Yugoslavia during the period when the British were backing Mikhailovic and his Chetnik army. At a later date, when Allied allegiance had been transferred to Tito and his Communist Partisans, Glanville had been a leading figure in the regrouped British mission. Finally exposed, he had admitted that he had first been recruited during his prewar Cambridge days and kept on ice until 1945, when the KGB decided his credentials were now impeccable enough to justify activating him. He had finished his war service in Vienna, but had been invited to join MI5 on his return to civilian life.

Because of his international reputation in medieval studies, Glanville had frequently been asked to lecture at foreign universities. His dossier listed three tours of the States, as well as several visits to East Germany, Poland and Italy. The KGB had chosen well: his cover was watertight, enabling him to come through the major security scandals of the sixties unscathed. He had been positively vetted and given clearance on three separate occasions, and until the moment of his exposure had been regarded as a valuable agent. In particular it was noted that he had supplied one of the first breakthroughs leading to the destruction of the Baader-Meinhof gang. At home he was a respected Establishment figure, widely tipped for an eventual knighthood, although his homosexual activities were known to the authorities. On occasion MI5 had arranged for his tastes to be catered to while he was abroad ostensibly on their business; it was thought better to know who he was with rather than risk a KGB frame-up. The way in which he was finally uncovered contained a degree of irony, and certainly reflected little credit on the efficiency of the Firm: he was arrested by members of the Metropolitan vice squad for an act of gross indecency in Hyde Park during a routine sweep. Even that might have been suppressed had it not been for the fact that his casual pickup in the act proved to be a KGB officer traveling with a Soviet trade mission. When arrested, the Russian insisted that he had deliberately sought out such a liaison in order to obtain asylum and defect: he made sure he gained sanctuary by denouncing Glanville. Faced with a virtual fait accompli, Glanville, in turn, collapsed under prolonged interrogation and admitted the extent of his duplicity.

All this had taken place within the first month of the new Labour government taking office. After a great deal of pious agonizing that had reached Cabinet level, Glanville was granted immunity from prosecution, a decision justified by the time-honored cynicism that it was not a propitious moment to rock the boat, and by the fact that he had been cooperative.

It was not until Hillsden had studied the files for the second time that he spotted an isolated reference to Jock. At the time in question operatives had always been given numbers rather than code names. He remembered Jock's serial as well as he knew his own, and it suddenly jumped out at him from a page of transcript. Glanville had been in Bonn the year that Caroline disappeared and the East Zone network blew up. From Bonn he had gone on to Salzburg, traveling as the senior member of a British cultural mission.

Hillsden read the verbatim piece of interrogation several times to make certain he had missed nothing. There was only the one isolated reference to Jock, which struck him as odd, since most of Glanville's evidence had been detailed and explicit. He thought it over and decided it was worth discussing with Control.

When he entered the inner sanctum, he found Control fiddling with an electric coffeemaker, one of the latest designs that measured and ground the beans before filtering the brew.

"Little perk I treated myself to," Control said. "Trouble is, I haven't a clue how to work the damn thing. Those amazingly clever Japs are too clever by half for me. That's why I never volunteered for a tour in the Far East. What am I doing wrong?"

"I'm a Nescafé man myself."

"It says on the instructions that it does everything but drink the stuff for you. Now, what I've been trying to work out is, do I press this button first, or this one?" He poked at the machine with a hand rheumatically-swollen at the knuckles. "Pressing the right button at the right time is the secret of a peaceful life, wouldn't you agree?" The remark seemed aimed at Hillsden rather than the machine. Control crossed to his desk and spoke into the intercom. "Amanda, can you come in here for a moment, please?" The machine started to emit a noise like a burglar alarm. "Oh, God, now what's happening? Perhaps it's an omen, Alec, warning us to stay clear of Glanville. It *was* Glanville you came to see me about, wasn't it? I heard you'd been asking for his files."

Before Hillsden could think of a suitably casual reply, Amanda appeared. She raised her eyebrows at the noise coming from the machine and removed the plug from the wall socket.

"Brilliant," Control said. "Why didn't I think of that? That must be the reason why you're a top secretary with an inflation-proof pension, and I'm merely a humble head of department."

"I've told you before, that plug is faulty. I've been onto maintenance, but naturally they haven't done anything about it. Though I don't know why you bought that contraption in the first place," she added at her most arch. "My coffee's not good enough for you, I suppose?"

"One must move with the times, Amanda dear."

"Before you move with anything, you should read the instructions."

"You know how hopeless I am at understanding classified information." The banter between them suggested an old married couple. "Let's dispense with automation for today and settle for your own worthy brew."

"How do you take it?" she asked Hillsden.

"Black with a dash. No sugar."

"I'm glad somebody watches their weight" was her parting barb as she returned to her lair.

"She doesn't always approve of me," Control said as the communicating door closed. "One should never challenge women in the kitchen or criticize them in bed. Two golden rules. How is the wife, by the way?"

"Fine."

"She understood about the funeral, I hope?"

He reminded Hillsden of old newsreel shots of Stanley Baldwin, turning on the same bland smile, the air of I-know-what-is-best-for-all-of-us.

"She went, reluctantly."

"I knew you'd persuade her. Getting along better these days, are we? I seem to recall there was a slight domestic hiccup once upon a time."

The image of Baldwin remained, Baldwin advising the King to toe the line.

"That's all over and forgotten."

"Good. I always think we need a quiet domestic life in our line of business. Something natural to fall back on."

"I'm sure you're right."

"I made certain of it by remaining a bachelor."

"Belfrage also turned up," Hillsden said quickly.

"Really? Now, what was it you came to see me about? Glanville, wasn't it?"

"Not specifically. What we are all concerned about: Caroline's murder." Two can play your game, Hillsden thought.

"Ah, yes," Control answered without any change of expression. "It was just that you mentioned Glanville before."

"No. *You* mentioned it."

"Did I?"

"And you're quite right, I have been reading his file. You see, I don't think we'll get anywhere with Caroline's case by ordinary police work. My hunch is, we've got to look further back for the real answers."

"But why Glanville?"

"He met Jock once, and for all I know, Caroline too. I'd like to take another shot at him."

"Touchy subject. He disturbed all sorts of beasts in our jungle. Nobody's too happy about Glanville. He's still a psoriasis on the body politic."

"All the same, I'd like your permission to tackle him."

Control sucked in his breath and shook his head. "I don't think we can challenge his immunity, not after the Prime Minister's statement in the House. That's not tinder we want to relight; the resulting blaze might scorch us all. You've read his confession. Very full. He went a lot further than Blunt, but I can't recall that Caroline was ever mentioned."

"Exactly. That could come under deliberate errors and omissions."

They were interrupted by Amanda returning with the coffee. "Only powdered milk, I'm afraid. We didn't get fresh today. The milkmen are on strike. It's their turn this week." Hillsden noticed that she swung her skirt as she retired again.

"I ought to change her," Control said, as though reading Hillsden's thoughts, "except that we're used to each other. Toleration of another's moods is not to be despised when you reach my age. Have you noticed that this stuff doesn't dissolve? Like the powdered eggs we got in the war. What extraordinary things they were—almost secret weapons— but I did discover they made excellent glue. If I'd been bright, I'd have patented the idea. That's apropos of nothing. Too much change all the time, too many changes." Then, without a pause; "But you were saying about Glanville?"

"Despite your worries, I still think he's worth another go. Discreetly, unofficially."

"There's no such thing."

"Aren't we meant to be a secret organization?"

Baldwin stared back at him; Baldwin the smoother of troubled brows, ready to shed crocodile tears.

"But dependent on our masters' largesse, Alec. And we've been told to lay off."

"Who by?"

"Need you ask? Voices on high."

"I take it you mean *new* voices on high?"

"They're still feeling their way, Alec, and new brooms always want to sweep cleaner than the old. Incur their displeasure this early in the game and they can turn very spiteful. They'd have no hesitation in being ruthless when it comes to fixing our future budget. Indeed, they'd welcome a reason for cutting us down. As you must have gathered, they don't set much store by our activities as it is. It's *their* dirty linen now, don't forget. They inherited the *merde* as well as the power and the glory."

"The reference to Jock was never followed up in his interrogation. I want to find out why. This is a new situation, we're entitled to chase new leads."

"When one lives on the charity of others, Alec, one is only entitled to what they decide. It's my job to protect us from the winds of change, to take the wider view. You're too close to it, too involved."

"I was waiting for you to say that."

"Sometimes one has to state the obvious."

"There's nothing obvious about Caroline's murder."

Control had been stirring his coffee through all this; now he sipped at it and grimaced. "It's my firm belief that Glanville's larder is empty. If I didn't think that, I'd be willing to take a chance."

"Somebody was keeping tabs on her all the time she was in that place. We know that, and it wasn't just a social worker."

"You're not suggesting it was Glanville who made those solicitous phone calls, surely? He's gone to earth, counting his remaining blessings, he wouldn't put himself at risk again."

"So he's definitely off limits, is he? You still haven't given me a straight answer."

"Haven't I? I thought I had," Control said, his future defense already prepared, a man incapable of working a coffee machine but adept at manipulating any mechanism that protected his rear.

16
AUSTRIA

JOCK SAID, "I told you it was true. Have I ever lied? This place is like something dreamed up by Bram Stoker. I don't suppose it's ever been known as the house of mirth."

"Wrong author," Hillsden said smugly. "That was Edith Wharton."

"Oh, full marks, Alec. Flaunting your superior literary knowledge again! Very sharp. You should enter for a television quiz show."

"God, you two," Caroline said. "You're both so bloody touchy tonight. And if either of you so much as mentions flies to me, I shall scream."

"Who's touchy? I'm in a great mood. It's just that Alec can't bear not having the last word. I was just boning you both up on local history. I've discovered one or two other gruesome little details about our present address."

"How gruesome? I've had quite enough for one day."

"Well, this place has had a checkered career and a variety of occupants, ranging from a fifteenth-century bishop of hideous disposition, to robber barons and the distinguished order of the SS. We're probably rather a letdown. I suppose what really fascinates me is that cruelty is passed on from generation to generation."

"Why should that be so unusual? We pass on diseases; even in the act of love we can accomplish that. That's always seemed to me one of God's nastiest inventions."

"You're confusing love with lust, Alec. Righteous moral citizens who never sit on dirty toilet seats are immune."

"Why do men always bring conversations down to the lowest common denominator?"

"You want to answer her, Alec, or shall I?"

"Let's change the subject. What were you saying about this place?"

"Ah, yes. I started to tell you about the 'bottle.' "

"Bottle?"

"Yes, and once again I'm indebted to my learned friend, Herr Dr. Lehmann, for putting me wise. We're all aware of the dungeons, but what we didn't know is the existence of a superdungeon, the definitive dungeon, from which there could be no escape."

"Where?"

"In the floor of the Keep. Sealed over now for safety, but apparently there's a chamber twenty feet deep and shaped like a bottle; the sides narrow up to a neck just large enough to squeeze in a man—or a woman, for that matter. They weren't too particular in those days. It dates from the aforementioned bishop; he designed it, doubtless for the greater glory of God."

"Good night!" Caroline said. "You're sure it's sealed now?"

"We've all walked over it many times without knowing. According to Lehmann, legend has it that one poor bastard survived eleven years inside it. He came up white as a slug and blind."

These morbid scraps of information were related over the last dinner they all had together in the castle, the night before Caroline left for Berlin. It was their custom to dine in the main hall. This had been paneled in the latter half of the nineteenth century, and the original windows had been given the Gothic treatment. The walls were hung with huge portraits of past Teutonic dignitaries—the kind of utterly undistinguished works of art that usually find a last resting place in town halls. During the war SS officers had used them for revolver practice and most of the canvases bore scars; the eyes in many of the portraits had been neatly drilled by some accurate marksman, so they now resembled characters in a horror movie. The leaded windowpanes had been etched with initials, hearts and sentimental messages. Even the lid of the damp and tuneless Steinway standing on a raised platform at one end of the hall had not escaped desecration.

As they talked their voices bounced back from the vaulted ceiling decorated with dusty coats of arms. They ate, seated far apart like sparse guests at a canceled wedding, at a massive oak table; this too had been scored by past invaders. The decaying splendor of their surroundings was not matched by the food served; the Austrian station was not high on the Firm's pecking order, and they constantly envied their CIA counterparts with seemingly unlimited funds.

On this final night they had decided to mark the occasion with some bottles of decent wine. The cook was a pleasant Bavarian woman who worked by one rule: that quantity was always preferable to quality. Caroline had nicknamed her Scheherazade. "If we stay here long enough," she used to comment, "we could write *A Thousand and One Nights of Veal.*" But that night they drank more than they ate, with Jock making most of the conversation.

"I've thought a lot about the mentality of killers," he remarked.

"Can we change the subject again?" Caroline pleaded.

"Why? It's fascinating. I can't help thinking, for example, of past guests at this very table. I mean, look around you. When the SS were in residence, they sat here in these same chairs, doubtless eating the same food, drinking too much out of boredom, loneliness, all the usual ailments that soldiers are heir to; taking potshots at the art gallery before going downstairs to tear off a few more fingernails. The point I'm trying to make—"

"Yes, get to the point, for God's sake! Either that or go to bed," Hillsden interrupted. His eyes went to Caroline.

"I'm getting there. The point is, they can't all have been monsters."

"Why not?"

"Well, statistically it's unlikely."

"Balls. They didn't join the SS to become humanitarians."

"Can I finish? Okay, I grant you that the majority of them presumably enjoyed their work; at the same time you have to admit that they were also capable of leading totally ordinary lives. They had girlfriends, wives, children."

"I don't have to admit anything of the sort. If you mean that some of them carried family photographs in their wallets and cried at Brahms' 'Cradle Song,' it proves bugger all."

"You're oversimplifying, as well as using foul language in front of a lady. You can't deny that killers live on two entirely separate levels. I think of those splendid Aryan types—our past enemies and present allies"—he raised his glass to one of the defaced portraits—"sitting here, a little pissed like me, having their acorn coffee, a final belt of schnapps and then going to their rooms to write letters home. '*Liebe* Gretchen, how I miss you and our little *kinder.*' But the following morning they were at it again, attaching electrodes to genitals, thumping kidneys with rubber truncheons."

"That doesn't strike me as being an exclusively German characteristic. What about the Gulag and all those liberated African dictators doing their best to keep the tradition going?"

"I didn't say the Krauts had a monopoly. Did I say that, Caroline?"

"I wasn't listening. I switched off."

"God, don't let's throw stones in glass houses. We British—correction, *you* British—have never lagged behind the field. Look what you did to us poor Scots at Culloden, look at the Moors murders, your unenviable record as child floggers."

"So? History always repeats itself. Nothing new in that. The first time it's tragedy, as Marx said, the second time it's comedy."

"How deeply you've read, Alec. I envy you the instant quote for every occasion."

"My only party trick."

"Level with me, Alec; you haven't really read all the books you claim, have you? You took out a lifetime subscription with the *Reader's Digest* as a child."

"How did you guess? You're right. I'm the most unforgettable character I ever met."

"And I'm going to bed," Caroline announced. "I have to make an early start in the morning. I'll leave you both to swap insults."

With exaggerated politeness both men rose to their feet and kissed her good-night. After she had gone they opened the last bottle of wine, though perhaps only Hillsden was conscious of the symbolism, and stayed up until they had finished it. Their conversation ranged over a lot of dangerous ground, but always skirted around the topic that was uppermost in both their thoughts—two of history's accomplices chewing old fat.

"The end of an era," Jock said. "Unlike this wine, we've seen better years, and now it's over."

"Not for you. For me, maybe. I don't relish the thought of going back to being a bloody pen pusher behind a desk."

"Control won't keep you there."

"Take a bet?"

"No, you'll soon be off to pastures new."

"I doubt it. I'm considered an emotional casualty. Isn't that the reason I'm being sent home?"

He waited for Jock to pick up the cue, but he merely held his glass up to the light. "A little sediment. Like us, Alec. We're the last of the vintage. Why do all the fucking novelists portray us as romantics keeping the world safe for IBM and General Motors?"

"Maybe because they're in the business of writing fiction."

"Don't they know that we're squalid licensed criminals, permitted to do the unthinkable in the name of patriotism? Some people make a living trading in commodity futures; we earn a crust trading in human futures. There's precious little romance in that."

"Is that all you believe?"

"More or less."

"You just said 'patriotism'—doesn't that mean faith in our system as opposed to theirs?"

"That's just the crap politicians put about. Depends which side of the blanket you were born on. We're all serving the same lost causes." Jock drained his glass. "No, I couldn't go back home."

"Never?"

"Never's a long time. Let's just say I'd need a real incentive."

"Don't you miss England at all?"

"Why would I miss England? I was born in Glasgow, in the dear old Gorbals, where the coppers patrolled in twos and beat the shit out of you whenever they got a chance, and Saturday night was the night for getting a broken bottle in your face if you spoke out of turn. See, unlike you, I don't believe in fictions: I only remember facts. No, there's nothing I miss back there. All that grayness, all that newspaper-fed ignorance, all that bloody envy, and the women looking as though they're only fertilized with bromides. I like my women to be young, full of ripeness, something to bite on."

"You've been out here too long, Jock. The cult of the vampire has got to you; it's all these dark, forbidding forests."

"Don't you believe it. Finish the bottle."

"You've finished it."

"Have I? So I have, my apologies. Know your trouble?"

"Which one?"

"You're too set in your ways, you only see things through a married man's eyes. Don't you ever long for release?"

There was an edge to his voice that made Hillsden cautious. He was familiar with Jock's technique, especially when he'd had a few drinks. Like a skilled acupuncturist, he was always liable to insert the probing needle when one least expected it.

"We're both married. Married to this bloody job."

"But you must have dreams. There must be moments when you long to enter the dark forest and lose yourself completely."

"What makes you think I haven't already?"

"But you didn't stay there, you didn't journey on into the center. I'm talking about total submersion."

"And you're also pissed."

"You think so?"

"Not smashed, just pissed. Let me ask *you* something for a change. Have you ever been in love?"

"No."

"Don't you think you've lost out on something?"

"No."

"What makes you so sure?"

"You."

"You think I'm not a good advert for it?"

"Well, are you?"

They were skirmishing close to the minefield now. Hillsden wondered what part Jock had played in getting him sent home. There was no real friendliness in the face staring at him across the table. He thought, All men are enemies when it comes to love; why am I wasting what little time we have left, sitting here while part of me dies like those flies in the room above?

"Perhaps you're right," he said. He got up, surprised to find he was steady on his legs and stone-cold sober.

"Give a good report of me when you get back to the old country. Tell them Jock is keeping the flag flying, that his buttons are polished and he's never late on parade." It was one of those moments when, despite his smile, despite the forced humor, Hillsden could believe in the Saturday-night ritual of the broken bottle ready to be pushed in the face of anybody who stood in his way.

"Just do one thing for me: take care of her. Although I haven't been let in on the secret, I presume you have a good reason for sending her back to Berlin?"

"Not my decision, old son. Came down from on high, and once she leaves here Berlin will be running her, not me."

Later, when the castle was quiet, he padded from his room to Caroline's, like any other adulterer. They made love and were ignorant, in Yeats' sad phrase. But whereas, before, sadness had been a bond, an added fillip to lust, that night it was a dead, unspoken thing. A vehement premonition laid siege to Hillsden's heart. Naked beside Caroline in the single bed with a duvet tucked around them like a swollen toga, he charted the weeks and months ahead. The coldness he felt was the coldness she was going to: he had never been warm in Berlin. It, too, was a dungeon shaped like a bottle, everything enclosed by the Wall, and something told him that Caroline was going in blind.

17

SINCE THE END of his old life and the beginning of public notoriety Glanville had been forced to change his address three times, finally settling in a small Lincolnshire farming community situated between Woodhall Spa and Tattershall, part of that flat countryside adjacent to the Wash which, during the war, had been peppered with air bases. He had purchased a cottage with a view over the fens towards the red Norman tower of Tattershall Castle, taking up residence under the assumed name of Plimpton, a disguise that was soon penetrated by the locals. There he lived a solitary existence, visited by few of his old friends and denied the easy sexual pickings of the past. The cottage was isolated from the nearest village, having once been attached to a now-derelict pumping station. The freehold included an acre of black fen soil criss-crossed by dikes, a feature that allowed *Private Eye* an easy play on words when, as was inevitable, they traced him to his hideout.

There was an unseasonal sprinkling of frost on the ground the morning Hillsden arrived, making the dark plowed fields around the cottage glisten like opencast coal mines. A small wooden bridge straddled the dike separating Glanville's land from the road. There was a crude notice board with the words PRIVATE PROPERTY—KEEP OUT stenciled in amateurish lettering, which he took to be Glanville's own work. He parked his BMW on the grass verge, punched in the code for his intruder alarm, then crossed the bridge on foot. A dead rat floated belly-white upwards in the dike, an image that scattered childhood memories of Kenneth Grahame's lovable inventions. As he opened the iron cowgate, a flock of seabirds driven inland by the weather rose lazily into the air, then settled again with angered voices. The early sun picked out the distant castle tower, reminding him once more of how far he had come since the days in Austria. A thin twist of smoke curled from the cottage's single chimney, and he noted that Glanville had begun to fashion flower beds close to the front door. An old woman's cottage, he thought. The curtains were drawn, but as he rapped on the door he could hear music being played, then the voice of a radio announcer beginning a news bulletin. The locks on the door were new.

Most of the newspaper photographs blazoned on the front pages at the time of Glanville's fall from grace had depicted him as something of an aesthete, with the typical profile of a public-school career diplomat —the mask of bogus superiority, Waddington had termed it, which wasn't wide of the mark. A hint of cruelty, perhaps, beneath the thinning but carefully groomed hair; the look of a man to whom social success had always come too easily, though the faces of treason, like those of murderers, always fitted after conviction.

Now as the door was partially opened, held by a security chain, Hillsden was confronted with another version of the man, familiar but different. The sparse hair now had a yellowish tint to it, and the face below was hollowed and bearded, giving Glanville the appearance of an actor Hillsden had once seen play Don Quixote. The features had been printed from the original negative, but in transit the image had been scored and aged.

"Didn't you read the notice?" Glanville asked. It was a prissy voice, cultured, slightly sibilant. "I don't receive anybody except by appointment. Why can't you frightful people leave me in peace?"

He was wearing a patterned silk dressing gown with a foulard of the same material partially masking his scraggy neck.

"I'm not from the press."

"It makes no difference who you are, my answer's the same."

The smell of fresh coffee, pungent, aromatic, drifted out from the single ground-floor room.

"We have something in common that I'd like to discuss."

"Didn't you hear me? I do not receive uninvited visitors." A trace of anxiety had crept into his voice.

"I appreciate that, but I'm sure exceptions can be made. You needn't look so worried. This isn't an official visit."

"I still have no idea who you are."

"But you can guess. I've driven a long way, and that coffee smells good."

Glanville peered past him through the crack in the door to the BMW parked on the road.

"I came alone, if that's what you're worried about. There's only me. Just a chat, that's all I want. It won't take long."

"Have you proof of identity?"

"Now, you know better than that. We're birds of a feather, you and me, Mr. Plimpton, and we can break all the rules when it suits us. You're not going to get rid of me that easily, so why not let me in? It's bloody cold on this doorstep."

"If you are who I think you are, I've told your people all I have to tell. And if you're genuine, you'll also be aware that I was given firm assurances that I wouldn't be troubled again. I've paid my debt to society."

"Well, that's just dandy. I've often wondered what it would be like to have nothing on my conscience. You're a fortunate man, Glanville. Fortunate, but becoming a real irritant. I wouldn't put too much faith in that chain, if I were you."

"If you threaten me or use any force, I shall inform the police."

"They might be a while getting here. Now, let's stop pissing about, shall we? Be a good chap and open the door. I'm not going to get rough, that's not my style. All I want is a talk. You're going to get pneumonia standing there in your nightie."

Glanville stared at him with real hatred. "Do I have your word on that?"

"Sure, and my word is better than yours used to be."

Glanville closed the door and detached the security chain.

"That's better. Let's keep it friendly." He walked into the warmth and stamped his feet on the flagstones. Glanville kept his distance, putting a scrubbed pine table between himself and Hillsden at the fire. The table was littered with papers and a brimming ashtray.

"Writing our memoirs, are we? What're you going to call it, 'A Queen in Exile'?"

"That sort of cheap jibe doesn't impress me."

"It wasn't meant to. I take my coffee with milk, by the way. No sugar."

Glanville wrapped his dressing gown tighter and moved to the Aga cooker, lifted the coffeepot, poured two mugs and left Hillsden's on the corner of the pine table.

"You'd have made somebody a good wife." The first sip burned his lips. "Perhaps you *were* a good wife—or was it the other way around in your case? I'm naïve about such things." He sat down at the table, flexing his legs, feeling the circulation returning. He reached for the pile of loose papers, but Glanville was there before him and gathered them up. "Don't be nervous. We can either enjoy this together, as the whore said, or just go through the motions. You choose."

"I've had assurances—"

"And guess what? I don't give a damn what assurances you've had from whatever source. To me you're just another vicious old queen. Mind you, I've nothing against queens, as long as they don't frighten the horses, but what really gets up my nose are the ones like you who have their cake and eat it."

"I find you very offensive."

"How perceptive of you to notice. It's deliberate on my part. See, I have no idea what your memoirs will contain if they ever see printer's ink, but I doubt whether there'll be a chapter telling how several of my friends went to their deaths as a result of your efforts. You'd call it horses for courses, no doubt, but I'm not so sophisticated as you, nor as understanding as some of your chums in high places."

Glanville sank down in a chair, leaving his own mug of coffee untouched.

"That's right, get comfortable, warm your old bum against the Aga, answer politely and this will soon be over. As I said, I'm not the type to get rough, but I'm quite skilled at heavy wrist slapping."

"All this won't go unreported, you know. I shall file a complaint. You've no right to utter threats."

"You're absolutely correct. This is a free country," Hillsden replied, but in truth he was regretting going in so heavily from the start. Everything about Glanville brought old angers to the surface, a deep resentment that to all intents he had got off scot-free. The next time he spoke he used a more conciliatory tone. "I repeat, there isn't going to be any violence. All the same, I wouldn't file a complaint if I were you. You may think you're safe, that confession has absolved some of your sins, but it wouldn't take much to change that. We could still make life very difficult for you, give you so much aggro that you'd long to escape to your spiritual home. Fancy changing this for a nice one-room apartment in Moscow, do you? We could fix that, too. Who knows? Maybe you'd be given a nice Russian boyfriend to ease the boredom of your twilight years—assuming you can still get it up, that is. We're in a rough game, you and me. There are no written rules."

He leaned over and helped himself to one of Glanville's cigarettes. "Now, curiously, all I want from you is just something that will jog my memory. Give me that, and I'll leave the rest to history. I won't bother you again." He struck a match on the leg of the table. "Does the name Nicolson mean anything to you?"

Glanville hesitated. "I knew a Peter Nicolson once."

"I'm not looking to dredge up a list of past boyfriends. How about a *Mrs.* Nicolson?"

Again the hesitation before "No."

"Okay. Let's try Oates. Caroline Oates." He watched Glanville's face through the cigarette smoke.

"That does strike a vague bell."

"At one time she was Dinnsbury's girl Friday. You remember Gunga Dinnsbury, I'm sure. He ran you for a time."

"Yes. Frightful old pedant. Always smelled of cheap cologne."

"Well, we don't all share your exquisite taste, and he wasn't getting paid as much as you. Good. We've made a start. Shows you're willing to try. Now, be a little more definite. We want straight answers, don't we? No evasions. Did you ever meet her with Dinnsbury?"

"I could have done. Though I doubt she would have made any lasting impression. She was hardly my type." He sucked his lips in so that they virtually disappeared.

"Right, let's leave that for a moment. Now, I want you to jump ahead and think about Austria."

"Austria?"

"Yes, you've heard of Austria. Land of the White Horse Inn, lederhosen and strong young thighs." He found it difficult to keep his voice even. "You were there with a British cultural mission."

"Oh, yes, that's correct. One amongst many."

"And you met a friend of mine, a close colleague who's now dead. You met him in Salzburg."

"I can't be expected to remember everybody all those years ago."

"You mentioned this person during your interrogation. He was known as Jock."

"I didn't know him as Jock," Glanville said a shade too quickly.

"No, you wouldn't, would you? In those days we used numbers for operatives. But given your position of trust at the time, you would have known he ran our Austrian station. That was your reason for meeting him. I won't press the point, but there's a fair chance you were ultimately responsible for his death. Miss Oates was one of his people. Since you're on record that you met him, it's conceivable that you also met her."

He waited, but Glanville remained silent. "You see, what interested me when reading your file was a curious inconsistency. You were so explicit about most details of your double career, and yet that particular section seems fudged, not as crystal clear as the rest. I'm not asking you to search your conscience, just your memory."

"I had eighty-five hours of questioning. If they missed anything, it was your people's fault, not mine."

"Or there's another explanation. You could have a continuing reason not to fill in those missing gaps. Isn't that a possibility?"

"If you wish to think so."

"Oh, I do. I have a very suspicious mind, and the object of our little chat here is to try and rectify the omissions. So I'll ask you again: how much personal credit would you claim for destroying our Berlin network at that time? Don't be modest."

"You know as well as I do that I passed on certain information. I have no idea how it was eventually used."

"No, I can see how a man of your sensitivity would shy away from the results of his crimes. I said, don't be modest. It's my hunch you were primarily responsible for blowing the whole gaff."

"I was only one of many links in a long chain."

"Who was running you on the other side at that time?"

"Why ask what you already know?"

"Remind me."

"Henze."

"Ah, yes."

Glanville lit a second cigarette from the stub of the first. Hillsden noticed that his bony fingers were nicotine-stained.

"What method did you use when contacting him?"

"A dead letter box. Are we only going to go over old ground?"

"I'm a methodical man. Now let's go back to Caroline Oates, the girl who made little impression on you. Shortly after you had your last known meeting with Jock in Salzburg, she was ordered back to Berlin. That was her last trip. They took her there, and that was the beginning of the end. You can follow that, can you? So what I'm asking is, did Henze ever reveal to you what it was they were both onto?"

"Is it important now?"

"I'll decide what is or what isn't important."

"Not in so many words. All he told me was that he thought your lot were getting too close to something big. It was then that I began to feel that my own position could be vulnerable."

"Why specifically?"

"One develops a second sense, surely I don't have to tell you that?"

"So you took steps to protect your valuable rear, if you'll pardon the expression."

"I did what we all do in such circumstances, what you would have done. I took certain necessary precautions."

"You betrayed Henze, in other words? You began the whole cycle of events."

Glanville looked away. "Isn't betrayal what this endless game is all about? It wasn't just me, I wasn't the only one. There were others. Others with more to lose." He seemed to catch himself out and stopped abruptly.

"You can't quantify death, Glanville. Once you're dead, the game's over. But you left something out. Before they blow the final whistle in our game, they sweat you. And worse. They sweated Caroline Oates. Sweated her in a way that makes your eighty-five hours child's play, first in East Berlin and later in Moscow Centre, where the health-farm techniques are more sophisticated. Even so it took them the best part of six months to clean her out. You see how gentle we were by comparison? And we didn't throw you out as a wheelchair case either."

Glanville stared at a point above Hillsden's head.

"Did you know that?"

"Know what?"

"That when a trade-in was finally arranged they returned her in a very poor state of health."

"No, I didn't know that."

"Oh, come on, sweetie, you're not trying again. You knew she'd been traded."

"I did hear something of the kind, but by then I wasn't being kept fully in the picture."

"But you knew she'd come home?"

"Yes, but I had no idea of her circumstances."

"Didn't her return worry you?"

"Why should it worry me?"

"Why indeed? Because you're lying, aren't you? It didn't worry you for one very good reason: you knew she had come home a vegetable, so she didn't present any risk. You still thought yourself safe."

Glanville fingered the foulard at his neck in the way that women play with a string of pearls. "If that's the way you wish to interpret it. As I told you, I didn't know her, so why should I fear her?"

"But in our game we don't need to know people to fear them, do we? It's enough if they know *us.* Let me ad-lib a possible scenario for you. There you were, still a respected member of the Establishment, still on our payroll with no discernible stain on your Hawes and Curtis suits—"

"Kilgour and French, as it happens," Glanville interjected, suddenly offering a glimmer of spunk.

"I sit corrected. You had the necessary intellectual and moral arrogance to justify your actions, you were better placed than most, and your pedigree and social contacts were superior. You had no reason to suppose that you would ever be rumbled—a fruitful double career drawing to its end, the almost certain prospect of a knighthood and a generous pension within sight. And then this woman, who you claim never to have met, but who you were aware of—this woman, Caroline Oates, discovers that Henze has been turned, a discovery that could lead her back to you. How does that strike you?"

Glanville shrugged, got up and put some coke into the Aga from an antique brass scuttle. It wasn't until he was bent to this task, his face concealed from Hillsden, that he answered. "All very inventive, but what does it matter now? We're all either dead, disgraced or exiled. Burnt-out cases. It's all over and done with."

"You haven't let me finish. There's a second act to my scenario, one I haven't invented. Unlike you, Miss Oates wasn't given the luxury of retiring in comfort, though this is the sort of cottage she once dreamed of. She came home a vegetable. A vegetable," he repeated, drumming it at Glanville's face as he turned from the stove. "Of no apparent use or threat to anybody. Notice I said 'apparent.' Yet somewhere, years later, somebody took a decision to eliminate what was left of her. Now, why do you think that was?"

"You mean she was killed here, in England?" Glanville's surprise seemed genuine enough.

"Yes. Not some corner of a foreign field, but in Farnham, to be exact. In a private nursing home."

"When?"

"Just over three weeks ago. You want to know how? She was injected with a fast-acting toxin, the sort that good SS men used to rejoin their beloved *Führer.*"

"That side of it was never part of my involvement," Glanville answered slowly. "My commitment was entirely idealistic. I hated that aspect of it."

"Nobody's suggesting *you* did it, sweetie. If I thought that, I'd kill you now with my bare hands. What I'm asking is, why? Why? What part of her poor tortured memory had escaped their worst efforts? What could she have known that still frightened them?"

"I can't imagine."

"Well, I have a third act. Not watertight, partly circumstantial, but worth listening to. They were worried enough about her, this prematurely senile woman strapped into a wheelchair and all but forgotten by the rest of the world, they were concerned enough to make regular inquiries about her condition."

"You mean they went to the nursing home?"

"Not until the day they murdered her. No, somebody telephoned from time to time. Then—and this is where my conjecture comes in— whoever called got the impression that she was miraculously on the mend, that she might still be able to bring them down with the one bit of information everybody had missed, ourselves included. There has to be a very good reason, wouldn't you say, to murder somebody who couldn't brush a fly off her nose?"

"It's inexplicable to me. Horrible and inexplicable."

"You see how lucky you are by comparison? You can still let strangers in at your door and not fear them. I didn't arrive with a hypodermic, I came for help, so search your memory once again. What name did you hold back? The name of the someone so securely hidden that you knew you were on sure ground? Give me that for Caroline's sake."

"I don't know of any such person."

"You're scared, Glanville. Look in the mirror. It's all there in your sweating face. You're scared, and you're still lying. And for what? For nothing. The world hasn't changed for the better because of your squalid little betrayals. Why are you still protecting them? Did they protect you? They fed you to us."

134

"You're just trying to trap me."

"You think so? How d'you think we got onto you in the end? Simple. We were running Henze by the time Caroline went back to Berlin. We caught him red-handed and he turned as easily as a trout in the pan."

"No, you're making it up. That's bloody mad. I'm not going to be tricked by something as crude as that. If it was true, you'd have picked me up sooner."

"You were more use to us left undisturbed. It was just bad luck all round that you got a hard-on in the park that night and then panicked. The vice squad did us all a bad turn. A tragedy of good intentions, sweetie. Instead of blowing your boyfriend you went and blew your own cover."

Glanville shook his head violently. "I don't believe this is an unofficial visit. You're trying to pin something new on me. Your bloody outfit has slipped up again and you're looking to blame it on me."

"Why are you getting so excited if you've got nothing further to hide? Don't you believe in British justice? You can't try a man twice for the same crime. We always knew your hands were only slightly grubby, that you only killed by proxy. Henze was ours, I promise you. We were running him, and through him we were running you. You want me to prove it? Better sit down again." He waited, smiling, as Glanville did as he was told. "We told him to make sure you were entertained, so he pimped for you. My memory's better than yours, so if you want names, I'll give you some. How about starting with Leif Otto Flindt? Aged nineteen; occupation, waiter in the Hauptbahnhof Hotel, Bonn. He liked you to shave his legs along with other delights, didn't he? Then there was Peter Florin who worked in the post room of the West German embassy in Paris. But he didn't last long, did he? Just a few odd nights. He scared you by asking too many questions. I must admit he wasn't one of our better selections, though they do say that buggers can't be choosers. After that you were more cautious—until you fell in love with young Werner. You wrote poetry to him. Rather turgid stuff, we thought, inferior Houseman. We had a lot of fun passing it round the Firm. We even composed his love letters to you, which was even more fun. But please don't think I'm sitting in judgment on your life between the sheets; it's just to add weight to my case, to convince you that we never believed Henze betrayed Caroline and the others. We had a tight vise on him, so it would have been tantamount to signing his own death warrant. Now, equally, and this might surprise you, I also don't think it was you. What I do believe, however, is that you have a pretty good idea who it might have been. So throw me a crumb, Glanville—just a crumb and I'll leave you alone forever."

"Why should I trust you? What guarantees will I have, even assuming that you're right?"

"None at all. It's too late for bargains, sweetie. But be afraid of me, be fearful of what I could do to ruin your Shropshire Lad retirement benefits. I wouldn't have any qualms about it."

"If you'd turned Henze as you claim, why didn't he supply the missing answers?"

"Henze is dead. Shot in the back of the head as he was leaving his house to take the dog for a walk. They're all dead except you and me, Glanville—Caroline, Jock, Henze, the entire East Berlin network. Caroline was the last. The last and most unnecessary murder on the face of it, but you and I know that nothing like that is done without a purpose. Those inscrutable masters we all serve for different causes always have a purpose."

"I've only your word for it that she is dead. There's been nothing on the news or in the papers."

"You mustn't take me for an amateur, sweetie. Do you like looking at pretty pictures? I brought one for you."

Hillsden produced a buff envelope and held it out. "Go ahead, take a peep. Only make sure you don't let me see it too."

Glanville took the envelope reluctantly. Very slowly, as though expecting it to explode in his face, he eased a finger inside the flap and withdrew a portion of the photograph inside, then quickly pushed it back. "What a filthy trick!"

"We're in a filthy game, sweetie. That was once a pretty girl, though not by your standards, but what price prettiness when you reach the autopsy table? When they cut you open and stitch you up again, they don't try for needlepoint prizes." He retrieved the envelope and pocketed it.

Glanville sagged in his chair, head in hands. "I'm not well. I've been through a lot these past months."

"True, none of us are in the peak of condition, are we? But while your heart's still ticking, tell me if that picture helped jog your memory. Don't worry: if you faint I'll catch you. I can't promise to give you mouth-to-mouth resuscitation, but I'll massage your wrists and still be here when you come around, asking the same question for as long as it takes. You weren't the end of the daisy chain, Glanville, you were somewhere in the middle, so tell me who your other dancing partners were. The ones still in place. Where are they? In Bonn, Salzburg, Berlin, where?"

"Closer to home, but I'm only guessing."

"Guess, then!"

"You mentioned one."

"Who?"

"Dinnsbury. He could have been one of them."

"Bullshit! He went out with a clean bill of health. You're still playing games with me. Caroline wasn't killed by dead men. I want to know who's still around."

"I swear to God I don't know."

"Yes, well, we don't have a Bible handy. How were you contacted here in London?"

"Mostly by dead letter boxes, sometimes by telephone. I never met any of them face-to-face."

"What sort of deal did you make, Glanville?"

"Deal?"

"Isn't that what I said? They were kind enough not to put you in the dock at the Old Bailey and let justice take its course. How did you buy your way out of that? Being just somebody from the sticks, I'm anxious to know, I might need the password myself one day. The old-pals act, was it? Somebody from the same school who knew somebody from the same school who pulled the necessary strings?"

"I told them everything they wanted to know."

"You turned Queen's evidence—very apt in your case—but that wasn't your ace card, was it? That came after. What was the deal?"

"I've been publicly ruined, haven't I? It was leaked to Fleet Street. Does that smack of a deal?"

"I'll ask you again, because you don't seem to be listening to the question. Who did you protect?"

"For the last time, I don't know. There was no deal, nobody protected me. I wasn't that important."

"Well now, that's an admission."

"You may think I was, and perhaps at one time I did too. I acted from principle, not for personal gain."

"Go on, you'll make me cry in a minute."

"You're so smart, aren't you, so quick with the witticisms? Well, you weren't smart enough to ask the question of the one person who might have told you. You should have asked your friend when he was alive. *He* knew."

Hillsden was pulled up short for the first time. "Who're you talking about?"

"The one you called Jock."

"Jock knew?"

"That was my impression. That time I met him in Salzburg I was under orders to find out if the East German Präsidium had been penetrated. Naturally, I let him think I knew more than I did, that London had sent me to get an update. For some reason my visit made him very agitated. He was adamant that whatever my authority, he couldn't comply. When I insisted, I remember he said, 'It's too delicate. London should know that.' I pressed him and he told me he suspected that Moscow was getting a day-to-day playback on the whole East German operation, and that everything pointed to the fact that the leak was back in London. 'We're getting closer,' he said, 'we just need to put the last piece of the puzzle in place. If we jump the gun we'll blow it.' He refused to give me names; all he said was, 'When this balloon goes up it will make the Philby thing seem like a children's tea party. It's right on the bloody doorstep.' "

"What did he mean by that?"

"How would I know?"

"Then what happened?"

"I reported back to Henze, and he insisted that I meet with this man Jock again. It proved difficult, but finally an appointment was made for us to bump into each other at a reception for the American Trade Fair in Vienna. I kept the date, but he never showed. Instead I got a message at my hotel saying there had been a change of plan. Later somebody telephoned with a safe address I was to go to the following night."

"Jock phoned you?"

"I don't think so. Somebody with a foreign accent. I went as instructed, but when I got there the place was swarming with police and I drove past without stopping. Afterwards I learned a man had been shot there." Glanville lit yet another cigarette. "End of story. No further contacts, no explanation, nothing."

"Did you ever discover who was shot at the rendezvous?"

He shook his head. "I didn't take those sorts of chances. It was never wise to make too many inquiries. I assumed it was this man Jock."

Hillsden shook his head. "Jock wasn't shot in Vienna. He drowned in a boating quote accident unquote, in the same lake that claimed Ludwig of Bavaria."

"Well, I can't add anything else. Does that satisfy you?"

"I don't satisfy that easily, but you get eight out of ten for effort."

"Are you going to leave me in peace now?"

"I don't know how you define peace." Hillsden suddenly felt tired, which wiped all the menace out of his voice. He had the feeling that he was an actor left waiting for a cue, with the prompt corner empty.

Desperation had brought him to this place, and all he'd take away, he realized, was the pain of failure. Only the photograph in his pocket, the one he could not look at himself, kept the hatred alive.

"I've paid the price," Glanville was saying, "whatever you think of me. In the last analysis it all rests on the spin of the coin. Like the Varsity Boat Race. I chose the Surrey side and lost."

Somewhere a train whistled, the sound traveling over the flat fields.

"Yes," Hillsden said, getting up to go. "But there are prices and prices. Aren't you fortunate the race was run here? They don't give you a choice in Moscow."

18

AT ALMOST THE precise moment that Hillsden closed Glanville's front door, the first of a series of bombs exploded in various parts of the country.

The initial target was the reception area of the BBC's Television Centre in Wood Lane, close to Shepherd's Bush. The devastation was considerable. Twenty-seven people were killed, including a party of old-age pensioners from Luton who had just arrived as an invited audience for a popular quiz show. Many of them were so badly mutilated that they could only be identified by such possessions as wristwatches or jewelry. The total casualty figure was close to seventy. The police later formed the opinion that the bomb had been concealed in a 35-mm film can, one of many such packages routinely delivered by motorcycle dispatch riders. Other than signing for the deliveries, the reception staff paid little attention to the riders themselves, who in any event wore regulation, feature-obliterating crash helmets. The bomb had been detonated less than five minutes after the rider had left the Centre without challenge.

Perhaps the most disturbing aspect of the subsequent outrages was the absence of any discernible pattern. They occurred at roughly half-hour intervals over the next three hours. The second bomb wrecked much of the façade of Brompton Oratory, causing a traffic jam that stretched all the way back to Heathrow Airport, paralyzing the city.

Here, mercifully, the casualties were few. The third bomb gutted a synagogue in Leeds—cynically during a funeral service—and caused eleven deaths and twice as many hideous injuries.

These incidents were horrifying enough, but it was the last bomb that claimed the media headlines. This was exploded in the canteen of a U.S. Army Air Force base while the staff were playing host to a large party of disabled children. Seventeen U.S. personnel died, including four wives of serving officers, but it was the toll among the children that aroused worldwide revulsion. Twenty-three were killed outright, and a further nine died in hospital. It was as if they had not suffered enough in their sad little lives, for many of them were spastics. The bomb had been packed with three-inch nails, which inflicted appalling wounds. Some of the television-newsreel footage was deemed too horrendous to transmit, though the following morning one of the national tabloids devoted its entire issue to photographs of the carnage, and the *Times,* flouting tradition, placed its leader on the front page, which compared the incident to the war crime perpetrated by the Nazi SS at Lidice. From all sides there were demands for the death penalty to be reintroduced.

The Prime Minister was at Chequers, but as soon as he learned the extent of the campaign, he returned to Downing Street under heavy police escort to preside over an emergency meeting of the full Cabinet. Arrangements were made for him to broadcast live to the nation that evening over the entire BBC and IBA television and radio networks. The Director General of the BBC issued orders for all scheduled programs to be canceled. Not to be seen lagging behind, the IBA countered by withdrawing all commercials. Both networks broadcast continuous news bulletins. The Archbishop of Canterbury, the Catholic Bishop of Westminster and the Chief Rabbi issued a joint statement calling for a national day of mourning and prayer; flags on all public buildings were flown at half-mast; and a Book of Remembrance opened at the American embassy in Grosvenor Square; by the end of the day it had been signed by over three thousand people. Police leave throughout the country was canceled and the armed forces put on full Red Alert.

Shortly after the first reports were made public, an orderly crowd started to gather in Whitehall, and queues of volunteer blood donors formed at hospitals all over the country. Another crowd, estimated by the Metropolitan Police to number twelve thousand, assembled in the Mall outside Buckingham Palace. There was no violence and the crowd sang "Land of Hope and Glory" and other patriotic songs, although the Monarch was not in residence, but was traveling on the royal train during a tour of the north. The Queen sent a personal message of sympathy to the American ambassador. Security measures for the entire Royal Family were doubled, but this did not deter the Prince of Wales from piloting an RAF jet to the stricken American air base—a spontaneous gesture that further enhanced his universal popularity.

At the Cabinet meeting the decision was taken to dispatch contingents of the SAS to every major city. In London mobile units of the Special Patrol Group were placed at strategic points and police marksmen posted on the roofs of all government buildings. In addition, a squadron of light armored cars established a base in Hyde Park. Sentries at Buckingham, Kensington and St. James' palaces were issued with live ammunition. The public were advised to avoid all museums until security checks had been carried out. Not since the General Strike of 1926 had there been such a spontaneous mobilization of the forces of the Crown.

No single organization claimed immediate credit for the outrages, but inevitably, given the historical precedence, they were widely assumed to be the work of one of the Irish terrorist groups; as a result the Irish Tourist Board office in Bond Street was sacked. But this was an isolated reaction, later traced to members of the National Front, and for the most part the large Irish population of the British Isles was not subjected to any undue abuse, though in Belfast Loyalist mobs carried out revenge attacks in the Catholic Bogside area. The Irish Minister for Home Affairs flew secretly to London for urgent consultations between the two governments and promised the utmost cooperation. That evening most of the pubs, theaters and cinemas were deserted, as people stayed close to their television and radio sets, anxiously awaiting the Prime Minister's speech.

In the event the speech was an anticlimax, for even the emotion of the moment could not produce any drastic change in his basic personality. At the best of times he was an uneasy performer in front of the cameras, and the text he read off on Autocue was the product of several uninspired minds, hastily drafted, redrafted and generously spattered with the flatulent rhetoric that most politicians employ on such occasions.

"Bring back De Gaulle," Hillsden remarked, watching at home with his wife. "Bloody pathetic! Why couldn't he, for once, say something vital and original instead of just spouting the same fucking platitudes?"

"Don't swear."

"What d'you mean, 'Don't swear'? Listen to the prick."

"How can I listen if you're shouting?"

Hillsden jumped up from his chair and poured himself a sizable tot of whisky, spilling ice cubes on his wife's prized Oriental rug. Behind him the P.M. faltered, momentarily losing his place on the Autocue. "We shall spare nothing . . . rather, we shall spare no effort to bring the perpetrators of these monstrous crimes to justice, and you may rest assured that my government will never be intimidated by such acts of wanton terrorism."

"Shitting himself," Hillsden said, between gulps of whisky. "Scared shitless—just look at his face."

"I wish you'd be quiet. And I hate that language."

"I have already given instructions," the P.M. continued, "that the security forces, under my direct orders and with the full backing of my Cabinet, are to be given much wider powers of search and arrest. Following this broadcast I am going straight to an emergency debate in the House to ask that the existing Suppression of Terrorism Act be strengthened; and it is my belief that these measures, which, with my known abhorrence of any diminution of civil liberties, I seek reluctantly, will be welcomed and supported by all the Opposition parties. This is not a time to play politics—"

"So why mention the subject?" Hillsden shouted at the screen.

"—but a time to unite the entire nation, a time for resolution. I know I speak for all of you when I say that today's tragic and terrible events have brought home the grim reminder that the very fabric of our civilized society is threatened. You have a right to look to your government to protect every citizen of whatever race, color or creed, and I shall not fail you. I ask you all to remain calm in the sure knowledge that everything that can be done *is* being done and will continue to be done. Our hearts and prayers go out to those who have lost loved ones, and especially our thoughts are with the parents of those children, and with the relatives of the American forces stationed in our country, who were so callously struck down while performing an act of Christian charity. God save the Queen."

The P.M. was left staring at the cameras for a few seconds until his image was replaced by a picture of the exterior of No. 10 Downing Street as an announcer intoned: "That was the Prime Minister, the Right Honorable Herbert Greenwell, speaking live from Downing Street. The nine o'clock news now follows."

"Hardly 'live,' " Hillsden said. "That's an exaggeration."

"I thought he spoke very nicely. What else could he have said?"

"Are you really asking me? You can't be that bloody dim." He waved his arms, sloshing what remained of his drink.

"Mind my rug, you've already dropped ice cubes."

"Oh, sod your rug! Look at what's on the screen. Those plastic bags are filled with the remains of children. Get your bloody priorities right, woman!"

He saw her face change color and the tears start to well up in her eyes, causing the mascara to rivulet her cheeks.

"I'm sorry, I'm sorry," he said. "I didn't mean to take it out on you. Don't cry. Please, I'm sorry, it's just that things have been getting on top of me lately. Business hasn't been good, they're talking of firing some of us. But that's no excuse, I'm really sorry."

He tried to put his arms around her, but she evaded him and rushed out of the room. He gave himself another slug of whisky before going in search of her.

She was locked inside the bathroom. He stood outside the door and spoke to her in his normal voice. "Margot? Come on out. I've said I'm sorry. Don't stay in there, please." There was no response. He leaned his head against the closed door and tried again. "Darling, don't be silly, don't make it any worse than it already is. I just can't stand the sight of that man, he gets up my nose. Thinking about those poor little kids and all the others just made me see red. Come on, stop crying, dry your eyes and come out. I promise you, I'm over it now, and I'll make it up to you."

Her eventual response was muffled.

"What? I can't hear."

Another minute went by before she unlocked the door. They stared at each other, intimate strangers, bruised by twenty years of marriage.

"You always look so young when you cry," he said gently.

For the second time he tried to embrace her, but again she walked past him and into the bedroom.

"Darling, don't let's keep this up. Whatever differences we have, whatever I've done to you over the years, this isn't the night to quarrel. Look, I've apologized, and I meant it—believe me, I meant it. All we've had all day is reminders of death, so don't let's you and me fight it out to the finish."

She sat at her dressing table, took some cleansing cream from a jar and dabbed at her mascara-streaked face. "Until next time," she said.

"What does that mean?"

She wiped off the cream with a tissue.

"What does that mean?" he repeated.

"Just that you're always sorry, but it always happens."

"What does?"

"Us," she said. "Our little deaths."

Hillsden came further into the room. As she removed the last of the cream from around her eyes, she raised them to look at his staring reflection in the dressing-table mirror. "Anyway, it doesn't matter." She got up and began to remove her clothes. He had the feeling that it was no longer any concern to her what effect her actions had on him. She might have been a total stranger undressing on a holiday beach.

"Can't you even feel angry?" he asked. "Get your own back on me? At least that would prove there was something left between us. Anything would be better than this. Do *something*—hit me, get it out of your system."

Her clothing lay on the floor where she had stepped out of it, and again he had an image of death: in the tumbled garments there was a certain similarity to the television pictures of the victims, the look of something that had once been human.

"You'd like that, wouldn't you?" she answered, reaching for the nightdress he had bought her on her last birthday. "It would get you off the hook."

"Oh, darling, what a stupid thing to say."

"Yes, well, perhaps I am stupid. You should have married somebody more your equal."

With her shiny face devoid of any makeup, he thought how vulnerable she looked. Now she folded back the bedcovers and got between the sheets, immediately turning her head away from him on the pillow. He sat on the nearest edge of the bed and touched her bare shoulder. "Darling, look at me. People can't be perfect all of the time. We have to talk, have rows, make it up, live through the good and the bad."

"I thought we'd done that," she said, her head still turned to the wall.

"I wish you had more friends."

"Well, I don't. You've seen to that. I've never been good enough to meet your friends; you've made that very plain over the years. You've never shared that part of your life with me."

"Not for any deliberate reason. I might say I've never felt you showed any real interest in what I do. I guess I don't have a very interesting job. Selling wine was never my first ambition in life, but at least it's paid the rent, given us a roof over our heads. I promise I'll make the effort from now on. We'll go out more, do more things together, begin again."

She pulled herself upright in the bed, leaning against the buttoned headboard that, like themselves, had seen better days. She stared at him; thinking that the worst was over, Hillsden smiled, but her face remained the same.

"I have been talking to somebody," she said. There was a sudden defiance in her voice.

"Well, good, I'm glad. Who?"

"Nobody you know. A man."

"Okay. I guess you're entitled."

"Oh, not what you're thinking. A doctor. I've been seeing a psychiatrist."

The confession took him by surprise; even after a lifetime of concealing his real emotions he was still not able to control his expression of disbelief. "I thought you didn't believe in them."

"Maybe I still don't. But at least it's somebody who listens to me."

"And does it help you?" Hillsden asked, recovering.

"Yes."

"Well, I'm glad. He has all the answers, does he? All the answers I can't supply."

"No, there are no answers."

"So what do you talk about?"

"That's my business. I pay for him out of my own money."

"How long has this been going on? Am I at least allowed to ask that?"

"Quite a while. Once a week for the past three months."

"And has it helped?"

"It helps not to be alone."

"That's great. As long as you're getting your money's worth."

He got up from the bed and, after placing her discarded clothes on the back of a chair, left the bedroom and went downstairs. The television was still on; he stared at a close-up of Bayldon being interviewed at Westminster, pontificating as usual, saying nothing new; just stale echoes of his master's voice reached Hillsden as he poured himself another whisky: "Terrorism will never succeed," "Our resolve is as firm as ever," "The situation is under control."

You pathetic clown, Hillsden thought; nothing in life is ever under control. There was violence even in suburban bedrooms, the terror of loneliness behind drawn curtains, love and hatred mixed together like volatile explosives, with memories the detonators.

When finally the interview came to an end, Bayldon was succeeded by pictures of some of the victims: family snapshots, wedding pictures doubtless prised from grieving relatives. An announcer's off-screen voice listed them, giving intimate details of better times beyond recall. Brides, sons and daughters, frozen in life and now in death, filled the screen. One young girl in particular, described as "a former Miss Blackpool," was caught in the perfection of youth. She wore a one-piece white bathing costume, and the contrast of this against her flawless tanned skin was almost too much for Hillsden to bear. He was overwhelmed by a longing for times past, when endless romantic love untainted by the pain of living had seemed attainable; when the texture of a girl's naked skin had been the only thing to be desired. Her image was replaced by another, the face of an American airman, shiny-cheeked, the epitome of those idealized young men once painted by Norman Rockwell. The airman had died trying to save one of the crippled children, a girl half his age.

Hillsden switched off the set, and only then realized, for the first time since her murder, that it had been some hours since he had thought of Caroline.

19

GENESIS

"IN THE END it all comes down to people, doesn't it," Caroline said. "Individual people, one person. You can open your legs to a cause, but the masses can't make love to you, can't make you *love*. You have to take a man into your bed."

"I'll have to think about that. Bit too deep to take in at first go."

"Or too obvious."

They were sharing a single bed in an anonymous little *Gasthaus* tucked away in the pine forests that bordered the small Austrian village of Krumpendorf. Hillsden had selected it. "I stayed here just after the war, when you paid in bars of soap, or a packet of cigarettes. You could live like a king for a whole month if you came up with a pound of coffee."

"All illegal, presumably, furthering the black market?"

"Oh, yes, totally. Strictly against Army regulations, but everybody did it from the General on down. Nobody drew any pay: you didn't need to. It was a very strange feeling being around here just after the war ended. Unreal. Almost as unreal as this."

It was the start of the affair. They had booked in under false names in two separate rooms. The rooms had rough-plastered white walls and double windows, and were heated with baroque tiled stoves burning

146

sweet-scented pine chips. As an added precaution, they ate at separate tables whenever they took a meal in the small dining room. For the rest they had devised a plan whereby one or the other would leave the hotel first; then, after an interval, the other would follow to a prearranged rendezvous in the forest. When the weather was fine they spent most of the day there, picnicking and making love in the open air. It was only at night, when the staff had retired, that Hillsden risked going to her room, stealing back to his own just before the staff were up and about again.

"Tell me about it. When you say 'unreal,' do you mean the life was unreal or the situation?"

"Both. Certainly the life. Suddenly it was all over. They blew the whistle and there we were, bloody relieved we'd come through it, of course, but plunged immediately into a new role. We were the masters, the proverbial conquering army occupying enemy soil. When you walked into a place like this, for instance, the locals all stood to attention. Unnerving in a way; it took some getting used to. There was a great deal of forelock touching and groveling; they fell over themselves to tell you that they had never been Nazis, never joined the Party."

"Did that apply to the women too?"

"No, they were a different problem."

"Why are you smiling?"

"Some joker had ordered there was to be no fraternization. *Streng verboten, meine Herren!* You will not fornicate with the enemy. The British Army of the Rhine will renounce sex from 0700 hours."

"Keep your voice down," Caroline whispered. "And did you?"

"No fear. Went at it like stoats. I mean, you can imagine, can't you? Half a million of the sex-starved licentious soldiery wandering about the countryside and told not to pick the flowers. The whole stupid edifice collapsed within weeks."

"But wasn't it strange to fraternize with women who a little while previously you would have killed?"

"We didn't kill women. Not intentionally, anyway."

"Don't split hairs. You know what I'm getting at."

"No. It's remarkable how quickly that side of it returns to normal."

"But what was their attitude?"

"The same."

"It's all fascinating. Tell me more."

"Why are you so curious?"

"Because I want to know all about you. See, I was still at school then, when you were deflowering all the Rhine maidens. You forget that."

"No, I don't." He leaned over and kissed her breasts. "How could I?

You realize we're going against orders right now. Breaking all the rules —the Firm's, the Church of England's, my own, all simultaneously."

"You don't look very guilty."

"I am. Guilt encircles me like floodwaters round a swan's nest."

"Very poetic. Did you just think of that, or have you been saving it for an occasion like this?"

"Don't be like Jock. He's always ribbing me about my literary tastes. It was all my own original work."

"I don't want you to feel guilt where I'm concerned," Caroline said.

"Maybe I'm not cut out for adultery."

"Takes two. I didn't exactly discourage you. And I wish I'd met you sooner. . . . Did you have many affairs during that time, after the war?"

"Not many, and I wouldn't call them affairs. Three, to be exact."

"In this hotel?"

"No."

"I'm glad about that. What were they like?"

"How about if I turned the tables and asked you the same question?"

"Ask me."

"No, I don't want to know."

She squirmed closer to him, entwining her legs in his and he felt the heat of her body against him.

"Tell me more about yours, then."

"God! you're persistent. They were just episodes in another landscape. Funny."

"What?"

"I was thinking. I suppose all the deceits started then. We were like the blind—two people trying to read each other by touch. There was the language thing, you see. My German was minimal then, and none of them spoke English. I'll tell you how strange it was. One of them, I forget which, took me into her home to meet her parents. They stood the entire time; it was grotesque. The mother said nothing, but her father jabbered away at me nonstop, and every so often he would bow. It took a while to latch onto what he was trying to say. I finally caught on: he was giving me his daughter, telling me how honored they were that I was going with her. When I left, I put half a pound of coffee on the table and her mother came forward and kissed my hands. I never saw any of them again after that."

"Why?"

"Guilt once more. Or call it shame. I thought how awful it must be to want something like half a pound of coffee beans so badly that you'd actually trade your daughter." Hillsden stared down at her. Her lips, kissed bare of color, endlessly invited a love he had all but forgotten. He remained amazed by the suddenness and intensity of his feeling for her. From the moment he arrived at the Austrian station there had been no other choice to make. Now it seemed impossible to believe in a time when he had not loved her. He likened his love to a plant that, incredibly, forces its way through concrete—in his case penetrating the slab that had for so long entombed him beneath a failed marriage. From this moment onwards there would be a different kind of guilt to carry forward: the regret that they had not found each other sooner.

"What about hatred?" Caroline asked, cutting into his thoughts. "Maybe that came into it, too."

"Hatred?"

"Yes. Isn't that a possibility, bearing in mind what the war was all about?"

Before answering her he reached down by the side of the bed to pour them both another glass of hock. He was in a cramped position, and as he passed Caroline her glass the wine slopped.

"Damn! Here, have mine."

"No, this is fine. Rub some behind my ears for luck."

"That's only champagne."

After a silence he said, "You think you *ought* to hate—that's what you've been indoctrinated with for years—but it's not so easy when the smoke clears. You can't hate misery itself, only what causes it."

It was Caroline's turn to remain silent for a while. "The smoke hasn't cleared for me, that's the difference between us," she answered finally. "I have to keep it alive; otherwise I couldn't go on. See, I don't have any courage; hatred's all I've got."

It was as if the plan of retribution instilled in her in the nursery had carried her through the years, just as some people hoard love letters even from those who have betrayed them.

20

THE MOOD OF the country remained volatile, and a further symptom of the general unrest was the emergence of a breakaway and more militant faction of the CND movement calling itself CANS (Committee Against Nuclear Suicide). They seemed to surface overnight with a well-organized sit-in at the main U.S. Strategic Air Command base, where the new generation of atomic missiles had just been made operational. It was here that the still unidentified terrorists struck again with devastating effect. Some two hundred twenty pounds of explosives, hidden in a mobile hamburger stand serving the demonstrators' camp, was detonated by remote control, causing a massive crater. Nearly forty demonstrators and seven members of the police force were killed outright. In the aftermath of panic an American soldier guarding the perimeter opened fire with an automatic weapon when the hysterical crowd attempted to rush the security fence to escape. The result was an additional five dead, including a child eighteen months old. Since the soldier was empowered to act as he did under the new emergency regulations, he was subsequently exonerated—a verdict that intensified the already large body of anti-American feeling.

Once again the *Times,* joined this time by the tabloids, devoted its entire front page to a leading article calling on the Queen to dissolve Parliament and for a coalition government to be formed. The Foreign Secretary flew to Washington, where he was tongue-lashed in no uncertain fashion by a President already under siege by a hostile Congress and in the middle of an election year he was dubious of surviving. Public opinion in the United States was already clamoring for a return to an isolationist foreign policy and the withdrawal of American forces in Europe.

On the world markets there was a heavy run on sterling; against the dollar the pound dropped below parity for the first time in history, and the Bank of England had to intervene on a mammoth scale to stabilize the situation. The minimum lending rate was raised to an all-time high, and the government rushed to reimpose exchange controls.

The violence was not confined to the British Isles; acts of terrorism —bombings, kidnapping and murders—erupted all over Western Europe, jumping across frontiers with the ferocity of a forest fire. There was much talk of a new terror network, that terrorism's old guard had been supplanted by a younger generation of renegades; the erstwhile limited, parochial aims had been discarded, and in their place the security forces detected an overall strategy directed against NATO and other defense-related targets. Most disturbing of all was evidence of cross-pollination between the unholy alliance of three main groups, apparently masterminded from one source in the Eastern bloc. As the lengthening trail of violence criss-crossed Europe—first England, then

Belgium, now Italy, then back to Germany and across to France—the antiterrorist forces, sharing intelligence, found many common factors, but their successes were few.

Back in England most of the known IRA suspects and other assorted sympathizers had been rounded up in the first forty-eight hours following the initial attacks, but apart from odd hauls of small arms and ammunition these operations produced little. There was an Orwellian chill to the political air which, transmitted to the general public, produced the feeling that the old order was about to disappear for good. Battered by the economic situation and unable to provide any long-term answer to the terrorism, the fledgling Labour government had its back to the wall. On two occasions the Speaker of the House suspended the session following turbulent scenes on the floor. Under its emergency powers the government had banned all rallies, demonstrations, marches and meetings of more than fifty people, adding to the sense of a society under siege and enraging various civil liberty groups. There were several attempts to act in defiance of this ban, and one such demonstration of several thousand students resulted in a bloody pitched battle with the police.

Given such a situation, it was not surprising that the death of Glanville merited only a paragraph or two on the inside pages, with terse headlines such as LONELY END OF A TRAITOR and LAST HOURS OF A SPY. He had been found, apparently dead of a heart attack, by a friend. The official statement said that foul play was not suspected, and that the funeral would be private, but as with so many of the official statements being put out at that time, it was a lie.

Like Caroline before him, Glanville's body had been probed by the cutting edge of Hogg's analytical mind as well as his dissecting scalpel.

"A nerve gas, according to the illustrious Hogg," Control said.

"Not his heart?"

"No, Alec, but then his heart was never in the right place, was it?"

Hillsden felt compelled to acknowledge the joke; one could never be quite sure about Control's sense of humor.

"To be strictly accurate, the heart stopped, as it usually does when the time comes. Glanville's time came when somebody squirted an aerosol can in his face. Simple and effective, just like a halitosis spray, although in his case the relief was more lasting. D'you perceive a pattern, Alec?"

The second use of his Christian name in the space of a few minutes disconcerted Hillsden. Familiarity, where Control was concerned, usually had a price on it.

"What sort of pattern?"

"You're younger than me, of course—not that that's any criterion, it simply means one has more to remember. And I do have an excellent memory—mostly for trivia, I suspect. The memory of a mind capable of solving the *Times* crossword most days, but unable to comprehend the method of mending a fuse. However, occasionally something of pith and moment swims to the surface. Like, 'What matters in waging a war is not righteousness but victory. Close your hearts to pity. Proceed brutally.' Any idea who said that?"

"Napoleon?"

"Warm. No, it was our old friend Adolf, a few days before he went into Poland. He was talking about the propaganda pretext for launching a war. Credibility he dismissed as unimportant, on the basis that the victor is never asked afterwards whether or not he told the truth. And he was right, utterly accurate in his evaluation of human nature."

Hillsden listened politely; he had no idea what Control was leading up to. The veiled reference to encroaching senility didn't fool him. He thought, What am I being set up for?

"But that's by the way. I've been giving a lot of thought in recent days, as I'm sure you have, to what's behind this current wave of terrorism. I think we can assume that it is Moscow-financed, if not Moscow-inspired. Their aim has always been to disarm everybody but themselves. So what has changed? Nothing has changed. It is as if Stalin, Beria, the Gulag, the Wall, indestructible Gromyko, never existed. We have learned nothing—no lessons ever memorized, all the textbooks ignored."

He moved to the window, putting himself in silhouette. "Divide and conquer, Alec. Different methods, different groups carrying them out, but still working from the same original blueprints. Don't do for yourself what others will do for you, but be ready to walk in afterwards and collect the spoils. As usual, their timing is impeccable. We're ripe, Alec, ripe for plucking, though, of course, those in Whitehall are reluctant—or, should we say, unable—to grasp the fact."

It was the longest speech Hillsden had ever heard him make, and he wondered why he had been singled out to hear it. Control turned to face him again and smiled. "Naturally, I would always deny this conversation ever took place."

"I wasn't even here."

"These somber thoughts are prompted by the fact that I was summoned to the presence this morning. An audience with the Right Honorable Mr. Bayldon, no less. Having kissed the ring, I then had my trousers taken down and was given six of the best, followed by an extremely disagreeable lecture on the failings of the Firm. I didn't care for any of it one bit. Not one bit. I haven't been talked to like that since I was at prep school. Not a student of history, our incumbent Home Secretary. He doesn't discern any clear pattern, and declines to be educated on the subject. When I could get a few words in, I tried to point out that what is happening now was undoubtedly planned a long time ago, the seeds planted in a rank herbaceous border to flower at regular intervals. All the varieties: a few fellow travelers, some hybrids and, right in the center, the dedicated perennials that never wither on the stalk."

Control seemed pleased with the metaphor, as though he had just discovered a hidden talent for words.

"Of course, over the years we've managed a little uprooting. Modest weeding out, nothing spectacular, but enough to disrupt the overall pattern. And perhaps, without knowing it, we got—we are getting—a shade too close to the core. And if you go along with that, if unwittingly we *have* stumbled too close, that would be enough. Not that we do actually have the puzzle solved, but that Moscow *thinks* we do. Hence the stepping up of the pace, because they can adapt in minutes, whereas we go through the laborious democratic process, and that takes years."

He paused, looking down at a photograph of an elderly couple whom Hillsden took to be his parents.

"We are all justifiably mystified about Caroline's death. So far, that is. But now we have a second death on our hands—Glanville's. Two burnt-out cases suddenly disposed of, and no apparent connection between them. Except that true students of history, such as you and I, know there is always a connection. To continue my hypothesis, perhaps Moscow thinks we are on the brink of making that connection."

"Yes." Hillsden nodded in agreement.

"If you go along with me thus far, that brings us full circle to you and your connection with both of them."

"Hardly with Glanville."

Control smiled for the second time during the conversation. "I beg to differ. On the face of it, Alec, you were the last person to see him."

"What gives you that idea?"

"A device known as a bug. It's your voice on the tape, Alec. You were careless. You even uttered threats." The smile was erased.

"I wouldn't be so stupid as to kill Glanville."

"Ah, well, *I* know that, but others might not take your word for it in the circumstances. After all, you were stupid enough to go against my orders, I must remind you of that."

"Why would anybody go out of their way to pin that on me? A tired old queen, a self-confessed traitor, scarcely worth swinging for."

"Politics, Alec, politics. The art of finding scapegoats. Glanville didn't die in his sleep: he was murdered. Hogg has established that. Isolated and identified the nerve gas used. It was of British origin, of a type issued to the Firm. Questions are going to be asked, questions that have to be answered. It's known as justice, the upholding of the law. No man, not even a traitor, being above it, or denied it. That's what sets us apart from less civilized societies."

"Is that why you were carpeted by Bayldon?"

"No, he was dealing with wider issues. The subject of Glanville was mentioned, but only in passing, and since I wasn't asked to elaborate, I didn't. But we can't be certain that sleeping dog won't be roused in the near future."

"So what are you trying to tell me? That as and when the facts become known, I'm going to be offered up as a sacrifice?"

"Now, you know me better than that."

"I don't know you at all," Hillsden said savagely. "And I don't like riddles. I enjoyed the history lesson, very illuminating; now come out in the open and say what you mean."

"It's complicated, Alec. Like an Iris Murdoch novel. Have you read Murdoch?"

"Some."

"I'm quite passionate about her. Especially *The Severed Head*. One of her best; the interplay between characters, like an intricate dance, choreographed by a master. Naturally, I would never put myself anywhere near her level, but I do have a certain . . . aptitude, put it no more than that, for survival in a maze. We lead such complicated lives. Are we the hunted or the hunters? Who are we really working for? Ourselves, them, the others? Or just from a sense of anger against the whole mishmosh? Ever ask yourself those questions?"

"Frequently. A few moments ago, as a matter of fact."

"And what answers did you come up with?"

"None that made much sense."

"Yes," Control said, going to the window again and this time running a finger along the sill to collect the day's residue of London grime. "But in your case I'd say there is one straightforward answer. Anger. You've always struck me as being an angry man. You hide it well, but I've frequently sensed it was there just below the surface, like a blind boil in adolescence, poised to erupt. You're angry now, of course, irritated by my circumspection. . . . Well, I said it was complicated."

"Glanville was alive and lying when I left. That must have been evident from the playback."

"You were digging in somebody else's plot, Alec."

"What the hell does that mean? Did you bring me here just to hear gardening hints?"

Control turned, rubbing the side of his nose. "Don't waste your anger on me, Alec. I'm your friend, perhaps one of the few you have at this moment. And you're going to need your anger. You're going to need a lot, real and faked, because you're going back."

"Back where?"

"To where it all began, Alec. To where it all began."

21

BELFRAGE WAS NOT the most satisfying and certainly not the most
accomplished of lovers, though it would have offended him to be told
that his technique was in any way lacking. He was also prone to postcoi-
tal guilt, and Pamela was astute enough to realize that the guilt provided
the initial stimulation as well as the resulting melancholy. Increasingly,
she felt the sacrifice demanded of her by Gunther was too high a price
to pay; she devised a kind of Pelmanism to stem her boredom while Sir
Charles panted his way to an unshared conclusion she was obliged to
fake.

When Pamela thought about the various stages in her sexual education, most men, with the exception of Gunther, had bored her in bed.
Her teenage experimental years had been haunted by those fearfully
correct public school types more anxious to make a good impression on
Mummy and Daddy than give her what she craved. Supine beneath Sir
Charles and waiting for the moment when he would finish his exertions,
she would recall their strangulated voices and permanent but wasted
erections, the way they had kissed her with chapped lips, their hands
pressed hard against her breasts while they pleaded for selfish, quick
relief. Sir Charles was merely an older version of those distant swains.
A cousin had been the recipient of her first, total favors: both of them
limp from tennis, he with a face swollen from hay fever, two novices in
a summerhouse, pretending a knowledge that soon proved less than
comprehensive. But from her point of view it had been a necessary
watershed, the initial pleasurable taste of deceit, a preparation for
grosser treasons to come. Because, of course, she had been schooled to
save herself, to survive crossing over from the weald of youth unsullied
until that supreme moment when, on Daddy's arm, she walked—to the
accompaniment of Mendelssohn—towards the old con trick of love,
honor and obey. Seeing others go that tired old route, she had determined not to be trapped in the same cul-de-sac.

The aged parents' biggest mistake was to allow her to finish her
education at UC. Still, she had always been Daddy's girl, and what she
wanted Daddy delivered. There, on the sprawling campus at Berkeley,

159

covering an area as large as the town she had been reared in, her search for nirvana ended. It was not only another world, where the tanned natives spoke her language in a foreign tongue, but a world in which intellectually, politically and sexually she came of age. The cricket blazers had been replaced by T-shirts stenciled with the slogans of dissent, the summerhouse exchanged for the back seats of Chevrolets and vintage Thunderbirds. More confident hands removed her bra, more agile minds instilled in her an awareness of what was wrong with the society that had spawned her. The whole experience was a revelation. She discovered that she was no longer an endangered species from a country spent and dulled from two world wars, but part of a movement on the march that was going to wipe the slate clean and begin again— a movement that made up the rules as it went along, and broke them again just as casually if they proved ineffective for its needs. She found herself accepted in a virtually classless society that mockingly rejected every attitude that she had hitherto never questioned. Brought up in the belief that there would always be a status quo, she was astounded to be told that there was no status quo. She started to breathe in that heady American contempt for authority and found it exhilarating. The prospect of being included in possible violence, combined with the politics of destruction, was a consummation devoutly to be wished.

Naturally, none of this was accomplished overnight. In the beginning, her accent, the way she dressed and the amount of pocket money she could fling around set her apart. When she caught on that acceptance could not be bought, she strove hard to slough off her old personality, for she was desperate to be accepted. Previously she had never had any political awareness. It had been taken that when eligible to vote, she would vote as Daddy voted, which was straight down the line, true-blue Tory. At home the conversation had always been about Them and Us, and Them embraced every shade of pink, however faint. The extent of her involvement in social issues had been to sign a petition supporting the retention of fox hunting; from age sixteen she had owned a fur coat. Now, as she lost her English bloom in the California sunshine, daily becoming more and more obsessed with the need to shed everything she had once held sacred, she joined every protest and signed any petition likely to foment trouble. Like most converts, she embraced the new faith more resolutely than those born to it. She went out of her way to cultivate the friendship and respect of the student gurus, sitting at their feet (or on their faces, if that was the required entrance fee), and steeping herself in their nihilistic philosophies. What they preached in the sullen aftermath of Vietnam seemed the only way to save her generation. There were to be no more wars, except those of their choosing.

It was during this second stage of her development that she met Gunther, seduced first by his mind and then by his exciting, casual brand of sex. It was Gunther who put romanticism in a political context, Gunther who demonstrated that Marxism held the one great prize: salvation through violence. Spread-eagled beneath him, she awakened to the lure of chaos. It seemed all so perfect, so logical, such a stunningly original idea to further a revolution in the midst of such affluence, to plan a golden state within the Golden State. Especially the way Gunther described it. He revealed how he and others had brought a new strain of revolution from Europe to the New World and the way in which, once germinated, the plant would proliferate. "This is only the beginning. We haven't got started yet."

The future he pictured for her was a more potent drug than the top-class shit they smoked together, and just as he perverted her mind he perverted her sexual tastes, making her more and more dependent on him. He taught her the merits of patience, the need to go under-ground. "You're doing it all the wrong way. Never show your real hand. Always play the cards they want you to play. Be an exemplary student. Don't sign any petitions. Don't join any student body or organization. Fade into their background, make them feel secure with you. Be what they expect you to be, and you're halfway there." She believed every-thing he told her, obeyed his instructions to the letter and reversed the process she had begun.

She was besotted with him. Not only was he a compelling teacher, he practiced what he preached. Although he knew most of what there was to know about her within a short space of time, she could ferret out little knowledge of his background. He was German, from Hamburg, the son of wealthy middle-class parents he despised and had cut himself off from. There was scant humor in him, as she quickly discovered; he was serious about everything. When they were alone together, he would often remain silent for hours, refusing to engage. His intensity fascinated her as much as it frightened her on occasion; gradually she began to assume for herself the same qualities she admired in him, thinking that by emulating him he would find her more attractive. From the way he used and educated her body she realized he had satisfied himself with many others before her, but there was no way he could be drawn to discuss his past affairs. Likewise there was nothing tender about him; he was as far removed from the ideal lover she had once fantasized over as a teenager as was possible to imagine, but the more casually he treated her, the more she desired him. The prospect of losing him was unthinkable; there was nothing she would not do to keep him.

During the second summer they were together he announced they would take a holiday abroad. Naturally, he had not bothered to consult her, nor did it ever enter her mind to challenge his decision. The arrangements had been made; they were going to Brazil; Gunther knew best; it was all marvelous.

On that holiday she was to discover just how effectively he had destroyed her previous convictions. In the beginning he seemed more relaxed than she had ever known him, but his moods could change quickly, and it came as no surprise when at the beginning of the second week he withdrew into his shell again, becoming nervous and irritable with her. "We're moving on, this place bores me," he said suddenly. It was a statement of fact: there was no question of asking her opinion.

They packed and checked out of the hotel within the hour, and drove in a rented car for four or five hours until they reached a remote village. Not once did he give any indication of their eventual destination. They arrived at dusk and obtained a squalid room in the only hotel. She was tired and hot after the journey, but the shower in the room produced nothing but a thin trickle of rusty water; this and his refusal to communicate the reason for their sudden move finally irritated her beyond measure.

"Why the bloody secrecy?" she shouted. "This was meant to be a holiday. I loved the other place. Now, without telling me why, we drive for bloody hours to the back of nowhere. Why? Give me a reason."

"My plans changed. I have to meet somebody here."

"Who?"

"You'll meet him tonight."

"What if I don't want to?"

"You'll meet him tonight," he repeated. "You'll do as you're told, and you won't ask any more questions."

She sulked until an hour later, when he announced that they were leaving.

"I'm not getting back in that bloody car again. I'm hungry, I want something to eat."

"You will eat. Just get in and don't argue with me."

This time the journey was short, a matter of four or five miles up into the hills. They came to an isolated villa, tucked out of sight from the road, and which appeared to deserted. There were no lights in the windows and the surrounding garden was neglected. Gunther parked the car at the rear of the villa, and as he cut the engine she heard a dog barking. It was not a friendly sound. As they walked towards the rear entrance the door suddenly opened and they were confronted by a young man she guessed to be roughly the same age as Gunther. He was heavily built, bordering on obese for his size, with a fat, babyish face. He held a Doberman bitch on a choke chain of the type used by prison guards and police, the sort that could be swiftly slipped free. The animal reared on the chain, snarling at them.

"She's okay," the youth said. The accent was sibilant and difficult to place. "It's just that she doesn't make any distinction between friends and enemies." He gave a command, and the Doberman immediately became placid.

Inside, the youth led them into a room whose wooden shutters were closed. As they came into the light Pamela got a better look at him. His skin was olive-colored, and she thought his origins must be either Mediterranean or South American. The most disturbing feature about him was his lips, which seemed not to fit the rest of his face—swollen as though bee-stung was what came to her mind. Despite his bulk he moved lightly on his feet like a trained boxer. There was something repulsively attractive about him, especially when he smiled, as he did now.

"I guess you're hungry? I prepared something." He pointed to a meal of cold meats and wine laid out on the table.

"Since Gunther isn't going to introduce us, I'm Pamela."

"Oh, I know who you are. Please eat."

He handed her a plate and she helped herself while he poured wine for them. She waited for Gunther to offer some explanation, but he said nothing. When he and the youth had taken some food and wine for themselves, they left the room abruptly, closing the door after them. The Doberman remained with her. She threw it a piece of meat, but the bitch ignored it.

Although hunger forced Pamela to eat, the food did nothing to stifle her queasiness. At the back of her mind she couldn't help thinking that she had seen the youth somewhere before; there was a vague familiarity about him. She listened for their voices but could hear nothing, and she was afraid to move with the Doberman's eyes never leaving her. When she had finished she placed the empty plate and wineglass by the side of her chair. Fear and the irritations of the day had exhausted her, and after a while she dozed off.

When Gunther shook her awake she was in the middle of a disturbing dream about her parents. "Are we going now?" she asked, as old fears immediately returned.

"No, we're staying here for the night."

"Why? What is this place? Why did we come here? What's happening?" She spat out the questions in one breath.

The youth was nowhere to be seen. "And who is he?"

In answer Gunther gripped her forearm tightly enough to restrict the circulation. "Just do as you're told and don't ask questions that don't concern you. We're staying, and that's all there is to it. Now go to bed."

She noticed that while she was asleep their luggage had been brought in. Still holding her by the arm, he propelled her towards the door, picking up her suitcase on the way. She was led into the hallway and up the stairs and shown into a bedroom. Like the rest of the house, it was sparsely furnished with few comforts.

"Are you coming to bed?" The fear of angering him further had softened her voice.

"Later."

"I'm frightened," she said. "I don't understand any of this."

"There's nothing to be frightened about. I'll explain it all later. Trust me."

But when he had gone, trust was the last thing she believed in. Before undressing she examined the room. The wardrobe and chest of drawers were empty, and the only thing she found was a single paperback novel on the bedside table. It was written in Spanish, and with its lurid cover appeared to be a cheap thriller. She heard the Doberman padding about on the landing outside as she got into bed, then a long silence. Once again she fell into a twilight sleep. The noise of a door slamming wakened her; it was followed by the sound of a car driving away. She sat up in the bed and screamed Gunther's name. She heard footsteps coming up the stairs, and a moment later Gunther appeared in the doorway. "Are you mad? What're you screaming for?"

"Because I was scared. I've been scared ever since we got here. I don't understand what's going on. I thought that was you driving away, leaving me alone with that character and his hideous dog."

"Well, I didn't drive away. I'm here."

"Is he coming back?" Gunther shook his head and sat on the edge of the bed. "But isn't this his house?"

He stroked her hair. "It's a place he uses."

"Please tell me what it's all about."

"Just be patient."

"Why did we come here at all? We were on holiday."

"I had to come. I was ordered to."

"Ordered? Who ordered you?"

"He did."

She stared at him. "That fat boy? Why would you be ordered about by him?"

"It's just as well he's not around to hear you call him that. He's very touchy about his looks."

"What is he? Are you in some sort of trouble? It's to do with drugs, isn't it?"

He smiled. "What a lot you still have to learn, baby. No, it's nothing to do with drugs."

"Then what is he to you? He has to be somebody very special to bring you to this dump in the middle of nowhere."

"Oh, he is, he is very special. You're very privileged. You met somebody that the police on three continents would give anything to catch up with, somebody who's done what you and I have only talked about." He waited for her reaction, but when her expression remained blank, he could not contain himself. He said with sly, winking pride, "You met Raoul, the one the newspapers call the Salamander."

"That was him?"

"He'd be pleased you didn't recognize him. Now do you understand?"

"No, it still doesn't make any sense. . . . Unless you've been lying to me all this time."

"Not lying, just waiting until I was sure you were ready for the next move. You see, baby . . . Here, have this, you need relaxing." He lit a fat joint and allowed her to use it first. She took it gratefully. "I can tell you now that he had grave doubts about your coming with me, but I convinced him you could be trusted. I talked well for you. If I hadn't —if he had the slightest doubts—you wouldn't be alive now. I couldn't have saved you. He doesn't take chances; that's why he's survived and most of his imitators haven't. But he has to recruit new blood, to keep the momentum going."

Even when the drug started to flatten out her fears, she still had little real comprehension of what he was telling her. It was only much later, after they had made love, that she learned the extent of Gunther's involvement. He explained his role in the fat boy's network; explained that through him, she, too, was committed, her credentials entered in a passport that would never be shown, that from this moment onwards her real identity would be buried forever. He reminded her of some of the fat boy's past successes: the bomb in the railway station at Turin, the assassination of the Israeli ambassador to Peru, the hijacking and eventual destruction of the British Airways 747 in Kuwait. "Those are just the ones they credit him with, not the complete list. Sometimes he simply passes on an idea, makes sure all the necessary arrangements are in place, but plays no active role himself. He could be a thousand miles away when the bomb goes off. Such a brilliant mind for producing chaos —you might almost say he was born for it. And so far he's had a charmed life, despite what you might have read in the papers they've never got anywhere near him. It's two years since they even had a reliable sighting. You never contact him, he contacts you. He has no possessions, nothing."

"What about the dog?"

"You're right. He does have her. He's fond of animals, but not so fond that he wouldn't use a bullet on her if she proved a threat. Tonight was a good example of the way he operates. He's never used this place before, and he'll never use it again. It was merely put at his disposal by his paymasters."

The way Gunther told it, he could have been describing a saint rather than a hired killer. "There's just one thing that might destroy him. You hit upon it without knowing. His Achilles' heel is, he likes his food too much. He's had surgery on his face several times, and probably the next time you see him—if you ever see him—he'll be different again. What can't change for him is his appetite. You were right on target. He's a fat boy."

"What about the other?"

"The other?"

"What does he do to relax?"

"Oh, you mean this? My guess is he's neuter; he gets all his kicks from his work."

"It seems odd," she said, "to call it work. Death from nine to six. Who payrolls him?"

"I don't think he cares too much whose signature is on the check. There's no shortage of commissions. Talents like his command a high price."

"What will we be asked to do?"

"Who knows? When he's ready, when he's decided, he'll tell us. Maybe next week, maybe not for months, maybe never. Until then we're on ice. But he'll always know where we are."

The holiday over, they returned to UC and the following year got degrees in their respective subjects, being regarded as ideal students more concerned with pursuing the American ethos of success than meddling in politics. They made their separate ways to Europe, Pamela going home to England and Gunther to his native Germany. He provided her with ample funds and briefed her on what to do and what to expect on her return. It was only then, for the first time in their affair, that she learned whom they had been recruited to serve. She took it in with a mixture of fear and excitement; at that time it still seemed like a marvelous game they were being permitted to play, containing no more danger than the drugs they habitually used.

Gunther had told her that in his absence she would receive her future instructions through the personal advertisements placed in the window of a small tobacconist's just off Wardour Street. The first message would be placed on a specific date, and would alert her to keep a prearranged rendezvous with her control. She was to be run by a covert KGB officer in the Russian embassy using the code name Albert.

Pamela was welcomed back by her family and endured the suffocating atmosphere of home life in the country for a few weeks, making the effort for appearance' sake, but with no intention of picking up old threads. Once the conventions had been observed, she told her parents that she was determined to make a life of her own, a decision they privately welcomed, for they admitted to themselves that her stay in California had changed her. She moved back to London, taking a small flat that Gunther had picked for her, and began her secret life. On the appointed day she went to the tobacconist's shop. There, amid the postcards giving details of lost pets, secondhand cars, camera equipment and the services of whores masquerading as French teachers and masseuses, she singled out the card meant for her: DARLING PLEASE MEET ME USUAL PLACE THURSDAY MORNING. I STILL LOVE YOU. ALBERT.

The predetermined first rendezvous had been in the Snowdon Aviary at Regent's Park Zoo. Anxious to make sure nothing went wrong, she was among the first to be admitted when the zoo opened its gates, and went straight to the aviary. After nearly two hours no contact had been made, and she was forced to leave and use the toilet, returning as soon as possible to resume her vigil. Again no one approached. Her fears increased; she became convinced that the fault was hers, that she had somehow misunderstood her instructions and had failed the first test. She remained in the aviary until lunchtime, then fled, by now traumatized into thinking that every new face had menace in it.

For the next week she visited the shop every day, but it wasn't until Saturday that a second message appeared: DARLING SORRY COULDN'T MAKE IT LAST TIME BUT WILL DEFINITELY MAKE AMENDS MONDAY. DON'T THINK ME A SNAKE IN THE GRASS.

She agonized over the meaning concealed in the wording, finally deciding that she was meant to go back to the zoo, but this time to the reptile house. Once again she took up her position at opening time, and willed herself to stifle a lifelong horror of snakes. As she wandered around staring at the inert exhibits in their glass-fronted cases, she thought how far she had come in such a short period, and wondered if she would ever know peace again.

"I think you dropped this," a voice said.

She turned to find a man standing beside her. He held out a packet of peanuts of the kind on sale at various points in the zoo for those wishing to feed the animals. She took it from him. He was of average height, probably in his middle thirties and wearing reasonably well-cut clothes, somebody who would pass unnoticed in a crowd.

"Thank you," she said, not knowing how else to react.

"Snakes are much less sinister than one imagines, aren't they?" the man said, then walked on and out of the building before she could frame a response. Clutching the bag of peanuts in her hand, Pamela resumed her tour of the exhibits, not daring to follow him until a reasonable interval had elapsed. He was nowhere to be seen when she got outside, and she took a taxi back to her flat.

Not until she was safely inside did she examine the bag of peanuts.

Tucked away in the bottom of the bag was a small, folded piece of paper. On it was typed: "You will shortly receive an invitation for a country weekend. Accept it."

Having read it several times, she was conscious that it was not something to be kept. It seemed too absurd and melodramatic to emulate those scenes in spy movies where the heroine swallows the secret code, so she dropped it in the kitchen waste disposal along with the remains of her breakfast and shredded the lot. She wished Gunther were with her.

Two weeks of increasing strain and uncertainty went by before anything happened. Not knowing what else to do, she paid irregular visits to the tobacconist's shop, but there were no further messages. Then she received a plain envelope containing a first-class railway voucher to a market town in the heart of England. The voucher was dated for a particular train on the coming Friday, and attached to it was a typewritten note: "You will be met and taken to Brampton Abbots. Enjoy yourself." The name of her destination meant nothing to her.

The only aspect she was certain about was the kind of clothes to pack; here her upbringing stood her in good stead. On the day she caught the designated train. The first-class carriage was not full, and she found herself being eyed by a young man of roughly her own age who had stockbroker written all over him. Before the train had left the outskirts of London he behaved true to form and began a conversation. After exchanging a few pleasantries, and just when she was preparing to freeze him out he suddenly remarked, "I say, it's just occurred to me. Forgive me for asking, but you wouldn't be going to Brampton Abbots by any chance?"

"Yes. Yes, I am, as a matter of fact."

"Terrific. So am I. My name's Jeremy Ross."

"Pamela," she said.

"Ever been before?"

"No, I haven't."

"Oh, you're going to have a great time, Pamela. Old Marty doesn't do things by halves. Amazing pad he's got there—squash courts, swimming pool, Jacuzzi, the works. You'll meet the most extraordinary people, and it's anything goes. He doesn't stint on anything, old Marty. I daresay it's all written off to expenses, paid for by his somewhat grotty magazine, though I better not shout that about. Do you ever read it?"

"I pick it up sometimes," she lied.

"You want to watch out he doesn't try and put you in it. He's always on the lookout for new faces, and not always the faces."

By a process of deduction she pieced together the identity of her unknown host: Jeremy's leering remarks about the magazine had given her the first clue. A Martin Gattey published an immensely successful *Playboy* rip-off, and had gone to great lengths to establish himself as something of a character. Although the magazine itself was little more than a pale imitation of Hefner's original, Gattey paid his contributors well, and the nude layouts went as far as the law allowed. He was constantly in the gossip columns, and his well-publicized weekend parties always featured a strange mixture of show-business personalities, the odd stray politician and luminaries from the world of sports. The origins of Gattey's undoubted wealth were somewhat obscure; it was generally thought that having come to England as a refugee just after the war, he had made his first fortune in property before turning his attention to Fleet Street. His efforts to acquire a national newspaper having been balked, he launched *Bachelor,* which, much to his competitors' surprise, proved an immediate winner.

"Any idea who else is going to be here this weekend?" Jeremy asked.

"No."

"Nor me. Still, who cares? We're both here, and surprise is the spice of life, I always say. What d'you do? I bet you're a model, no?"

"Wrong, I'm afraid."

"Curses. You're certainly pretty enough." His approach was so gauche that she wanted to scream. "Let's have another guess. You're one of those frightfully worthy types who work for charity."

"Just a secretary. Very dull."

"Well, anytime you want a change of scenery, let me know. Our office could do with a gee-up. Now, what about me, what do I do?"

Apart from boring the arse off people? she thought. "Oh, you're easy. Either merchant bank, probably owned by your daddy, or else stock-broking."

His face fell. "I say, it can't be that obvious, can it?"

She only half listened for the remainder of the journey while he kept up his nonstop sexual innuendo. When they reached their destination, they were met by a uniformed chauffeur driving the latest Bentley.

"Didn't I tell you?" Jeremy remarked, after greeting the chauffeur as a familiar. "You have to hand it to him: Marty knows how to do it."

After a twenty-minute drive at high speed they arrived at the house. Whatever lack of taste Gattey displayed in his magazine, it certainly wasn't repeated in his life-style. The mansion they approached through a tree-lined avenue was genuine Queen Anne, and had been lovingly restored regardless of expense. Gattey had built an additional wing in keeping with the main structure to house the Olympic-size indoor swimming pool and games complex. When she was taken on the obligatory tour for new guests, Pamela saw that Jeremy had not exaggerated: there was something for everybody.

Gattey himself proved to be urbane and witty. She had been expecting vulgarity combined with an immediate pass, but was pleasantly surprised and quickly disarmed by his unforced charm. There seemed to be staff everywhere, and when she was taken to her room she found it furnished in impeccable taste. When greeting her, Gattey had made a point of stressing the informality. "We only have two house rules, Pamela. Don't frighten the peacocks and no gambling for money. Apart from that, you're here to enjoy yourself. Dress as you like, take a swim, hot tub, play a little tennis or squash, use the sunbed, or say to hell with it and do nothing. I want you to feel relaxed. Good to have you here." It all seemed far removed from any scenario dreamed up by Gunther or the Fat Boy, and she wondered when the true purpose would be revealed.

She was not kept in ignorance long. When she went down to join the thirty or so other houseguests for lunch, the first person she bumped into was the man she had met at the zoo. Something warned her not to betray that they knew each other. Gattey introduced him as Andrei Shmari-nov, a director of a Polish newsprint company with whom he did business. The man she knew as Albert kissed her hand with exaggerated courtesy but showed no further interest, and it was Jeremy who took her in to lunch.

The moment she entered the dining room it became quite obvious that whatever else the weekend held, nobody was likely to go to bed hungry. The food was served with that casual lavishness that only the very rich can afford, in strict contrast to some of the boring house parties she had been forced to attend as a teenager. Perhaps the only giveaway was the fact that the male guests were outnumbered two to one; Gattey had assembled a bevy of stunningly attractive girls, most of whom seemed to know their way around. She recognized several of the men: a tennis superstar, two well-known television personalities and a rising Labour politician who gave the impression that if he couldn't lick the rich he certainly had no objection to joining them.

The sun came out during lunch, and their host ordered coffee to be served on the terrace. After a decent interval tennis partners were recruited and she went upstairs to change. Rejoining the others, she noticed that "Albert" was taking photographs of some of the girls. She played two sets of doubles before going off alone to explore the magnificent grounds. Although she was under no illusions about the real purpose of the gathering, the men seemed personable, Jeremy excepted, and Gunther had been away a long time.

It came as no surprise to her that "Albert" appeared in an isolated part of the garden out of sight of the main house. Briefly, pointedly, he described what was required of her.

"We need to take out certain insurance policies for the future," he said. "I assume you have no objection to seducing one of our fellow guests?"

"No. Providing it's a man. I wouldn't fancy the other."

"It's a man."

"Which one?"

He gave her the name.

"Fine," Pamela said. "No hardship, he's quite dishy. Is he expecting me to make the first move?"

"He's expecting to get lucky with somebody, that's the main reason he's here. How you do it is up to you. Just make sure of him, that's all. I want you to use this." He passed her a mini–tape recorder the size of a cigarette packet. "Are you familiar with these?"

"Not really."

"It's all set. You just press this one button. It runs for three hours. It's important that you use his name; we must have positive identification on the tape. Tomorrow I want photographs of you together."

"You mean photographs of us on the job?"

"No. But that might be needed later, on another occasion. Is everything clear?"

Pamela nodded. "What do I do with the tape?"

"I'll collect that from you before we leave. Don't follow me now and ignore me as much as you can." He walked away abruptly.

She continued to wander around the garden until she had decided on the best and least obvious approach to make. Returning to the house, she first secreted the tape recorder in her bedroom, then rejoined the party by the swimming pool. As luck would have it, the opening move was made for her when one of the girls suggested a session in the Jacuzzi —a suggestion eagerly accepted by the men. Pamela gave the lead by being the quickest to strip naked. Once in the Jacuzzi, she casually edged herself close to the man "Albert" had selected as her potential lover, and when their nude bodies touched beneath the turbulent water, the message was immediately received and returned.

Dinner that evening was even more sumptuous than lunch. She sat opposite her prey and used every opportunity for subtle eye contact. By now she was confident he was hooked. When the meal was over and most of the guests retired to the private cinema to watch one of the latest releases, she sat next to him. In the darkness Pamela found that the situation evoked the remembered eroticism of her teenage years; it was a long time since she had experienced such sexual anticipation. Nothing was said; everything was understood between them.

When eventually he came to her room he proved to be an inept lover by Gunther's standards, though she introduced him to variations that he confessed he had never sampled before, and in a very short time he was clay in her sensual hands. The fact that the hidden tape recorder was running heightened her own sexuality, and it was a simple matter to obtain the damaging indiscretions that had been demanded of her. She felt confident that "Albert" would be more than satisfied with the results of her first assignment.

ALL that had happened at the beginning of her secret life. There was no repeat invitation to Brampton Abbots, and she received instructions that there was to be no further contact between her and the man. Instead she was directed to take up a lucrative and responsible post that had been arranged for her as an interpreter with the EEC in Brussels. There she was reunited with Gunther, but none of her colleagues were aware

172

of the liaison and it was generally supposed that she was a bachelor girl intent on playing the field. Gunther led his own life, coming and going at irregular intervals; she was aware that his own involvement was deeper and more frightening than hers. From time to time she read reports of the Fat Boy (privately she always thought of him by that name): supposedly he had been sighted in Cairo, then given credit for one of the bomb outrages in France.

Pamela was quite happy in her new job and gleaned various useful pieces of intelligence, which she duly passed on to Gunther. Her social life was anything but dull. The Commission was a hotbed of lobbyists and fringe politicians, all of them pulling down generous expenses and living away from home; she seldom had difficulty getting them to divulge classified information now that she had the taste for deception, though the necessity to be constantly on her guard had been drummed into her by Gunther; given the transient, cosmopolitan population of the Commission, there was always the danger of partnering somebody from the other side.

When she questioned Gunther about the future, he was deliberately evasive. "They're never in a hurry. I happen to know they're very pleased with you so far, so your time will come. Just keep your nose clean until they select your next target. They seem to think you have special qualities."

The target was finally identified as Sir Charles Belfrage, whom she first met at an OPEC reception, the apparent chance liaison having been carefully stage-managed by Gunther. She went to the reception with an Arab boyfriend, for this was a preliminary skirmish and she was under orders not to rush things.

She found Belfrage to be a diplomat cast from a well-used mold, in appearance not unlike Eden, but with craggier features and more humor in the eyes than Eden had ever possessed. There was also something about his manner that suggested to her that he had not always moved in the right circles, and when she did her homework she found he had come from a middle-class background not unlike her own. At their first meeting he was gravely polite, a man trained to listen and keep his private thoughts private. All the same, she came away with the feeling that she had made a positive impression on him.

With Gunther's connivance, she and Belfrage met again at a gala performance of *The Magic Flute* given in aid of African Famine Relief. This time she was careful to go alone, and they bumped into each other in the bar during the first interval. Belfrage offered to get her a glass of champagne, and they chatted until the bell rang. The conversation was

173

resumed during the second interval, and it was then, having discussed a mutual love of opera, that Belfrage offered to leave her his privilege seats when he returned to London. "I shall need to know where to send them," he said casually.

Admiring his style, she gave him her address and telephone number. She was confident that he would make the next move, and just over a month later, when he returned to Brussels as part of his official duties, he duly rang her. It had already been decided by Gunther that she was not to be readily available, but she let him know how much she appreciated his kindness for the tickets.

"If I'd known you were coming over, I'd have kept this evening free," she said. "Unfortunately, I can't get out of a prior date at such short notice."

"Of course not, I wouldn't dream of asking you to. Perhaps another time?"

"I'd love to see you again. It's such a relief to meet somebody who doesn't always talk politics."

"Well, as long as you haven't forgotten me," he said. "There *is* just a chance that I might have to stay over longer than planned. The French are being their usual boring selves where we're concerned."

"Well, if you do, give me another ring. I don't have anything else planned this week."

He made sure he prolonged his stay; the hook was now firmly in place. They dined together at one of the less fashionable restaurants, chosen by Belfrage for what he termed its "relaxed atmosphere and excellent wine list." To any interested observer he might have been a father taking out his daughter for a celebratory dinner. Their urbane conversation, mostly concerned with the arts, contained no innuendo on his part, though Pamela was certainly conscious of his skill in getting her to talk about her background. They shared a taxi back to her apartment, where he dropped her off, making no attempt to extend the evening. When they parted he kissed her on the cheek.

The following day she received a gift of flowers. The accompanying card read: "We must try to take in La Bohème next time," and carried no signature. She knew better than to write and thank him for the bouquet.

After that it was only a matter of time; on his next visit, with nothing openly discussed between them, she finally admitted him to her apartment and her bed. He had been netted and landed.

"My sweet, I can't keep making such frequent visits," he told her. "Not only is it too risky, but there's too much going on back home."

"I understand."

"On the other hand, I have to see you again. You've had a devastating effect on me, I must tell you that. I've no rights in the matter, and I don't want to deceive you about my domestic situation. That can't be touched, so if you can't live with that—and there's no earthly reason why you should—I'll have to grin and bear it. I can't pretend it'll be easy, after what's happened, but that's my problem."

"I do want to see you again. That's very important to me. You're so different from everybody else. I find most of the young men of my own age so boring. They never have anything to talk about except the obvious."

"Well, then, we'll have to find a solution. There is one answer, of course. It's selfish of me, but I'll put it to you."

"What's that?"

"With your qualifications I don't think you'd have too much trouble finding a similar sort of job in London. I could help by pointing you in the right direction. One gets to hear of openings."

She was careful not to jump at the idea. "I do have to support myself. I guess I've been spoilt here. And there's a question of finding somewhere to live."

"Well, naturally, I'd help there. I could take a little flat for you."

"I'm not the type to be kept," Pamela said. "That's not my scene, and it wouldn't be good for you either." She knew that this was what he wanted to hear.

"You're too good for me. Well, understood. Would you have any objection to my getting a pied-à-terre, somewhere discreet, which would be handy for those times when we could see each other? No strings, of course."

Again she played hard to persuade, using arguments that were sweet to his ears. She explained that even though she adored his company and the fact they were so good in bed together, she couldn't let him put his marriage and career at risk. "I understand your position, believe me. I know there's no question of your getting a divorce. It isn't that, and I don't want to lose you, but I'd rather it finished now than bring any trouble on you."

He countered by saying he was besotted with her, that she was the best thing that had ever happened in his life, and that there was no way he would willingly give her up. After a second and emotional bout of lovemaking, she promised to think it over.

"You played it perfectly," Gunther said. "Keep him in suspense for a while longer, then give in. Go back, let him start to tie the noose. I'll take care of all the arrangements. There's a safe house you and I can use, and I'll join you there. Eventually, it would be a good thing to let him know you've got a boyfriend; it'll keep him on his toes. And make him pay; wrap your legs around his neck and squeeze him dry."

So it began. Belfrage could not believe in his good fortune. Apart from the unexpected flattery of believing he had seduced a girl young enough to be his own daughter, there was the added bonus that she came from his own class and had no discernible ulterior motives. It led him to take risks that in any other context he would have rejected as absurd. He entered into a second sexual childhood with her. Under her tutelage he was introduced to cannabis ("Let's keep off the hard stuff," Gunther said, "hold that in reserve"), which Belfrage found the most daring thing he had ever attempted. For the first time in a decade he took exercise, suddenly made conscious of the contrast between his body and Pamela's. There was a new buoyancy to his walk, and his staff found that his sarcasm, long a byword in the department, was gentler.

With Pamela he invented a number of code words, some as warning notes to be sounded during telephone calls made from his office, others for conveying endearments, and when they were alone together he called her Squirrel. It was "My darling, sexy Squirrel," or "My bushy-tailed little Nutkin," as though all his sublimated thoughts had been culled from an obscene version of Beatrix Potter. Pamela suffered these and other infantile expressions of his passion. His pillow confessions revealed that he had long entertained, but never enacted, certain sexual fantasies; she set herself to fulfill these for him, and in the process further enslaved him. (Lady Belfrage, it appeared, had never been prepared to cater to anything more than the missionary position.) In Pamela's pliant embraces, long-dormant conceits surfaced; he pushed aside the training of a lifetime, discarding his Civil Service mask the moment she entered his bedroom. As their relationship deepened and she gained his complete confidence, subtly assuming a naïveté he found especially endearing, she was able to move closer to her real targets.

She took her cue when he let slip that Lady Belfrage cared little for the intricacies of his career. "Penelope likes the ends, naturally, but not the means. I don't want to be disloyal to her, but she's never really pulled her weight; she doesn't set a good table—otherwise I might have risen through the ranks faster to a somewhat more exalted position. Not that I'm complaining. I could have done better and I could have done worse. Point is, right now, with my sexy little Squirrel sharing it with me, I consider my life fulfilled. Just to be able to kiss that pretty little Black Forest and call it my own. It is all mine, isn't it?"

176

"Of course," she said, keeping the boredom out of her voice. "Tell me more about what goes on in your wonderful, exciting life. I love hearing you talk about it, it all sounds so romantic."

Belfrage took flattery of this kind as a cat takes butter on its paws. "Not really, Nutkin. Romantic's hardly the word I'd put to it. Duty is very humdrum most of the time. All the talk about walking the corridors of power sounds good, but it doesn't mean overmuch when you're actually doing the walking. A few perks, of course; it opens a few doors, but the rest is tabloid fodder. You know what we British are like: we cherish our mystiques."

In the beginning all she managed to wheedle out of him was innocuous enough, if occasionally mildly libelous. "Don't leave anything out," Gunther insisted when she reported back to him. "We'll decide what's important and what's not." He was the one now in contact with "Albert"; Pamela was considered too vulnerable.

Sometimes Belfrage's old fears resurfaced and he would talk of ending the affair. It was then that she needed all her skills. She had learned that if she cried it had a devastating effect on him; he could not deal with tears. "You're the only man who's ever made it happen for me" was her best ploy, since it went straight to his basic conceits as a lover. The abject volte-face that inevitably followed such episodes left him ever more in her thrall.

As the relationship continued she delved deeper, starting in the past and working slowly forward to the present day, though he was always circumspect. "Tell me about the Cliveden set," she would say. "Was it true what they said about that Cabinet minister? Wasn't he supposed to have dragged-up as a maid and served at table?"

"I seem to remember there was supposed to be something of the kind, years ago. A lot of very odd goings-on at that time. The trouble with politicians is they're never satisfied. It's not an original thought, but power does corrupt. Some of them travel so far from their origins that they start believing they're beings set apart, not answerable to anybody, least of all their constituents."

She used all her wits to get him to talk about security matters, approaching it casually one night when they were watching a news item on television: an Opposition backbencher had once again reopened the question of MI6's fallibility. The name Dinnsbury was mentioned several times in the interview.

"Has anybody like that ever worked for you?"

"Like who, Squirrel?"

"Spies and people like that."

"No, my sweet. I'm not directly concerned with the cloak-and-dagger brigade, thank God. All that comes under quite a different department —though I must admit I did come across that awful piss artist Maclean a couple of times."

"Really?"

"Yes. Met him in Washington, I remember. He was bad news. Can't think how he got away with it for so long. I'm sure I'd have spotted him and his cohort if it had been up to me. I can usually detect anything that's ginger beer."

"Ginger beer?"

"Queer. Just using the old vernacular. What d'you call them nowadays? Gays, isn't it? That's always been a misnomer to me. Generation gap, I suppose, like a lot of other things. But not between you and me, eh?" He kissed his favorite part of her body.

"I'm sure you would have been brilliant," she cooed when he had finished. "Do you think there are still people like them?"

"Like who?"

"Maclean and people."

"Why are you so fascinated?"

"I don't know. It's just that I've never met anybody except you who really knows what's going on."

"You are a divine little Squirrel, d'you know that? Divine. But I'm not as important as you like to think. No, things are tighter now. Not much tighter, I don't suppose, but at least one gets the impression that somebody's minding the shop. We all have to be vetted."

"That's nothing to do with vets, is it?"

"No, sweetness. Like a medical checkup, except they probe the old brain box instead of the prostate." He chuckled at his own joke.

"Have you been vetted?"

"Oh, yes. They've rattled the skeletons in my cupboard, but it was mostly bare."

"What would happen if they found out about us?"

"God, don't even talk about it. Touch wood quick." He reached out for the bedside table.

"Tell me what skeletons they did find, then. Have you always been unfaithful?"

"No, I can honestly say I haven't. The occasional fling, like anybody else, but nothing serious. Nothing like us, I mean. My darling, what they're mostly concerned about is any connection, however remote, with the Reds. And like most chaps of my generation—we're talking about the Thirties, don't forget—I joined a few Left-wing groups, subscribed to the Left Book Club and so forth: very small beer. But now you're the only little body hidden away, and you're not bones, my darling, you're beautifully covered. Look at your sweet boobies and sweet little tummy and that little forest I'm going to kiss again right now."

While he performed what he believed he did to perfection, she looked down at his balding patch and went through the motions of responding, knowing that it was important to him to think himself a tiger. After all, this was when he was at his most vulnerable, the times when she could extract the most.

In the aftermath of one bout of lovemaking when they were taking a bath together, he let slip a passing remark about the death of Bayldon's chauffeur, and she pounced on it. "Darling! it could have been you in that car."

"Yes, I suppose so. One of the hazards of the job today. Anybody's a target."

"Weren't you scared?"

"I wasn't anywhere near when it happened, Squirrel. I was more distressed about the poor man."

"They should give you protection."

He soaped her back and breasts. "The only person I need protection from is you."

"You don't take it seriously, and I'm worried about you."

"Darling, I carry an umbrella, not a gun. They're not after characters like me; the bastards are more likely to blow up women and children. You be sure and take care of yourself. If you're out shopping and there's a bomb scare, just don't take chances. It's frightening what they're capable of."

"What d'you think will happen if it doesn't stop?"

"That's a good question. Now do my back, sweetheart. We're living in very dodgy times: there are very sinister forces at work. Added to which there could be another major shake-up in the offing. Don't ask me what because I'm not allowed to say, and indirectly it might involve me."

"You're not in trouble?"

"No, course not. I just happen to have had some contact with the character who's held responsible. Just depends how much leaks."

All this was faithfully reported to Gunther.

"Press him, get more details."

"It's not that easy. He's not stupid, you know."

"Then think up some more bedroom games to soften his brain."

"You don't care what I have to go through, do you?"

179

"Not particularly, no. What really upsets you is that I'm not jealous, isn't it?"

"Who cares whether you're jealous?" she said, but there was no conviction in her voice, and his smile angered her further. "I hate your guts."

"Good. I like you to hate. Keeps you wanting me."

His hands, so unlike Belfrage's, still had the power to excite. When he ran them over her body, it was as if she was programmed to respond, whatever her innermost feelings.

"Not now. Don't you even care that I'm just come from his bed?"

"No. What's that got to do with it?"

"Sometimes you disgust me."

"Or do I make you want it more? You can't hide anything from me, remember?"

Such was the chaos of her life: she was alienated from her past, uncertain of her future. When, from duty, she paid the occasional visit to her parents, it was like entering a foreign country. She carried her secret like an unwanted child. In a curious way she had developed a sort of affection for Belfrage; for all his shortcomings as a lover, he was kind and considerate, romantic in his old-fashioned way, and there were even moments when she despised herself for deceiving him.

She was most successful with him when she was not trying so hard, when she allowed a splinter of compassion to enter into their relationship. Often the concern and pity she expressed was genuine, though she was at pains to conceal this from Gunther.

His demands grew ever more insistent. "You're not trying hard enough," he accused her. "Don't you realize we're working to a timetable? We have to have results."

Returning to the small house in the mews where the treacheries bloomed between kisses, she often felt that she was pressing Belfrage too hard; he might well be a fool in love, but he was too schooled in discretion to be a pushover.

"I worry that you're in danger," she said to him. "That I might lose you one day and all this would end."

"If it ends, it won't be my doing, Nutkin. That's the way of things, don't think I don't know that."

"That wasn't what I meant. Every day I read about people like you being killed. Only yesterday they shot that diplomat in front of his wife and children."

"I keep telling you, I'm not in the front line. I'm just a back-room boy. I might walk out of here and get run over by a bus, but that's another matter."

"You told me a lot of your work is secret. You said that."

"Yes. To a degree. But then most government work is, sweetie. There's no such thing as open government. That would spoil all the fun. We can't have the electorate knowing what we're up to." He laughed at his own cynicism, but she refused to share the joke. "You are a silly little Squirrel, and it's very dear of you to worry about me. I promise you I can take care of myself."

Her continued lack of success led to more violent scenes with Gunther. "Look, we know he has certain inside tracks, can't you get that into your head? He liaises with MI5. I've been told he was consulted when our people got rid of that woman Oates, for reasons you're familiar with."

"He always maintains that he's just a civil servant."

"Oh, Christ! how fucking naïve can you get? They're *all* civil servants, you brainless bitch! That's just a smoke screen. I'm telling you your geriatric lover-boy is right there in the thick of it, so don't argue with me!"

"He's not that geriatric," she said in a sad attempt to get back at him.

"I'm not so sure that I trust you. I'm putting in a bug." Using her key when the house was unoccupied, he installed the device. "As much to keep tabs on you as on him. Just remember that everybody in this game is expendable."

22

VARIOUS RUMORS, EVER more bizarre, went around the Firm when Hillsden suddenly disappeared from circulation. It was, everybody agreed, "a rum do," and although the Firm had survived defectors, scandals and the vagaries of governments in the past, nobody could remember anything quite so odd or unexpected. *"Très misterioso,"* Fenton remarked more than once in his usual pedantic fashion, but it was Waddington who was the most perplexed. Events that had no logical explanation always taxed him more than catastrophes. Earthquakes and the like he could cope with. It was, as he often said, the unexplained slamming of a door that made him think twice. He felt a sense of personal betrayal.

One theory, put into circulation by Ms. Glazer in Reception, was that Mr. Hillsden was suffering from a terminal disease. She based this on the fact that she had observed his complexion changing color in the weeks preceding his disappearance. "I can always see death in people's faces," she said with morbid pleasure. "My hairdresser just died of AIDS, and the last time he did my highlights, I told him, I said, 'You don't look very well.' Because I could see the change in him. And lo and behold, three weeks later he was gone. Snuffed it. Only thirty-two. Makes you think, doesn't it?"

"What it doesn't make me think is that it could have any connection with Alec," Waddington replied.

Rotherby, who had always considered Hillsden his social inferior, offered the uncharitable explanation that there was no real mystery. "He was probably given his marching orders, if you ask me. For the simple reason that he just wasn't up to it anymore. After he came in from the cold, he seemed to have lost his touch."

"He wouldn't just leave without saying anything," Waddington said.

"You don't think so? I would have thought that was very much in character. Probably wanted to avoid standing a farewell round of drinks."

"That's one of your typically shitty remarks. You're not exactly famous for throwing a party every day of the week."

The speculation continued for a month, but when no official explanation came down from Control, Waddington asked for a personal interview. He was well aware that from its inception the Firm had been founded on the old boys' network, and built into the very fabric was the old boys' reluctance to share anything with subordinates. Whispers and vague hints were the order of the day—anything to avoid being positive. So he went in with both feet. "Alec and I were working closely together. If there's something sinister, I've got a right on a need-to-know basis."

" 'Need to know' is one of those frightful American expressions, isn't it?" Control said with much cracking of knuckles. "I always think we should pay more respect to our mother tongue. But since you've asked me the question, I will say that Hillsden's departure is not going to leave another unhealed sore in the public mind."

"That's too clever for me. What is that meant to signify?"

"We don't draw straight lines here, Waddington, nor are we in a particularly honorable or humanitarian profession. We practice a strange kind of virtue, which earns us little praise when we succeed and an avalanche of blame when we fail. On the whole it's best if we keep our cupboards locked."

"Then there is something to hide?"

"My dear Waddington, the day we have nothing to hide will be the day we all depart."

"Okay, let me put it another way: could this be the beginning of a purge? I'd like to know because I'm behind on my insurance premiums."

"Alec did not leave under a particularly large cloud, but neither did he exit trailing a halo. Not for the first time, he trod on somebody's toes and it was felt to be of mutual benefit for him to move on."

"He was booted, in other words?"

"Your words, not mine."

"And you concurred?"

"I saw the advantages for all concerned. You're not married, are you, Waddington?"

"You know I'm not."

"Of course I do. Marriage and our trade are never an entirely happy combination. Alec was married. I think that added an extra strain."

"I still don't understand why he disappeared without a word to any of us—me especially."

"Embarrassment, possibly?" Control said, ending the interview.

Ignoring the implicit warning, Waddington drove out unannounced to Wembley (his prior phone calls going unanswered), only to find a FOR SALE notice posted outside Hillsden's house. The local newsagent informed him that the papers had been canceled two weeks previously, and that, as far as he knew, the Hillsdens had packed and gone without leaving any forwarding address. He followed through with the estate agent handling the sale of the house, but was told that all inquiries had to be channeled through Mrs. Hillsden's solicitors; the house was legally in her name.

Before Waddington could make further searches, he was summoned to another meeting with Control. This time the dialogue was one-sided.

"Obviously you're hard of hearing," Control said, "so this time I'll speak loud enough for it to penetrate. Hillsden has left us for good. As far as we're concerned he never existed. There is no trail to follow, the trail ends here. You know all that it is necessary for you to know."

THERE was a basis of truth in Control's guarded explanation, though the timing of Hillsden's departure with the final breakup of his marriage was coincidental.

183

After accepting the plan Control had devised, it seemed to Hillsden as good a moment as any to write finish to a relationship that had long since been stripped of pleasure. All the same, he was relieved when Margot offered only token resistance. Despite her going through the motions of acting the wronged wife, he suspected it was merely a show put on for convention's sake; in the books she borrowed from the library, the tabloids she studied so avidly, the women were always exploited; all her emotions were secondhand. The fact that he made no demands, and that there was to be no division of the spoils quickly stemmed her tears. The sale of the house would realize a sizable sum, certainly enough to provide her with more capital than she had ever dreamed of. She could foresee the prospect of spoiling herself; there were holidays she had always wanted to take, luxuries she had long coveted. For the first time in years she felt something approaching affection for a husband who had become a stranger to her. It was as if, in leaving her, he had done her a good turn.

Once the formalities had been agreed, including his undertaking that she could have any divorce her solicitor suggested, their last days together were placid. As they discussed the final loose ends they might have been planning the perfect beginning to a life rather than the end of something.

"What will you do with yourself?" she asked. "Where will you live when you leave here?"

"I haven't decided. Maybe abroad. I haven't any firm plans."

"You've certainly made a clean sweep of it, giving up your job as well. What will you live on?"

"Oh, I'll drop into something eventually."

"It's not a good time to go looking." Their roles had been subtly reversed; now it was her turn to show concern for him.

"Probably stay in the same line of business," he said with hidden truth. "I know a bit about wine and people will always want to drink, whatever state we get in. Never know, I might go on the road as a commercial salesman."

"Yes, you'd like that, you always said you were fond of traveling," she agreed, having had no conception of his past life, and only a passing interest in what it might now become. Her thoughts were concentrated inwards, though on the night before he left for good she made the effort to prepare a decent meal. They slept side by side for the last time, and when he departed the following morning she kissed him as she might a child going off to school. It wasn't until an hour or so later, having phoned the estate agent and her lawyer, that the full extent of her freedom came home to her. Only then were her tears genuine.

HILLSDEN'S freedom was more circumscribed. He left London and took a train to Leeds. There he checked into an anonymous commercial hotel, choosing the cheapest he could find. He carried a minimum of baggage, just the clothes he stood up in and half a dozen clean shirts. The hotel had no restaurant, and he took all his meals in junk-food establishments. There was an established routine to his days: after leaving the hotel early in the morning, he headed for the public library, taking up his position on the steps with a line of other out-of-works. When the doors were opened, he went straight to the reading room and studied the daily papers, scouring the *Jobs Vacant* columns. He pointedly discouraged any approaches by his fellow searchers. Leaving the library, he walked the streets until lunchtime, then usually went to a cinema, only emerging when the pubs were open. His evenings were spent in solitary drinking, and a close observer would have noted that he invariably chose those pubs that had a preponderance of homosexuals among their regular clientele. His attitude often made him a less than welcome visitor to such establishments, since all subcultures have their own rituals and outsiders are inherently suspect.

Matters came to a head one night when a particularly outlandish queen decided that Hillsden needed to be flushed out.

"Are you waiting for somebody?" the queen said.

Hillsden turned around slowly. "What?"

"You keep looking at my friend, so I thought perhaps you were waiting for somebody, that's all."

"No."

"Just wondered if you were looking for fun tonight."

"I'm not looking for you, that's for sure."

The queen bridled. "Oh, we're very grand, aren't we, Doris? Are you just passing through, then? Because if you are, you're taking a fucking long time about it. And spoiling the fun. We don't want to look at your mournful boat-race every night! Mirror, mirror on the wall, you're not the fairest of them all."

Despite the blatantly camp speech the queen was heavily built and dressed in a tight-fitting and elaborately studded leather outfit with bits of paramilitary gear draped about it. He had spoken loudly enough for others in his group to hear, and now there was an expectant silence as a dozen interested faces turned towards the scene.

"Just piss off, will you?" Hillsden said. "Go and romance somebody else."

The knowledge that he had an audience spurred the queen on. "Listen to Mother Teresa, girls! Don't flatter yourself, I'm not about to pull a faded old pensioner like you, dear. Oh, sorry, I didn't mean to tread on your foot."

"You're pushing your luck, chum."

"Oh, we're going to be chums, are we? That's nice. Did you hear that, girls? I trod on her foot and it was love at first sight."

He brought his booted foot down again, and Hillsden reacted with frightening speed and force, hitting him three times in quick succession, the first blow with the flat of his hand landing on the bridge of the queen's nose and breaking it. Blood spurted across the bar. The other blows were chopped to the back of the neck as the queen buckled over and stayed down. Several of his friends rushed Hillsden as the pub erupted. He bottled the first to reach him, but was then overwhelmed. They kicked and beat him senseless, and he knew nothing more until he came to in a police cell. Later that day he was brought before a magistrate and charged with causing grievous bodily harm. Described as a salesman presently unemployed, he pleaded not guilty. Bail was refused, and he was remanded in custody for seven days, the magistrate asking for a medical report. At the end of the week he was again remanded, and his case sent for trial at the County Sessions. There, a month later, he was found guilty on the evidence of the bartender and five other witnesses. Although taking account of his previous good character, and the fact that he had been subjected to a great deal of provocation, the judge was not constrained to be lenient. He lectured Hillsden at some length from the bench on the need for tolerance towards minorities, and sentenced him to twelve months' imprisonment, with six months suspended on the condition that he seek psychiatric help on his release. The case was widely reported in the local papers, and subsequently written up in *Gay News,* a periodical that enjoyed national circulation.

In prison Hillsden shared a cell with an embezzler, who gave him some useful tips on the use of stolen credit cards. The nature of his offense was soon common knowledge among the other prisoners in his block, and the resident homosexuals plotted to get their own back. Allocated work in the prison laundry, he suffered a multiple fracture of the bones in his left foot when one of them dropped a heavy steam iron, apparently by accident, as he was passing. He spent the remainder of his term in the prison hospital, but his foot had still not completely healed when he was discharged.

On his release Hillsden returned to the same hotel, only to find that his custom was no longer welcome. The management handed back his few possessions, and he spent his first night sleeping with other vagrants and meth drinkers on an abandoned building site. The next day he joined the shuffling queue awaiting opening time at the local Salvation Army Mission, and managed to secure a temporary bed in one of the dormitories there. His foot still required attention, and he passed many of the subsequent days attending the out-patients department of a National Health hospital. Varying this routine, he obtained casual employment in the kitchens of an Asian restaurant, all the time burying his old personality and paying less and less care to his appearance, so that soon he became indistinguishable from the rest of the large floating population living from hand to mouth in the city. Bored with the life of a *plongeur,* he moved around, taking any menial job that paid cash with no questions asked, staying just this side of the law, working only long enough to earn himself a few nights in a proper bed and a couple of square meals, then drinking away the remainder. These bouts of drunkenness landed him another night in the cells, and when, in court the next morning, it was discovered he had no regular means of support, he was remanded in custody to await a report from the Probation Officer.

"Why did you leave your last permanent job?" he was asked. "I see you were with a firm of wine merchants for several years." The officer assigned to his case turned out to be in his late twenties, bespectacled, stooped, with an undernourished look. He offered a cigarette, the last one in a crumpled packet. Hillsden took it without comment.

"I was fired."

"For what reason?"

"No reason. I was made redundant."

"That's a reason."

"Depends which way you look at it."

"You must have received redundancy pay, then. What happened to that?"

"She had it."

"Who?"

"The wife."

"Where's your wife now?"

"No idea."

"You haven't kept in touch?"

"No. It's over. Last I heard she was getting a divorce."

"Do you have any children?"

Hillsden shook his head.

"What about relatives?"

"What about them?"

"Haven't you any family you can go to?"

"No, they're all dead."

"Look, Hillsden, you're obviously an educated man. You must see that the life you're leading at the moment can only have one end. You're either going to kill yourself with drink, or else find yourself back in jail. Is that what you want?"

Hillsden did not answer, staring past him.

"At this rate, drifting from job to job, it's got to end badly. I can't help you if you refuse to be helped."

"When your luck's out, it's out. It's all right for some—like those bloody queers. They seem to do all right, tarting themselves up and poncing about like they owned the place."

"Yes, well, we know your views there. That's what landed you in clink in the first place. No good harboring those sort of resentments, that's not going to get you on your feet again. The point is, do you want to be helped?"

"Depends."

"There are places and organizations that exist to help people like yourself. But I have to warn you they're not holiday camps. I see from your record you were told to see a psychiatrist. Did you?"

"No."

"Why not?"

"They confuse you even more."

"Well, what I'm prepared to do, if you'll cooperate, is to arrange for you to go to a hostel I know of that takes cases like you. It's run by a charity, so don't expect the Ritz, but you'll have a roof over your head and some pocket money. If you want to pick yourself up off the ground, now's your last chance."

"Where is this place?"

"Just outside Plymouth. It's run by the Brothers of Mercy."

"Won't pick myself up by being on my knees all day, will I? How religious is it?"

"You're expected to attend services, but they don't ram it down your throat. So, what's it to be?"

"How long will I have to stay there?"

"Just as long as it takes to get back your self-respect. But if you don't

188

make the effort, they'll kick you out. There's plenty more where you come from. I'm doing you a favor, Hillsden. If you say yes, I'll get you a railway warrant and a few quid to tide you over. Do you have your National Insurance card?"

"Stolen."

"Do you remember your number?"

"No idea."

"I'll get it from records. So what's it to be?"

"Okay. I'll give it a try," Hillsden said after a pause. "Not my idea of heaven, but probably better than hell."

23

EVERYTHING HE KNEW about the game warned Calder that he was being used again too soon after the last assignment. With regrets he left the tidiness of his Swiss apartment and drove across the Italian border to Milan before taking the tortuous coast road with its endless succession of tunnels into France, crossing the frontier above Monaco. His instructions were to check into the Hyatt in Nice, where he would be inconspicuous among the package tours. The contact would be made there.

It was early evening when he finally reached Nice, and the rush hour along the Promenade des Anglais was in full swing, the Fiats and Citroëns tail-gating one another as far as he could see through the insect-spattered windscreen. As he approached the hotel an Air Algeria jet made an alarming tight turn and came in low over the water to land, flying parallel to the road, wings seesawing as the mistral gusted, before leveling off just prior to touchdown. Distracted by this, he thought that he had passed his destination, then realized that the Hyatt had been taken over and renamed since his last visit. They should have known that, he thought; why wasn't I told? Lack of attention to such details irritated him.

A well-dressed whore was just taking up her position at the entrance to the hotel's underground car park as he eased the Mercedes down the ramp. (He always parked the car himself; he liked to know exactly where it was in case of need.) Having looked around, he backed it into the bay nearest to the hotel elevator, the rear fender just touching the garage wall. Before leaving, he checked the cars in the adjacent bays, noting the license plates of those on either side of his vehicle.

As expected, at reception he found that a double room with balcony overlooking the sea had been reserved for him in the name of Müller, which matched one of his many false passports. When he filled in the police *carte d'identité,* he listed an address in Hamburg as his permanent residence. There was a message waiting for him in his box, which he did not read until safely in his room; it merely said "La Ribote. 20.00 hours." He flushed the note down the toilet. The room was functional rather than luxurious, designed for the universal unisex taste, with large double-glazed windows that effectively muffled the constant roar of traffic seven floors below.

While he prepared to take a shower he heard children running up and down the corridor, then shouts in Arabic. Naked, he examined the contents of the mini-bar, selected a miniature bottle of Chivas Regal and poured it into a toothbrush glass. A notice on top of the television receiver advised that he could have a choice of feature films cabled to his room for a modest charge. Two were listed as "adult entertainment"; he selected one of these, rang the hotel operator with his choice and then took a shower.

The film had started by the time he finished in the bathroom, and he lay on top of the bed, enjoying his whisky and watching the shadow play of counterfeit lust. The heroine and her lover, drenched with studio rain, were writhing on a tennis court. A tennis court, of all places! Wouldn't be my first choice for a spot of humping, Calder thought. Pornography always had to go to ludicrous extremes to justify its existence. The two actors tore at each other's clothes, collapsing like freshly caught fish into the tennis net as they continued copulating in the red mud of the court. Then the director zoomed in closer as the simulated climax approached; it was like being in an operating theater observing two bodies being cut open. Suddenly the images disgusted him; he had wanted some diversion before the appointment he had to keep, but the frenzied pictures on the screen depressed rather than stimulated. He switched off the set and opened the sliding windows. Hot air mixed with traffic fumes rushed at him as he stood, still naked, staring at the distant beam of the lighthouse on Cap Ferrat. Below, on the deserted shingled beach, a dog ran through the spume as though crazed.

With his usual thoroughness Calder had packed a lightweight conservative suit of German origin. When dressed in this, he took a copy of *Stern* from his suitcase, together with a packet of West German cigarettes and some book matches from a Hamburg restaurant. Downstairs in the lobby he changed some deutsche marks into francs before using the directory in the public phone booths to look up the address of La Ribote. It would never have occurred to him to ask the concierge for directions.

Outside, the same whore was parading, but now she was wearing a different outfit, a sure indication that she had already pulled her first trick of the night. He walked past her without returning her smile, going several blocks before hailing a cab.

La Ribote proved to be a modest bistro off the tourist list and mostly patronized by locals. There was no menu as such, merely a blackboard with half a dozen specialties of the day chalked on it. Calder selected a table at the rear of the room with an unobstructed view of the door, noting that the only other exit was through the kitchen. Opening his copy of *Stern,* he ordered a bottle of the house red while he waited, giving the order in guttural French. There was only one waitress, a jovial buxom woman, who extracted the cork from the wine with the expertise that he had always envied. He was careful to thank her in German, before apologizing and repeating it in French. He smoked one of his cigarettes, leaving the packet on the table. While sipping his wine he made a careful appraisal of the diners and was alert to each new arrival. He had no idea whom he was to meet; he knew only the coded greetings they would exchange.

Then Gunther entered, walking straight to Calder's table and addressing him in colloquial German. "Sorry I'm late, but I had to visit my mother in hospital."

Calder answered in German, the language they were to use throughout the meal. "I hope she's recovered from the operation."

"Yes, thank you, she's on the mend now, but it will be a long road back." He accepted the glass of wine Calder poured for him.

"Your mother's good health."

They studied the menu and ordered, both choosing the same dish— steak cooked with a particularly succulent variety of local mushrooms. During the meal their conversation was confined to trivia, and it wasn't until they reached the coffee-and-cognac stage and the other diners had thinned out that Gunther finally mentioned the reason for their meeting, approaching it with a wariness that Calder understood and admired.

"Things are going quite well in England."

"Good."

"Have you been keeping up with the latest developments?"

191

"I stay in touch."

"We've had a few successes and got them guessing. The Irish connection comes in very useful. They're always the first to be given credit."

Calder nodded. He wished the German would get to the heart of the matter; the meeting was going on too long for his liking.

"It's extraordinary how lucky we've been with the political scene. The change of government couldn't have come at a better time. They don't know what's hit them, and of course everything they're forced to do works against them."

"What exactly did you want to see me about?" Calder asked as a police car sirened past outside.

"We have something coming up in the future where we might need your expertise."

"Not in England, I hope? I couldn't go back so soon. That would be very foolish."

"No, no. On your home ground."

"I don't operate there, you should know that."

"It isn't what you think. It's not your usual sort of work."

"What, then?" He was getting irritated now—the German was treating him like a junior.

"If we succeed we would want you to debrief somebody."

"Who?"

"It's better that you don't know until the trap is sprung. We're aiming to bring somebody out. If we succeed, your help would be invaluable. There would be no risk as far as you're concerned. By the time you come into it, the risks would all have been taken."

"I don't operate in the dark. Either I know the whole story, or it's not on. I don't work any other way."

Gunther took this calmly, pouring himself another cognac. "Why d'you think the meeting was arranged here?" He looked at Calder over his glass. "It would have been just as easy to have had dinner in Zurich and save us both a journey. If our masters don't hear from me tonight that everything is agreed, I very much fear you won't have a home to go back to. While you've been away certain measures have been taken to ensure your full cooperation." He smiled and sipped the cognac.

Calder was careful not to show any reaction to the threat. "Is it anything to do with the girl?"

"What girl?" Again the bland, blank smile.

"Your girl. She is yours, isn't she?" Calder said, letting him know that not all the aces were in one hand. "When she's not being farmed out, that is?"

"You won't get to me that way. I'm not the jealous type. And don't let's waste time fencing with each other. You'll be paid as usual."

"Okay, you can't give me chapter and verse, but at least prepare me. Is the object of the exercise to turn him or her?"

"Perhaps 'turn' is the wrong word. We think we have a good chance, with your help, to learn a few more missing pieces of the puzzle we have to solve. He or she doesn't fall into a conventional pattern."

"When will it happen?"

"When we make it happen." Gunther drained his glass. "I must get back to the hospital," he said in a louder voice. "It was great seeing you again. Have you anything you want me to tell Mother? Will you be visiting her?" He got up from the table and signaled for the check.

"Yes," Calder said. "Tell her I'm not too happy about the treatment, but I'll go along with whatever she wants."

"She'll be pleased." He examined the check, then handed it to Calder. "Very reasonable. Thank you for inviting me, I've enjoyed it." Then he left the restaurant.

24

THE BROTHERS OF Mercy were an amiable fraternity, though it had been said, uncharitably, that several of them could have been described more accurately as sisters.

The home where Hillsden and some twenty other social misfits were given sanctuary, three meals a day, regular but not compulsory prayer meetings, and some amateur brainwashing by a visiting shrink was one of those sprawling English country houses that nobody except institutions or big business can afford to keep up these days. The Brothers owed their existence to the largesse of a long-dead Chicago meat-packer, whose widow cared more for the human soul than for hog bellies. Basically Tudor, the main building had been "improved" by a series of Victorian architects, but with the passing of the years and the superior taste of a departed gardener who had concealed most of the horrors with Virginia creeper, it had settled into the Devon landscape and seemed at peace.

The rooms were high-ceilinged and cool. Some still retained William Morris wallpapers, and a few were hung with passable nineteenth-century paintings, mostly dogs savaging stags, bishops and their acolytes at play and other examples of bygone enthusiasms. Hillsden's room was on the top floor, and had patently been for the exclusive use of domestic staff in less egalitarian days. Being right under the roof, it was stiflingly hot when the sun shone, but had the compensation of providing a fine view down a valley dotted with wind-twisted pines, through which the sea could be glimpsed.

The inmates ate in a communal dining room that had once been the ballroom. The food was adequate, if plain; all the vegetables were grown in the walled kitchen garden on strictly organic principles. To aid the digestive processes for all this roughage, one of the Brothers read passages from the Bible during meals. For recreation there was a large billiard room housing a professional-sized table, the baize cloth eaten away in places so that the balls often performed startling trajectories. There was also a well-maintained conservatory and, in the grounds, one of those fake grottoes so beloved by the Victorians, together with a crumbling folly and an animal cemetery festooned with miniature gravestones.

Since it was a privately run establishment, the rules were refreshingly few and owed nothing to the dictates of the Ministry of Social Security. The residents were an odd bunch, as was to be expected, but they seemed to Hillsden to have been selected with reasonable care and deemed capable of being returned to society in a wholesome condition. There were a few drug addicts, but the majority were alcoholics and dropouts. Hillsden deliberately kept himself distanced from them, although he was careful not to carry his aloofness too far: silence in itself could be suspicious. The serene atmosphere and well-meaning efforts of the Brothers to bring about social and spiritual salvation might easily have lulled him into carelessness; in different circumstances he would have welcomed the change of pace.

He made a point of faithfully attending the therapy sessions—to all intents the sincere supplicant anxious to make amends. The house shrink was a desperately earnest individual with a slight speech impediment, so that every time he evoked the name Freud (to whom he owed his existence) it came out as "Floyd." In order not to disappoint him Hillsden invented elaborate fictions about an unhappy childhood dominated by a drunken father, eking out the details like a long-running soap opera. For the rest of the time he was left to his own devices, though expected to do his quota of domestic chores and to assist with the gardening. The Brothers ran the home on the basis of mutual trust; the inmates were on their honor not to abscond or stray into the nearby villages and there fall from grace. Since most of them had never had it so good, the system worked reasonably well.

Hillsden spent his spare time wandering along the cliffs above the sea. Many of the beaches formed part of private estates, and although technically open to the general public, they were mostly inaccessible except by boat. In the fine weather of that summer they looked as inviting as any Caribbean island, though the Channel water remained ice-cold even on the hottest days.

Sitting among the gorse and bracken of the cliff tops, sliding grass strands through his teeth to taste the juice of summer, he had plenty of time to ponder the route he had traveled so far. Below, the tides came and went, washing the sand as the Brothers hoped to wash his soul, but he doubted whether a life of deceit could ever be completely cleansed. Now it was a matter of waiting. The trap had been baited, it was only a question of whether it would entice an animal of the same breed as himself. Control had been confident of success, but as the weeks passed Hillsden became more and more skeptical. When the plan had first been put to him, he had few second thoughts about accepting it. Caroline's death had decided the remaining course of his life; until then he had never believed himself capable of her kind of hatred. The only thing that had ever driven him had been a vague, unstated loyalty towards a system, rather than a sense of "my country right or wrong." He had often thought how comforting it must be to have the unshakeable convictions of a Philby, to make a decision early in life and never renounce it, to prefer exile to home. But when the time came, there had been no anguish in the severing of old ties; leaving his wife had been like parting from somebody one meets on a holiday that one hasn't enjoyed.

These were his recurring thoughts as the days of waiting came and went. He had no idea how and when he would ever be contacted, and in the meantime was content to rebuild his physical strength. His injured foot was finally on the mend, and the Brothers' placid routine, combined with an unaccustomed life of leisure in the open air, replenished and prepared him for whatever lay ahead.

He had noticed that occasionally a few picnickers chanced the perilous footpath down to the beach, bringing with them the indestructible plastic flotsam of the twentieth century that the fish cannot eat and the sea cannot absorb. He was perched in his usual place one morning when a girl arrived below. She placed a brightly colored towel on a cluster of rocks just clear of the tidemark and, thinking herself unobserved, proceeded to disrobe. From a distance she seemed like a naiad as, nude, she ran into the gentle, lapping waves. She waded in up to her waist, holding her arms high as the first chill of the water tested her resolve. The action lifted her breasts, and she turned, exposing her body to Hillsden's gaze, before lunging backwards into the sea and striking out with the graceful movements of an experienced swimmer.

Hillsden sank lower into the tall, burnt grasses so as not to be detected, watching the girl sport in the dazzled water. He could not avoid acting the voyeur, and watched her with the manic concentration of an adolescent. When finally she emerged from the sea and stretched out below him on the patterned towel, he felt the pain of her beauty like a knife thrust. With her wet skin glinting before the sun dried her, her breasts, the perfect triangle of her pubic hair, she seemed unreal, somebody conjured from the depths of a dream. He watched her for fully fifteen minutes before easing himself out of her possible field of vision and returning to his room. There he found he could not sublimate the emotions she had aroused: the image of her body had been burned into his consciousness.

The following day he went back to the same spot, arriving earlier than he normally did, and this time made the descent to the beach, positioning himself on the blind side of the cluster of rocks she had used. He had reasoned that the girl was probably on holiday, and that having found such a perfect location she would return. His surmise proved correct. She came at the same time as the previous day, and was immediately aware that her solitude was now shared. Hillsden behaved like Mann's tragic character in "Death in Venice," casually observing her as he read a newspaper, though deliberately avoiding any eye contact as she arranged her towel and beach bag on the rocks. She disrobed out of sight, but this time emerged wearing a minuscule bikini. The sea was rougher that day, and her swim was not prolonged. It was only when she came out of the water that they acknowledged each other's presence.

"How was it?"

"Freezing," the girl said. "Have you been in?"

She had the accent of a deb, the sort of voice Hillsden had often heard at the end of a telephone line when ringing a Tory M.P.

"No, I'm not brave enough."

She showed no inclination to continue the conversation and went to her own place among the rocks.

He took up his position again the day after, but she failed to appear; disappointed, he assumed that her holiday was over. After two more days he resigned himself to the fact that it had been a pleasing diversion, allowing forgotten lusts to resurface; now the dull routine of the waiting game resumed. Then on the fourth day she returned.

As he slithered down the last few yards to the beach she turned and greeted him with a smile. "I'm sorry if I seemed abrupt the other morning," she said.

"Were you abrupt? I didn't think so."

"It wasn't until afterwards that I realized we'd met before."

"Really?"

"Yes, weren't you at that last party of Timmy's?"

"Timmy who?"

"Oh, God! If you have to say 'Timmy who?' then I've obviously got it all wrong. Don't you know Timmy Clark?"

"Sorry, no, he doesn't ring a bell."

"Oh, dear. You're always doing this, Wendy," Pamela said.

"It's Wendy, is it? Well, I'm James, and I apologize, Wendy, for not knowing your friend Mr. Clark. Was it a good party?"

"Yes, as a matter of fact."

"Pity I missed it."

There was something about this opening gambit that grated on him; it was a little too glib. Not that he was complaining; he was glad the ice had been broken and that her mistake had given him a slight edge. After they had exchanged the inevitable comments about the weather, she stretched out on her towel and opened the book she had brought with her.

"I've been trying to improve my mind. My boyfriend thinks I don't read the right books."

"What is it?"

She held it up for him to see. "Ivy Compton-Burnett. Have you ever read her?"

"Years ago I tried a couple." Hillsden studied the photograph of the author on the back of the jacket: there was more than a generation gap between the severe face of Miss Compton-Burnett under her Edwardian hairnet and Wendy's generous curves that he had only to drop his hand to touch.

"Yes, she can be heavy going at first, but once you get into her I think she's marvelous. There was a bit I was reading in bed last night. D'you want to hear it?" She raised herself up and moved even closer to him, her bikini top concealing nothing. After finding the place, she read aloud: " 'Oh, must we be quite so honest with ourselves, my dear?' 'We do not know how to avoid it,' said Terence. 'That is why there is horror in every heart, and a resolve never to be honest with anybody else.' Don't you think that's stunning?"

"I'm still trying to work it out. It certainly sounds profound. Is there ever horror in your heart?"

"Sometimes, I guess."

"What was the other bit? 'Never be honest with anybody else.' Yes. Well, honesty's always relative, isn't it? It depends who we're with and what we want from them."

"Yes. Was I that obvious?"

"What are we talking about now?"

"That bit I gave you about Timmy Clark. I don't know a Timmy Clark. I just made that up."

"You just had to talk to me, was that it?"

"That's about it, Mr. Hillsden," she said slowly.

He realized that they had finally caught up with him, and made an effort not to let her see the surprise he felt. He gave them full marks for an original approach. "And we can also take it that your name isn't Wendy?"

"You got it in one."

Hillsden got to his feet. "Well, congratulations. You had me fooled. And there I was, thinking you found me irresistible."

"You're not going, are you? We've still got a lot to talk about."

"You mean you want to tell me about all the horrors in your heart?"

"No, I thought we could discuss a change of scenery for you. I'm sure the Brothers of Mercy aren't really your cup of tea."

"Since you know so much about me, you must know I'm out of all that, on the shelf."

"You could be taken down off the shelf, surely, if the price was right?"

Hillsden stood looking down at her. "Just tell whoever sent you to leave me alone. I'm not in the market." He started to walk away.

"Wouldn't you like to know what happened to your Caroline?" Pamela said.

That stopped him. He turned to face her again.

"And Jock, and all the others? Wouldn't that tempt you?"

"Who sent you?"

"I'm acting for a prospective buyer."

"Listen, Wendy, or whatever your name is, don't press your luck. You're a pretty girl, but don't think you can just smile and flash your tits and I'll roll over and beg. You're a long way from help, and I still know a trick or two, even though I'm retired. It wouldn't take much to drown you. The tides around here are known to be treacherous; even the strongest swimmers get into difficulties."

"Yes, we thought of that. Take a look behind you."

Hillsden swung around and scanned the cliff tops. A figure stood up in the bracken and he saw the glint of a rifle barrel.

"He's also been listening to everything we've said so far." She produced a two-way radio from her beach bag. "So just relax, Mr. Hillsden, you're not dealing with amateurs."

The man on the cliff top ducked out of sight again, only to reappear a few moments later on the pathway leading down to the beach. The gun was not in evidence, but he carried a canvas tennis bag and was dressed in shorts and a T-shirt as though he had just come from a game. As he got closer Hillsden judged him to be about the same age as the girl, but unlike the girl, he did not suggest a clean-living, outdoor English type.

While he waited for their next move he tried to figure the odds. If they had done their homework, they must be feeling fairly confident of landing him. From their point of view he was, after all, ripe for plucking: out on his ear, with a prison record, no visible means of support, doing penance with the Brothers. In spite of the initial surprise—he had to admit that the girl had done a good job—he had his wits about him once again. He needed to change tactics; it would be wise to lose some of his previous cockiness and play more of the role they doubtless expected of him. Not that the advantage was all on their side. He doubted whether they had intended to play the ace marked Caroline quite so early in the game. From past experience he knew that they, too, must be nervous.

He stood his ground while the young man slithered the last few yards to the sand and joined the girl, placing the tennis holdall by the side of her towel and unzipping it to let him see that the rifle was close at hand. Hillsden recognized it as standard NATO issue, but adapted to take a silencer.

"Let's all sit down, shall we?" the young man said. "Get ourselves comfortable. We have a great deal to talk about." Hillsden thought he detected traces of a German accent buried in the correct English. "We can either keep it all friendly, or we can play rough, as you suggested to Wendy here. It's the same treacherous sea for you as well, Mr. Hillsden."

"You've already heard what I have to say. I'm not in the market."

"No, that's true. You're here on the beach."

I'm right, Hillsden thought. Anybody with that heavy a sense of humor has to be German.

"Let's talk about what we both know, shall we? What we both fully understand. We both know that your previous employers, like those I work for, don't let us go easily. They have a long reach and no real gratitude for past services. Once we cease to be useful to them, we're expendable. Full retirement is never part of the contract. Now, what I have the authority to discuss is a way of relieving you of certain anxieties about your future. A new way of life, shall we say? Something better than the charity you're currently living on. I'm sure finance, or lack of it, has entered into your reckoning, hasn't it? Or do you intend spending the rest of your life looking over your shoulder, never knowing when your old friends will decide you're an embarrassment they would rather do without?"

When Hillsden remained silent, the German stroked the barrel of the rifle and went on, "Surely it would make sense to consider an alternative? Wouldn't you agree?"

"What am I supposed to consider?"

"Some traveling, a new home, a more secure future."

"In return for what?"

"Oh, come now, Mr. Hillsden, you're not that naïve. The word is cooperation."

"Or betrayal."

"Didn't they betray you? You paid your dues, and how did they show their gratitude? I think you'd find my people much more generous. How generous? Well, to begin with, twenty-five thousand pounds generous. Paid into a Swiss numbered account, just to show their goodwill. After that, depending on how cooperative you prove, other equally generous installments."

Playing for time, Hillsden looked down at his feet and traced patterns in the sand with a piece of driftwood. It was vital that he not give them the impression that he had been expecting their approach. What happened next would be crucial.

"I'm not so sure I have anything worth selling. I've been out of the field for a long time."

"That's a risk our people are willing to take, a risk they're willing to pay for."

Again Hillsden took his time about replying. "Do I have any choice? Now that you've found me, won't your people have the same long reach if I refuse to go along?"

The young man smiled. "It's the same leopard, just different spots. The only time we'll ever be secure is when we're dead."

"How do I know they'll keep their side of the bargain?"

"It wouldn't be to their advantage not to. You can work that out for yourself. And don't underestimate your worth. They wouldn't have sent us here to make the offer if they thought you had nothing to give."

"And afterwards?"

"How d'you mean?"

"When they've got all they want, what happens then?"

"That's up to you. You'll have the money, you can go where you want."

"I'd need protection."

"That could be discussed."

"Protection at both ends. If I go along, I want to disappear for good."

"Of course."

"How would I be sure of getting the money?"

"I see we're beginning to make progress. You're asking practical questions. I like that; I'd do the same in your position. How? The first installment is already in a numbered account. You will get the number with your new passport and identity. I think you'll find our arrangements are watertight."

"How soon do you want an answer?"

"Why not give it now? You have to appreciate our position. If your answer proved to be no, it would present us with certain problems. You might be tempted to turn the tables and sell the information about our offer elsewhere. I'm sure you take my meaning. If, on the other hand, I've managed to convince you, there's no time like the present. All the arrangements are in hand."

Hillsden hesitated one final time. Certainly they were thorough: he was being given no chance to contact anybody, and the gun in the tennis bag was a reminder that the choices were all theirs. "If you mean we start now, I've got no decent clothes, no luggage," he replied, playing his doubts to the end.

"I repeat, we've thought of all that. We have clothes for you. You will be traveling as Wendy's father—a good touch, don't you think?" Again the smile without warmth. A cold breeze suddenly blew in from the sea.

"You came down here this morning as usual, and this time you took a swim. But as you said, the tides here are very treacherous. A man like you, depressed, not in the peak of condition, who knows what was in your mind? Your old clothes, washed up somewhere along the coast, will highlight the tragedy. How does that sound?"

"As though you were never in any doubt about what my answer would be," Hillsden said.

"I have your new clothes in the car. You'll be traveling as a Mr. Coburn, recently widowed. Black tie, we thought, and a black arm band, to show respect for the dead."

25

KILLING PEOPLE HAD never cost the Fat Boy a single night's sleep. He carried a score of hatreds like loose coins, to be spent on the sheer pleasure of the act. Plastic surgery had cut away some of the puppy fat from his jowls and altered the shape of his nose, but his enthusiasms had been left intact.

For some months now he had been dormant in Libya, motionless but alert, waiting for the time when he would once again be called upon. During his temporary retirement false trails had been laid, bogus clues planted about his whereabouts. Even so, he was amused to read that he had still been credited with several hits. There was gratification in that; he needed the assurance that even when he was absent from the scene his existence was felt.

The initial stages of the English plan had gone well, with a run of luck that had surprised even him, and he regretted that he had not been part of it. Tripoli was a secure base, but he was not sorry to be leaving. The local fanaticism worried him; he felt more at home with the Russians, whose emotional pulse beat at the same slow rate as his own; with them nothing was ever done on the spur of the moment. They used him as he liked to be used: for the difficult assignments where there was most risk.

Now he sat with his KGB control on the terrace of the Quaddan Hotel, listening with the respect he gave to few as the details of his new assignment were explained. Below the terrace balustrade a tribe of starving cats prowled; from time to time he threw them scraps from his breakfast plate. When the British had been in residence the cats had prospered; legend had it that a wealthy spinster had left a will in their favor and their numbers had multiplied to plague proportions. Now the survivors, despised and neglected, had reverted to the wild. The Fat Boy felt an affinity with them; they lived, as he did, by their wits.

"The selected target has outlived his usefulness, and we have to make certain that as we move on to the next stage there are no loose ends. We missed him once, unfortunately, but I'm sure you won't make the same mistake."

They plotted the assassination as casually as others might discuss the need for minor dental surgery. The Fat Boy would be working alone, as he preferred, and only one contact would be necessary. He was told who.

He considered this. "We met briefly, a long time ago."

"Are you happy with the choice? There are certain special advantages."

"I can live with it, providing I run the show."

"Of course. Equally, you must understand that nothing must lead back to us. When it's over, London will take steps to implicate our hosts here." The Fat Boy shared the humor of this; it was the sort of cynicism he enjoyed most. "Moscow is increasingly of the view that these people are more trouble than they're worth. They have no system, no long-term aims that we share; they're simply a gang of hysterical amateurs unable to see further than their pathetic Islamic revolution. As if that was important. And witness the way they go about it." He reminded the Fat Boy of the St. James' Square incident, when a young British policewoman had been gunned down by a member of the Libyan legation. "A prime example of their unreliability. Can you imagine us making such a mistake? Though, of course, had it happened in Moscow they would never have left Russia alive. The British have gone soft; they deserve all they get."

The more they talked, the more the plan appealed to the Fat Boy; ideas began to take shape. He plotted his best approach, what steps should be taken to put it into operation, the type of weapon best suited to the job and—perhaps most vital of all—the necessary safety measures to be taken when it was over. These were the details that, from long association, they trusted him to decide. The reason he had survived so long was that he had always studied his own Dow Jones index of fear and dealt in futures. His prime value to the KGB lay in the fact that no connections had ever been proved. To the West's security forces he was a jack-of-all-causes, somebody who operated without any consistent pattern, thus clouding his real motives, or those of the people who ran him. It was an arrangement that satisfied both parties; he worked best alone; all he needed was to be pointed in the right direction.

The briefing over, he left Tripoli the following day, starting out on a complicated journey designed to cover all the spoors and which eventually would take him to the place where someone had been selected to die.

HILLSDEN also had thoughts of murder. On the boat journey over to France he likened his situation to that of Dr. Crippen and young Ethel

Le Neve: they, too, had set out in the same way on a journey into the unknown. The girl he knew only as Wendy stayed close to him the entire trip. They paced the deck together, watching England disappear. He wondered when he would ever see its coastline again. The German had not accompanied them, but had taken a flight from Heathrow to Paris. From there he would make his way to Cherbourg, their port of arrival.

"Could you ever leave for good?" Hillsden asked.

"I already have as far as loyalty's concerned."

"That was easy, was it?"

"Not difficult. England's finished. It's only a matter of time before we take over completely."

Before they were a mile out into the Channel the sea got choppier, and the girl proved to be a bad sailor. "Let's go to the cabin," she said. "I think I'll lie down for a while."

"You're always better off in the fresh air, you know."

"So they say, but I have to lie down."

He accompanied her below. In the cabin adjacent to theirs a group of football fans playing a noisy game of poker shouted ribald remarks as Hillsden and the girl passed their open door.

"You can't be sorry to leave that sort behind," she said when they were alone. She went to the washbasin and splashed her face with cold water.

"They seem to be coming with us."

"You know what I mean." She lay down on one of the twin bunks, then wrinkled her nose in disgust. "Urgh!—the smell of these blankets."

"Don't you like getting closer to the people?"

She made no answer, and as her eyes closed, some of the hardness in her face disappeared. Hillsden damped a hand towel and laid it across her forehead. The unexpected coldness jolted her.

"I thought it might help."

"Thank you."

She closed her eyes again, holding the cold towel in place with a manicured hand. Hillsden sat on the opposite bunk and watched her. He remembered what her body had looked like on the beach and wondered who had first corrupted her with the old forgotten lies. Asleep, she looked strangely vulnerable; it required an effort of will to believe that there was any menace in their association. Nothing, he had learned, ever turned out the way one imagined. Keeping watch over her, his thoughts traveled back to Caroline—Caroline asleep in his arms. He was suddenly appalled by the thoughts that clamored to be admitted; as though reading what was in his mind, the girl opened her eyes and stared at him.

"It's passed now," she said. "Lying down did the trick." She searched his face. "You know, you're different from what I'd imagined."

"Didn't they brief you?"

"You can't bring somebody to life just by reading about them."

"What's different about me?"

"You're attracted to me. I never allowed for that."

"What makes you so sure?"

"It was there in your face when I woke up."

"Is that so very odd? You must know you're attractive."

They stared at each other across the narrow cabin, and he wondered, What is the chemistry between us—is it just the old physical con trick that traps us all, or the fact that neither of us is a stranger to treachery? He detected a change in her, the nuance of excitement in her voice. "Assuming you're right," he said, "there's not much I can do about it, is there? Wouldn't that be going outside your instructions? Prisoners are not usually allowed to make love to their guards. Unless, of course, you're a free agent in these matters?" He was aware that the dialogue intrigued her; there was, after all, a chink in her professional armor, and it amused him to work on it.

"Is that how you think of yourself? As a prisoner?"

"Isn't that what I am?"

"Don't you trust us?"

"Oh, my dear," he said, the age difference between them coloring his voice, "trust isn't a word to be found in the dictionary we both use."

He knelt in the space between the two bunks and drew her head down to his. She offered no resistance. At such close range she looked younger than ever, and he knew that for these moments, at least, the initiative had passed to him. It wasn't that he had any real intention of taking it further, but that the novelty of the situation intrigued him. Then it occurred to him that perhaps her seasickness had been feigned, and that she had planned the whole episode. To test her, he let his hands trace the outlines of her breasts, and again she allowed the intimacy.

A sudden shout from the cardplayers in the other cabin broke the spell. "Lock the door," she said.

He hesitated before getting to his feet and securing the flimsy catch; when he turned back she was already taking her clothes off. He remembered her glimpsed nakedness on the beach, but here in the confined space of the cabin her beauty seemed unreal; he had no defense against it. After they had kissed for the first time, he apologized for his clumsiness, "You'll have to forgive me, I'm out of practice." This was the one betrayal he had never worked out in advance.

She said nothing, but helped him remove his clothes, pausing to touch gently the pale scar on his shoulder. The last thing he had expected from her had been tenderness; it was as if in the moments before everything changed forever they had suddenly become human to each other. She opened the tightly made bed, and together they arranged themselves under the blankets, taking him back to the dark, remembered games of childhood; life hadn't moved far, after all, from the cupboard beneath the stairs where deceit had first been practiced. He had to remind himself that it wasn't love he felt; love was supposed to happen without a sense of shame or guilt. I once swore I'd never betray the memory of Caroline, he thought, but he could not prevent his body responding to the urgency of the girl's movements beneath him, and they struggled towards love of a kind as the promise was obliterated.

In the aftermath, they remained cramped together on the unyielding mattress listening to the mindless profanities that punctuated the poker game. She touched his scar again, tracing it with cool fingers. His own hand rested on her damp breasts and he stroked the softening nipples, feeling the slow pulsing of her heart. Guilt crept back over the threshold like a cringing dog.

"What a strange pair we are," he said.

"Why strange?"

"Well, given the circumstances. Or perhaps you were granting me the condemned man's last wish?"

"No. I wanted you, isn't that enough?"

"You know how they'd describe this in official reports? They'd say 'Intimacy took place.' Funny that a word for the closest form of friendship should have been corrupted to mean illicit sex—though I suppose in our case it fits the bill perfectly. To be intimate without friendship."

"Do you always analyze your lovemaking?"

"I haven't for a long time." His arm was cramped and he eased it out from under her, almost falling out of the bunk in the process. "These things weren't designed for passion, were they? A pity we didn't make it on the beach when I first saw you, when you first showed yourself naked to me. You knew I was there, didn't you?"

"Of course."

"Who's running you?" he said suddenly, hoping to catch her off guard, but she was equal to the ruse.

"You don't expect me to tell you that."

"No, but you can't blame me for trying."

"How much longer before we dock?" she asked.

He twisted his head to squint at his wristwatch. "Just over two hours by my reckoning."

"I won't be going with you all the way. He takes over when we land."

"What's journey's end for me?"

"I'm only told the minimum I need to know." She eased herself away from him. They heard a bottle being smashed, then more raucous laughter. "Listen to those yobs," she said. "They're hardly worth betraying."

He could almost believe that he was back in the Army: the cabin reminded him of a barrack room; the clamor on the other side of the closed door sounded like just another mess dust-up. But in those long-gone days loyalty had been an unbroken chain.

"Is he the regular boyfriend?"

"Why do you want to know?"

"Just curious."

"I live with him," she said, "whenever he gives me the chance."

"He's German, isn't he? One of the new democratic breed."

"If you say so."

"Oh, come on, Wendy! You're not in *Peter Pan*. We're not playing nursery games, there's no Mr. Darling in our futures. No need to be coy with me. A little while ago you were happy enough to have me inside you. Even if it didn't signify eternal love, it's some kind of bond, isn't it? We're two of a kind, you and me; the only difference between us is that you've got your Never-Never-Land to come. I've been there once and now I'm going back."

"If you tell them what they want to hear, you've got no problems."

"What about you? What will you do when you're offered the choice?"

"That's never going to happen. I've already chosen the winning side."

"How wonderful it must be," Hillsden said without sarcasm, "to have no doubts." The previous spurt of anger had aroused him again; there was something about her youthful arrogance that made her infinitely desirable. He pushed her back into the mattress and took her again, and this time he was the one in control. In the act of possessing her it occurred to him that only the oblivion of sex had the power to briefly smother all fears, and for once he could understand the frenzy of the rapist. He wanted to force an admission from her; not the words true lovers use—that would be asking too much—just something approaching affection to carry with him in the months to come. The girl writhed, moaning beneath him, but he knew the sounds she made were not for him exclusively, and when they finished he felt lonelier than ever.

Neither of them spoke for fully five minutes; then she said, "Do you think we'll ever meet again?"

"If I knew that, I'd know everything."

"Yes, I suppose so. Silly question." She eased herself out from under him and swung herself out of the bunk. "I could do with a drink. Shall we go back up on deck?"

"Whatever you want." Hillsden watched the gentle movement of her young breasts as she picked up her clothes. There was a kind of agony in her beauty, and he thought of all the wasted years, those that had gone and those that were still to come.

When they had both dressed and checked each other's clothing, she allowed him to kiss her briefly before they left the cabin.

"It was a kind of friendship, a kind of intimacy, wasn't it? It's important for me to believe that at least."

"Yes," she said.

Several empty beer bottles careened across the aisle as the boat rolled. As Hillsden reached to steady the girl, one of the poker players shouted, "Given her a knee-trembler, have you, Dad?" and the laughter followed them as they climbed towards the deck.

"What's your poison?" Hillsden said as they entered the noisy bar.

"I'll have a double vodka. Nothing with it."

"Supporting home industries, are we?" But the joke was lost on her. All the tables were occupied, and when finally he managed to get served, they took their glasses outside.

"What shall we drink to?"

"Good-bye to all that, if you have any sense." She stared past him to the day-trippers in the bar. "Look at them! Swilling down their duty-free beer and onion-flavored potato chips. You can't pretend it's any great loss to turn your back on those."

"If only it was that simple," he said. They stood in silence by the rail, watching as the French coastline slowly emerged like a theatrical transformation, while overhead the gulls screamed a shared loneliness.

An hour later when they disembarked, the French authorities showed no interest in the arrival of Mr. Coburn and his daughter. Having cleared Customs and Immigration, they walked to the dockside car park. Waiting beside a black Citroën, the German kissed Pamela and embraced Hillsden in true Continental fashion, the charade acted out with conviction for the benefit of any onlooker.

They took the *autoroute* back to Paris, traveling well in excess of the speed limit whenever the German judged the road safe from police patrols. Lulled by the soft suspension, Hillsden dozed in the rear seat.

Occasionally the two in front exchanged a few sentences; twice he thought he heard the word "London" mentioned. The German slewed the Citroën off the *autoroute* at the exit for Charles de Gaulle Airport and deposited the girl outside the Departure satellite. She kissed him through the open window, then walked into the building without so much as a glance at Hillsden. Before she disappeared they had moved off, descending the helter-skelter ramps to the main road again. Skirting Paris to the south and taking the route to Troyes, the German kept his foot down all the way; they stopped only once to fill up with gas and have a snack.

"Where are we heading for?" Hillsden asked while they ate, and when he was ignored he repeated the question in German.

"You'll find out when we get there."

"Listen, stop treating me like I fell off the back of a lorry. As far as I'm concerned, you're just the delivery service, you and your girlfriend. So stay in character, act the chauffeur and tell me where we're going."

The German wiped his plate clean with a piece of bread.

"When I trade, I'll trade on my own level, not with office boys," Hillsden continued. "And I want to see the money first. That was the deal."

Before answering, the German took a gulp of coffee and swilled it around in his mouth. "What makes you think you're in a bargaining position? You're on a fake passport miles from nowhere with no money. That's not a healthy way to travel. Finish your coffee and let's get going."

They drove for another three hours through the Haute-Marne, finally stopping at nightfall outside a nondescript commercial hotel in the small town of Tettingen a few miles from the Swiss border.

"Before we register, let's say good-bye to Mr. Coburn. Give me your passport." Hillsden handed it over. In its place he was given a West German counterpart issued in the name of Ernst Sauckel, a jewelry salesman born in Coburg.

"From now on, practice your German," he was told, "but you'd better let me do all the talking. We stay here overnight, then make an early start in the morning. I want to cross the border when most of the heavy trucks are going through; that way we attract less attention. We're sharing a room, by the way."

"How cozy. But not the same bed, I hope. Unlike your girlfriend, I'm particular who I sleep with." If he had hoped to score points, he was disappointed.

"If you fucked her, you did me a favor. She's not a good lay. Like the rest of your bloody race, she just lies down and takes it."

The German paid for their board in advance, and they had a simple, well-cooked meal before retiring. The twin-bedded room was sparsely furnished but scrupulously clean, with a shower and toilet partitioned off in one corner.

"No television. We'll have to find something to talk about instead. What's the going rate for chauffeurs these days?" Hillsden said, but the sarcasm was ignored. The German took the bed nearest to the door and lay down on it fully clothed.

"Oh, dear, don't some of us brush our teeth?" Hillsden said. "I'm going to take a shower, so look the other way if you think you'll get overexcited." He stripped and soaped away the scent of the girl, but nothing could remove the returning guilt. When he had finished he turned out the light.

"Leave it on."

"Sorry. Are you afraid of the dark? I'll tell you some German fairy tales until you go to sleep. Like how you took Stalingrad."

"Don't be too smart, save your energy. You're going to need it in the days to come."

Hillsden stared at the moths circling the ceiling bulb, pondering the truth of what had just been said. From past experience of interrogations, he had no illusions about what lay ahead. He wondered whether, in the final analysis, some kind of faith helped, and not for the first time in his life regretted that he had none. He tried to recall childhood prayers, a test of memory more than one of belief, and it was the memories of those lost years that he carried with him into sleep.

They left just after dawn, crossing the border with empty stomachs. As at Cherbourg, the formalities at the Swiss frontier were accomplished without incident. After an hour's drive they stopped for breakfast at one of those spotless Swiss roadside eating houses where the waitresses serve customers with the precision of a Rolex. When they resumed the journey, Hillsden unknowingly traveled the same route taken by Calder when he returned from murdering Caroline. Like Calder, he tried to memorize salient landmarks as they wound upward through the mountains. There was a regulated neatness about Switzerland that irritated him even as it impressed: the cows dotted about the lush pastures looked like the wooden farmyard animals he had played with as a child. The car had no air conditioning, and as the sun came out he had to fight to keep alert. The German drove with skill and concentration, and it was obvious that he was familiar with the terrain. It was only when they descended into the last valley that the German relaxed his grip on the steering wheel and eased his foot off the accelerator, so that they coasted to the entrance gates of an estate. As Hillsden watched, two blond youths appeared from a lodge house and checked the Citroën before opening the gates.

Once the car was inside the grounds they both came forward for a closer inspection. "Any trouble?" one of them asked. He peered into the open window, and Hillsden caught a whiff of a very feminine cologne.

"Do I ever have any trouble?" the German answered.

"Perhaps because you're not pretty enough," the blond said. He waved the car on.

At the house Hillsden was greeted by a man in his late fifties, smartly dressed in a gray flannel suit of impeccable cut, who looked as though he should be on the cover of *Forbes*. He held out his hand. "Welcome, Mr. Hillsden. You've come home at last. My name is Hansel."

"As in 'Hansel and Gretel,' no doubt," Hillsden said just before he was struck a crippling blow from behind and his world disintegrated into darkness.

THE jumping-off ground was West Germany. The Fat Boy spent a week in Hamburg refining his plan, then signed up for a coach tour of London and its surroundings, purchasing his ticket from a travel agency selected at random. He equipped himself as the average tourist, dressing from head to toe in the type of clothing he knew would be indistinguishable from that worn by his traveling companions. The tour was advertised to last ten days, and gave those participating the option of remaining with the main group or making their own arrangements on arrival. Thus, he calculated he had seven days in which to accomplish his mission.

The journey over from Hamburg to Dover was pleasant enough. His fellow tourists were the average mixture of young and old, all intent on having a good time and getting their money's worth; the main topic of conversation on the coach was the exchange rate. The Fat Boy took holiday snaps with his Leica whenever they halted for a meal, but unlike the others he had no film in his camera; he regarded Kodak's famed products as a prime security risk. He had not been in England for three years, but he was confident of his changed appearance and he was carrying nothing incriminating. He neither smoked nor drank, and despised the use of drugs. Apart from murder and love of food, he had no vices.

The group arrived at their London hotel almost on the scheduled minute. The Fat Boy took the single room allocated to him, deposited his baggage, then went out and bought all the newspapers he could find. It was always important to know what was going on in a capital city; the most carefully laid plans could come unstuck through a totally unrelated incident. He noted that there was to be a protest march of unemployed on one day of his stay, as well as a state visit of the President of Nigeria; both events would mean widespread traffic jams and diversions, vital factors to know when effecting any getaway.

Not wishing to appear suspiciously aloof, on the first evening he made a point of eating with the rest of the party, and used the opportunity to drop false hints about his movements during the coming week. After watching the ITN news bulletin and an episode of an appalling sitcom, he slept soundly for eight hours. Then, after braving what was erroneously termed a "Continental breakfast," he ventured forth complete with Leica, guidebooks and the authentic look of an innocent abroad.

He first went to the National History Museum in Brompton Road and, after spending an hour there, visited the adjacent Victoria and Albert, giving a careful portrayal of a dedicated Anglophile in both places. Then he had coffee in a nearby café before walking as far as Harrods. There, as a necessary test, he asked a policeman the best route to the Tower of London; having been courteously directed, he descended into Knightsbridge Underground station, but instead of buying a ticket he used one of the public phone booths. Dialing the operator and assuming an Irish accent, he made a hoax call to the effect that a bomb had been placed in Marks and Spencer's Oxford Street branch. Such amusements gave him something akin to sexual satisfaction, and it was with a lighter step that he emerged into daylight again and strolled down Sloane Street. Despite the overall drabness of the British, he couldn't help remarking that many of the young girls had an insolent prettiness about them; the rich were the same the world over, and he longed to dent their arrogance. His route took him to Sloane Square Underground station by the side of the Royal Court Theatre; from there he carefully measured the time it took him to walk at a normal pace the length of Eaton Square. It was never part of his planning to rely on getaway cars; mechanical things were too fallible and usually required a collaborator—two extra risks he despised.

He passed the entrance to the mews, noting the number of cars parked outside the trim houses, then made his way back to Sloane Square by a different route, well content with his morning's work. There was a revival of Orton's *Loot* playing at the Royal Court, and he bought a ticket for that day's matinee. Orton's flaunting disregard for sacred cows was pleasantly relaxing, in tune with the Fat Boy's mood; he enjoyed having his own beliefs dramatized as entertainment. The fact that the audience laughed in ignorance merely highlighted the basic decadence he was committed to destroy. When he returned to the hotel to take the evening meal in company with other members of the tour, he felt supremely confident, and on the following day joined the scheduled visit to Kew Gardens. The important thing was not to establish any rigid pattern.

On the third day he left the hotel early and went straight to Liverpool Street station, where he caught a train to Stratford-atte-Bow, home of the famed Cockney Bow Bells, in the East End of London. It was a place he had never visited before, but he made his way to the street market without hesitation: he had a photographic memory for maps and had done his homework. Although it was nearly fifty years after the event, some scars of the Nazi Blitz were still in evidence; old bomb sites still gapped the tattered side streets. Even the postwar high-rise buildings looked as though they were about to collapse; with their pitted and graffiti-scrawled walls, their broken windows and shabby paintwork, they formed part of a city under constant attack. The Fat Boy got the impression that in the course of a few miles he had crossed an unmarked frontier into foreign territory; the faces that jostled past him had no marked characteristics—they were composed of a score of different ethnic races as though they had been scattered together in haphazard fashion. He moved among them with heightened awareness, conscious that here he would be more conspicuous and therefore had a greater need for caution. It wasn't that he doubted the reliability of his instructions, for he had confidence in his backup organization, but his own built-in instincts for survival urged extra care.

Threading his way through back streets, he came at last to the address he had been given. The single-fronted shop was sandwiched between two emporiums selling cheap lines of clothes. It purported to be a jeweler's, but displayed only a few transistor radios and replica watches of dubious origin. The window was pasted with signs announcing a closing sale with amazing reductions, which had long since failed to impress the locals; everything in the district was a con aimed at the unwary.

Having observed the shop from a distance before crossing the street, the Fat Boy went inside. Opening the door triggered off a bell, and after a pause a Pakistani shuffled into view from a rear room.

The Fat Boy produced a single gold cuff link from his pocket. "You were recommended as being able to mend this for me."

The man fixed a watchmaker's glass into one eye and examined the link professionally.

213

"It's possible," he announced. "But expensive."

"I wasn't expecting you to do it for free."

"Cash."

"How much?"

"For something special like this, five hundred."

"Is that the going rate?"

"For the risk I'm taking, that's the price."

The Fat Boy's manner changed abruptly. "Listen, you fucking wog, the risk is to keep me waiting. Just close up the shop and get what I came for."

The man hurried to obey, locking the street door and reversing his OPEN sign, then led the way into the rear room, which obviously doubled as his sleeping quarters. A gas stove stood next to a sink piled with unwashed crockery, the remains of a meal lay on a table, and in one corner was a camp bed. A small dog of indeterminate breed bedded in a cardboard box cringed as the two men entered, baring its brown teeth in a pathetic imitation of a snarl. The man crouched down and flung the dog to one side; it whimpered and hid itself under the sink as he delved under the layers of old newspapers lining the box and produced a standard-issue German police revolver wrapped in oiled paper. His hand shook as he gave it to the Fat Boy, who tore off the protective paper and expertly released the magazine. He thumbed the first bullet into his palm, examined it, then replaced it and snapped the magazine back into position. After satisfying himself that the serial numbers had been filed off, he threw a bulky envelope on the table.

"Don't upset me by counting it, Sooty. Just show me the other way out. And remember, if anything goes wrong, you'll wish you never got off the boat. You go first and tell me if it's clear."

The man opened the rear door and looked outside. "Is good."

The Fat Boy slipped the gun into a pocket and stepped out into a service alleyway. He walked back to the main street and caught a bus to St. Paul's. There he transferred to the Underground, leaving it at Bond Street. He walked from Bond Street to Oxford Circus before catching another bus to Hyde Park Corner. Only when he was satisfied that nobody was tailing him did he return to his hotel. Safely back in his room, he checked the gun more thoroughly, then removed the Leica from its case and replaced it with the gun. He took the case with him when he went down to dinner. After the meal he watched live television coverage of a football match in the bar before retiring.

For the next two days he joined the others for the scheduled sightseeing tours. They were taken to the Tate Gallery, Hampton Court and

Windsor Castle. On the afternoon of the day before they were due to depart he excused himself on the pretext of a stomach upset, saying he would rest in his room. He was asked whether he wished to see a doctor, but declined, telling the tour director that he had suffered from bilious attacks since childhood and always carried a proven remedy with him. The man expressed regret that he was going to miss the highlight of the trip, a visit to the National Theatre.

An hour after the rest of the party had left for their final outing, he dialed a local number from his room. A girl answered.

"Do we still have a date tonight?" he asked.

"Yes. Everything's as planned."

"What time do you have now?"

"Six-thirty-two exactly."

He checked his own watch. "I shall be there at nine," he said and hung up. Then he took a shower and changed into pajamas before ringing room service and asking for an order of toast and a bottle of mineral water. When the waiter appeared he was lying in bed, and explained he was feeling off-color. The waiter commiserated with him and was well tipped for his concern.

The Fat Boy ate a piece of the toast and drank a glass of the water, passing the time until eight o'clock. Then he dressed and left his room, ignoring the elevator and using the stairway. The lobby was crowded with an arriving party of Scandinavian students, and he slipped through them and out into the street unnoticed. All he carried was the camera case.

By 8:45 he was in Sloane Square, and arrived at the entrance to the mews at precisely 8:59, just in time to see Pamela walking away from the house. The key had been left for him in the front-door lock. He turned it with a gloved hand and, entering quickly, mounted the carpeted stairs two at a time.

Belfrage had the television on, watching a symphony concert. They were playing the Grieg Piano Concerto. Before he reached the head of the stairs the Fat Boy had extracted the gun. As he entered the room Belfrage had his back to him and was in the act of pouring himself a drink. The Fat Boy shot him twice as he turned. The whisky glass hit the side of the television set as it flew from Belfrage's hand, but did not break. The Fat Boy walked over to where Belfrage lay on the thick pile carpet and shot him once more between the eyes at point-blank range. Then he turned up the sound on the television and left the house, dropping the key just inside the door before closing it. From start to finish the entire operation had taken less than a minute.

He strolled back to Sloane Square in leisurely fashion and took the Underground to Putney. There he crossed Putney Bridge, pausing halfway to observe the river traffic. With his arms resting on the parapet, he let the gun fall into the Thames, then continued on his way, and caught a bus back into London. By 10:30 he was once more in his hotel room. When the tour manager returned an hour later to pay a solicitous visit, he received him in bed, and they discussed the play he had sadly missed.

The coach left for the return journey to Hamburg the following morning, and it was generally agreed that the tour had been excellent value for the money.

26

" 'SOURCES CLOSE TO the Prime Minister' can happily conceal a multitude of sins if judiciously used," Bayldon observed in his usual half-apologetic manner when in the presence of his Leader.

"Yes," the P.M. said, "pity it can't conceal the whole bloody lot."

He stared out of the windows of the Long Hall at Chequers. Rain had misted the fields beyond the formal garden, but he could still make out half a dozen figures moving in the distance.

"Fat lot of use having top security when they still allow a right of way within sniper distance. Any decent shot with telescopic sights could pick us off at random. Still, that's England for you. I sometimes wonder if we're not entirely mad."

"Probably goes back to the Domesday Book," another member of the Cabinet murmured. "Preservation of ancient civil liberties and all that."

"Domesday Book is about right," the P.M. replied, with emphasis on the "doom." "And we seem to be writing a second edition." His eyes roved to see how many of the group appreciated his heavy humor. Replete after a lunch served by members of the W.A.A.F.'s, most of his Cabinet were smoking the free Jamaican cigars that were always handed around at official functions, and their brandy glasses were full. "Right, let's get back to business." He turned to Bayldon. "Are you saying,

Toby, that there's another security scandal brewing up? Is that what you're hinting?"

"Not exactly, George."

The use of Christian names was allowed at closed sessions, though frowned upon in any contact with the media.

"What, then? Spell it out."

"It's now been established that Glanville was probably murdered."

"If it's been established, it can't be probable, can it? I've said it before, and I'll say it again—and this applies to all of you. Either make exact statements or don't make them at all, especially in the House. The Tories have got the bit between their teeth and they'll pounce on anything that looks like waffle. So let's have it, Toby. Yes he was murdered, or no he wasn't?"

"Well, let us say that the forensic boys have determined that he died as a result of being exposed to a nerve gas. Now, it's also possible that this was self-administered, though doubtful. I'm told he was a potential suicide. The factor that disturbs me is that the nerve gas was one of ours."

"Are we still making it?"

"No, it was one of the early, experimental types."

"Authorized when the Tories were in?" the P.M. asked hopefully.

"Difficult to pin down an exact date. You know how cagey they are at Porton." Bayldon cleared his throat. "The other disturbing thing is that the information appears to have been leaked to the Opposition. My office tells me they're going to raise the matter at Question Time."

The P.M. exploded at this. "I don't bloody believe our present luck!"

"In fairness to Toby," the Foreign Secretary interjected, "it has to be said that when we were sitting on the other side we were overjoyed to be the recipients of a leak."

"It doesn't help to state the obvious, Sam. What some of you don't seem to realize is that we're sitting on a powder keg. Look at the latest opinion polls. It's not the terrorist campaign that'll bring us down, it'll be us pissing on our own doorstep if we're not careful. What I want to know, and fast: is Glanville the tip of another iceberg? Who had the best reason for killing him—us or the Russians?"

"On the face of it, if one is being logical, I suppose the Russians," the Foreign Secretary said. "On the other hand, the last person known to have seen him was somebody from MI6."

"How do we know that?"

"Glanville's hideaway was bugged."

"Who authorized that?"

"I did."

"Why?"

"It's normal practice, George. In any situation such as Glanville's, surveillance is kept up. I saw no reason to part from tradition in his case. The man was a self-acknowledged traitor."

The P.M. grunted. "Are the Yanks aware of any of this?"

"They're usually not far behind us."

"I've already got them round my neck night and day. Just one more scare and they'll pull out."

"There's a large body of opinion within the Party—in fact, within the country as a whole—that would welcome such a move, George."

This comment came from the Minister for Social Services, the Right Honorable Graham Lewisham. Like Bayldon, he had only been elevated to Cabinet rank so that the P.M. could keep tabs on him. In the customary slugging match that always took place when the next Leader of the Labour Party was being chosen, Lewisham had come close to securing the necessary majority on the first ballot; only the most devious behind-the-scenes bartering and payoffs had ensured the P.M.'s emergence as the outright winner on the second. Lewisham was the darling of the Far Left, one of nature's born snipers, a brilliant self-publicist who possessed great appeal for grass-roots members. Although one of his pet hobbyhorses was the corrupt Tory-controlled press, he was a past master at manipulating the media for his own ends, and never missed an opportunity to appear on television. The media had fallen headlong into the trap, and faithfully presented him as the bogeyman of the Left; he was, after all, "good copy" and they gave him more space and air time than his intellect warranted. He operated on the tried and tested method beloved of all demagogues: that what's important isn't the quality of the half-truth, but the number of times you repeat it. His command of unsubstantiated statistics was impressive, and his speeches were spattered with references to the "democratic process"; he was a champion of open government and for worker participation in boardroom decisions. He was at his most dangerous when seeming to be most rational, and he had unlimited ambition.

"If you want to quote 'the country as a whole,' Graham, you might also remember they only gave us thirty-eight percent of the vote, so I don't think we should feel too sanguine."

"It was part of our manifesto that we would end our dependence on American nuclear weapons."

"I don't need reminding of what was in the manifesto; I wrote most of the bloody thing! Unfortunately, events have overtaken us. This is not the time to rock the boat. The country is in a highly nervous state—and not because of the presence of Yank missiles in our midst, but because of terrorist attacks. Once we get that situation under control we can turn our attention to the wider issues. Agreed?"

He looked around the room and received a general consent. Lewisham, however, was not finished. "I hope we don't achieve that admirable aim, George, through the establishment of a police state. We've already taken the widest emergency powers ever seen in times of peace."

"That's my point: we're *not* at peace. How can you say we're at peace when practically every day acts of war are being committed against the civilian population?"

"Certain information which has reached me, and which I am in the process of checking, points to CIA involvement." The CIA conspiracy theory was one of Lewisham's favorites; it always assured him of a full house when he spoke at universities. "Be that as it may, the point I am trying to make is that I firmly believe our strategy is being deliberately, cynically manipulated. By our present actions we are betraying our own working class."

"Fine, duly noted," the P.M. said. "But I tell you this much: if you can bring me cast-iron evidence that the Yanks, in an election year, have set about killing scores of their own servicemen and wives stationed in this country, then I'll personally supervise the removal of every nuclear warhead. But until that time, we've got to get the economy right and bring back some law and order. And it might interest you to know that since we took these emergency powers our popularity has moved up a couple of points."

Lewisham was not to be silenced. "A workers' militia might be even more popular."

"Try telling that to the man in the street. I think you'd find he'd rather put his trust in the SAS. Let's move on, shall we? Toby, where do we stand?"

"I don't want to usurp anything Sam might be going to say," Bayldon began, with a nod towards the Foreign Secretary, "but in recent days the police have made considerable progress. The Special Branch carried out widespread raids at dawn yesterday morning in Norwich, Southampton and Liverpool, as a result of which over thirty arrests were made and a very large cache of weapons and explosives were uncovered. My latest information is that we might have a real breakthrough."

"What sort of breakthrough?"

"One of the suspects arrested is wanted by the Israelis in connection with the Munich murders. It's been the view of the police all along that although there could well have been some coordination with the IRA, this current wave of attacks is the work of much larger, regrouped Red Brigades, almost certainly financed out of Russia. Do you want to add to that, Sam?"

The Foreign Secretary got to his feet. "Yes, I think in broad terms that's also the view of MI5 and MI6. I met with both Directors just before I came here, and according to information they're getting back from our people in the Eastern bloc, the KGB have been pushing out big funds recently. Apparently there was a power struggle inside the KGB six months back, the outcome of which was that a new hard-liner gained control and immediately instigated a tougher line. Our problem has always been keeping ahead of them, and there I do think the Yanks have a genuine grievance. It's no good pretending our own security has been watertight. At times it's been like a sieve."

"Yes, well, we'll come back to that. But I'm slightly confused," the P.M. said. "Toby mentioned Israel, now you're talking about the KGB. Have I missed the connection?"

"It all points to a carefully orchestrated campaign aimed at forcing our hand. The Russians don't mind who they use. They're only too delighted if others do their work for them. Their peace offensive failed miserably—after all, the missiles are installed—so they've switched tactics, and to that extent they've succeeded. We're not the only ones to have suffered, as you well know; every NATO country has had its share. It comes back to Graham's hope. What they're up to is to create the sort of climate which will make the Yanks pull out, because of our instability."

"That is a complete distortion of what I said," Lewisham interrupted.

"Well, in so many words."

"No. Quite the reverse."

"Don't let's argue the toss," the P.M. said abruptly; he was not prepared to suffer another Lewisham lecture. "At least some progress has been made, then, and God knows we need a few lucky breaks. Now, what about our intelligence? Are there any more Glanvilles about to crawl out of the woodwork?"

"Don't tempt fate," Bayldon said.

"Well, he's the Fifth Man," the Foreign Secretary replied. "And the five were all of the same generation, so we can only cross our fingers and hope that it's five down and no more to go."

But at that very moment the Secretary to the Cabinet entered the room and handed the P.M. a note. When the P.M. finished reading it, his expression made it obvious that the crossing of fingers had not proved effective. He rounded on the Foreign Secretary. "You said something earlier regarding Glanville, something about the last person to see him being an MI6 man. What was his name, do you remember?"

"Hill-something, I think."

"Hillsden?"

"Yes, that was it."

"Well, you spoke too soon. This is from Special Branch. They've every reason to suspect that Hillsden's defected."

27

THE DREAM WAS muddled, bordering on nightmare, but never quite slipping over the edge into that all too familiar bottomless pit. Sometimes he was in a field, not unlike the dark fens surrounding Glanville's last resting place, and he was digging with his bare hands, digging for dear life but making no discernible progress. Then, like pages flipped in a photo album, the landscape changed and he was standing by an open grave. Everywhere was as quiet as during those elongated moments on Armistice Day just before the guns sounded the end of the two minutes' silence, with the crowds in Whitehall turned to stone. He could see into the grave, but there was no coffin, and as he looked the hole filled with water. He saw what at first he took to be his own reflection, but as he knelt on the newly disturbed earth at the edge of the grave the surface of the water was rippled by a sudden wind and the image fractured. As the water cleared again he could discern the upturned hull of a boat far below. Then, as though disturbed by hidden currents, the hull slowly rotated, releasing a body trapped beneath it. But instead of the body rising to him, he was drawn down into the dazzled bottle-green depths, bubbles streaming past him like tracer bullets until his outstretched diver's hands touched and turned the corpse. At the moment of contact, lumps of bleached flesh parted from the bone, the features coming away whole like a mask, eeling past him. He twisted to catch a last glimpse of Jock's drowned face before it was lost in the darker waters beneath. Then he was on dry land again, climbing in a spiral, his feet slipping on stone steps. There was light above and a figure beckoning to him at the top of the steps. He climbed without making progress, hearing himself shouting Caroline's name, but in the end it wasn't Caroline who stood waiting to receive him, it was Belfrage. "Are you feeling better now, Mr. Hillsden?" Belfrage asked, except that it wasn't Belfrage's voice. He opened his eyes to brightness to find the man called Hansel bending over him.

"I must apologize for what happened. Quite unforgivable, and the man responsible has been disciplined. No lasting damage, I hope? Such an unfortunate welcome."

As the last strands of the dream receded, Hillsden gradually focused on his surroundings. He was lying on a bed in a room he had never seen before. It appeared to be night, for the curtains were drawn and lights were burning. Attempting to sit upright, he was stabbed by a pain that seemed to fill his head.

"The trouble is that today we're dealing with a new breed. They lack any sense of moderation; it's all so violent. They seem to think that brute force solves every problem, whereas you and I know it achieves little or nothing."

Hillsden struggled to comprehend what he was saying, but the words came to him through a fog.

"I've had some food prepared for you," Hansel continued, "but if it's not to your liking, do let me know. I would hate you to think that my hospitality was lacking in any way. I'll leave you to enjoy it. When you've fully recovered we'll talk again." He paused by the door. "Oh, I brought you the English papers, too."

Left alone, Hillsden examined himself with care. Apart from the ache at the base of his skull he appeared to be in one piece, though he continued to move with caution. The thought of food revolted him, but he sipped the glass of wine that accompanied the meal on the bedside tray. It was some time before the initial dizziness wore off and he was able to take stock of the situation. "We're being picked off one by one," Control had said, and it seemed closer to the truth now. Not that he imagined they intended to kill him so early in the game. Equally, he could find little of comfort in Hansel's explanation. It was standard practice to present two sides of the same coin: we're all familiar with that technique, he thought. There's one to hit you and one to pick you up and dust you off; it speeded the process of disorientation. Now, as some of his old alertness returned, he began to tick off his options, taking them in sequence from the moment when Control had first outlined his scenario.

"As I see it," Control had said, "it has a certain logical progression. That's why I believe they'll take the bait. But if I'm right, when they come looking for you, don't make it easy for them. Strike a hard bargain, as hard as the traffic will bear. Show them you're angry, let them think you're doing it for the money, to get even after the way you've been treated. So much more plausible a motive, don't you think, than idealism? It is, after all, the way we capitalists traditionally operate—for personal gain. What they'll want to know is how close we are to finding the last piece of the puzzle that began with Philby, and there you'll have to box very cleverly, since we're no closer than we ever were. I know how you hate the journalistic clichés, but we're stuck with them, and the word 'supermole' is common currency. Call him what you will, he's still intact, still calling the tunes. You and I have no illusions there. How else could Glanville have escaped his just deserts for so long? Somebody considered him neutered until you overstepped the mark."

"But you were the one who first warned me off."

"I was acting in your best interests. I've never believed that Glanville was God the Father, Son and Holy Ghost. He was protecting whoever protected him. A maze within a maze, Alec. But you chose to ignore my good advice. That's the impulsive streak in you. It's held you back, Alec, denied you the promotion your talents deserve. Our lords and masters feel uneasy with individuality. They like the status quo, the comforting warmth of what was shall always be, forever and ever, amen. I sometimes think they will us to stumble and fail; it's something that gives them more power over us. They can never quite come to terms with the fact that we are a secret organization. They like to hold all the secrets in their own hand. That's the essence of the political mind: not government of the people, but against the people. 'Trust the people'— Churchill's father said that, but it wasn't a vote catcher and it did for him. He died of syphilis," Control added, as though, Hillsden thought, there was a connection between Lord Randolph's philosophy and his social behavior.

"Are you trying to tell me that somebody on our side had Glanville killed?"

"I think it's more than possible, don't you?"

"No, that's too deep for me to take in right away."

"Surely not? Given the history of his generation of fellow travelers, and the fact that many of them were so incestuously joined? The romance of those interwar years, the seduction of following a cause that gave them an affinity with the working class? It was the salve they could apply against privilege. They used their privileges, but at the same time they were ashamed of them; they needed, as old Somerset Maugham once said, to get down in the gutter and roll in the common dirt. But in the end, if a choice has to be made, it's the privileges that have to be protected, not the cause."

"Okay, but why wait until now?" Hillsden persisted. "Why grant him amnesty in the first place? He didn't suddenly become more dangerous. What he knew he knew from the beginning, so why not dispose of him earlier?"

"Maybe the fuse was relit with Caroline's murder, and this time it started to burn too close to the source. I daresay you're right. *He* didn't suddenly become more dangerous; perhaps *you* did."

"What did he tell me? Nothing of any great value. Just a reference to Jock—something Jock had told him, and we can't bring Jock back from the grave to testify."

"He was scared, though, when you turned up on his doorstep. Class again, Alec. You weren't of his class, and that automatically betokened menace. In Glanville's world he only felt secure dealing with his own kind. You have to remember that the whole dismal package has always been tied together with an old Etonian tie. Whoever had him killed didn't like the idea of a scholarship boy knocking on the last door. It was somebody with inside knowledge, somebody who had marked your card. That's why I've proposed this present course. You have a particular reason for wanting to lay Caroline's ghost."

"Not her ghost," Hillsden said. "I don't believe in ghosts. But a chance to find her killer—yes, I'd go back for that."

"You're under no compulsion, of course; the idea can die here," Control said half apologetically, Stanley Baldwin surfacing one last time. He cracked his knuckles.

"It would have to be made watertight."

"Yes, naturally. But I don't think it's beyond our capabilities to devise a convincing scenario. You start with the reputation of a maverick."

"And what do I take with me?"

Control stared at him as though he was suddenly confronting a stranger. "Oh, I'll let you raid the larder for some juicy tidbits, bones with meat on them. Real bones with real meat on them, but ones that we've no further use for. I'd hardly send you out empty-handed."

"I'd be working alone, I take it?"

"That depends on where your journey ends."

"And when they've finished with me?"

"We'll arrange a trade—after a decent interval, naturally. It wouldn't do to move too quickly. And I'd see to it that you got to keep whatever they paid you. I'm sure it will be more generous than our pension."

Except that nothing was ever generous in the profession they followed. All the price tags had been fixed long ago and there were no end-of-season sales, no bargain basements for the fainthearted.

The effort of memory had pushed the pain in his head further back. He got off the bed and tested his legs, going to the window to pull back the curtains. The room overlooked a large terrace, floodlit at intervals down to the lake. He could detect the chug of an outboard motor, though the double-glazed windows muffled the sound. Examining the rest of the room, he came back to the bed and picked up one of the English newspapers that Hansel had provided. It bore that day's date. The headlines were mostly about the current unrest and the government's inability to get on top of the situation. Then an item tucked away at the bottom of the front page caught his eye and broke his dream. Under a caption that said "Diplomat found murdered" was a photograph of Belfrage. He read the report twice, but the preliminary details were few, the news having only just made the early editions. The only part of the story that struck him as odd was the address where the murder had taken place, described as a pied-à-terre in Belgravia. From what he knew, Belfrage kept a small flat in Westminster close to his office and a country house just outside Oxford. He remembered the night they had both waited for Hogg's verdict on Caroline, the same night that Bayldon's car had been blown up; perhaps, after all, that had been meant for Belfrage and now somebody had made sure of him the second time around. But who would want to kill Belfrage? First Caroline, then Glanville and now Belfrage, he thought, and from all three there is a path back to me.

He sat and waited for Hansel to return, trying to discern the flaw in the patchwork of deceits. Instinct told him that nothing was ever that simple; there had to be something beyond the evidence. He traced back along the route he had traveled so far. Every avenue he explored led, inexorably, to only one conclusion—a conclusion so monstrous that he could not allow himself to entertain it. But it refused to go away.

"WILL the Prime Minister assure this House there is no substantial cause to suppose that the recent tragic death of a prominent civil servant is in any way linked with a breach of national security?"

The eagerly awaited question was delivered to a packed House of Commons, and the Prime Minister fielded it as best he could in the circumstances, giving the usual and inconclusive denial that custom demanded and his scant briefing allowed. Two supplementary questions from his own backbenchers were likewise deflected.

As soon as Question Time was over, the P.M. returned to Downing Street to preside over a meeting of his inner Cabinet, which was also attended by Control, the Commissioner of the Metropolitan Police, and that unique triumvirate known as the Three Advisers who had ultimate responsibility for the Positive Vetting system. The Prime Minister was in no mood to be smoke-screened. Control bore the brunt of his opening attack.

"Before we go any further, I want a straight answer to a straight question. Notwithstanding the statement I've just made to the House, am I to believe there is a direct link between the late Sir Charles Belfrage and an officer of your department who recently disappeared and may well have gone over to the other side? True or false?"

"I wouldn't call it a direct link, Prime Minister. They maintained normal contacts when the occasion demanded."

"Normal contacts?"

"Yes, sir."

"That could cover anything from sharing a McDonald's hamburger to pissing in the same pot. I'd hardly call anything in your sphere of operations *normal,* so don't give me jargon, give me the facts."

"I think the Home Secretary will recall he consulted both men following the death, in somewhat blurred circumstances, of one of our ex-operators."

"Can we call them what they are, secret agents?"

"As you wish. Officially, it's a term we try to avoid, Prime Minister."

Bayldon slipped a memo to his leader, and the P.M. glanced at it, then returned to his attack on Control. "I can recall a time when, *officially,* your position didn't exist. And to this day we *officially* maintain that your department is only a figment of the popular imagination. Weighing your meager successes against your embarrassment of failures, it could well be that at some future date the fictions should become facts. At the moment, however, to return to the specifics, we are talking about a woman called Oates, I believe?"

"Yes, Prime Minister."

"And in her case there *is* a clear connection with this possible defector—"

"Hillsden," Bayldon murmured.

"—this man Hillsden?"

"Historically they served in the field together, but in recent years he had no contact with her."

"So that's link number two. But we also know that the net spreads even further, taking in that other old nancy traitor Glanville. Link number three. Equally, it isn't the best-kept secret that Belfrage and Glanville were up at Cambridge together, and that for a certain period Belfrage was a member of the Communist Party." He swung around on the Three Advisers and tapped his yellow dispatch box. "I'd like to think your information is as accurate as mine?"

The senior member of the trio, an ex-admiral not easily intimidated by politicians of any grade, looked him straight in the eye. "Yes, he made no concealment of that."

"And you cleared him, not once but on three separate occasions?"

"Where such admissions are freely given, we usually allow youthful indiscretions, providing there are no other adverse pointers. As I'm sure you are aware, Prime Minister, at least two members of your own administration followed the same undergraduate route, and of course their integrity is beyond question. One has to remember the temperature of the political waters at the time such affiliations were made. In the Thirties we had Spain, and during the last war the epic of Stalingrad— all very understandable if viewed in those contexts."

It was the report of a seasoned survivor, and the P.M. knew better than to pursue him further. Instead he now framed his venom in more general terms.

"Gentlemen, let me educate you all. A ruling class on the run is capable of anything. Some of you people don't seem to have grasped that your world has changed. We're running the ship now, and if certain remnants from the old order think they can still call the tune, they have to be disabused of that notion. So let me make certain things crystal clear. This government has no intention of letting its authority be undermined by the incompetence of those charged with maintaining the security of the realm in all its aspects. Quite apart from this present flap, we are faced with an unprecedented wave of terrorism. What I want is an end to excuses, an end to the deliberate withholding of vital information, and a start made on producing positive results. My own private office supplies me with more intelligence than I have so far received from you gentlemen, and that is not a situation I am prepared to tolerate a moment longer. That said, let us recap. We have the death of Miss Oates, the murder of Glanville and now the murder of the unfortunate Sir Charles. The common link would appear to be this man Hillsden, so the question to be answered is 'Why?' " He turned to the Commissioner. "I suppose it would be too much to hope that the Special Branch have come up with something?"

"Since there was no evidence of robbery, Sir Charles appears to have been the victim of a deliberate assassination carried out by a professional. The only other factor that has come to light is that in all probability he was leading a double life."

"Are you saying he was a double agent?"

"No, sir. I mean he was having an affair. His wife was apparently unaware that he kept a secondary residence, though of course we shouldn't necessarily connect his extramarital activities with any security problems."

"In my opinion the two frequently go together. A man who is unfaithful to his wife has demonstrated that he is devious and not to be trusted. He was dealing with classified material, was he not?"

"Yes, almost exclusively."

"Christ, what a bloody mess! Do we know who the other woman is?"

"No, he seems to have been remarkably discreet. At the moment his charlady is our prime source of information. She claims to have come across articles of clothing which in her opinion were not his wife's; in addition, and perhaps more damning, she says he kept pornographic photographs in the flat. All hearsay, because nothing was found."

"Was he being blackmailed, do you think?" Bayldon interjected.

"There's always that possibility. We're checking into his bank accounts."

"Well, let me put my false teeth on the table," the P.M. said, with traces of his original Northern accent coming through. "I don't want anybody to be under any illusions where my government is concerned. I don't give a damn about the old boys' network. If the stables have to be cleaned out, let's get it over and done with, and to hell with who gets their fingers burned," he ranted, jumbling his metaphors. "I've watched enough Tory cover-ups in my time, and I don't intend this administration to be nobbled by a bunch of high flyers and fellow travelers. If anybody's going to do any muck-spreading, let it be us rather than Fleet Street. Cut the shit from under them, in other words."

It was a passionate, if somewhat disjointed, battle cry, and as he consulted the papers in his yellow box the Three Advisers exchanged sympathetic glances with the Commissioner.

"Now, I want an update on the terror campaign. I've got a summit meeting in Washington coming up, and the Yanks are still feeling very bloody-minded where we're concerned. Give me some good news for a change. Maurice couldn't make this meeting"—a reference to the Secretary of State for Northern Ireland—"but I have his latest report. As far as the IRA are concerned, the gloves have come off. The Army is now empowered to operate on a shoot-to-kill basis. That's off the record, but the facts will shortly start to speak for themselves. We're bound to get some flak, but public opinion has hardened in the past month and I'm prepared to weather any storms."

"Does Dublin know?" somebody asked.

"Yes," the Foreign Secretary answered, "and they're prepared to play it our way."

"But we need results here at home," the P.M. continued. "We've got to restore public confidence. We need to show that we're getting on top of the situation, that we're not a soft touch."

"We've already taken very wide powers," Bayldon said. "I think politically we have to tread carefully. Our own backbenchers are already very touchy."

"They'll be a bloody sight touchier if we lose the next election. My main concern is our own intelligence. As far as I can make out, every bloody department is as full of leaks as a sieve." Once again he addressed the Three Advisers: "Your system could do with some tightening up. We all know what's happened in the past. God Almighty, just look at the record! Members of the Queen's personal staff, senior officers of the Met, and a buggers' charter in the Foreign Office."

"Always a difficult line to draw in a democracy, Prime Minister," one of the three murmured.

"I agree," Bayldon said.

"You may agree, Toby, but at the rate we're going on there won't be a democracy to draw a line in."

"It's also a question of manpower, Prime Minister," the Commissioner said. "My forces are very stretched at the moment. At any given moment I've got a third on picket duties. And I have to warn you, sir, that the next set of figures are going to show a hefty increase in crime. I need to put more men on the street."

The discussion went back and forth without any conclusions being reached. However, just before the meeting broke up, the Prime Minister received one small consolation. A message was brought to him from the Cornish police: articles of clothing identified as belonging to Hillsden had been washed up near Falmouth, and an intensive sea search of the area was now being mounted.

"Well, that's something," the Prime Minister said. "With any luck the bastard committed suicide and saved us the cost of a trial." But he noticed that Control did not share the joke.

28

THE OTHERS AGREED that they had seldom seen Waddington so angry. "I don't buy it," he said vehemently. "They can say what they like, but nobody's going to convince me that Alec was the suicidal type."

"Oh, I don't know," Rotherby countered, just to be difficult; baiting Waddington was one of his keenest pleasures. "A natural progression. He was passed over, passed by, and now he's passed on. Not that he ever struck me as having anything much to live for."

"You do talk the most unutterable balls."

"Well, he failed with the Firm and he failed in the old matrimonial stakes. That's a full house in my book. He'd just had enough."

"What about Glazer's theory?" Fenton chimed in, attempting to lower the temperature. "That has more of the ring of truth about it."

"Glazer's theory?"

"Yes, you remember. She insisted she had second sight, that she could see the Grim Reaper in his face. Terminal condition. If she was right, that might explain everything."

"You're both assuming that the evidence is conclusive. Just because his clothes are washed up on a beach proves bugger all."

"Dead or alive, does it matter? He's tasted the last of our summer wine."

Waddington was not to be placated. Through a contact in Special Branch he tracked the progression of Hillsden's decline and fall. Apart from the incident in the first prison when he suffered an injury to his foot, there was nothing sinister on his record sheet. As far as Waddington could ascertain, nobody in the prison had been aware of Hillsden's connection with the security service. This was further established when he located the Probation Officer who had arranged Hillsden's stay with the Brothers of Mercy. Waddington journeyed down to Plymouth, and on the pretext that he was a relative he was successful in interviewing several of the Brothers. What they were able to tell him of Hillsden's state of mind and general demeanor while he was under their care further convinced him that any question of suicide was doubtful. He was given permission to talk to some of the other inmates, but all he could glean from these conversations was that Hillsden had formed no real friendships; he had kept to the rules and to himself.

Before returning to London, Waddington made other inquiries in the district, and later drove on to the Falmouth area where Hillsden's clothes had been washed up. Despite prolonged searches, both the Coast Guards and the Air-Sea Rescue units had drawn a blank. He came away even more convinced that his instincts were right.

Waddington never learned how news of these activities reached Control, but within a few hours of his return he was summoned to the presence.

"I'm at a loss to understand you, Waddington," Control said. "And I can't help thinking what a waste it would be if this excess of zeal on your part—misguided zeal, in my opinion—were to blight what has hitherto been a promising career. But blighted it most certainly will prove if you continue to flout quite explicit orders."

"He was a friend, and I don't believe this suicide story."

"Is it of any consequence what you believe?"

"It's of consequence to me."

"Let me explain the facts of life, Waddington. I'll try to keep them simple, since you appear to need some simple guidance on how to conduct yourself. Amazing though it may seem to you, you are not the only one perplexed by recent events. It has perhaps escaped your notice that our very existence is currently under threat. Our activities, our lack of success, are under close scrutiny. We are being looked at with jaundiced eyes. Every move we make is suspect. There is a growing feeling in Whitehall that we have been given too much rope in the past, that we have abused our powers and must be brought to heel. We are accused of complacency and grave errors of judgment at senior levels, and I emphasize the word *senior*. I can reveal to you that the Prime Minister has ordered a Commission of Enquiry, and its brief is to give particular reference to our methods of recruitment. I gather that it is felt—and in view of past events one can't argue with this—that we attract the wrong types."

Waddington listened with growing irritation. "What's all that got to do with Alec's disappearance?"

"Kindly allow me to finish. We are a necessary evil, only tolerated at the best of times if we keep our heads down and don't make waves.

The harsh reality is that, with the exception of the film industry, for which we provide lucrative fictions, nobody likes us. You see, it has never been clearly established who our real enemy is—he varies, according to which government is in power. The Tories have never forgiven us for betraying their own class. Labour governments distrust us for seeing Reds under their beds. Either way we can't win. Officially we are always neutral, serving whichever government is democratically elected."

"Yes, I am aware of our historical role."

"But are you aware that if we do our job properly, we can't be neutral? It's a contradiction in terms." Control carefully squared the blotter on his already neat desk. "It's a dangerous time to step out of line, Waddington. It was Hillsden's mistake to do that."

"You know, don't you?" Waddington said.

"What do I know?"

"What happened to him after he left here."

"I know some of it, as indeed you do, having disregarded my advice."

"Alec wasn't the man to just walk out."

"People do, you know—saints as well as sinners. There are no hard-and-fast rules. Still, I'm sure you have a theory of your own."

"Well, for a start, I don't buy suicide. If he's dead, then it wasn't by his own hand. I think he stumbled onto something, some echo from the past that came to light after Caroline's death. I was closer to him than anybody, don't forget. What else could make him behave so out of character? Don't tell me he was caught doctoring his expenses or stealing the petty cash. He didn't suddenly rape one of the secretaries. None of that fits. Nor was it like him to pick a fight with some flagrant old queen in a gay bar."

"There you're wrong. That was proven. He served a jail sentence for it."

"Then he had a reason. Alec *always* had a reason. He played it strictly by the book. And he cared, he bloody *cared*. Caroline wasn't just a name on a card index to him. He loved her. You know it and I know it."

"Sometimes," Control said, at his most unctuous, "love is the greatest betrayer of all. That's why the divorce courts work overtime."

"God, you're smug! Doesn't any of it matter to you?"

"You're not going to let it rest, are you, Waddington?"

"Damn right I'm not."

"Then perhaps you should know a little more, though I doubt whether it will do you any good. I can't tell you what the end of the story is, because I don't know it. Nor do I necessarily believe what I've been told. The difference between you and me is that I've never been surprised that a man suddenly changes completely the direction of his life—certainly not in our line of business. We don't lead natural lives. We are asked to carry out dishonorable acts for what we believe are honorable causes. But often the dividing line is blurred."

There was a note of tiredness, of resignation, in Control's voice, as if he, too, had been exhausted by the burden of a lifetime's service to deceit. "I can tell this much, because in all probability it will be public knowledge very shortly. I'm given to understand that sufficient evidence will be produced to charge Hillsden, dead or alive, with the murder of Sir Charles Belfrage. So, for his sake, let's hope he is dead."

29

PRIVATELY, HILLSDEN NICKNAMED the two blond goons Fortnum and Mason. The joke was nothing much, but it helped. He took it that one of them had been responsible for the violence on his arrival, and was in little doubt that their only function was as musclemen, to be kept in reserve as and when required. Hansel had been at some pains to excuse their behavior, but he dismissed this as being part of the old cat-and-mouse technique. They wore more or less identical clothes, and both moved with limp, insolent ease, as though they had based their characters on gangster movies. He marked them down as very butch gays, and the more dangerous as a result. They brought him his meals and accompanied him during exercise periods in the grounds. He was locked into his room at night, but otherwise allowed the freedom of the villa, though one or the other of the blonds was always present. He made no attempt to engage them in conversation. The courier who had taken over from the girl at Cherbourg, and whose name he had never learned, was no longer in evidence.

Hansel made no attempt to begin the preliminary debriefing, and Hillsden tried to rationalize this. He had no illusions about what eventually lay ahead. It wasn't a rest cure they were offering; they would want full value for their time and money, and he tried to fathom reasons for the delay. The more he went back over the sequence of events, the more he became convinced that they must have had advance notice of his intention to defect. He based this on the speed with which they had moved. From the moment when the girl had first made contact with him on the beach, they had wasted no time in spiriting him out of the country. Because of this he found the subsequent lack of urgency more puzzling. Long familiarity with Moscow Centre's methods dictated that there must be a reason for the hiatus. Somewhere there was a warning to be heeded, and he spent long hours trying to decide what it might be without coming up with a satisfactory answer. He kept returning to the episode with the girl on the boat: why? She was an enigma, an alien piece of the puzzle, somehow she did not fit the overall picture. Why had she given herself like that? He could not bring himself to entertain the idea that it was just a shared physical urgency, like some quick adolescent rutting, taken and forgotten, so that often there was no recollection of the partner's face.

What was it she had said? "You're different from what I'd imagined." Didn't that betoken prior knowledge? "You're attracted to me." And that had been true. As much as anything else he needed to explain it to himself; the mystery of his own motives gnawed at him, but at the same time he was aware of the dangers in trying to be an amateur psychologist. There were no normal patterns of behavior in the world he inhabited; one always had to guard against applying ordinary standards. Then again, why agonize over it? Perhaps there was nothing to discover, no hidden meaning beyond the lusts and angers of the body. Weren't there some who could still eat a hearty breakfast when only minutes away from death in the electric chair?

Other considerations also troubled him. So far Control's scenario had been played out by half the cast exactly as predicted, but he had been prevented from acting his role.

When not deliberating on these imponderables, he used his time to rehearse the interrogations that inevitably lay ahead. There were moments when he persuaded himself that the hiatus was merely part of Hansel's standard KGB technique. They were sweating him, he decided. First the shock of violence, followed by a period of uncertainty, the constant presence of Fortnum and Mason to keep him guessing about the next move. The Firm seldom resorted to physical force, or at least he had no firsthand knowledge of it, though rumors abounded that the Special Branch could be less than gentle. The usual form was to go in heavily the first day, while the subject was still emotionally crippled by the enormity of the step he had taken: round-the-clock sessions by a team of skilled interrogators, no letup, no sleep, alternating the styles, now friendly, now aggressive, sometimes compassionate, sometimes crude, the object being to keep the subject off balance. Of course there were exceptions. Waddington had always admired Philby's stamina, the way he had stonewalled the best team the Firm had ever fielded; to some the man was still a folk hero, granted the grudging admiration of fellow professionals for having licked the system.

With these thoughts in mind he did everything he could to keep himself alert, though he made a point of shamming nervousness: he wanted his hosts to believe they were scoring points.

Nothing happened until the afternoon of the third day. He was locked in his room finishing his lunch when he heard the sound of a speedboat on the lake. Going to the window, he saw the bright hull of a Riva arcing towards the mooring at the bottom of the terrace steps. There were two figures in the boat, and as the noise of the powerful engine died away, Fortnum and Mason walked down to the water's edge and assisted the male passenger onto dry land. He was bearded, immensely tall and wore a brown leather trench coat. Sunlight glinted on his spectacles as the trio came towards the house. The new arrival looked around fifty, though beards made such guesswork suspect. Like many tall men, he walked with slumped shoulders, and there was something vaguely familiar about him.

It was some twenty minutes before the door of his room was unlocked and Hansel ushered in the stranger.

"My name is Walters," he introduced himself. His handshake was cold and firm. "I apologize for the fact that you have been kept in suspense. We had good reason, I assure you." There was hardly any trace of an accent, though his delivery was stilted, as if his English had been learned from a textbook. Now that they were face-to-face, Hillsden suddenly remembered who it was he was reminded of. The connection was bizarre in the circumstances, but the lupine, bearded face, the eyes all but blanked out by thick pebble glasses, brought to mind that strange doyen of the Bloomsbury set, Lytton Strachey. As the thought struck him he imagined how scathing Jock would have been about such a literary comparison, and it needed an effort of will to keep a straight face.

Walters turned to Hansel. "You don't need to remain. I will tell you when we are finished." Hansel nodded and withdrew. The visitor took off the heavy trench coat and folded it before placing it over the back of a chair. Underneath he wore a well-cut suit made of tweedy woolen cloth.

"Before we discuss anything else, let me dispose of our side of the arrangement. As agreed, a sum equivalent to twenty-five thousand pounds sterling has been deposited in a numbered account with the Kreditanstalt, Geneva. The number will be given to you on completion of our task. You will find you can trust us."

"Can I also trust you to give me a clean passage out when this is finished? That was the other half of the deal. I was promised a once-and-for-all. After you've got what you want from me, I'll be marked forever. My people aren't too well disposed towards defectors. Whatever you think of their general capabilities, they have a long arm. Retirement to the ski slopes would be too close for comfort."

Walters nodded as though agreeing with the wisdom of this. "We are not yet at the point where that decision needs to be taken."

"Then the sooner we get started, the better. Your lot have wasted enough time as it is. For all I know, London is already looking for me." It was difficult for him to discern anything in Walters' expression; it was like staring at a fright mask. "I'm ready if you are." He felt an enormous relief that the waiting was finally over.

"Yes. I appreciate that. Unfortunately, Mr. Hillsden, the original arrangements are no longer viable. Certain events have taken place which force a change of plan. We are going to have to move you to somewhere safer. What you just mentioned is all too true."

Hillsden stared at him, but could see only his own reflection in the thick glasses. "What events?"

"They are indeed already looking for you, though not for the reason one might have expected. Your absence has been noted for another crime."

"You're lying."

Walters shook his head and his spectacles caught the light. "No, we haven't got time for lies, Mr. Hillsden." He picked up his trench coat and took a folded newspaper from one of the pockets. "As you will see, you have made the front pages." He held out the newspaper and Hillsden took it from him. There on the cover of that day's *Standard* was a fuzzy photograph of him in Army uniform. It had been taken years ago but was still a reasonable likeness. Occupying equal space was a formal studio portrait of Belfrage. The headline read: MI6 MAN LINKED WITH DIPLOMAT'S MURDER, and underneath the story began:

Scotland Yard today issued a warrant for the arrest of Alec Hillsden, reliably stated to have been a one-time MI6 agent who left the security service last year in suspicious circumstances, charging him with the recent murder of Sir Charles Belfrage. Sir Charles, a distinguished and senior civil servant in the Russian Section of the Foreign Office, was callously assassinated in his Belgravia flat. Informed sources state that his death had all the hallmarks of a political murder with security implications.

On his dismissal from MI6, Hillsden was given a prison sentence after being arrested and found guilty on a charge of causing grievous bodily harm. After release from prison he is said to have become a vagrant, drifting in and out of various menial jobs. He was subsequently arrested on a second occasion and this time remanded for a psychiatric report. It is understood that he received treatment in a West Country mental home, from which he disappeared in mysterious circumstances shortly before Sir Charles' murder.

Since then his whereabouts have been unknown, but according to a Scotland Yard spokesman, Hillsden is now believed to have escaped abroad, after having engineered a fake suicide by drowning. Interpol have been alerted.

"Have you read enough?"

When Hillsden said nothing, Walters took the newspaper from him and refolded it. "In the circumstances I think you'll agree a change of plan is necessary. We must move with all due speed. All the arrangements are in hand."

"How do I know that isn't a fake? You could have had it specially printed." But even as he said it he knew the real answer. The past and the present fused together, and he realized the trap had finally closed on him: Control had set the whole thing up. It could only have been Control, and he cursed himself for never having suspected it before. The bait had been too clever, too generous, and he had fallen for it.

"You flatter yourself. Why would we go to such ludicrous lengths? We already have you."

"But how could I have murdered Belfrage? You've only got to look at the dates. Nothing fits."

"Whether you did or didn't is of little consequence to us. What matters is that London *says* you did. Your only chance lies with us now."

"What if I don't agree?"

"I realize this has been a shock to you," Walters said, "but you have no option in the matter. As of now, you don't exist except as a hunted man. Without us you are lost. At this moment every police force in your Western democracies is looking for you." He lingered over the word "democracies." "We, on the other hand, can still hold out the promise of a future for you."

"That's your idea of a safer place, is it?" His mind raced to think of an alternative, but he had been boxed in. Control had seen to that. He realized now why there had been no urgency on their part; they had been waiting for Control to put the end of the plan into effect.

"I suggest we don't waste any more time arguing the matter, Mr. Hillsden. Your travel arrangements are prepared. As soon as it is dark we can begin your next journey. Look at it this way: it is, after all, a journey home of sorts."

There was a finality to Walters' small smile, the smile of the jailer who, though an inmate himself, knows that at the end of the day he is free to walk through the prison gates.

30

IT PROVED TO be another acrimonious Cabinet meeting, the third in forty-eight hours, with an array of television cameras recording the arrivals of Ministers at No.10. The stench of panic was heavy.

The latest crisis had come from nowhere, like a hurricane that never shows on the satellite pictures and strikes without warning. As with other examples of what has been termed "the British disease," the trouble began casually enough with what at first seemed a minor incident in a Wolverhampton factory under contract to the Ministry of Defence to make vital components for the Army's latest tactical atomic field gun, a project shrouded in secrecy. The story that finally emerged was that a West Indian welder employed in the machine shop accused one of his white colleagues of making a racist remark. In the scuffle that followed, the white workman fell into an inspection pit; some eyewitnesses maintained that he had slipped, others that he was pushed by his assailant.

The facts were never conclusively established, but the man was taken away in an ambulance suffering from concussion. Shortly after his admission into hospital he had a massive brain hemmorrhage and died on the operating table without regaining consciousness. When mention of the incident was included in the six o'clock news bulletin, the reaction was swift and horrifying. That same night the home of the West Indian in Wolverhampton was firebombed. He and his wife and their two small children perished in the ensuing blaze, and it was quickly confirmed that the fire had been started by a Molotov cocktail thrown from a passing car.

Within hours of this tragic development hitting the headlines there were spontaneous and violent race riots in parts of London, Bristol, Birmingham and Wolverhampton. Despite police reinforcements being rushed to the areas, the savagery could not be contained and continued throughout the night. The police came under attack from both black and white rioters, and after urgent representations from the Chief Constables concerned, the Home Secretary authorized the use of tear gas and rubber bullets to bring the mobs under control. It was the first time such measures had ever been used on the British mainland. When a semblance of order was finally restored, the countrywide death toll was twenty-three, the majority of them black. In the Brixton district of London alone the damage was estimated to run into several million pounds, one whole street having been reduced to rubble. In the course of making hundreds of arrests, the police had also suffered numerous casualties, and a Chief Inspector subsequently died from his injuries. First reports from the various hospitals and emergency services indicated that the use of rubber bullets had been responsible for three of the civilian deaths.

Predictably, public reaction was mixed, though the majority of the population shared a sense of horror and unease: the unthinkable had crept nearer. Every national newspaper, with the exception of the *Guardian* and the Communist *Daily Star,* called for immediate and draconian measures to be taken by the government. The more rabid of the tabloids demanded that martial law be proclaimed and the Army sent into the stricken areas to prevent further looting. This was resisted by the Commissioner of Police, who insisted that he could muster sufficient men and had adequate existing powers to deal with the situation. All police leave was again canceled; units of the Special Patrol Group and marksmen from the crack police D11 section were positioned at strategic points on twenty-four-hour duty.

The Trades Union Congress General Council met in emergency session and passed a resolution condemning what it termed "unprecedented police brutality towards the black community," and called upon the government to immediately ban any further use of rubber bullets. A second resolution called upon all member unions to stage a nationwide one-day general strike, with protest marches in all the major cities.

It was in this volatile atmosphere that the Prime Minister presided over the Cabinet meeting. Arrangements had been made for him to address the nation over all television and broadcasting channels that

239

evening. He was on a very short fuse and in no mood for compromise. "I don't want any time wasted discussing the methods adopted by the police," he began. "The order was necessary, and was given by the Home Secretary with my full blessing."

"I'm sorry, Prime Minister," Lewisham said in his usual unctuous fashion, "but I have to insist that we do discuss and indeed question that decision." He bunched his papers together like a woman patting butter, and took in the others around the table. "This Cabinet was constituted on the clear understanding that all major policy decisions would be a matter of collective responsibility. I only agreed to serve under that condition. It is a question of principle, and I stand on it."

"What principles would you have used last night when the firebombs were being hurled?"

"With all due respect, that remark has no relevance."

"I'll tell you how much relevance it has! There was a bloody good chance that the police would have been overwhelmed. When the request came in, two chief constables stated that otherwise their men would have to withdraw and leave the streets to the mobs. At one point in Brixton they were outnumbered by fifty to one."

"Nevertheless, the Cabinet should have voted on it."

"You live in a bloody dreamworld, Graham. What do you mean, 'vote on it'? You think we could have asked for a cease-fire while you made up your mind? People were dying out there."

Lewisham regarded him without any change of expression. "There are clear indications that the police used last night's tragic events as an excuse to continue their known bias against black communities, one of which I have the honor to represent. The use of tear gas and rubber bullets was a monstrous overreaction that calls for immediate condemnation. I never thought I would see the day when a Labour government sanctioned the use of arms against the working class."

There was a general lowering of heads and shuffling of papers around the table.

"It's typical of you to make such an accusation," the Prime Minister retorted. "You know as well as I do that we had no option. And it wasn't a declaration of war against the working class. It was the proper response, the *only* response, a studied and necessary step to contain mob violence."

"It is the word 'necessary' that I question. That has yet to be proved, and I wish to put my profound disagreement on record. I also want an undertaking that any further decisions of a similar nature are not authorized without the backing of the entire Cabinet."

"Is that intended to be an ultimatum?" the Prime Minister asked at his most glacial. "Because if so, I am quite prepared to accept your resignation."

His bluff called, Lewisham reached for his dispatch case and began to collect his papers together. He rose to his feet. "Very well. You will have my letter stating my reasons for resigning as soon as I return to my office."

There was silence as he left the room. The Prime Minister gave no outward sign of concern, and consulted the agenda. "Item One. Emergency powers. I'll ask the Home Secretary to speak on this, and then I want a short go round the table. We've got a lot to get through."

LATER in the day the Prime Minister had a secret meeting upstairs in his apartment with his Press Officer, one of his oldest and most intimate associates. They had been together ever since he had first stood for election back in the Forties, and knew each other's weaknesses and strengths.

"We're in a right bugger's mess, Charlie. First of all, how should we handle Lewisham's resignation? You've seen his letter, haven't you?"

"Yes. Bloody little hypocrite. Won't do him any good."

"Maybe not in the long term, but we shouldn't underestimate him right now. He's capable of making a lot of waves. You can bet your life he's already fixed himself some time on television. You'd better draft me a reply. Rather you than anybody downstairs. Don't thank the bastard for past services, because he's given none."

"Right. Will do."

"Have you had any soundings back yet?"

"I was straight off the mark, phoning round the country, and although there's a strong feeling of disquiet—I wouldn't put it any stronger than that—most of our people approve of the action taken. Predictably, the race-relations industry is having a field day."

"Aye, well we have to live with that. What do the Whips think?"

"They've been ferreting, and I've spoken to all of them. If you're forced to a division in the debate, the Tories will abstain."

"How about our own lot? That's what I'm more concerned with."

"The estimate is that about seven will vote with Lewisham, but you'll scrape home with the help of the odds and sods."

"What's the mood in Fleet Street?"

"Well, you saw how they handled it this morning. With the two exceptions, most of the Lobby correspondents believe you'll get a clear run. I might have to do a bit of horse-trading."

"Such as?"

"Well, they're all sniffing around the Belfrage case. They can smell another major spy scandal. I was thinking that an inspired leak might not come amiss. It could divert some attention from the present crisis if we threw them that bone. You know how they drool over that sort of thing."

The Prime Minister shook his head. "Bad idea. Don't like it. Dangerous. We've got enough on our plate as it is. If it was traced back to you, we'd be dropped in the shit. Plus it would give Lewisham even more ammunition."

"Okay, just a thought. I should tell you there has been a development in the case."

"What?"

"Somebody's come forward saying he spotted Hillsden on the Channel ferry—some football fan. Reckons he saw Hillsden with a young girl. The police are checking it out, but if true, it substantiates that he has defected."

"Just concentrate on Lewisham. I wish *he'd* bloody defect. Now I've got to get on with my speech. I'm due at the Palace in an hour."

He rang for his private secretary to bring him the draft of his speech. While deciding on its final form he received an update on the riot situation. Two more of the seriously injured had died in hospital, but there had been no further outbreaks and the situation was described as "stable." He again discussed with the Commissioner of Police the question of bringing in the Army, but it was left that the Commissioner would merely liaise with the GOC Southern Command for the time being, and that the Army should be used only as a last resort. The Commissioner advised the Prime Minister that he would be sealing off Whitehall, Parliament and Trafalgar Squares an hour prior to his broadcast, and that the proposed demonstration organized by the TUC would be diverted to Hyde Park.

None of this gave the Prime Minister any comfort, and it was with a sense of unease that he set off for his audience with the Monarch. He drove from Downing Street to Buckingham Palace with a strong police escort, noting that crowds had gathered along the route. Most of his anger was reserved for the Judas in his midst. He had always known that Lewisham was a supreme political opportunist, and had discounted his token loyalty; even so, their public rift had come sooner than expected. Promoting him to a Cabinet post had seemed the best way of keeping him neutered, and it was savagely ironical that outside events had provided the man with the perfect motive for resigning. Lewisham's pious breast-beating on behalf of the working classes was transparently bogus, but it was a clever public-relations job. The P.M. had to admit that it fooled a lot of people and commanded admiration in many quarters, especially with the militant Left. Like every Labour leader before him, he had always known that the real challenges to his authority would come from within the Party. In one sense it was a relief that the fight was now out in the open, but he wished that the timing had been of his choosing rather than Lewisham's. The race issue was always an emotive flag to wave, and he had no doubt that Lewisham would now unfurl it, rallying a sizable ragbag of fellow travelers. That was one aspect of the Tories that he envied: their ability to close ranks and emasculate their own malcontents. He reflected that for once old Harold had been right when he said that a week was a long time in politics. Not even a week, only twenty-four hours, he thought, as his car swept through the Palace gates and the anxious crowd waved.

31

AWAY FROM THE Kremlin itself, in another part of Moscow there is a highly restricted area close to the old Khodinka airfield. Inside a cluster of buildings enclosed on all sides by electrified barbed-wire fences and patrolled night and day by killer dogs, the day-to-day business of the GRU is carried on. Unlike the KGB, its sister and rival organization, the GRU—or, to give it its innocuous official title, the Chief Intelligence Directorate of the General Staff—has never been anxious to advertise its existence or activities.

The external walls of its headquarters have no windows, and the occupants are likewise faceless to everybody except those who come within their clutches. No vehicles are allowed within the inner precincts, a rule that is applied without exception, whatever the rank and standing of their owners. All visitors are screened by the most advanced electronic equipment, and even the smallest metallic object, whether a nail file or cigarette lighter, is immediately confiscated. Standards of security have been elevated to paranoiac heights.

On that particular morning the First Deputy of the Illegals Section, Colonel-General Lemzenko, had assembled three key members of his staff, including his own deputy, Lavrov, to discuss the imminent arrival of Hillsden. The First Department (Passport) had been responsible for providing Hansel's network with a complete set of false papers. Hillsden had first been taken in the Riva across the lake at night to a rendezvous point where Walters handed him over to a colleague. He never saw Walters again.

The next stage of his journey was in a limousine with CD plates, which took a complicated route to Geneva. There he was secreted inside the residency of the Soviet Trade Mission, where the final touches were added to his papers. Before being photographed for the documentation, his appearance had been subtly altered—his hair cut and dyed, his clothes exchanged for ones of Russian origin, lifts added to his shoes to give him extra height, temporary caps fitted to his front teeth. He assumed the identity of Valentin Savin, born in Latvia, citizen of Petrograd, an expert in environmental pollution attached to the Ministry of Agriculture with diplomatic status. As soon as the transformation was completed, he was flown out of Switzerland without challenge, traveling on a scheduled Aeroflot service to Moscow and accompanied by two GRU officers ostensibly working in Trade Representation. Under surveillance day and night, he had no opportunity to make contact with the outside world.

Since Lemzenko was anxious to establish first claim, on arrival in Moscow Hillsden was driven straight to the GRU headquarters. There, after being allowed to remove the false caps from his teeth, he was given a meal of caviar, followed by some cold and unappetizing chicken, together with a carafe of wine that his palate told him was imported French. Halfway through the meal he was visited by Lavrov, who behaved with stiff politeness.

"It is to be hoped our collaboration will be fruitful." Lavrov spoke English well, albeit with an accent. "Are you in need of anything?"

"I'd like a change of shirt, some toothpaste and something to shave with."

"These will be provided. Do you smoke?"

"I've given it up, but in the circumstances I'm prepared to start again."

"Which brand?"

"Benson and Hedges?"

"Ah, yes. I have smoked these myself when in London. They have no strength, but as you prefer. You have not eaten your chicken. There is something wrong with it?"

"Yes. It appears to have been cooked in axle grease. Don't you get enough of our cheap EEC butter these days?"

In answer Lavrov picked up a fork and tasted a piece of the offending chicken. "I find it totally acceptable. You have been spoiled, Mr. Hillsden."

"Not for a long time, and not irrevocably, I'm sure. Why have I been brought here? Why not the Centre?"

"We have our reasons. You should be flattered."

"Oh, I am, but still curious."

"It is for your own protection, a measure of the price we place on your value to us."

"The deal was that I would sing my song, be paid, and allowed to disappear."

"You have been paid. The transaction was honored, the money deposited in a Swiss bank. You have my word for that."

Hillsden returned the bleak smile. "Very comforting. Except that I am not at liberty to spend it."

"Once your situation changed, we had to take other measures for your own safety. As to your song, as you put it, well, we have still to hear you sing. Enjoy your excellent Russian chicken, Mr. Hillsden. When you have finished, you will be shown to your sleeping quarters. I hope you get a good rest. We want you to be your old bright self in the morning."

He smiled and left the room. As the door opened and closed Hillsden glimpsed two guards stationed in the corridor. A short while later another officer appeared and escorted him to another, adjacent block. There he was ushered into a cell furnished with a simple bunk, a chair and a small table. In one corner was a washbasin and a chemical toilet. There was a full packet of Benson and Hedges cigarettes on the bed, together with a towel, a tablet of soap, toothpaste and toothbrush. As he broke the cellophane wrapping on the cigarette packet he noted with grim amusement that alongside the government health warning were the words "Duty Free."

"How about matches?"

The officer felt in his pocket and produced a box.

"I was promised a razor."

"It will be brought tomorrow."

When he had been locked in, Hillsden set about examining his surroundings in more detail. He took the chair to the barred window, which was set high in the wall, and attempted to see what lay beyond. He found that his cell faced an inner courtyard. The mattress on the bed appeared to be standard Army issue; the one blanket smelled of stale sweat. A single cold tap fed the washbasin. He sluiced his face and brushed his teeth, but the aftertaste of the chicken could not be dislodged. After smoking one of the cigarettes and folding the blanket to form a pillow, he lay down on the bed fully clothed. There was no light switch, and he shielded his eyes against the glare of the naked overhead bulb. There was a small air vent in the ceiling, and he took it for granted that the room was bugged.

Sleep eluded him as he wrestled with the full implications of Control's duplicity. He felt a sense of despair at his own stupidity. All the clues had been there, under his nose. He could see them now and cursed his previous blindness. Why hadn't he suspected more when warned off Glanville? That should have alerted him, as should the apparent ease with which the German and the girl he knew only as Wendy had traced him to the Brothers of Mercy. In his obsession to uncover Caroline's murderer he had neglected normal precautions and allowed his guard to drop. At the same time he was aware that Control could not have been working alone; there had to be others. What had Glanville said? That remark of poor old Jock's: something about "close to your own front door" or words to that effect. How cynical Control's own remark "They're picking us off one by one" now appeared. It all slotted into place, and of course Control had always been one step ahead.

There was also Belfrage to consider. How much had he been implicated? If only he had thought it through, even the way Control had stage-managed Caroline's funeral had been suspect. Hillsden acknowledged he had been outmaneuvered at every turn, constantly confiding his strategy to the very man who was the instrument of his destruction. He tried to clear his mind of a sense of something past and unspeakable until fatigue finally closed his eyes. Sometime during the night he was jerked back to consciousness by a scream close at hand, but whether it was himself or the cry of another human animal he had no means of telling.

THE same officer woke him with a cup of coffee and a safety razor, an old-fashioned affair with a double-sided blade that Hillsden had not seen for years. It reminded him of his father during the war when blades had been in short supply; somebody had come up with a home sharpener, and it became a matter of pride to get as many shaves as possible from a single blade.

The officer remained in the cell while Hillsden shaved, then took the razor away with him. Shortly afterwards a uniformed guard brought him his breakfast: black bread and a piece of strong-smelling cheese, together with a second cup of coffee.

"You're spoiling me."

"Is what you eat in England?"

"It's not our typical breakfast. More a plowman's lunch."

The guard remained by the door while he ate.

"What's the matter? Are they afraid I might cut my wrists on the cheese?"

The man did not answer.

"You disappoint me. I've always been led to believe that humor was the strongest Russian characteristic. Where did you learn to speak English?"

"Here."

"I was making an English joke about the cheese."

The man stared at him.

"You should make a note of that. Might come in handy one day when you need some British breakfast table talk—relaxes your hostess, creates a good impression. How do you Russians start the day?"

The man regarded something on the ceiling as though Hillsden's words might be capable of corrupting him.

"Pity you didn't bring me *Izvestia.* We like our morning papers. I could have done the crossword, looked at the stock market prices, enjoyed the gossip column. I bet your gossip columns are more fun than ours. No scoutmasters on grave charges, no royal scandals or other examples of Western decadence, just jolly stories about clean-living members of the Politburo describing their prostate operations."

The moment Hillsden finished the meal the man removed his plate and coffee cup and retreated. Later a different guard brought a clean shirt. The collar size was correct. Then they left him alone for most of the morning; it wasn't until just before noon that the cell door was unlocked and he was taken under escort to a room in another block. There he was greeted by a man who introduced himself as Colonel Abramov. They sat opposite each other with a bare table between them. Abramov wore an impeccably tailored uniform with numerous decorations on his chest, and, like Lavrov, spoke excellent English. He smoked cheroots, and several times during the session ash dropped on his uniform. This seemed to offend him; on each occasion he got to his feet and flicked the ash away with a silk handkerchief.

"I have feelings for what you are experiencing at this moment," Abramov began. "Those who change sides always feel themselves to be isolated in the beginning. Excuse me, do you wish one of these?" He offered a leather case.

"I stick to cigarettes."

"Both are bad habits. We should know better. But one can't surrender all vices. And one should never forget that none of us is immortal."

"Are we going to talk philosophy?"

"We're going to talk about many things, I hope, Alec. May I call you Alec?"

"Call me what you like. Do you have a first name? Let's start off equal."

"My first name is difficult to pronounce in English, and there is no real equivalent. Why don't we settle for your calling me Victor?"

"To the victor belong the spoils."

"Ah, yes, the guard told me that recent events have not destroyed your sense of humor. But then, it's a characteristic of your countrymen to find humor in adversity. Is that true? I'm interested."

"Yes, there were a lot of laughs at Dunkirk. They eased off at Yalta, I believe."

"Look, Alec, please understand that there are no pressures, no time limits. And I want you to know that I understand your present position. I've often tried to imagine myself in your circumstances. How I would feel if I severed the umbilical cord. I sense it must be like losing one's entire family in a single accident. Is that far off the mark?"

"I haven't had a family for a long time, so I wouldn't know. But if you are so concerned about my welfare, Victor, why not a decent room with a view of the Kremlin? I thought I was here as your guest, not as a prisoner."

"Unfortunately, this building is not equipped with hotel facilities. But after we have disposed of the necessary debriefing, I think I can promise you better accommodation." He stood up to brush the ash from his uniform jacket. "We have lots of interesting discussions ahead of us, discussions we are both going to enjoy. Slowly, piece by piece, Alec, we are going to remake you. But first we have to remove your remaining doubts."

Hillsden watched him light another cheroot. There was something odd and sinister about these opening moves, and he knew he must make a concentrated effort not to be taken in by the surface friendliness. "What makes you think I still have doubts?"

"I've made a study of converts. You're not religious, are you?"

"I believe in an avenging God."

"The point I was going to make is that in my experience there is always a moment when the convert hesitates on the brink. He has brought himself to the point of irrevocable choice, and then old loyalties pull him back. It's not unlike the beginning of a love affair. We are attracted, perhaps we are desperate to possess the other person, but there is a still, small voice that urges caution. We have been there before, and perhaps we have been disappointed, or even betrayed. You and I must have no such hesitations between us."

Hillsden thought: At one point in my life I must have wanted something better. Is this where it all ends, darkness always at noon? Koestler knew about that, and in the end he took it to the only logical conclusion. But how many gods had to fail along the way? None failed me, because I believed in none to start with. I never had what Koestler must have had: that moment in time when everything is assured, when faith obliterates doubt. I've lived with deceit as an alcoholic lives with booze, and after a while you don't taste it, there are no kicks, just a dull necessity. You can't suddenly sign the pledge, go cold turkey, because that option is never on offer. If they dry you out, it's for a purpose, a preparation for something worse. It was never going to be as simple as Abramov promised; nothing ever was with the Russians. Their minds don't work like that, they know how to wait and let human chemistry do its work for them.

"Where would you like to begin?"

"As you wish."

"You don't have a rank, do you?"

"Not one that I still use."

"But you were in the British Army? Let's start there."

Now it begins, Hillsden thought. The long journey to Xanadu. "I was called up in 1943," he began, but Abramov interrupted immediately: "You didn't volunteer?"

"No, I wasn't that keen, I waited for my conscription papers to arrive. I first reported for initial training at Warley Barracks with the Essex Regiment. Infantry training didn't appeal to me, I must say. I wasn't one of Nature's square bashers. After six weeks they weeded us out, and I was selected as possible officer material, but I refused to go to OTC."

"That means?"

"Officer training course."

"Why was that?"

"I didn't want the responsibility. I was a reluctant soldier: I just

249

wanted to survive. So instead they posted me to the Intelligence Corps on the Isle of Anglesey, Field Security Section."

"Why Intelligence Corps?"

"It was a simple choice they made. Any odd man out either got the I Corps or the Pioneers. I spoke passable school German and French, and, of course, the King's English, which was rare enough, I found. My fellow conscripts were the usual motley group—lawyers, the odd reject from the teaching profession, most of us misfits that the Army couldn't place anywhere else. When we completed Corps Training, I got a posting to London, Grosvenor Square."

"A very smart address."

"The Army had commandeered several of the houses vacated during the Blitz. Even then our intelligence services always went for a Mayfair address if they could get one. Once there, I was directed to take a short refresher course in languages at Saint Paul's School. At the time I had been earmarked to be dropped in Occupied France. But by then, for reasons best known to themselves, they decided I was worth more than Field Security. At the completion of the course they sent me to Weybridge, where MI6 had one of their funny finishing colleges for agents."

"Funny?"

"Not funny ha-ha, funny peculiar. A touch of Kafka mixed with an Ealing comedy."

"I don't understand."

"Can you imagine a play by Gogol rewritten by P. G. Wodehouse?" Abramov shook his head.

"It was a sorting house for eccentrics."

"This was standard practice?"

"We couldn't have won the war without it."

Abramov continued to look puzzled. "Who was running it?"

"He's dead now. Felix Warren, ex–Indian Army, naturally known as 'Bunny' Warren."

"Why do you say 'naturally'?"

"It's a British habit to give nicknames. Anybody called White is known as Chalky, all the Clarks are Nobby, the Millers are Dusty and so on. Think of rabbit warren and you get to Bunny. Bunny rabbit, see?" He smiled, but Abramov was obviously still baffled. "By now I had achieved the exalted rank of WO2—Warrant Officer, equivalent to company sergeant major in the infantry. Then, having earmarked me for France, they behaved true to form and sent me to Cairo. I flew there in a converted Stirling bomber. A very dodgy flight. On landing, we all had to piss into the hydraulics to get the frozen undercarriage down."

"Why Cairo?"

"You may well ask. I never did find out. I kicked my heels there for three months, mostly sticking flags in maps to show the location of approved brothels. At one point there was talk of pushing me into Yugoslavia, but nothing came of it. Then I got shipped home again on the SS *Empire Ken,* a murderous bloody boat built for three hundred, but they crammed more than four times that number in her. We landed at Liverpool."

"What year was this?"

"Early '44. On arrival I got instructions to report to Section Five at Saint Albans. That was Philby's old hunting ground."

"Who was running that setup?"

"Felix Cowgill."

"Another Felix?"

"Just coincidence."

"What were your duties there?"

"Devising and planting deception material, supervising the operations of agents in the field, liaising with the various Allied governments in exile. I stayed there until September '44, and then went across to France attached to 30 Corps. I was with them until we moved into Germany, and ended up in Flensburg."

"Doing what?"

"Mostly farting around trying to trace ex-members of the SS. According to the local populace, nobody had ever been a Nazi, they were all spotless innocents, and the entire SS consisted of one platoon. From Flensburg I went to Hamelin, the Pied Piper town, still trying to root out war criminals. It was police work rather than intelligence, but by then, with the war over, the whole thing was screwed up anyway. Everybody wanted out. The place was swarming with draft dodgers who were now running the civil government. The black market was flourishing, everybody was corrupt, in it up to their necks, and the Yanks were shipping out stuff by the truckload. The currency was cigarettes and coffee; nobody used money. I had a high demob number, so I didn't get out until January '47."

"Where did you spend the remainder of your term?"

"Austria. Villach and Vienna. Getting more and more bored and disillusioned. When I finally got back into civvies—"

"Civvies?"

"Civilian clothes. They gave you a suit not unlike this horror I'm wearing now, a shirt, socks, shoes and a trilby hat. I sold them all to a secondhand shop the moment I got back to London. I had a gratuity

—roughly two hundred pounds—and that was about it. I was trained for nothing, I'd missed out on going to university. For a time I served as a waiter in Soho. We still had rationing, and the place where I worked still had horse meat on the menu. That was a dead end, and I drifted from that to a variety of jobs: window cleaning, salesman for a publisher, even as a porter in a hotel for a time—you name it. Then I spotted an advertisement in the *Times* from a character who ran a cramming college in the Brompton Road."

"What is a 'cramming college'?"

"Very dubious establishment for parents desperate to get their idiot sons through the public schools' entrance exams. You had to cram their brains with sufficient knowledge to get them a Pass mark. This particular place was run by an ex-Army colonel, a weird old bod called Pryce-Sampson. I taught elementary German to a series of chinless wonders, depressing myself as much as them, and stuck at it for about two years. It was around this time that I met my wife, and at least the job paid better than being a hotel porter. The college folded when Pryce-Sampson crammed something other than knowledge into one of his pupils."

Once again Abramov stared at him without comprehension.

"Sexual assault on a minor. No, let me rephrase that, since 'minor' gives you problems. He fucked one of the pupils."

Abramov shrugged.

"It was then, purely by chance, that I ran into old Bunny Warren again in the street. He was friendly, and asked what I was doing. I must have told him some convincing sob story because a few weeks later I got a letter from the Department asking me to come and see them. The upshot of that was, they asked if I'd like to return to the fold. Your lot had put up the iron shutters by then and MI6 were on a recruiting drive."

"We were rather flattered by Churchill's description. Who was running MI6 then?"

"Dinnsbury. One of the old school. Superior brain. He ran circles around most of them—and round you for a time."

Abramov nodded. "We were very aware of Dinnsbury. Go on."

"Of course it was all new to me—the cold war, I mean. A different enemy, different tactics. I had to go back to another kind of cramming school. They kept me behind a desk for a year, learning the ropes. Mostly internal subversion, infiltration of the local Communist Party, and the trades unions. The only area left undisturbed was the Foreign Office, with ultimately disastrous results."

Abramov smiled for the first time. "Not that we complained. What section were you in?"

"Satellites Seven. It was the period of the atomic spies, as I'm sure you recall. After a year Dinnsbury decided I should be moved across to Counterintelligence. My throat's dry. Any chance of a drink?"

"Why don't we break here? You've made a good start."

"Nothing you didn't know already."

"A good story is always worth telling twice," Abramov said evenly. His handkerchief came out and he flicked ash droppings from his jacket. "Such a dirty habit, smoking."

"We're in a dirty business, Victor," Hillsden said as he was led from the room.

32

FOLLOWING THE RACE riots, the Prime Minister had formed an Inner Cabinet to deal with the new emergency. It had immediately been dubbed a War Cabinet by his growing number of critics. Far from being able to repeal the hated search-on-suspicion laws as promised in his election manifesto, he had been forced to give the police even wider powers, thus incurring the wrath of the National Council for Civil Liberties as well as that of his own Left wing. Deliberately rubbing salt into his embarrassment, the Tories had voted with him en bloc for the new Defence of the Realm Act; this had ensured its smooth passage through the House, forty members of his own party, led by Lewisham, having defied him. Deciding that any further use of rubber bullets would probably be political suicide, whatever the justification, the P.M. had ordered, in the strictest secrecy, a number of water cannon from the West Germans, and had agreed with the Commissioner of Police that these could be used as an acceptable alternative should the riots begin again. This decision had been confined to the Inner Cabinet, and so far security had held.

Even so, his worries remained. "I've never had such a good press," he confided. "As far as Fleet Street is concerned, I'm doing all the right things. Normally, that in itself would be enough to make me suspicious. They're not out to do me any favors. But I detect a genuine, underlying sympathy. I don't think it's cynical; I think the country as a whole is in a very odd mood. The only time I can remember having the same feeling was just after Munich. Relief, but underneath it all a conviction that we're living on borrowed time, that there's worse to come. I can't describe it any other way, it's a feeling in my gut."

"What I've got is a powerful whiff of CIA Number 5," the Foreign Secretary observed. "I don't think the Yanks trust us anymore. And if we're talking about covert operations, there's never been much to choose between them and the Russians. The so-called special relationship always looks moth-eaten when we're in office. I didn't notice anything particularly 'special' about it in Washington last week; the Secretary of State dressed me down like a headmaster. He intimated that they were seriously contemplating pulling their missiles out unless we stabilized our situation. I took that with a pinch of salt because he's an arrogant bastard at the best of times and devious as they come, but there's no doubt that in an election year an isolationist policy is a vote catcher."

"I used to think the old days were bad enough," the Prime Minister said, "when all we had to worry about was the bloody Tories and the TUC, but if you're suggesting that what we're facing now is an undercover Red plot financed by the CIA, then God help us! I'm sorry, but I can't swallow that."

"Did you ever swallow the conspiracy theory about Kennedy? And how about Watergate?" Bayldon asked.

"I'm not saying the Yanks wouldn't pee on their own doorstep, and I'm aware that they've stuck their fingers in a great many foreign pies. I remember Suez, for example."

"You voted against that."

"Yes, and I was wrong. Events have proved that, sad to say. But I keep coming back to this gut feeling. What I can't get to grips with is the fact that there's no discernible pattern. It's as if there's a whole army of subversives out there lighting a hundred different fires, and they're not confined to any particular industry or class. The present troubles cut across all the old class barriers. Unexplained murders, attacks on U.S. bases, synagogues, churches of all denominations, ethnic minorities— all combined with a well-orchestrated campaign to denigrate the role of the police. I can't believe they're all a series of coincidences. It's as though the whole countryside is a tinderbox and you've only got to throw one more match for the whole lot to go up."

"Well, I don't want to be the one to throw the match," Bayldon said, "but something else has cropped up. I took a call just before this meeting from the chief Defence correspondent of the *Express.*"

"Charlie Weaver, you mean?"

"Yes. Now, I wouldn't describe him as our most ardent supporter, but I've always found him to be disturbingly accurate and nonpartisan. I only accepted his call because he insisted it was for my ears alone. After I'd heard him, he said he was only prepared to sit on it until eight o'clock tonight, but was giving us a chance to consider our position."

"Well, come on, then, out with it."

"He says the *Express* has received letters and photographs linking Glanville and Belfrage, some of them as recent as last year. Naturally, the first question I asked was whether they could be fakes. He swore not. Says the photographs have been subjected to all known tests. He wasn't so adamant about the letters, because obviously they're easier to forge, but some of Belfrage's were written on Foreign Office notepaper, which isn't exactly reassuring."

"Anything else?"

"Unfortunately, yes. The bombshell is that the letters implicate Lewisham. If they're genuine, then our good friend the Honorable Member for Forthill South has been in the pay of the KGB since 1975. The date fits because, as Weaver pointed out, having done his homework, that was the year Lewisham went to Moscow with a TUC fact-finding mission."

The revelation produced stunned amazement around the table. The Prime Minister broke the silence. "The letters have to be a fake. Our Graham may be our Judas, but he's too fly, too fond of himself, too ambitious, to risk ending his career that way."

"What do I tell Weaver, though?"

"If they publish, Lewisham will issue a writ for criminal libel."

"They might be prepared to take their chances in court."

"Did Weaver reveal how they came by the material?"

"No."

"Can we get them under the Official Secrets Act?"

"Doubtful. The Glanville case has already been well aired, and where Lewisham's concerned it doesn't apply. If you want my view—"

"Well, of course I do if it's pertinent."

"Lewisham is a dangerous animal to be on the loose," Bayldon said succinctly, "especially at a time like this. Dirt sticks, and fake dirt often sticks as firmly as the genuine article. He did you a good turn by resigning. We could return the favor by giving Weaver the green light. If Lewisham was still in the Cabinet it would be a different matter, but if he comes a cropper as an individual he won't necessarily foul our nest. On the contrary, it might take him off our backs for a while, give him something else to think about."

The Prime Minister took his time before replying. The idea was certainly attractive in many ways, but he hesitated to give it his blessing. There was a cottage industry in ministerial memoirs, and a long line of Brutuses in the Labour Party; ex-comrades had a compulsion to whitewash themselves at the expense of old colleagues. He suspected Bayldon went home to write his diary every night with the aim of publishing it the moment they were out of office. He had no intention of giving anybody future ammunition. "No," he said finally, "I don't like it. On the other hand, any attempt to muffle the press without good cause would be equally dangerous." He fixed his eye on Bayldon. "Just tell me one thing. When you had this discussion with Weaver, did you tell him you'd be taking it to Cabinet level?"

"Not in so many words, George."

"Well, what words *did* you use?"

"As I recall, he more or less took it for granted that I would be dumping it in your lap."

"They're such cunning bastards, all of them. Show me a straight journalist and I'll show you a rattlesnake." He put his hands together in front of his face in an attitude of prayer and was silent again. "I tell you what you do," he said after a pause. "Call their bluff. Go back and tell Weaver that you've reported the matter, but that this government will never obstruct the course of justice. They must take their own decision according to their own legal advice. Point out that in this matter Mr. Lewisham will certainly act as a private individual in his own defense. And depending on the outcome of any civil litigation, then and only then will this government consider whether questions of national security demand that we take the matter further."

"Brilliant, George," the Foreign Secretary exclaimed, and there was a general murmur of approval.

"Yes, I thought so myself. Let the buggers cook their own goose. In the meantime, and before it hits the headlines, I'll have a private word with my opposite numbers. Make them privy to it and spike their guns as well. You leave that to me. I know just how to put it."

"Troubles shared are troubles halved," Bayldon said.

"Or doubled," the Prime Minister replied, having the last word, as was his right.

IN the event, discretion and the P.M.'s cunning persuaded the editor of the *Express* to exercise caution. Weaver's story ran with banner headlines, but was confined to details of the association between Glanville and Belfrage. Lewisham was never mentioned by name, but the report stated that there was strong evidence implicating an ex–Cabinet Minister. Predictably, this led to widespread speculation in the rest of the media, though, as with the *Express,* nobody was prepared to risk prosecution by actually naming names. It was left to *Private Eye* to dot the *i*'s and cross the *t*'s: in its typical buccaneering and often near-suicidal fashion the satirical magazine went ahead and nominated Lewisham as the most likely candidate for the honors.

Lewisham immediately instructed his lawyers to apply to the courts for an injunction banning the entire issue, and although the judge granted the plea, some fifty thousand copies of the three-hundred thousand print run had already been snapped up. Black-market copies changed hands at inflated prices, especially in the vicinity of Westminster. Before the television debates began, Lewisham slapped in a writ for criminal libel, but this did not stop the usual batch of pontificating "experts" (most of whom had a personal ax to grind, if not a secret life to conceal) chuntering on at inordinate and boring length about the erosion of civil liberties. There was much talk of "the public at large being gravely concerned," whereas in fact the public was only too anxious to read about dirt in high places, which they always suspected existed and liked nothing more than to have confirmed. Once the writ had been issued, the mass-circulation dailies were able to comment on Lewisham's reasons for issuing it without fear of retribution. The editor of *Private Eye* entered a defense of justification to the writ and announced the magazine had every intention of fighting the case. The stage was set for a major courtroom drama.

But there was drama of another kind in the Cabinet room. Although the accusation against Lewisham produced the odd crocodile tear for appearance' sake, those Ministers who in the past had suffered from his insufferable arrogance prepared to dance on his grave. That was their only comfort, since the rest of the news continued to be as depressing as ever.

Even God seemed to have it in for the government. The elements were not being kind. A prolonged drought, the worst since the beginning of the century, had necessitated the introduction of water rationing in all but the northwest of the country—an unpopular move, since, far from being a nation of shopkeepers, England is a nation of gardeners, the inhabitants happier to forgo a bath than neglect their herbaceous borders.

There were no great expectations; it was the worst of times.

33

HILLSDEN'S UMBILICAL CORD had not yet been completely severed, but the slow process of cutting him loose from past associations continued inexorably. With painstaking, cold, analytical skill, Abramov emptied the secret places of Hillsden's mind of all previous loyalties. Gradually he was brought to the stage where such truths as remained could be extracted as easily as pulling milk teeth from a child.

Their relationship was that of poacher and gamekeeper; respect was tinged with old enmities. The past was like a dense forest, and as he was persuaded to penetrate deeper into the heart of it memories tore at Hillsden like thorns. Somewhat to his surprise he found it was a journey he could only make with pain, tracing the old maps of his life back to those first landmarks of deceit. Abramov made him travel the same tortuous route more than once, prompting him to remember long-buried names, places, dates, endlessly probing, demanding, flushing out forgotten motives, bringing him face-to-face with truths he had believed were hidden forever.

At the end of every long session he was returned to his cell; it was a reminder that although they were hearing his confession, they were not prepared to grant absolution. The effort of keeping back some parts of his own awareness told on him. It was during the nights that the strain became intolerable; he often hallucinated, and curiously it was to recollections of childhood that he returned most frequently. The walls of his cell sometimes appeared to open out, allowing him glimpses of lost freedoms, glimpses of halcyon days: the crowded beach at Weymouth, where his first family holidays had been spent, the tide receding far out to sea, exposing rippled sand colandered with a million worm holes. At other times he revisited city streets of a homeland gone forever where he and others had played a simplified form of baseball. Then faint images of his dead parents would appear. But the most persistent picture, and the one that evoked the keenest sense of loss, was that of a small girl he had loved and been rejected by at the age of nine. Often her features blurred, the face of innocence assuming first the characteristics of his wife, then of Caroline, as though some unseen operator was projecting three slides simultaneously, producing an overlapping composite of hideous menace: the face of his childhood sweetheart suddenly transformed into Caroline's death mask. The nightmare progression accelerated until he became the rapist violating the body of the child while Caroline and Margot looked on, joined together as silent, condemning witnesses. It could not be said that he was happy or unhappy; such clear-cut attitudes no longer had any meaning for him; he was merely something suspended in time, more akin to the object in the famed experiment of the dog's head than anything human.

He had no means of telling whether Abramov was satisfied with the progress being made. He was never praised for his efforts, nor did Abramov betray any satisfaction when he had prised loose a valuable fragment. No written record was made, but he was certain that the dialogue between them was being recorded by hidden microphones. The sessions followed no regular pattern; sometimes he would not be summoned until the afternoon; on other occasions they would begin as soon as he was awake; once Abramov came in the middle of the night and the interrogation lasted until daybreak. He was aware that this was designed to keep him uncertain, on edge and thereby more vulnerable: tiredness had always been an essential weapon in the armory of debriefing.

By the end of the second week they had reached the point where he had joined Jock and Caroline in Austria. It was the moment he had dreaded most of all. Because of Control's treachery he had felt little compunction in revealing the existing setup in London, but now, as they approached the shallows and depths of the only relationship in his life that had any lasting meaning, new fears surfaced.

Abramov pounced at once. "You say Control ordered her back that last time?"

"Yes."

"What makes you so sure?"

"She told me so herself."

"But you never knew the reason?"

"No."

"Didn't you try to find out? After all, you were having an affair with her. Lovers are not supposed to have secrets, and your affair could hardly have been purely physical, given the circumstances. You were both in the same game. After your physical needs had been satisfied, surely you exchanged confidences of a more cerebral nature? I don't believe you didn't know."

"Well, it's true. And you know why. It's standard procedure not to reveal sources if you're working alone. The resistance forces always operated that way during the war. The various links in the chain only knew as much as it was necessary for them to know. I could only guess."

"All right, what did you guess?"

"I was on the way out by then. Control felt it politic to exclude me, for reasons which only became apparent at a later date."

"Because you'd broken the rules?"

"They were his rules, and I had transgressed them. He considered me too emotionally involved."

"And were you?"

"I was in love with her. Love warps judgments, doesn't it?"

"The human variety, perhaps," Abramov replied. "Not love for a cause."

"You'd know better than me about that."

"And her feelings towards you, what were they?"

It was a question he did not want to answer. "Maybe she kept her true love for a cause. Like you said."

"So you accepted Control's decision?"

"I didn't have any choice, even though I didn't understand it at the time."

"Did you suspect that Jock had any part in the decision?"

"Not directly. But he was running the show locally. Presumably, like me, he had to go along with Control's decision."

"What was your relationship with him?"

"I thought he was good at his job, dedicated, tough, professional, with no illusions. I always felt he was a street fighter, a good man to have on my side. My relationship with him? As intimate as he allowed. He never let anybody get really close. That was his method of survival—except that he didn't survive."

"Were you surprised at his death?"

"Not surprised, no. We're never surprised, are we, that our trade holds terminal dangers? It's part of the fine print in the contract. No, surprise would be the wrong word. I wondered who had betrayed him, and I would have wished him another death."

"What would you say if I revealed that your mistress performed that function?"

"Are you saying that?"

"I'm asking the questions."

"If she did, and I'd need some convincing, I imagine you gave her no choice. Whatever she told you, I know she didn't volunteer."

"Why are you sweating?"

"It's hot in here," Hillsden said, looking him straight in the eye.

"Tell me about Jock's relationship with her. How intimate was it, would you say?"

"They weren't lovers, if that's what you're trying to suggest."

"That wasn't in my mind, but apparently it's in yours."

"It was a team effort," Hillsden said, angry with himself for allowing Abramov to ruffle him. "I was always the low man in the team. I told you: she was Dinnsbury's girl in the first place. He was the one who promoted her, though it was Jock who badgered him to post her to the Austrian station. I only came in later. Then, after Dinnsbury was retired, Control took over."

"So are you asking me to believe that you had no real knowledge of what she and Jock were onto?"

"I knew they had both been instrumental in breaking the Munich ring, but I'm sure you know all that."

"Don't decide what I know or don't know. Don't try and anticipate my questions. Just answer them." The cheroot smoke hung between them, thick and acrid. "You're not doing so well today. For some reason, you're not cooperating as well as usual. Why is that?"

"I'm doing my best."

"Let's stay with the love of your life. When she was taken, who did you suspect had betrayed her?"

"I was in the dark like everybody else. All London knew was that the entire network had gone up the spout. There was always the possibility that Henze had been turned twice. We considered that; it was the most rational explanation at the time. But when Henze was killed, we were back to square one. Of course, you might have turned him again, and then killed him anyway, just to throw us off the scent."

"We might, yes. It's an interesting theory."

Hillsden detected the barest change of expression on Abramov's face; it was a nuance, nothing more, but for the first time since the interrogations began he had the feeling that he had touched the right button. "When Jock died, our last real chance of finding out vanished. You made a clean sweep. All we were certain about was that Caroline was taken soon after she arrived in Berlin, so you must have had advance information. The speed with which it happened meant you were expecting her. She was too good to be taken unawares. So who tipped you off? No harm in telling me now, surely? It's all yesterday's news."

Abramov stubbed out his cheroot. "We'll come to that in due course," he said, getting to his feet and signaling that the session was at an end.

THERE were many things Hillsden did not understand. His debriefing was not following any normal line. An increasing sense of unease crept into his veins like damp in a wall. During the last session Abramov's attitude had noticeably hardened, and he searched for some plausible explanation for the change, but could pinpoint no single factor. Despite the long hours they had spent together he was still no closer to discovering the man's true intent. From the very beginning the fact that he was being handled by the GRU and not Moscow Centre remained a mystery. He had always assumed that the KGB had been responsible for Caroline's destruction, yet now this was open to doubt. It would be a mistake to underestimate the suspicion and hostility that existed between the two complementary but rival organizations. There had always been a relentless power struggle between the military and the Politburo, with the KGB in the middle: Big Brother keeping tabs on Big Brother, paying off old scores, drip-feeding the acids of past hatreds.

The vital question was deciding to what extent Control had betrayed him. He could almost persuade himself that Abramov knew only part of the story. If he was correct, if Control was being run by the KGB and not the GRU, it would go a long way towards explaining Abramov's line of questioning.

On the other hand . . . Go back, he thought, you've missed something. Take it step by step. List the sequence of events.

One: Obviously Control set me up to protect himself. And others? Yes, in all probability.

Yet . . . Rider to One. Wouldn't it have been simpler to eliminate me on the spot, as with Glanville?

Two: But he didn't. Why not? The opportunity was there. Instead he went to the lengths of devising a complicated defection scenario.

Unless . . . unless he decided my elimination on home ground would be too dangerous. Close to home, it would certainly have prompted others to pick up where I left off. Wadders, for example.

Three: It all began with my visit to Glanville. Up until that point Control behaved normally towards me, although ambivalent about Caroline, anxious to sweep her case under the carpet.

Four: There's something I missed with Glanville. Or interpreted wrongly.

But . . . Control could not be certain that I'd missed it. Therefore.

Five: Taking no chances, he acted on the assumption that I did know.

Six: How best to disarm me? Use Caroline's murder. Good psychology. Play on my known relationship. He knew I couldn't resist the chance of avenging her. And he was right, I played into his hands, suspecting nothing. The wheels were set in motion to remove me once and for all. And at the same time . . .

Seven: If his plan succeeded, it would make bloody sure I was discredited. Whatever happened in the future, my word would count for nothing. He was safe. Clever. Diabolically clever.

Eight: The first part of the plan works a treat. Then, to make doubly sure and cut off all escape routes, Belfrage is eliminated and I am made the prime suspect, stitched up, the sack weighted so that I never rise again.

Which brings me back to Abramov. How much of all this does he know or suspect? Some, any, all? So far he has given me no indication that he knows Control masterminded the whole thing. Which means that either he genuinely does not know that Control is Moscow Centre's baby, not his, or else I am being played with, lulled into a false sense of security.

He paced the cell during this silent monologue, moving around the four walls as much to exercise his muscles as his brain. His reason was at its highest tension, and he could find no peace.

THE next sessions assumed a different form. Abramov abandoned specifics; instead the discussion was on moral and political attitudes in general terms. Hillsden was alert to the fact that more than ever before he needed to keep his wits about him. In such circumstances philosophical discussions were suspect.

"Would you agree that life is significant only when it is dangerous?" Abramov asked at one point.

"Isn't danger always relative? So-called safe suburban normality seethes beneath the surface. There's danger in not keeping up with the hire-purchase agreements, if you bring it down to the mundane. Danger in crossing the streets, in going to bed with the door unlocked—even danger in smoking too many cheroots."

"I take your point, but what we are talking about is the ultimate mystery of human personality: the enigmas of pain and suffering, of good and evil, of life itself, and of death. Those are the wider issues."

"*Crime and Punishment,* in other words."

"How well read you are, Alec."

"Oh, yes. Steeped in your Russian classics."

"I'm delighted to hear it, but for the moment let us confine the question to *our* dangers, the dangers we have elected to live with. Those dark processes that demand we must submerge our real selves and bury conscience. To live always with the thought that we may be faced with the choice of killing or being killed. The very process that brought you here. By taking that final step your life took on an added significance, surely?"

"Obviously."

"And added dangers."

"Yes."

"Let me put it this way: we are more often known by our masks than by our faces. Your mask, for example: what does it tell me? Does it denote a man who will accept exile with good grace? Or is it the mask of somebody who still has doubts? If I peeled it off, would I reveal uncertainty?"

"I can't go back, if that's what you mean."

"That isn't exactly what I meant. Given the choice, would you deny me or God?"

"I've never been convinced of the existence of God."

"Yet I'm told that every man becomes religious when the knife is at his throat," Abramov said, with the closest he ever came to a smile. "But again you've avoided the question."

"I can't deny anything until I know what it is I'm being asked to deny."

"All previous beliefs, loyalties, friendships, every particle of your past life."

"Haven't I already done so? Betrayed those I worked with, trampled on beliefs, renounced loyalties. Isn't that what these past weeks have been about?"

"We hope so," Abramov said. "For everybody's sake."

HILLSDEN was left alone for a whole week. He took this to be another aspect of the deliberate war of nerves. It was the universal technique: prolonged interrogation followed by a period of isolation that was designed to induce paranoia.

The next time his cell door opened Abramov greeted him with unaccustomed friendliness, a veritable hail-fellow-well-met. "I'm sorry we have missed our regular sessions, but I have been awaiting instructions. Certain decisions have been taken regarding your future."

Hillsden was escorted from the cell, but this time they did not go to Abramov's office. Instead he found himself taken to the center courtyard of the GRU complex. There an unmarked official limousine was waiting.

"A change of venue, you'll be pleased to hear," Abramov said.

"What have I done to deserve this?"

"You're a valuable prize, a feather in our cap—isn't that the expression the English use? And, as such, you merit special considerations. So far you have passed all the tests with flying colors. Now you get your reward." The use of native colloquialisms chilled rather than reassured.

With Abramov at the wheel they drove at high speed out of Moscow.

"You don't have to observe the law?"

"What law?"

"Isn't there a speed limit?"

"Not for us."

"You're not telling me that in Russia there's one law for the rich and one for the poor?"

"What I like about you, Alec, is your sense of humor. I'm not rich. We have no such divisions in our society."

They traveled for an hour or more until eventually they entered a forested area, and massive trees shuttered out the thin sunlight. Hillsden was reminded of a sequence in a film he had seen long ago; he could almost make himself believe that the serried pines and silver birches concealed a waiting troop of cossacks who would shortly break from cover and bear down on them. All the dark myths of a Russia that never changed surrounded him; he became convinced that this was the last journey he would ever make.

After another mile or so they left the main road, turning onto what was little more than a cart track. Here the forest thinned out, and eventually after a bumpy ride they came to an isolated house in the middle of a clearing. At first glance Hillsden had the impression that it was abandoned; there was an air of neglect about it, as though it had no resident occupants, but was merely a staging post.

"This is where your new life begins," Abramov said. He reached into the rear of the car and took out a briefcase.

"Is this to be my permanent home?"

"No. Just a temporary stay while we prepare you for the next development."

265

"Am I being fattened for the kill?"

"Fattened, yes, but not for the kill. From now on it will be much different. You have joined the elite."

They were greeted by a plump, middle-aged woman who looked as though she had been the original model for Mother Courage. It was a peasant face, with cheeks the texture of blood oranges, but she was not dressed like a peasant, and Hillsden was agreeably surprised to hear her welcome him in passable English.

The interior of the house was furnished with heavy, old-fashioned pieces, and there were a few dark oil paintings from a bygone age on the walls. A tiled stove stood in the middle of the comfortable main room. It looked like a summer-stock set for *The Cherry Orchard*.

"A nice change, eh?" Abramov said. "You will be very happy here. Madame Vyatkin will take good care of you."

"Tanya," Madame Vyatkin scolded Abramov. "He will call me Tanya. You drink vodka? Mr. Hillisdent?" Her mispronunciation of his name again gave him the impression that they were all actors in a play. He half expected to hear the sound of a woodman's ax outside.

"Yes," he answered. "Vodka would be very acceptable."

She brought a carafe and glasses. "I prepare the food. When you have drunk and are hungry, you eat very well, Mr. Hillisdent."

"Hillsden," Abramov corrected this time.

"Isn't that what I said?" She glared at him before retiring to the rear of the house.

Abramov poured the vodka. "Let us drink to your wise choice."

The vodka was the genuine article, and from long abstinence Hillsden felt the impact immediately. He broke out into a sweat as the alcohol reached his stomach.

Abramov opened his briefcase and took out a sheaf of papers. "While you rest here and get yourself in good physical shape, I want you to study and learn this." He handed over the papers.

"What are these?"

"Something we have prepared for your first public appearance."

Hillsden looked at the first typed page. Before he had read more than a few lines he realized what he had been given. "I have to learn this? What for?"

"The press conference we shall be giving you in due course. As I said before, you are a valuable prize. We want to show how proud we are of you, and it's always better to rehearse these occasions, don't you think? That way we avoid any possible misunderstandings or mistakes. You have been brought here to give you some peace and rest before the

266

event. In your room here you will see that we have provided new clothes. Tanya is an excellent cook and very reliable. She'll take good care of you."

"You mean I say this word for word?"

"We think that would be best. Somebody will be here to help you with it—somebody who knows the procedures and, at the same time will be an agreeable companion for you. We wouldn't want you to be lonely."

Abramov looked past him and nodded. Hillsden turned, expecting to see Tanya, but instead another man stood in the doorway. It took him a second or two to recognize what had once been a familiar face, and he felt his heart begin to pump faster at the shock.

In the doorway Calder gave a slow smile, then advanced into the room.

"Hello, Alec," Calder said. "Welcome to the club."

For the second time since he left home Hillsden knew he had got everything wrong.

"Hello, Jock," he said.

34

"WHEN WE DEAD awaken, eh?" Jock said, pouring the vodka. "Or do you believe in ghosts?"

"I do now."

They were alone together at last, with only the lost years to separate them. Abramov had gone back to Moscow and the shock of the sudden confrontation had worn off slightly, but Hillsden still could not grasp the true significance of Jock's reappearance. He had aged reasonably well, though the well-cut Western suit could not totally disguise the beginning of a belly. The voice had thickened, and only occasionally betrayed traces of Jock's origins.

"Didn't bring you flowers, old son," Jock said, raising his glass, "since I was told you were in good nick, but I didn't come empty-handed. In my privileged position, which will shortly be yours, I'm allowed the English newspapers. The good old reliable *Sun,* complete with a staggering pair of tits on page three, just to reassure you that since your departure nothing has changed. Plus the *Guardian* and the *Telegraph*. A catholic cross section, catering for all tastes."

Hillsden fingered the newspapers in the way a blind man touches the sleeve of a long-lost friend.

"I also brought you some English cigarettes. Those Russian jobs will put you away. Real coffin nails. Probably because they don't have a government health warning on the packets."

"Proper little Red Riding Hood, aren't you?"

"How quickly you've penetrated my disguise. It's good to see you again, Alec. What shall we toast? The good bad old times or the better ones to come?"

"Whatever you think is more appropriate."

There was something about Jock's manner that struck a false note, and it occurred to Hillsden that for some reason he was nervous. This was out of character for the old Jock, who had always exhibited a take-it-or-leave-it manner.

"We've got a lot to talk about, a lot of catching up to do."

"Yes."

"Treated you well so far, have they?"

"Better, I imagine, than they treat most. I've nothing to compare it with."

"How were things at the Firm when you left? Got a decent wine list this year?"

He *is* nervous, Hillsden thought. Anxious to let me know he's up-to-date. They were like two old dogs circling each other in an alleyway, both anxious to stake out their territory.

"I followed the Glanville saga, of course. What a boring old queen he was. I was never happy about our using him. But as usual my advice was ignored. You can never be sure about queens. Are they going to react like men or women? And talking of women, what's the news of Caroline these days?"

He turned away to refill his glass as he mentioned her name.

"She's dead. I went to her funeral."

"Dead?" His eyes didn't quite focus on Hillsden as he came around. "That never made the papers."

"No. Somebody pulled a lot of strings to keep it out. She was murdered; unlike you, her death was not exaggerated."

"But who would want to murder Caroline . . . ?" The question remained unfinished.

"Were you going to say 'so long after the event'?"

"Well, yes. They exchanged her years ago. I imagined she was living out her retirement in some cottage by the sea. That was what she always dreamed about."

"Yes, she did, didn't she? No, when eventually they made the trade, she wasn't in good health. She spent her retirement, if you can call it that, strapped into a wheelchair."

"You wouldn't be kidding me, would you, chum?"

"I guess neither of us is here to kid each other."

"And she was definitely murdered?"

"Well, unless she somehow managed to take her own life while the balance of her remaining mind was disturbed. She was injected with a shot of DS7, that reliable, once-and-for-all painkiller."

"Jesus! So we're the only ones left from the old network."

"It seems that way, though until a short time ago I thought I was the sole survivor. You've got a few gaps to fill in for me."

"Too true, and we'll get around to all that, but I still can't take in what you've just told me." His amazement seemed genuine enough. "Where did it happen?"

"In a private nursing home—one of those places they call God's waiting room. She was a cabbage, there was nothing left of her when they let her come home. Whoever worked her over did a very thorough job."

"Did you see her?"

"No."

"Never?"

"No."

"Why was that?"

"I wish I knew now," Hillsden said slowly. "At the time I had my reasons. I suppose, in the end, we all betray the ones we love."

At that moment Tanya came into the room and announced that their meal was ready. They went through into a dining room and sat at opposite ends of a large table. Although it was the first decent meal he had been served in weeks, Hillsden had no appetite.

"Before we start down memory lane again," Jock said, "I take it you know the prime reason for my being here? I'm to give you a tutorial, show you the ropes, get you acclimatized. They've earmarked you for the top treatment—the works. You're going on television. You're going to have your own show."

"Am I that much of a catch?"

"They think so, and they want to steal a march on Moscow Centre. After all, they assigned Abramov to your case. He's one of their rising stars. The new breed. They kill you with kindness."

269

"You mean I should consider myself lucky? But why the GRU, why not the Centre in the first place?"

"Yes, I wondered that. Who knows, chum? The reason nothing in this country works is because the left hand is never allowed to know what the right hand is doing. But things are changing. They have to change. It's going to take time to get rid of the rest of the old pack, all those fossils propped up on Lenin's tomb during the May Day parade like exhibits in a shooting gallery. Well, they're getting thinned out, but it's a slow process. Still, they've buried three in recent years, so God is doing something right."

"Are you allowed to say things like that?"

"Chum, it's not like you think. You've joined the elite."

"Philby was the first one to say that. Do you ever see him?"

"God, no! Not my cup of tea. I did come across him once at the opera. The other two fell off the perch, but of course you know that. Anyway, I don't live here. Did you think I did? My deal was something different. You forget, I'm dead. They decided I was more use to them dead, so they let me back into the outside world."

"I see."

"I know this must be a surprise to you, but you were the last person I expected to see cross over. Not that you'll regret it in the long run, and you chose your moment well. It's all coming to an end back home —only a matter of time. Things are rough and they're going to get rougher—take my word for it."

"I always took your word, Jock."

"Believe me, this is the only game in town. Will the little wife be joining you at a later date?"

"That's over. It was over a long time ago, as far back as Austria."

"Well, when we get you organized we'll have to arrange a party. Man cannot live by defection alone. Two things the revolution never did away with: a little of what you fancy"—he charged his glass again from the bottle of Tokay that had been put out for them—"and a little of what you fancy. I still fancy both." He downed the wine in the same way he had disposed of the vodka, and Hillsden noticed that the small surface veins on his cheeks had gradually reddened. "A change of scenery hasn't changed any of that."

"Tell me about the rest."

"Where do you want to start?"

"You're the one who died. Let's begin with your watery death."

"Did you like that touch? The lake was my idea. They provided a body and dressed it in my clothes, just like the man who never was—

270

remember that wartime ruse? I'm told I'm buried in Vienna's Central Cemetery, and that I even have a headstone provided by the British Council. I was going to pay a visit and take flowers one day, then thought better of it. Would have been a good scene in a Hitchcock film. That's about the only thing I miss, living in Switzerland: all the films are a hundred years old by the time we see them."

Jock's speech was hurried and slightly slurred. I was wrong before, Hillsden thought. It isn't just nervousness; he actually wants to talk. He's more interested in telling me his own story than hearing mine.

"You live in Switzerland?"

"Yes, didn't I mention that? Not at the beginning, of course. In the beginning they brought me here, like you. Via East Berlin. Aren't you eating?"

"I'm not hungry."

"They want you to look good on television."

"Go on, I'm fascinated. Why the decision to kill you off? There must have been a special reason."

"The reason, dear Horatio, is in our stars, if that's the right quotation. I always lacked your superior literary knowledge, didn't I?"

"I get the gist."

"It all began with one of those hopeless-from-the-beginning complicated fucking scenarios that London think up from time to time. I'm convinced they use a Ouija board. Control had only been in the top seat a matter of months after Gunga's departure, and I guess he wanted to make his mark. The idea was that Caroline would defect once she got to Berlin. Henze was to set her up. There was a feeling that Moscow Centre suspected that Henze had been turned, so it was to be a good-conduct pass for him. Then once she'd been turned she was to find out the identity of the supermole back home."

"That's right, they still believed in his existence in those days, didn't they?" Hillsden said blandly. "But go on about Caroline—how much of that did you know?"

"All of it. All of it from London's end, that is."

"And you went along with it?"

"No, I told them it was a lousy idea, but I was overruled. And that was the real reason Control wouldn't let you go in with her. He knew about your relationship, and he thought you'd talk her out of it."

"He was right. Had I known."

"So you were packed off home and Caroline did as she was told. Didn't any of this come out afterwards?"

"Not a word."

271

"Doesn't surprise me. Nobody wanted to take the can back. And what's another agent between friends? The whole thing went wrong immediately. Henze was killed shortly after she got there. She did manage to make contact, but there wasn't time to follow through with the rest of the scheme. She tried to go it alone—you know how single-minded she was. It wasn't just a job to Caroline, it was a personal vendetta. She was picked up a few days after Henze bought it."

Jock stared into his wineglass. Hillsden did not look at him. "And you?" he said, breaking the silence.

"They got me in Vienna, about a month later. And as you might have suspected, I was never cut out to be a hero, chum. Glasgow slums don't prepare you for that role in life. In any case, there aren't any heroes anymore, just mugs. I thought, Fuck it, who wants to be a mug, who cares? The whole bloody network had gone up in smoke. London weren't going to bail me out. No way. They were never going to trade me; I had too many stories to take home. So I did my own deal and settled for the terms on offer. I was to be killed off publicly, then, after an interval, used in a different way. It's worked out okay. The pay is good, I live well, they don't call on my services too often, I'm a respectable Swiss citizen now." He tossed off the rest of his wine.

"Did you ever see Caroline again?"

"No."

"Weren't you worried when they traded her?"

Jock took the empty glass from his lips. "Why would I be worried?"

"You said you had no idea they sent her back a vegetable. For all you knew, she could have made you a less than respectable citizen."

Jock shook his head violently. The veins on his cheeks were now quite prominent. "They don't work like that, chum. If they told her anything, they told her I was dead."

"Who were you dealing with? The Centre or Abramov's mob?"

Before Jock could answer, they were interrupted by Tanya. She looked at Hillsden's plate. "You don't like my cooking, Mr. Hillisdent?"

"It's fine. It's just that I'm not that hungry."

The answer did not placate her. While she cleared the table she made clucking noises with her teeth. "You don't eat, I get into trouble."

"I'll eat tomorrow."

"You made her lose face," Jock said when she had gone. "Never make them lose face, old son. Rule One. I learned that early on."

"I'il try and remember."

"Listen, you're home and dry. Give a good account of yourself at the press conference and they'll treat you like a king. Hey, it's good to see you again. Just like old times."

"Nearly," Hillsden said, thinking of the moment when the cameras would turn.

35

THE REHEARSED PRESS conference was skillfully stage-managed. The television coverage, simultaneously translated into a dozen languages, was relayed by satellite and given due prominence in Western Europe and the United States. Hillsden appeared relaxed and in good health, and gave the reasons for his defection without faltering. Trained observers could detect no signs that he had been drugged or otherwise forced into his confession. His statement was predictably laced with accusations of the aggressive intentions of the West and the threat they posed to world peace. He acknowledged that he had been an active member of MI6 and had carried out subversive operations against the USSR, which he now regretted. He went on to say that his decision to defect had stemmed from his gradual alienation from the warlike materialism of the West and his appreciation of the merits of the Soviet system. He stated that he had asked for and had been granted political asylum, and that it was his intention to apply for Soviet citizenship.

Whitehall made every effort to minimize Hillsden's importance, letting it be known that for many years he had been dealing with low-classification operations mostly concerned with internal security. Great play was made of the fact that he was wanted in connection with the murder of Sir Charles Belfrage, that he had a criminal record following his dismissal from the security services, and that he had undergone psychiatric treatment. More for appearance' sake than anything else, a formal request was made to the Soviet authorities for his extradition on the charge of murder, and nobody in the government was surprised when the request was turned down. In a tit-for-tat operation, six members of the Soviet embassy in London had their diplomatic status revoked and were required to leave the country in forty-eight hours.

And there, officially, the case of Alec Hillsden was left to die a natural death.

Unofficially, it was kept alive for a few more weeks in Fleet Street, the main beneficiary being Hillsden's ex-wife. His disappearance and subsequent emergence in Moscow had given her the one thing she had always secretly hankered after: a sense of being somebody set apart. After the initial shock, she had discovered there were material advantages to her changed status. At an auction organized by her solicitor, one of the Sunday tabloids secured the rights to her story and paid a five-figure sum for it. The turgid exaggerations of her otherwise banal history were ghosted into a four-part serial under the general title of A TRAITOR SHARED MY BED. As always, the combination of sex and treachery proved a copper-bottomed circulation booster. Margot bought a scrapbook and carefully pasted in it all her clippings; in a remarkably short space of time she had come to believe all that was being written about her. The spoils allowed her to run riot among the mail-order catalogs. She sent away for a collection of china birds, a complete set of Dickens bound in imitation leather, a bracket clock with Westminster chimes, and a custom-made luxury kitchen for her new apartment which, sadly, proved to be neither custom-made nor luxurious.

Fame, even of the most mundane variety, soon becomes addictive, and when interest in the Hillsden affair was replaced on the front pages by the next ten-day wonder, Margot experienced withdrawal symptoms. For the first time since the early days of her marriage, she began to frequent pubs, and it was at one in Mayfair that she met and shortly afterwards took as a lover a man considerably younger than herself who claimed to be a pilot with British Airways. In point of fact he was a chauffeur working for a car-hire firm, married, with three children, his single experience of air travel being a holiday charter flight to the Costa Brava. Nevertheless his bogus story left Margot unsuspecting during those times when his marriage had prior claim, and his prowess in bed gave her a new lease on life. It never occurred to her that she had exchanged one form of treachery for a more common variety, and the memory of Hillsden quickly faded.

Pamela, on the other hand, to her surprise, thought a great deal about Hillsden. Following Belfrage's murder she had left the country for a period, and remained abroad until Gunther got word to her that it was safe for her to return. Even so, he decided that it would be unwise for them to set up house again, and they both moved to different parts of London, only meeting in crowded restaurants patronized by the younger set.

On this particular night she waited for him in the latest "in-place," a small trattoria just off Knightsbridge that served indifferent Italian food at exorbitant prices to those snobbish enough to frequent it. He was late as usual, and as she sat waiting for him and surveyed the flushed faces at the closely packed adjacent tables, she could not help thinking how a well-placed bomb would thin their idiot ranks. She ordered a first course to pacify the equally snobbish waiter, then passed the time sorting through the contents of her handbag. She stared at the round plastic box containing her contraceptive pills and tried to remember whether she had taken one that morning. It was something that never changed —whatever the circumstances, women never escaped their physical destinies.

The party at the next table suddenly erupted as a hysterical girl spilled a glass of Coke down her smart little Laura Ashley print blouse. One of the young men at her table caught Pamela's eye and leered. "He's not going to show up now, petal. Why don't you join us?"

Smile, humor the twit. "I'm used to it. Thanks all the same."

"I damn well wouldn't leave you sitting there."

You damn well wouldn't have the bloody opportunity, she thought, her smile still fixed in place, hating Gunther for exposing her to the exchange. Outside, a unit of the Bomb Squad went past at suicidal speed, its siren screaming.

She turned her thoughts to Hillsden again, thinking back to the cross-Channel trip and their lovemaking. She wondered what life in exile was like, and whether the time would come when she would leave England forever. Hillsden had done it; he had crossed the Rubicon. She remembered the scar on his body, and the intensity of the memory surprised and troubled her. The mood was broken when the same young man rocked backwards on his chair and pushed his excited face closer to her. "I should give him up as a bad job if I were you, petal. You sure you don't want to join me? You look so forlorn sitting there on your own."

She stared at him without expression, freezing him out, seeing herself pulling the trigger without hesitation, the ruptured body blown clean off the chair and his stupid grin disappearing for good.

LESS than a mile from Pamela, the Prime Minister's car and police escort drove out of the courtyard of Buckingham Palace. The P.M. had just finished a lengthy audience with the Monarch, the third he had

275

requested that week. Tonight he had offered nothing but bad news. During the short journey from Downing Street to the Palace he had decided it was his duty to inform the Monarch that the country was in danger of becoming ungovernable unless further draconian steps were taken. The police forces were now so extended in their efforts to contain the widespread industrial violence that the breaking point was near. This left only the option of putting in the armed forces and declaring a state of emergency. He had learned that there was little to be gained by mincing his words; the Monarch preferred—indeed, invited—plain speaking. After he had related these somber facts, he had been asked whether he should consider the possibility of forming and leading a coalition government. He had replied, truthfully, that such a step was something he had considered and did not discount, but during the discussion that followed he admitted he could not give any assurance that he would be able to carry the majority of his Party with him.

"For the moment I have the broad support of the entire House, but I cannot conceal from Your Majesty—and it gives me no pleasure to have to admit this—that certain elements within my own Party already violently oppose the measures taken so far. How they will react in the days ahead is an open question. It grieves me to say this, but I must live with the facts of political life."

He had not mentioned Lewisham, nor had he been pressed to name names. But it was Lewisham in full cry, Lewisham the demagogue and potential willing martyr stomping the country, sniping at the government's actions, lighting the fuses of new discontents, grabbing the headlines, who was causing him sleepless nights. In recent weeks the man had been urging a General Strike to bring about the reforms he claimed were necessary. His skills as an inflammatory orator could not be denied. He had the gift of the public gab, and was never at a loss for a rabble-rousing piece of personal invective. His basic technique was to dangle the impossible hope of total equality for all, concealing the maggot in the heart of the carrot.

The Prime Minister had transcripts of all Lewisham's speeches brought to him as soon as possible, and on that night, arriving back at Downing Street, he was given the latest, delivered a few hours previously at a mass rally in Wembley Stadium. Having poured himself a generous drink, he sat down to study the transcript. It contained the usual diatribe about the emergence of a police state, and here Lewisham never neglected to use emotive comparisons with Right-wing repressive dictatorships. He constantly referred to the police as a paramilitary force that was being used as a political weapon to crush the working class. "The true voice of democracy is being deliberately silenced. The Tory gutter press prints only distortions and lies. But there is no lie they can print, no distortion of the truths I put before you, no smear they can invent against me or my family, that will ever divert me from the great socialist crusade I serve, have always served, and will continue to serve."

The Prime Minister's reading was interrupted by the flashing light on his hot-line phone. He picked up the receiver. His expression changed as he listened.

"He's what? Is it on the box now? Right, I'll come down to the press office. Call the Home Secretary and the Commissioner of Police and tell them to get here immediately."

He finished off his drink and hurried downstairs. Members of his personal staff were waiting for him in the press office, grouped around the television set. The familiar face of one of the BBC's news announcers filled the screen.

". . . We're hoping to go to Charles Sterling, who is at the scene," he was saying.

"Where?" the Prime Minister asked.

"At his father's house."

"God! Is that where it happened?"

"Yes, sir."

The picture on the television screen switched to a man standing on the pavement of a suburban street. The whole area was bright with arc lights. In the background the white tapes used by the police to seal off bomb incidents could be clearly seen; inside the taped area was a wrecked and smoking saloon car. Large numbers of uniformed police were milling around.

On camera, Sterling lifted his hand mike and began to report. "It would seem that the gunman or gunmen were concealed in a vacant house on the opposite side of the road when Mr. Lewisham arrived here following his appearance earlier this evening at Wembley Stadium. He had come to visit his elderly father, who lives in this house, number 74 Arcia Avenue. The terrorists opened fire with automatic weapons as soon as he stepped out of his car, and he received multiple bullet wounds. A short while ago he was removed to Croydon General Hospital after receiving emergency medical treatment as he lay on the pavement. According to the Incident officer in charge, his condition on arrival at the hospital gives cause for alarm."

Sterling paused as his voice was obliterated by the sirens of another police car and a fire engine arriving at the scene, then resumed: "The situation is still confused, and there are conflicting reports regarding the number of terrorists involved and their subsequent actions. The whole area has been sealed off, and a massive police operation is now in progress. I understand that armed police marksmen are involved. As soon as I have any additional information we shall be returning to the scene; in the meantime back to the news studio."

The studio announcer reappeared. "As viewers will have heard, the Right Honorable Graham Lewisham, the controversial Member of Parliament and until recently a Cabinet Minister, was tonight the victim of an assassination attempt. Unknown gunmen attacked him as he arrived outside his father's house in Croydon. His chauffeur, who has so far not been named, died immediately, and Mr. Lewisham received severe injuries. He is now undergoing emergency surgery, and his wife is on her way to be by his side. So far there has been no clue as to the identity of the gunmen, although it is well known that Mr. Lewisham has received many threats on his life. Since resigning from the Cabinet he has been an outspoken critic of the government, and in particular has denounced the tactics of the police in dealing with industrial disputes. We shall be breaking into our regular programs to bring you the latest bulletins as soon as we have any further information." He paused and looked off-camera. "I understand we have just received film taken at Wembley earlier tonight when Mr. Lewisham made another characteristically provocative speech."

"Turn the sound down," the Prime Minister said as one of his aides handed him a phone.

"The hospital on the line, sir."

"What's the latest? I see. How do they rate his chances? I see. Well, stay with it. I want to know the moment there's any development. And as soon as Mrs. Lewisham arrives, put her through to me here."

He hung up without ceremony and turned to the others. "Alfred, you'd better start drafting a statement for me to give to the press. Two versions, just in case. And I'll need to have something to present to the House tomorrow. Make it tough, whatever the outcome. What a bloody turn-up for the book!"

"What news from the hospital, sir?"

"Less than fifty-fifty. He was blown half to pieces. Two bullets lodged close to the brain. Where's Tony? Tony, call a full Cabinet meeting for first thing tomorrow. Everybody—no excuses, no exceptions."

Somebody else entered the room. "Prime Minister, there are television crews outside."

"They'll have to wait. I'm not making any statement at the moment, other than the obvious, which you can relay. Horror and disgust at this latest outrage—you know the bloody form." He stared at the image of Lewisham on the box. "Christ! This is all we needed. Michael, come with me: I want a word alone."

He exited, followed by his principal private secretary. His first call upon reaching his office was to ring the Palace and speak to the Monarch. That done, he rang his wife in the flat on the top floors of No. 10 to say he would be up most of the night, and asked her to organize coffee and sandwiches. Then, while waiting for Bayldon and the Commissioner to arrive, he tried to anticipate what further horrors lay ahead.

GUNTHER finally made his appearance, threading his way through the crush to where Pamela still waited. His arrival was noted with some distaste by the young man at the adjoining table.

"I've been here over an hour."

"So?"

"Well, don't apologize, will you?"

"My business took longer than planned. Come on, we're leaving."

"Leaving? Aren't we going to eat? All I've had is a first course, just to keep the table."

"I can't help that. I've changed my plans."

"What's happened?"

"Don't ask. Watch the late-night news if you want to find out. You're driving me to the airport."

"I didn't bring the car."

"Shit! Why not?"

"You didn't tell me to. Am I going with you?"

"Use your brain. Of course not. Where is the car?"

"Where I left it, outside my place."

"Then we'll have to find a taxi and pick it up. Get your things."

He snapped his fingers for the waiter, forgetting that the one way of ensuring bad service in a British restaurant is to treat the staff as staff.

DESPITE three hours of surgery, Lewisham died on the operating table. His wife was told that had he survived, the damage to his brain was so extensive that he would have been deprived of most normal functions. Mrs. Lewisham collapsed and had to be put under sedation. The Prime

Minister was informed within minutes and spent the rest of the night with the Home Secretary and the Commissioner, discussing the measures they agreed would be necessary to contain the inevitable repercussions. In view of the gravity of the situation it was decided to cancel all Army leave, and this directive went out to the Ministry of Defence. A maximum alert went into effect at all government buildings and an intensive watch put on all sea and air ports, but by then Gunther had slipped the net on the last plane to the Continent.

36

AS JOCK HAD predicted, Hillsden was treated well following the televised press conference. He was provided with an apartment, large by Moscow standards and situated close to the Novodevichy Monastery in an area reserved for privileged Party officials. It was on the fifth floor of a massive block. The furniture seemed prewar, the sort of anonymous tables and chairs his parents might have purchased when first married, suggesting a kind of sad permanence. They were the only things that gave him any sense of his past life. The flat was reasonably well heated and contained the basic essentials for bachelor life, including a small library of English novels that in the ordinary course of events he would have despised reading, but which he now found strangely comforting. As a housewarming gift, Jock arrived with a canary in an antique wicker cage, which Hillsden placed in the only window that gave him a clear view of the alien city.

"Answers to the name of Gromyko," Jock said.

"You're pissed, Jock. Canaries don't answer to anything."

"I'm nowhere near pissed, though I'm certainly pissed off. They're keeping me here for some bloody reason that so far hasn't been explained. I've been given an apartment like this on the third floor. Remember that play? Saw it once, didn't understand it. *The Passing of the Third Floor Back.* Somebody told me afterwards it was all about Jesus. I didn't get it. Too deep for me. I wouldn't say no to a drink if you asked me."

"I don't think there is any."

"Got to get you organized, old son. Have they given you any money?"

"Yes, but I've no idea where to spend it."

"I shall have to take you around, show you the ropes and the sights. You need hard currency to get anything halfway decent. Bloody rubles are no use. Wait here. Like MacArthur, I shall return."

He disappeared for ten minutes, returning with a full bottle of Johnnie Walker, which they demolished together. The evening ended with them singing the Eton Boating Song and "A Long Way to Tipperary" with forced gaiety, but when Jock had staggered back to his own apartment, Hillsden was left with the feeling that he had been in the company of a stranger. Perhaps, he thought, the scars formed during a lifetime of distrust were so deeply ingrained, like pitted pores on a coal miner's neck, that nothing could fade them.

He saw little of the other residents. The housekeeper who had been allocated to him came in daily to make his bed and keep the apartment tidy. In appearance she was not much different from the Cockney char-ladies toiling in the corridors of Whitehall, but she spoke no English (or at least showed no comprehension, he could not be sure which), and in the beginning his Russian was only sufficient for elementary pleasantries.

Abramov visited him once, and Hillsden took the opportunity to request some Russian textbooks. "Of course. I will arrange for this. You can have a teacher if you wish. I want you to be comfortable now that you are with us permanently. Likewise, if you wish to visit the ballet or the opera, this too will be arranged. We have the best. Your friend Calder could accompany you. How is he, by the way? Do you see much of him?"

"Yes, we spend time together, but he has his own life."

"I put him here in the same building because I thought it would be company for you. Do you find him changed?"

"I imagine we've both changed since we last met."

"His sudden reappearance must have been a shock."

"Yes, it was. Drowning is usually permanent."

"But then, the world is dull if it is always predictable, don't you agree?" Abramov moved to the canary and poked a finger through the bars of the cage. The bird fluttered in panic, shedding small feathers. "They are so stupid, these birds. Born in captivity, but they never get used to it." He remained by the cage, his back to Hillsden. "I think perhaps Calder is not enamored of Moscow. He prefers Switzerland. It's a dull country, I'm told. They've never had a war, of course."

"Not recently. A few centuries ago they provided most of the merce-naries for the rest of Europe."

"Is that so? You are telling me something I did not know. I can't imagine living in such a country myself. The very rich are obscene. One reads about them in Western newspapers and wonders why the revolution has been so long delayed. It will come. Nothing can prevent it. Like that African animal that runs in circles and eats its own entrails, the capitalist system will do the same. Then there will be a place for you."

He rapped on the side of the cage and the canary went into a new frenzy. "When you have settled down, you will find there are many compensations in our society. In the meantime, if you can bring your influence to bear on your friend, it would be a personal favor to me."

"I'm not his keeper."

"No, but I'm sure you take my meaning. He has a tendency to—what do you call it?—kick over the braces."

"Traces."

"Thank you. Not a wise course in his position."

"I'll do a trade with you," Hillsden said.

"What have you in mind?"

"In return for keeping an eye on Jock, there are certain gaps in my own life that I'd like filled."

"You mean you would like more agreeable company?"

"That, too, maybe, but I was thinking of something else. Now that I've severed all the old links, it would set my mind at rest to have the answers to certain questions." He waited, but Abramov gave no reaction. "Why was Caroline killed, for instance, and by whom?"

"You think that is worth knowing?"

"To me, yes."

"Well, we'll see. I'll bear it in mind. It's early days yet. Don't think about the past too much. The future is here."

As Hillsden had quickly learned, nothing happened swiftly in Moscow. More than two weeks passed before the textbooks were brought to him by a girl he guessed to be in her early thirties. She introduced herself as Sonya Aleksandrov, a professor of English at the university. "I am here to teach you. Do you have any Russian?"

"Not really. What I have is pathetic."

"Good. We can start from the beginning."

"It's shaming that with a few notable exceptions, the British seldom bother to learn other peoples' languages. I suppose it stems from the days when we thought we owned the world. You obviously speak my language very well."

"I think not. Maybe you will correct me when I make mistakes?"

Hillsden was not sexually attracted to her—she was too thickset and buxom for his taste—but she had a pleasant personality and was an excellent teacher, encouraging him extravagantly through the first stages. He began to look forward to her twice-weekly visits. She was also helpful in other ways, on one occasion offering to take him on a sight-seeing tour of the museums and art galleries. This was something he had asked Jock to arrange, but Calder showed little inclination for Russian culture, although they did visit the opera together.

"You can do better," Jock said during the interval.

"Better than what?"

"Your little schoolmarm."

"It's a strictly professional arrangement."

"For the time being."

"She's not my type."

"What is your type, Alec?"

"I thought you knew."

There was a pause. "I'm only saying this for your own good. You can't live alone, not in this place. You'll go mad."

"Well, when my Russian is fluent, I shall wander forth and chat up some of the local talent."

Jock shook his head. "No, it doesn't work like that."

"Well, don't worry about it. I imagine it will take care of itself one way or another."

"She's probably been planted on you," Jock continued when they were back in the apartment. "You should be careful."

"I'm sure she was planted; Abramov chose her for me. But since all we do is study Russian grammar, I hardly think she's going to discover anything new about me."

"Don't be too sure. They never let go," Jock said. "You'll find that out."

"You're bloody gloomy tonight."

"Operas are too long. And all those mountains of flesh, puffing out their tits like pouter pigeons." He reached for the whisky. "Don't mind, do you?"

"Go ahead. You provided it. You *are* giving it a bit of a thrashing these days."

"Yes, well, I'm bored with being kept here. I miss my own place, my own amusements. I might add that my amusements are a bloody sight younger than your professor. Switzerland isn't all cowbells and yodeling, you know."

"Why are they keeping you here?"

"Good question. They won't give me any answers. Has he said anything to you?"

"Abramov? No. But then, he's not running you, is he?"

"No. I'm being run from Zurich. Have been for years."

"Perhaps they're thinking of a special job."

"They could do that without my being here. That's how it's always been." He grimaced as he swallowed the whisky. "I think they water this stuff before they sell it to us. I wouldn't put anything past them. D'you notice any difference?"

"No, not really. I'm not a native connoisseur like you."

"Well, I tell you what, I'm going to arrange a party. A bloody good party. I'm not going to stagnate here. The old equipment needs some exercise. You want to come to my party?"

"If I'm invited."

"Course you're bloody invited. I owe you one. After all, I'm your best friend, aren't I?"

"You are now," Hillsden said, looking away to the canary in the cage.

HILLSDEN's fluency in Russian progressed slowly. He found going back to school difficult; his concentration wavered when Sonya was not present. He made a point of watching the television news bulletins in an attempt to improve his limited vocabulary, although their content, when he managed to understand them, irritated him. There appeared to be no restrictions on his movements, and armed with a guide book he took to walking long distances in an attempt to physically exhaust himself, for he had become a victim of insomnia, something he had never experienced before. During these sight-seeing trips he was conscious of being tailed, but since his journeys were innocent, he was never troubled. In the small hours of the night when sleep eluded him, he often wrote letters to Margot that subsequently he never posted. In one of those strange reversals of human nature, he found that he missed her and wanted to make amends for causing their marriage to become a wasteland.

But mostly his thoughts returned to the still unexplained mystery of Caroline's death. He often attempted to draw out Jock on the subject, but without success. Calder's behavior was becoming more and more erratic. After a few drinks—three seemed to be the optimum figure—the anger that lay just beneath the surface erupted. Often he lapsed into rambling, maudlin monologues about the injustice of his present situation that Hillsden only half listened to.

"I thought we were going to have a party to cheer you up?"

"What party?"

"Well, you were the one who suggested it."

"That's right. You're right. We both need cheering up. We used to have some good times back in Austria, didn't we? The three of us. Those were good times. Did we know they were good times, or is it only now that we think they were?"

"They were better times. But the past is a foreign country."

"That's very astute. I like that."

"Not mine, I'm afraid. Hartley wrote it."

"Hartley? Did I know him?"

"L. P. Hartley, the novelist. The full quotation is 'The past is a foreign country, they do things differently there.' It's the first sentence of *The Go-Between.*"

"You're so fucking well read."

"Not any longer." Hillsden waved a hand in the direction of his ragged library. "Apart from the Russian classics the good Sonya makes me study, I'm starved. I can hardly get excited rereading *Children of the New Forest* and *The Water Babies.*"

"Have you made a pass at Sonya yet?"

"No, I've resisted that. I thought you were going to take care of my sex life."

"I will. Haven't forgotten. But you're such a bloody romantic. I can lay on a bit of nookie, but I can't guarantee the romance."

"Haven't you ever been in love?"

"Tried it once. Didn't work. I can't get it up for love, old son. Have to have an element of fantasy. That's the only thing that turns me on. And afterwards, I can't wait to see the back of them." He turned the empty whisky bottle upside down. "Another dead soldier. Okay! Party time. Tell me your preference."

"I thought you knew my type."

"Remind me."

"You remember Caroline, don't you?" Hillsden said carefully.

"Course I remember Caroline. Hardly likely to forget her." He got to his feet still clutching the empty bottle. "But she's dead. Like you told me. You told me that," he repeated, weaving his way to the door. "I'll come up with something. Depend on old Jock. Procurer extraordinary to the Court of St. James and well-known Moscow pimp. Awarded the Order of Lenin, third class, for services to mankind." The bottle slipped from his hand as he groped for the door handle. Opening the door, he shouted into the long bleak corridor: "Awake, you prisoners of want!" and then he was gone.

37

THEY HAD OTHER such evenings, some more drunken than others, with Hillsden holding back, staying reasonably sober, gradually lulling Jock to reveal more of himself. The feeling that there was something bogus about Jock's account of the past grew in him like the first mouthfuls of rice in a starving child's belly. Progress was slow, for even when heavily in his cups, Jock seldom let his guard drop completely and the old instincts for self-preservation held firm. But Hillsden had all the time in the world now, and with each new session he edged closer to the center of the maze.

Finally, after throwing out numerous hints about his connections with Moscow's underground culture, and true to his often repeated promise, Jock announced that his celebrated party would take place. "My pad, I think. Not so many flights for the girls to walk."

"How are you going to smuggle them in?"

"You leave that to Jock. A wink is as good as a nod, old chum. And this is on me. Tonight we cement the Anglo-Soviet friendship pact. A splendid opportunity for you to try out your new prowess in Russian. Any sexual colloquialisms you lack, I'll supply."

Hillsden viewed the prospect with something less than enthusiasm, then on second thought decided there might be hidden advantages. Remembering his last conversation with Abramov, he requested a meeting, using the unlisted telephone number he had been given, and duly reported the arrangements for the party.

"Being the new boy, I thought I ought to ask you if such entertainments are allowed."

"I appreciate that, Alec, but you're not telling me anything I didn't know. We've already inspected the girls. They are both clean. I was hoping that perhaps you might have found Sonya to your liking, but obviously I judged incorrectly."

"Sonya's very pleasant and an excellent teacher."

"Pleasant, but not stimulating in the right way, I understand. Your friend Calder obviously has your best interests at heart, as indeed I do. You were quite right to check with me. Always feel free to come to me if you are in doubt about anything. Let's hope you like what he has found for you."

"You haven't forgotten your side of the arrangement?"

"How persistent you are, Alec. No. But for the time being, enjoy yourself."

When Hillsden presented himself at Jock's apartment, he found Jock waiting with two pretty girls, one considerably younger than the other. He was offered the older one.

"My inclination was to choose Inga for you, chum. I know you used to prefer the more mature woman, but as my guest, take your pick," Jock said in English. "If you'd prefer Katia, I'm easy. They're both Czech, by the way, and don't speak our lingo, so try German or your schoolboy Russian. In the sack they're both fluent in French."

The sexual innuendo, even though it clearly escaped both the girls, embarrassed Hillsden. "Fine." He greeted Inga in German, since he still felt inhibited about testing his Russian.

"We have eats and a plentiful supply of liquid refreshment," Jock said. He alternated between English and German. "Again, seeing as how there is only one *Schlafzimmer,* I'm quite willing to defer to you. Unless you fancy a foursome, that is?"

"No, you take the bedroom."

"Well, you can have it later. The night is young." He took some of the food and two bottles of wine and disappeared into the bedroom with Katia.

Left alone with Inga, Hillsden poured two glasses of wine and made polite conversation, still sticking to German. He discovered that Inga was a student at the university in the last year of a computer course. She said she liked Moscow, but felt homesick for Prague. Hillsden confessed that he, too, felt much the same way; he missed London. As he said it he wondered how much she had been told about him.

"This the first time I meet an Englishman," she said. If Abramov had briefed her, she concealed it well, he thought. He had always expected Jock to produce two whores, but there was nothing in her manner or dress to suggest she was a professional. Like most of the Russian women he had seen in the streets, she wore little makeup and her clothes were clean but dowdy, concealing rather than emphasizing the shape beneath them.

While they ate he questioned her about computers, confessing that he knew little or nothing about them. "I think they'd intimidate me. I hardly comprehend how television works, let alone anything more complicated."

She found this amusing. As he struggled to keep the conversation flowing he had a sense of déjà vu, his thoughts going back to that period just after the war and his first faltering attempts at fraternization. He remembered how Caroline had been intrigued by that part of his life, and thinking about her withered present lusts. There was something aseptic about a blind date; he found himself incapable of behaving as the situation demanded, and was conscious of Inga's growing perplexity at his hesitation.

"You wish me to take my clothes off?" she said suddenly, bringing matters to a head.

"I don't wish you to do anything you don't want to do."

His reply appeared to confuse her. "You don't like me?"

"On the contrary," he began in English, then apologized and continued in German: "It isn't that. You are a very attractive girl. But you mustn't think you're here to be treated as a whore."

"Are all Englishmen so polite?"

"All Englishmen don't find themselves in this situation."

"You are a long way from home, like me. It's natural to want to be with somebody, and if you like me, why not show me? I take my clothes off, then you stop being polite."

She stood up and began to disrobe, folding each shapeless garment neatly. There was nothing seductive about the process, yet he found himself strangely touched by her eagerness to make things easier for him. When she finally stood nude, it wasn't Caroline he compared her with, but the girl on the boat who called herself Wendy. Wendy, nude, with her firm tanned skin had been so positively Western, her body more akin to a photographer's posed simulation of perfection than anything he had hitherto encountered. But this quiet stranger, who now moved to him and kissed him carefully, was infinitely more human and desirable. He returned her kiss. The taste of wine was still on her lips. When he dropped his head to nuzzle the soft hollow between neck and shoulder that had always aroused him, he caught the fragrance of the scent she was wearing. It had none of the headiness of French perfume; it reminded him of summers past, of the bowls of dried rose petals mixed with sticks of cinnamon his mother had preserved.

As their lips parted she said something in Russian which he failed to understand. She drew him down to the faded cushions on Calder's sofa and began to loosen his clothing. When he was naked, she knelt between his legs and he surrendered himself to the wet warmth of her mouth. Their eventual lovemaking was more intense than he had experienced for years; it was as though their shared loneliness in the alien city consumed them both, as though they were true lovers without hope instead of strangers who might never meet again. She cried out as his flesh pulsed inside her to match her needs, and he felt her nails rake across the scar on his back. For some minutes afterwards he lay dazed, suspended in time, stupefied, the girl still trembling beneath him, murmuring inarticulately; he was conscious only of the racing of their closely joined hearts. Then they must have slept, for what he next heard was another, sharper cry that he could not place at first, believing it to be part of a dream. Again he heard it, followed by the crash of something falling in the other room. This time it roused Inga and they untangled their bodies, raising themselves to listen.

"What is it?" she whispered. "Is it Katia?"

"I don't know."

He got up from the sofa and went to the bedroom door. He could just make out Jock's voice mingled with another sound, the low moaning of somebody in pain.

"Jock? Everything okay? What's happening?"

Inga joined him and gestured for him to try the door handle. It was locked. Then he rapped on the door. "Jock! what's going on?"

There was silence for several moments before the key was turned in the lock. When the door was opened, Jock stood there naked, blocking their view of the room. There was blood on his chest and abdomen.

"Been an accident," he said. His speech was slurred.

Hillsden pushed him to one side. The naked body of the younger girl lay face downwards on the rumpled bed. The sheets were bloodstained in places, and under the lower half of her body was a larger stain, as though a bottle of wine had been spilled.

"Jesus Christ! What the hell have you done to her?"

He went to the bed and gently turned the girl over, bending to listen for a heartbeat. To his relief she was still breathing. A trickle of blood issued from between her thighs. As he swung around to face Jock, his toe stubbed against an empty wine bottle by the side of the bed. With a growing sense of horror and revulsion he saw that the neck of the bottle had blood on it.

"You sadistic maniac! You've nearly killed her. Inga! Get some towels and water. Quick as you can," he called in German. Jock sank down on his knees by the door. Hillsden went over to him and slapped his face. "What did you do to her?"

"Didn't mean it. Just an accident. Help me."

"Fuck helping you. It's that poor kid who needs help."

Inga returned with a bowl of water and a towel.

"Do what you can for her."

He went back into the other room and searched for his discarded clothes. As he pulled on his shirt and trousers he tried to decide what to do. The moment he was dressed he hurried down the bleak corridor to the next apartment and hammered on the door without thought of the consequences. There was an appreciable pause before the door was half opened. He could not see who was beyond it.

"Telephone, I need to telephone, there's been an accident," he said in what he hoped was intelligible Russian.

The door opened wider and he found himself facing an elderly man in a nightshirt. "Please," he insisted. "It's very urgent. I must telephone for a doctor. A girl is very sick." His Russian was just adequate enough for his needs.

The man studied him but said nothing.

"You have a telephone I can use?"

"*Da,*" the man said finally. He stood aside and allowed Hillsden to enter.

"Where is it?"

The man switched on a light and led him into a study. He pointed to a desk and waited in the doorway while Hillsden picked up the instrument. All he could think of was to dial Abramov's private number. It rang several times before it was answered. Something warned him to speak in English. As briefly as possible he explained what had happened.

"Is she dead?"

"No, but she needs a doctor quickly."

"Just stay there. Don't speak to anybody else. I will take care of everything."

Hillsden hung up and turned to the silent man in the doorway. "Thank you. Thank you very much. I am most grateful."

It wasn't until he was back in Jock's apartment that he realized he could have used Jock's phone. Inga was kneeling by the side of the bed. Jock was where he had left him. "How is she?"

"Very bad. Is a doctor coming?"

"Yes. Try to keep her warm."

He went over to Jock and pulled him to his feet. "Now listen! You're in deep trouble, do you realize that? Get some clothes on and leave all the talking to me when they arrive. Do you understand what I'm say-ing?" Jock nodded. He pushed him to one side, collected Inga's clothes in the other room, returned to the bedroom and handed them to her. Then he went to the small kitchen in search of utensils to make some coffee. He had no idea how long it would take Abramov to arrive. While waiting for the water to boil he made another trip to the bedroom, taking his own jacket to add to the blankets Inga had wrapped around the girl. He slipped a hand under the coverings to feel for her heart again, and found that her entire body was shuddering.

Jock was partially dressed by now, but seemed incapable of any coordinated movements. "What's going to happen?" he kept repeating.

"Who knows? Just pray you haven't killed her, that's all." He thrust Jock's shirt at him and returned to the kitchen. Jock followed him.

"Get some of this coffee down you and try to sober up before anybody arrives. How could you do that?"

"Just started as a bit of fun."

"Don't give me that, you perverted bastard! If that's your idea of fun, God help you."

"Who did you ring?"

"Abramov."

Jock swayed, spilling hot coffee. "Oh, Jesus, why him?"

"Because he was the only one I could think of."

"Oh, Jesus, what will I say?"

"It won't make any difference what you say. He'll see for himself."

"Chum, don't you turn on me. You have to help me somehow."

"What can I do?"

Suddenly Jock bent over the sink and vomited. Hillsden made no effort to comfort him, watching without compassion. He took a cup of coffee to Inga, and they waited by the bedside until Abramov arrived. It was the first time Hillsden had ever seen him out of uniform. He was accompanied by a man they took to be a doctor, who asked, "Where is she?"

Hillsden indicated the bedroom and the man went in, closing the door after him.

"Go to your own apartment with this girl and stay there," Abramov said to Hillsden. "Say nothing of all this to anybody." He turned to Inga and repeated the warning in Russian. "I'll deal with Calder."

"Can't we wait until we know whether she's going to be all right?"

"Your presence will only be a hindrance. Do as I say."

They left and walked up to Hillsden's apartment in silence. When they were inside, Inga said, "Who was that man? Was he KGB?"

"Something like that."

She began to cry, and he put his arms around her. "I'm frightened."

"You did nothing."

"But I was there. We were both there. That's enough."

"Get into my bed. You're cold and shivering."

"Don't leave me alone."

She got beneath the covers fully clothed, and Hillsden lay on top of the bed beside her, cradling and stroking her head until her sobs died away. In the stillness he thought he heard a car starting up far below. Gradually Inga drifted into a fretful sleep, but every time he attempted to ease his cramped body off the bed she reached out and clutched him.

THE following morning he made Inga breakfast before she left for her class at the university, but the horrors of the previous night had made them strangers again, and she scarcely spoke.

"Is there anywhere I can contact you if I have any news?"

"You heard what he said. It's better we don't see each other ever again. God willing, Katia is all right and we both get home to Prague."

"I'm sorry for what happened, but I'm not sorry that I met you. You'll remember your first Englishman for all the worst reasons, won't you?" He tried to kiss her good-bye, but she averted her face. "Take care of yourself," he said with sad finality.

"It's not up to me, is it?" were her last chilling words to him.

LATER that same day, having heard nothing, he decided to ignore Abramov's warning and went downstairs to Jock's apartment. He knocked at the door, but there was no answer. While he stood listening for any sounds of life within, he heard somebody coming up the central stone stairway and hurriedly retreated back to his own floor.

He remained in his apartment until hunger forced him to go out for a meal. On his way down to the street he knocked on Jock's door, but again there was no answer. All he could think of was to eat in the restaurant they usually frequented, in the hope that he might find him there, but he drew a blank.

He ordered from the menu, which was never going to merit a Michelin detour, and, while enduring the usual lack of service, went over again the horrendous events of the previous night. Jock's deterioration had been marked in recent weeks, but Hillsden had put this down to his frustration at being forced to remain in Moscow. True, his drinking had become more pronounced and his moods more erratic; the intervals between truculence and ugliness had telescoped, with a noticeable undercurrent of suppressed violence.

In the Austrian days Jock had always been argumentative, fond of having the last word, but he had never exhibited this darker side so blatantly. Sexually he had been something of an enigma, throwing out the odd oblique hint, but never revealing his true inclinations. Hillsden simply had concluded that Jock's sexual tastes had remained fossilized since adolescence. He used to buy girlie magazines, something that Hillsden and Caroline ribbed him about, but so did thousands of other men his age. There was nothing overtly sinister in that; the mid-twentieth-century obsession for the explicit portrayal of the female nude had spawned an international industry, as well as providing endless ammunition for the cause of women's liberation. Hillsden had once remarked to Caroline that it was all in Jock's mind. "I don't think he really *does* anything much. He *thinks* about it a lot, I'm sure, but that's about as far as it goes." Certainly, whatever the truth of the matter in those days, it had never impinged on Jock's work. Ironically, I was the one who incurred official condemnation, Hillsden thought; adultery blotted *my* copybook.

Yet it wasn't the past that monopolized his thoughts as he picked at the burned offering on his dinner plate, but the recurring image of Katia's violated body on the soiled bed twisted like some broken marionette. He did not think he would ever rid himself of the revulsion he had felt. Whatever Jock had done in that bedroom was beyond his comprehension; there was no starting point, no way in which he could imagine performing such acts on another human being. The disgust that rose in his mouth like bile owed something to his own behavior, the fact that while the horror in the adjoining room had been taking place, he and Inga had reached out for a kind of loving.

He pushed his half-eaten meal away, unable to swallow another mouthful, paid and left the restaurant. The street outside was deserted. Still preoccupied with the same train of thought, he was not aware of being followed until a black Volga limousine pulled up beside him.

"Alec," a familiar voice said. He turned to see Abramov behind the wheel. "Get in. I wish to talk with you."

He did as he was told.

"There are matters we have to discuss," Abramov said as they drove in the direction of Gorky Park.

"How is the girl?"

"The girl died. Her internal organs had been ruptured; she bled to death. You acted correctly, and for that I am grateful, but there was nothing that could be done."

"Oh, God!"

"God was not much help to her. The incident has caused a great many problems, and reflects very badly on me. The girl was Czech—you knew that?"

Hillsden nodded, still numbed by the news.

"Her father is a high-ranking Party member in Prague. Therefore the true circumstances of her death must be concealed. To the outside world she died in an automobile accident."

"What about the other girl?"

"She has already been spoken to and taken care of. She will not be returning home. She has finished her studies at the university and will take up a position of some importance in our East German headquarters —for her own protection, you understand," he added without any trace of irony.

"And Calder?"

"Calder is a more difficult problem. I will get to Calder in a minute."

"Where is he?"

"By now he should be back in his apartment. Suitably uncertain as to his future, which has yet to be decided. But it is you I want to discuss first. I have a proposition to put to you, which I hope will provide answers to a number of unresolved problems. This is your world now. You are one of us, Alec, and you must start thinking like one of us. So far you have not disappointed me; you have passed all the tests. But loyalty, like a delicate piece of machinery, has to be kept well oiled. We can never relax our vigilance if we are to succeed in our final aims. Nor can we ever shirk what that loyalty demands. Now, in the course of our many talks together, you have several times made it clear that you attach great importance to knowing the truth concerning the death of your ex-mistress. I have given the matter much thought and I am willing to make a trade with you."

Abramov brought the car to a halt and switched off the engine. "I will put the proposition in the form of a question. If I was to reveal to you the identity of the person who killed your Caroline, and if I was to so arrange matters as to bring you face-to-face with her killer, what would you do? How strong are your feelings?"

Taken by surprise, Hillsden stared straight ahead; with the engine no longer running, the windscreen had misted, blurring his vision. Abramov's question drained all strength from him; he might have been sitting in a doctor's surgery having just been told he had a terminal disease.

294

"I don't know," he said finally. "I can't give you an intelligent answer."

"Why not?"

"I've never killed."

"Not even in the war?"

"I wasn't that kind of soldier. You know I wasn't in a combat unit."

"Then how about Belfrage?"

"I didn't kill Belfrage. London framed me."

"There's always a first time. And you have the motive."

"That's the trade, is it? If you tell me, I have to go through with it?"

"Since you put it like that, yes, that is the trade. When I thought of it, the intention was to do you a favor."

"Presumably, her murder was carried out for a reason?"

"Correct."

"And, presumably, on your direct orders?"

"Not mine. I'm not a policy maker, Alec. The order came from another, higher source."

"So why do you—they—wish to dispose of the killer if he acted on orders and did such a good job for you?"

"On that occasion, yes. Since then he has not proved so reliable. Now he is considered expendable."

"I still don't understand why it has to be me. You must have better men for the job. What if I botched it?"

Abramov rubbed away some of the condensation on the windscreen with a gloved hand. "It's like many things in life, Alec. If one can resolve several problems at once—ours as well as yours—it has a certain poetic justice. I'm sure you, being a literate man, can appreciate that."

"Except we're not talking about poetry, we're talking about murder."

"I wouldn't put it like that. Would it influence your decision if I said that whether you are involved or not, by his subsequent actions the person concerned has sealed his fate? I don't take you for a stupid man. You must have guessed by now. No? Then perhaps this will help you make up your mind." He leaned over and, with the tip of a gloved finger, wrote CALDER on the misted windscreen in front of Hillsden.

It was very still in the car.

"Does that concentrate your thoughts?"

"I don't believe you."

"Why would I lie? Surely the events of last night must have convinced you that he is capable of such a thing? Think about that. Don't think about him as your friend, but as a man capable of inserting a wine bottle into the vagina of a young girl to satisfy some perverted desire. You saw it with your own eyes. Does that suggest to you somebody who would hesitate to inject poison into the woman you once loved?"

As Abramov smeared the windscreen with his hand, Hillsden sat motionless. "You can have time to think about it. Not too much time. The situation regarding the girl is delicate. We have to remove all the evidence as quickly as possible."

"How do I know you're telling me the truth?"

"I can convince you of that. I can give you every detail of his stay in London. He was under surveillance the entire time. He even murdered again there. A prostitute. It was reported in your London papers. That was for his own satisfaction, not ours. Ours he was paid for. If you want more proof, I can give you more. But if you're still unconvinced, I'll make a further concession. Confront him with it; let him tell you himself."

"Why would he do that? He'd never do that, not to me."

"He would if you offered him a deal."

"What sort of deal?"

"Something that in his present situation I think you'd find him only too anxious to accept. The deal would be that you've spoken to me on his behalf and saved his neck over the dead girl."

Hillsden shook his head violently. "I still can't promise anything."

"But you will try, Alec? I have great confidence in you. I know you'll try for my sake."

Abramov restarted the engine, swung the car around, and they drove back to Hillsden's apartment without speaking. The heater gradually cleared the windscreen, but the last thing to fade was Jock's name.

38

THE ONLY SOUND in the room was the tiny clicking noise the canary made kissing its own image in the metal mirror fixed to the bars of its cage.

Hillsden sat by the window and watched as it flirted and danced along the perch, the tiny head bobbing in ecstasy. It repeated the sequence time and time again, as though, he thought, love was only the reflection of oneself. Sitting there, a glass of whisky in his hand, it occurred to him how much easier life would be without choices.

In searching so long for the truth about Caroline's death he had become the prisoner of his own hatreds; hate had grown in him like a malignant tumor, strangling reason; hate had brought them all to this place where the final choice had to be made. What else but hate had persuaded Caroline to go back that last time? She had passed her hatred on to him, the baton in a relay race nobody could win. And what if Abramov's version was just another macabre joke in a long series instigated by Control? What if yet again he was merely being used as the instrument of another's will to pay off old scores? The present, not the past, was the foreign country he inhabited, where everything was done differently.

He stayed by the window, the rain falling like tears on the glass, as the room darkened and the canary preened and strutted. Since the conversation with Abramov in the car he had done nothing about contacting Jock, though he realized the confrontation could not be delayed much longer. Abramov had been insistent that the matter be resolved quickly. He reached to replenish his whisky, but there was no extra courage left in the bottle. At that moment he heard the knock on the door.

He picked his way across the gloomy room and opened the door. Jock said, "I kept out of your way as long as I could, chum. Got myself together finally. I'm all right now, back to my old self after the scare."

Nobody ever looks any different, Hillsden thought. Murder doesn't change us—only love and grief. He stood aside and let Jock enter.

"God, it's dark in here. All the lights fused or something?"

"No, I've been asleep."

"You're lucky."

Hillsden pressed the switch. The canary fluttered wildly, falling to a corner of the cage; a cloud of small feathers hung in the air.

"You frightened Gromyko. You should put a cloth over him when it's dark. That's what I needed the other night—except that in my case a sack would have been more appropriate. I don't know what the hell got into me, but it's never going to happen again." Jock's voice had the false gaiety of somebody who has walked away unhurt from a car crash. "All tidied away now. I had a very unpleasant session with our mutual friend. He read the riot act, not surprisingly, but promised to take care of everything. One thing I will say about them, they never get uptight about morality; all they're ever concerned with is preserving the image. I just have to keep a very low profile for a while, which I certainly will.

I don't want to live through anything like that again. But you were a brick, chum, a real friend in need. And you did all the right things. I shan't forget I owe you one."

Hillsden let him talk himself out, and his silence disturbed Jock.

"I know how you must feel, and I'm offering no excuses. There *are* no excuses for the way I behaved. It's not an excuse, but I guess I've been thrashing the hard stuff lately. Got myself tied in knots. No *In vino veritas.* The fuse finally blew. It's the bloody atmosphere of this place. I've never been happy here." He faltered again. "You're not saying much. Has anything happened to you?"

"I saw Abramov too."

"You did? When?"

"Last night. I came looking for you, but you weren't home, so I went out for a meal on my own. I was obviously being tailed, and he picked me up when I left the restaurant."

"Did he give you a rough time?"

"No. The conversation mainly centered around you."

"What did he say about me?"

"Presumably what you already know. He was mostly concerned with the death of the girl."

Jock seemed to crumble. "What are you talking about?"

"The girl died. Surely you knew that?"

Jock stared at him.

"What?"

"She's dead. Don't tell me you didn't know?"

"Are you kidding me? Of course I didn't know, I swear." He collapsed into the nearest chair. "Don't kid me, please. Not about that. Just tell me it's not true."

"I'm only telling you what I was told."

"Oh, Jesus!" He rocked backwards and forwards in the chair like an old woman. "Oh, Jesus, God!" His anguish seemed genuine enough, but whether it was for the girl or his own plight there was no means of telling. "I know I said I've sworn off the drink, but I've got to have one now."

Hillsden displayed the empty whisky bottle. "You're out of luck, I'm afraid."

Jock fumbled in his pockets for a cigarette, but was incapable of lighting it. "You've got to help me, chum. What's going to happen now?"

"As far as the girl's concerned, it's been taken care of. Officially, for the benefit of her Party-member father in Prague, she died in a car crash.

298

One of those unfortunate accidents with no witnesses. You're lucky they operate in the narrowest, most stiflingly brutal world imaginable. After all, they've had more than fifty years to perfect a system of deceit. On this occasion it's working for you. The other one, Inga, my girl, has been bought off, so you're safe."

"Is that what Abramov said?"

Hillsden waited for a show of remorse about the dead girl. He had made a pact with himself that what happened next would determine the rest of the story. But even as he watched, Jock started to recover and his relief was as offensive as body odor.

"I bet you had a hand in getting me off the hook. I bet you put in a good word for me, didn't you? For old times' sake. That's two I owe you."

"Yes. Funnily enough, we did talk about old times. About you and me. And Caroline." He struck a match and offered it to Jock.

"Caroline? Why Caroline?"

"As you once reminded me, they never close a file."

"What could he want to know about her?"

"It was mostly what I wanted to know. Little things that still nag at me. He suggested that you were the best person to ask."

"Why would he suggest that?"

"I imagine he thought you were better placed than most to know the truth. You've never really filled me in on your part of the story, have you, Jock?"

"Haven't I? I thought I'd told you most things."

"There are gaps, though, aren't there?"

"Chum, it's water under the bridge. I know you cared a lot about her, I cared about her too, but we can't bring her back."

"I didn't just care about her. I loved her."

Jock's confidence was returning now; he was wary, parrying the questions with a smile. "And we never learn, do we? Love complicates things, I've found. What do you want to know?"

"The end of the story."

"You told *me* the end of the story. The only reason I never went into detail about the rest was that, knowing how you felt, I wanted to spare you." He lit another cigarette from the butt of the first.

"Perhaps now I'm ready to be told."

"Why punish yourself, chum? What good can it do? It's not exactly a bedtime story."

"No, I don't suppose it is, but I'm not looking for comfort."

"Well, if we're going to get into it, I need a drink, chum. A large hair of the dog, despite all the good resolutions. That news about the girl really shook me. Let's continue this down in my place. I think I can put my hands on a bottle or two, and I still have a tin of beluga in the fridge."

Hillsden followed him out into the corridor that always reminded him of an institutional building: a vista of identical, drably painted doors, the perfect setting for any prewar black-and-white thriller. It always surprised him that he heard little or no sound from the other inhabitants. As they took the stairway to the floors below he tried to imagine the next few hours between them. There was no longer any room for maneuver; he was caged as surely as the frightened canary.

Jock's apartment had been cleaned up; there were no traces of the fearful chaos of the night the girl died. Even more than Hillsden's, the rooms were characterless, devoid of personal possessions—only a temporary halt for a transient.

"Do you mind switching?" Jock asked, producing a bottle of vodka.

"A small one to keep you company." Hillsden avoided sitting on the sofa, where he and Inga had made love.

"You know, chum, I can admit it now. When they told me you were defecting, I suspected something. I never figured you coming over. I had you down as the last boy scout." His manner was breezy, as though they were settling down at a school reunion to swap stories about old football games.

"I might say the same about you. Of course, in your case I had no reason to suspect anything; I believed you to be dead."

"My situation was different. And I was never a boy scout. When they took me, I hoisted the white flag quicker than you could say Baden-Powell. I never had any ideals. Did you have ideals when you started?"

Hillsden took his time answering. "I think perhaps I once thought our side played it cleaner than the rest."

"Never. No way. What we do, old son, whoever we do it for, isn't to further the detergent industry. Nothing we wash ever comes out pure white. We're gray people doing gray jobs; everything we touch is stained. Am I right or am I wrong?"

"I guess you're right."

"I *know* I'm right. *You* know I'm right. I was always in it strictly for the money. I wasn't going to end up like the rest. We've both seen them —pathetic old buffers with potbellies, wondering if their pension is going to stretch to a night on the town once a month. Can they afford the club subscription for another year? Wondering why everything they once believed in went down the tubes. Who retired in the mistaken belief that their efforts had made the world safer for democracy. And what did they get in return? A fucking CBE, if they were lucky, to keep in the glass case on the mock Georgian chest of drawers inside the mock Georgian semidetached with double-glazing and electric storage heaters in the hall. Christ! You think I was ever going to settle for that?"

Hillsden saw the house he had shared with Margot, the cold pattern of the wallpaper on the stairs, the bedroom where he had once believed love was safe.

"You think *London* was going to give me a golden handshake tucked away in a Swiss numbered account? The chance never comes twice, chum. You're the literary one. You know the crap they feed you: No man is an island, every man is a part of the whole, et cetera. Bullshit. Believe that and the bell tolls for thee, all right—the funeral bell, sweetheart. It's every man for himself. Always was, always will be. I spotted the con, the old Establishment sleight of hand. I just caught on earlier than you; that's the only difference."

He waved his glass in the air, excited by his own tirade, the vodka splashing on the faded carpet. "What does it matter who has the secrets? *What* secrets? Not the secret of eternal life—now, that would be worth preserving. But all the other shit—the next generation of missiles, the latest nerve gas, laser beams in space. Give it a couple of years and fifth-grade high school students are going to be designing death rays on home computers. They're going to make A-bombs as small as Sony Walkmans, chum. You think any of us can stop what's coming? The world's always been coming to an end."

"I never knew you were such a deep thinker, Jock."

"That's not deep thinking. I reserve that for number one."

"So you surrendered gracefully?"

"Yes, but don't get me wrong, I didn't blow the network. I didn't have to."

"Who did?"

"Have another drink first."

"I'm okay for the moment."

"You're going to need it. I warn you, you're going to find some of this hard to take. Some of your most cherished illusions are about to vaporize, old buddy."

"Assuming I still have any."

Jock regarded him for a moment. "For openers, what would you say if I told you Control betrayed Caroline just to get her out of the way?"

"Control?" Hillsden forced himself to sound and look surprised.

Jock nodded his head vigorously, delighted that he had scored with the first shot.

"Control?" Hillsden repeated. "Jesus Christ! Did you know that when we were all together?"

"Come on! I was playing it straight then. Control fooled me, as he's fooled everybody. But Caroline got too close for comfort, and since Control was running her direct from London, using me as the post office, he was ahead of her every step. She only had one ace in the hole."

"What was that?"

"I'll get to that. Let me tell it in the right order." He poured himself another drink. "Caroline was a loner, agreed? She fought a private war. You knew that. You may have slept with her, but I bet you never got all the way inside her head. Am I right?" Hillsden nodded. "It went back to the death of her father. Now, my theory is that through Glanville, via Henze, word got back to Control that his own position was getting dicey. So the devious bastard arranged to meet her in Salzburg and encouraged her to follow the leads she had. I think she had instincts about him even then. No conclusive proof, just the old female radar working. She boxed cleverly, I'm sure. She must have done; otherwise he'd have made certain she never left Salzburg alive. He went home confident that Berlin would do his dirty work for him. The last thing he had to take care of was you, and you'd already played into his hands by breaking the house rules."

"Is this all theory?"

"Theory, but backed up with hindsight. Since he couldn't be sure how much you knew, how much Caroline had shared with you when your heads were side by side on the pillow, the obvious answer was to get you home, under his wing. Back in London you'd be neutered. So you were ordered to pack your bags and Caroline went into Berlin."

"Where they were waiting for her? But what did she have?"

Jock focused again. "What?"

"You said she had an ace in the hole."

"Ah, that, yes. Don't rush things. Let me tell it in my way. She met with Henze—that much I do know. And he gave her something." Jock paused for effect, his eyes glinting over his glass as he took another drink. "A packet of photographs. Ten photographs, to be exact."

"Photographs of Control?" The word "photographs" triggered a switch in Hillsden's memory.

"No. And I'm saving the big surprise for you. God knows how or where Henze obtained them, but the fact is he did, and he passed them on to Caroline. He knew they were hot, but he hadn't grasped the real significance. Caroline did—immediately. They were the last piece of the puzzle, and dynamite. Not only could they blow Control clean out of the water, they could sink the entire Russian operation in England."

"Tell me, for God's sake!"

"Patience, patience."

"Did you see them, too?"

"I saw nine of them. And she was right."

"How did you get them?"

"Caroline posted them to me, using that safe address we had in Vienna. With Henze dead, she had to move fast. Sending them to you was too risky, so it had to be me, luckily."

"Why 'luckily'?"

"They proved to be my insurance policy later—and I'll come to that. The tenth one she banked herself—literally. She posted it to London, addressed to herself care of Lloyds Bank in St. James's Street where she kept her savings. I guess she thought she had a chance to get out, but they took her the next day."

It required an effort for Hillsden to stifle his impatience, but he was determined that Jock should tie his own noose and hang himself unaided.

"They took her, but for a long time they couldn't break her. And this is the part you're not going to like, but you've been through it now, you know the way they work. She had—everybody has—one vulnerable spot, and they found it." He swallowed his drink and hunched forward as though suddenly gripped with a stab of pain. "Wait, I have to pick up my own threads. When they got me, it didn't take me long to realize that Control had to be the one responsible."

"Why?"

"He was the only one, outside of you and Caroline, who knew the safe house in Vienna. Where was I?"

"They had just picked you up."

"Yes. Classic operation. Three o'clock in the morning. No knock on the door; they had a set of keys. Next stop East Berlin, where they started right in, working me over as if they were racing against a deadline." He no longer looked at Hillsden. "I found out I wasn't brave like you're supposed to be. You never know until you're actually faced with it, do you? They were good at it. Told me what they were going to do with Caroline if I didn't talk. Showed me pictures of other reluctant witnesses. Do I mean witnesses? Victims. The same old techniques the Nazis used—we talked about that in Austria, remember?—how you can bear pain for yourself, but not for others. I couldn't . . . couldn't even bear pain for myself. I didn't know they'd already worked her over. So when they offered me a deal, I told them everything. It seemed to

303

me the best thing I could do for her. We were kept apart, they never let me see Caroline. So my only excuse was, I thought I was saving her. I swear to God that was my thinking."

Hillsden waited. He thought, Why don't I pity him?

"I wasn't to know they'd pick up on something I mentioned casually. I don't even remember how or why it came up. But you know how thorough they are—the same questions repeated hour after hour. They didn't let me sleep for six days. Who knows what I said?" He stared at his empty glass. "Did we get through the bottle?"

"Looks like it. What was it you let slip?"

"I told them about the room."

"The room?"

"The room in Austria at the top of the tower where all the flies went to die. You said it freaked her out, that it was the only time she'd ever betrayed any sign of weakness. They've made a science out of collecting fears." He searched Hillsden's impassive face for some indication that he understood. "I couldn't know they'd use it. How could I have imagined it? I'd have to be one of them, think like them."

He reached for the second bottle, but did not open it. "Know what they did? They built a replica. Reproduced it like a bloody film set. And when they'd built it, they filled it with flies and put her inside. She lasted five days and then she broke. When they let her out, she'd have nailed Christ to the Cross all over again." There was a long pause. "And there you have it. Can you open this? I'm all thumbs."

Hillsden took the second bottle from him. His hand shook as he pulled the cork. After he had filled Jock's glass, he poured a small amount for himself. If Jock noticed, he gave no sign.

"At least say you understand."

"Yes, I understand what it must have been like." He swirled the colorless liquid in his glass, wishing everything else was as clear. "Presumably, part of your deal with them was the packet of photographs?"

"Yes."

"And the tenth one . . . did you tell them about that?"

"How could I? I didn't know about it then." Jock rose to his feet. "Got to take a leak." He weaved his way to the bathroom.

Left alone, Hillsden tried to put his thoughts in order. It was all coming closer, the strands of fog separating: it just needed a last gust to reveal the rest of the lost landscape. He topped up Jock's glass and was back in his chair before Jock returned.

"So how did you find out about it?" Hillsden asked, immediately returning to the interrogation.

"What?"

"The last photograph in the set."

"First of all, ask me who was on it."

"Okay, I'm asking."

"A girl and a man." By now his speech was slurred. "If I produced it now, you'd recognize them both. Boy, would you recognize them. Any guesses?" Hillsden shook his head. "Give you a clue. When was the last time you saw the white cliffs of Dover?" But still the penny did not drop for Hillsden. "All right, second clue: sea gulls." Jock waited, his face as flushed as a small boy who is bursting to betray a confidence. "They brought you over on a boat, didn't they?"

"*That* girl, you mean? Wendy."

"Is that what she called herself? Yes, you dozy prick, that girl!"

Hillsden gave him his moment of triumph, then said, "And was the man her German boyfriend?"

"No, you're not even warm. What did I say? I said it was dynamite. The German is not even in the same league."

"Control, then?"

"Give up, you'll never guess." Jock swallowed the contents of his replenished glass. "Look, let me take it slowly for you. Go back a bit. Henze gives Caroline the photographs. He knows who Wendy—Pamela, what-have-you—is, but he doesn't grasp the significance of the guy in the picture. Why should he? He's just a local boy from Berlin. Caroline, on the other hand, gets it in one. Okay, so far? Now, for a long time, nobody here knew of the existence of the tenth one—me included. They've got my set, they think they've got the lot. Then they trade Caroline. She goes home, and, as you told me, sadly she's a wheelchair case. She's stuck in a nursing home, I imagine. Incommunicado. However, unlike the Swiss, British banks play it straight. If you have an account with them, they send you regular statements. So, presumably, at some point, Caroline's efficient bank manager traced her whereabouts —maybe the Firm gave him the information, they'd consider a bank enquiry was kosher—and he included the photo in the rest of her mail. You with me so far?"

"Yes, it all sounds plausible."

"Let me ask you something. It always puzzled me—why you never visited her."

"Like you, I found out I wasn't that brave when it came to the crunch."

"If you had, you'd have spotted it. But somebody spotted it, and that person told Control."

"Who was it?"

"One of a small army, one of the hibernators nobody looks too closely at—little people serving large causes. Friend of the Matron's. Irish, clean as a whistle on the surface, takes the wafer three times a week, but her true passion is not the Cross, but hatred of the British. She spotted it."

"You still haven't told me what."

"Saving the best to the end. Let's suppose, just suppose, you'd been the one—*you,* not that old Irish biddy. Suppose you *had* paid Caroline a visit—that was always on the cards—and there on her bedside table beside the Mickey Mouse clock is this picture. Pretty girl, so you take a look. Normal enough. You take a closer look, and what do you see?" Jock paused for maximum effect. "Standing with his arm round the girl, none other than Her Majesty's present Home Secretary."

"Bayldon?"

"Bayldon, none other. Control's had him on ice for years. Now, knowing you, you'd have checked it out. You of all people would have wanted to know the reason Caroline kept something like that on display. You would have started to pull in the long daisy chain. Aren't I right? Course I'm right. And that chain would have led you, eventually, to the Right Honorable Mr. Bayldon. You were on the scent anyway, without that: Belfrage, Glanville. Your nose was pointed in the right direction, so Control had to start clearing the decks. After arranging Caroline's elimination, just in case she made a miracle recovery, he then set about disposing of the others, and you were on the list." He poured himself yet another drink, well pleased with the way he had told the story.

"So he had her killed for that?" Hillsden asked slowly as he prepared himself for the last question.

"Oh, depend on it, Control kept himself distanced. He let this side make all the funeral arrangements. He may run Bayldon, but he doesn't run those sort of risks. But even Control doesn't always get his own way. You weren't meant to survive. It was just that Abramov got to you before Moscow Centre."

"Yes, that was lucky in the circumstances." After the shortest of pauses he asked, "Tell me, what made you remember the Mickey Mouse clock?"

He waited, but no answer came.

"How easy was it, Jock? Easier than the little tart you killed in Soho, easier than the girl the other night? Is a hypodermic easier to use than a knife or a bottle? Or was it that she recognized you? Was that it? Come on, you can tell me. Have another drink and tell me how it feels."

"It wasn't like that." Jock's face had been suddenly drained of all color, like a print dropped into strong bleach.

"What was it like, Jock?"

"She wasn't there, chum. I did her a favor. She wasn't there anymore. You loved her; you'd have done the same. It was an act of charity."

"Like putting down an old dog, you mean? Is that what you mean?" He got up and walked to the door.

"Where're you going? Don't go! Chum, don't go. Don't leave without saying you understand. It was like I said, she wasn't there."

Back inside his own apartment, Hillsden sat by the window next to the canary, the room in darkness, staring out at the silent city. An enormous tiredness engulfed him like the dark waters of a lake, and he was suddenly aware of his heartbeats like a Mickey Mouse clock ticking away the minutes.

Some hours later when he noticed that the darkness was thinning, he returned to Jock's apartment, finding him sprawled and unconscious across the unmade bed, the empty vodka bottle cradled against his cheek. He said his name softly, but there was no response. He picked up a cushion and pressed it down on Jock's face, making sure that what remained of Caroline's hatred held it there until the faint, bubbling sounds died away forever. Then he replaced the cushion and, before leaving, made the necessary phone call to Abramov. There was one other matter to arrange before the long night ended.

POSTSCRIPT

THE MAN VARIOUSLY known as Calder, Miller and Müller was buried for the second time in an unmarked grave. No announcement was made of his death.

In accordance with the final bargain he had struck with Abramov, Hillsden was allowed to leave Moscow shortly afterwards and was given a villa close to a Black Sea holiday resort. While there he agreed to undergo a series of cosmetic operations that subtly but effectively changed his appearance, since it was tacitly understood that he still had an active role to play. During the time he was recuperating he was awarded the Order of the Red Banner for his valued services, and was granted Soviet citizenship. On the surface he appeared to be the devout convert, but in the secret chambers of his mind he nourished an older faith that had never been corrupted.

He lived a comfortable and privileged existence and was not without agreeable companionship. A month or so after his arrival Abramov arranged for Inga to join him. Abramov also conveyed the news that Pamela's German boyfriend had been killed when an explosive device —regrettably of Russian manufacture—that he had been preparing detonated prematurely. As to Pamela, she had been persuaded to take a long sabbatical in Brazil.

Another of Hillsden's perks was to receive Western newspapers and magazines. He looked forward to receiving them, and closely studied developments at home, keeping himself in training for the last race he had yet to win. Opening his airmail copy of the *Times* one morning he read that Britain's patchwork coalition had finally collapsed in the face of continual and increasingly violent unrest. The Prime Minister had resigned, and the Monarch had sent for the Right Honorable Toby Bayldon, as the most obvious and able choice capable of uniting the nation, to form a new government. It was reported that his selection had been welcomed on both sides of the House, and that in the country as a whole there was a widespread feeling of renewed hope.

ABOUT THE AUTHOR

BRYAN FORBES was born in London in 1926 and served in British Intelligence during the war. In addition to being a distinguished director of such films as *The L-Shaped Room, King Rat, The Wrong Box* and *Seance on a Wet Afternoon,* his published works include three previous novels and a biography of Dame Edith Evans. He is married to actress Nanette Newman, and they have two daughters.